"A panorama of Russia in our time"

That is how the *West Coast Review of Books* describes JOURNEY INTO FIRE. It is fiction but it reveals "real people, actual events and places . . . Stalin, Zhukov, and company . . . devastatingly clear portraits of human beings one is not likely to forget . . . blood and gut emotions that are often shattering in their impact."

It moves with Kolya (grandson of Eleanor, the heroine of *A Space of the Heart*) from pre-revolutionary days through the slaughter of World War I, the beginnings of the Russian Revolution to life as a leader of a collective farm and husband of Anna, the gentle surgeon; through prison and generalship in World War II into today's U.S.S.R. It is a story of the victory of the human spirit over despair and degradation and the nature of that triumph.

"Authentic!"
—*Library Journal*

"Affecting!"
—*Publishers Weekly*

Also by Patricia Wright

A Space of the Heart

Published by
WARNER BOOKS

JOURNEY INTO FIRE

Patricia Wright

A Warner Communications Company

WARNER BOOKS EDITION

Library of Congress Catalog Card Number 76-42413

ISBN 0-446-81525-X

This Warner Books Edition is published by arrangement with Doubleday & Company, Inc.

Cover Art by Larry Kresik

Warner Books, Inc., 75 Rockefeller Plaza, New York, N.Y. 10019

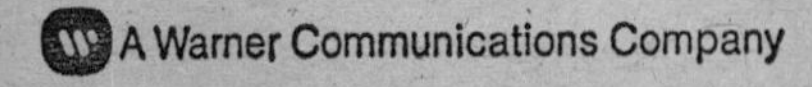

Printed in the United States of America

Not associated with Warner Press, Inc. of Anderson, Indiana

First Printing: September, 1978

10 9 8 7 6 5 4 3 2 1

Contents

PART ONE: The Hearth, 1911-15 9

PART TWO: Consuming Flames, 1917-21 69

PART THREE: The White Heat of Hope, 1923-24 181

PART FOUR: Steel from the Forge, 1928-34 211

PART FIVE: Cold Ash, 1934-41 281

PART SIX: Inferno, 1941-45 381

Epilogue, 1968 497

Historical Note 507

WESTERN SOVIET UNION & EASTERN EUROPE
FRONTIERS AS OF 1940
ARCTIC OCEAN
NORWEGIAN SEA
NORWAY
SWEDEN
FINLAND
WHITE SEA
Archangel
R. DVINA
LAKE ONEGA
GULF OF FINLAND
LAKE LADOGA
Leningrad
ESTONIA
BALTIC SEA
LATVIA
LITHUANIA
(UNDER SOVIET INFLUENCE)
U. S. S. R.
R. VOLGA
Moscow
R. OKA
EAST PRUSSIA
R. VISTULA
GERMANY
Vitebsk
Mozhaysk
Minsk
Smolensk
Tula
BELORUSSIA
Warsaw
Bobruisk
Bryansk
GERMAN POLAND
Gomel
Orel
EAST GALICIA
Saratov
R. VOLGA
Kursk
SLOVAKIA
PRIPET MARSHES
Kiev
R. DON
HUNGARY
Kharkov
R. DNIESTER
UKRAINE
Stalingrad
RUMANIA
Odessa
R. DNIEPER
Rostov
Astrakhan
Bucharest
CASPIAN SEA
R. DANUBE
CRIMEA
0 MILES 300
0 KM 300
BULGARIA
BLACK SEA

Part One
THE HEARTH
1911-15

Chapter One

The house stood a little way from the village. It was made of curling gray planks, shiny with age and leaning inward to the slope of the hill. In the translucent early morning light, with air so still it was strange to find the river continuing to flow, it looked as insubstantial as a watercolor. Yet somehow, year after year, it had survived the driving storms of winter, the snowdrifts piled up by gales sweeping unchecked across the Russian plains, the churning weeks of rain every spring and autumn.

So fragile did it seem to Kolya, determined to celebrate his name day by going fishing, that he preferred to climb out of the window rather than risk putting his shoulder to the stiffly sticking door. Sometimes days would go by without anyone daring to open it, and when they did, Kolya always contrived to be close by, hoping the balcony outside would collapse instead of merely giving its usual threatening creak.

Slanting rays of sun were just touching the black crests of the pines hemming in the village to the west, but the plain to the east was glowing with light reflected from curling fronds of mist. Kolya was usually too busy to take much note of the sights and sounds of the country in which he lived, but the shimmer of mist-covered river, the mauve smoke from the village chimneys further down the track and strange, magical glimpses of meadows as broad as the sky itself combined to send a thrill of pleasure through him. "My country," he thought, the first time he had consciously done so, and then with less truth but more assurance: "My century!"

Kolya had a special feeling about the twentieth century: he had been born in the first month of the first year of the new era, so his age always tallied with that of the century itself. Both he and the century were now eleven years old and he was sure the future was waiting with the same impatience as he for the thrill which changing scenes would surely bring. He was happy at Obeschino but he did sometimes wish his century would hurry things up a little—a really spectacular collapse of the balcony, for instance, would make a welcome change.

"Good wishes, Konstantin Aleksandr'itch, on your name day." The formal chorus greeted him through the village, even though nearly everyone called him Kolya the rest of the year. Spiced buns and little pastries were offered him, and since everyone stood by until the last crumb was eaten, he began to fear the brightening sun would drive all the fish into unassailable hideouts long before he could meet his friends by the bridge.

"Ah, little master, 'tis a sad thought we'll be seeing you no more this summer," scolded Fat Masha the washerwoman. "Why do you want to leave us for Petersburg, then?"

"Oh no, that's my sister Yelena, she's to be wed in Moscow." Kolya's mouth was full, he was anxious to be gone and his family was not in fact master here any longer, only the ramshackle house and orchard still in their possession. But old habits die hard, and although his father had the sweetest and gentlest of dispositions he held strong views on good manners, especially toward the peasants, and when necessary enforced them with a three-foot riding whip.

Fat Masha, who was never known as anything else, shook her head emphatically. "It is both of you going, your grandmother the old Barina will be taking you back with her as well, and then what will the boys here do, without you to lead them into mischief eh? It'll be a quiet summer with no one to fill the place with zebras!" She waddled off laughing. Obeschino had never forgotten the morning it had woken up to find every ox and bullock in the village paddock painted in foot-wide white and black stripes following Kolya's fascinated discovery of a picture book about wild animals. He had resisted the temptation to strap humps on the sheep or cotton trunks on the horses, but Z is for zebra and a large can of whitewash in the stables had proved his undoing.

When he finally reached the river his friends were equally emphatic about his imminent departure. "Petersburg! What kind of a stupid place is that to spend the summer?" Vanya Ivan'itch always thought places and things outside his experience stupid.

"You were coming to Oryol with us to help sell the winter's work for the village, Father said we would be away a whole three weeks." Petya looked sullen and genuinely distressed, for he and Kolya were true friends, even if Petya was the youngest of a sprawling family of drunks whose only occupation was to pickle the village cucumbers, while Kolya was constantly reminded of the behavior and standards expected of a gentleman, however poor his family might be.

"But I'm not going anywhere!" Kolya was bewildered and upset by the unexpectedness and, he felt sure, the falsity of these accusations. "It's my sister, she's to be married to some rich Moscow banker who wants our name and doesn't care if we hardly have a house to live in. Mamma says Obeschino should sound grand enough for them so long as no one comes to look at it."

They stared at him in disbelief. Luka, the oldest of the boys, gave a guffaw. "Think of young Lena wed to a Moscow banker! Yes, Barina, no, Barina, how about your new carriage, Barina? She'll be able to shut her own front door then, I daresay. Where has she met this banker, then, a day's journey as we are here even from a flea-bitten town like Yakovka?"

"Mamma met him last year," said Kolya, pale with anger. "And if you say one more word about not believing me I'll . . ."

"What'll you do, little Barin? Bite me in the bottom?" jeered Luka. He was a thick-shouldered seventeen-year-old who only joined the smaller boys because he enjoyed their admiration and his father was too shiftless to make him do more than chop wood for the stove.

Kolya hesitated. He knew Luka could break his ribs with one of his crushing grips, he had seen him do it, yet he feared the other boys' taunts almost as much as Luka's strength. "I'll fight you if it's the only way to make you believe me. I'm not going to Petersburgh, it's Lena and she's to marry a Moscow banker." His voice jumped uncertainly.

"*Bozhe moy!* My God!" Luka scratched his head, disconcerted and uncertain what to do next, a barin could scarcely be attacked without horrifying retribution. Kolya knew a wave of relief followed almost at once by surging excitement, had he known it, one of the purest excitements of all, that of outfacing an enemy.

"Let's fish!"

"Look at him go! What a whopper!"

"*Posmotrite,* look, there he is!" The other boys broke in with the chatter of tension removed, and they scattered cautiously along the riverbank.

Kolya established himself in the shadow of a blazing bush of broom and cast his line, but he was too upset to relax into the absorption of fishing. After about half an hour he quietly packed up his things, crawled backward through the bushes until he was out of sight and then hurried home, circling a field of flax to avoid the village.

It was still early and his parents were not yet down, but his grandmother, who was eccentric chiefly because she was English, or so his mother said, was already up and seated on the veranda enjoying the bright sunshine. She did not look seventy-nine years old, nor as if she had arrived only yesterday after days in the train—first from Petersburg to Moscow, then two hundred miles to Oryol before changing to the branch line for Yakovka and finally enduring a whole day of bumpy track to Obeschino.

Kolya did not grasp quite the extent of her journey, but he knew Grandmamma was very old and was vaguely grateful to her for getting up to give him the reassurance he craved.

"Kolya, my dear, happiness on your name day." She kissed him. "I am so pleased to be with you, the last time I greeted you on your own day you were five years old and I am sure you do not remember it at all." She had the most expressive eyes Kolya had ever seen, set in wrinkles to be sure but bright and young-looking under slanting eyebrows like his own, still hardly tinged by the gray of her exquisitely piled hair.

"I think perhaps I do," said Kolya doubtfully. "It was just before we came to Obeschino to live for always, wasn't it?"

A shadow passed over her face. She could remember the haste of their departure, the relief when it was discovered that the Tsar would allow the family to retire and live on the tiny remnant of their long-sequestered estates and not enforce exile to Siberia. It had been mercy indeed toward Kolya's father since he had undoubtedly sympathized with the revolution flaring through Russia that year of 1905, but sometimes she wondered whether her son Alseksandr would not have been happier a true martyr in the east. She roused from the easy abstractions of old age to find Kolya tugging at her arm. "Grandmamma, I'm not going back to Petersburg with you, am I? Papa told me it was Lena going to Moscow to be wed."

She slipped an arm around his shoulders. "Would you hate it if you came back with me?"

"I told them . . . I told them it wasn't me going," said Kolya in a small voice. He could think only of having to go back to Luka and confess the truth, of the retribution he would have to endure for deceiving his fellows.

"Who did you tell?"

He shook his head, it was something he would have to deal with himself, there was no point explaining. He looked at the ground, his mouth tight, and never knew how, for an instant, the years rolled back for his grandmother.

Ilena Vassilievna Berdeyeva had been a widow for thirty years, every day still a loss, a loneliness beyond describing, yet the time of her distant happiness still so close to her heart that she knew not an instant of regret. Now, just for a moment, in the slant of a child's head, the defensively tightened face, she saw, really saw after thirty years, the beloved face she was waiting, impatiently and confidently, for death to allow her to see again. A flash, and then it was gone: eleven-year-old Kolya was standing there, not Nicolai as he turned to leave the house that terrible morning so long ago.

Shock made it impossible to speak for a moment, and her sons had grown up so long ago that in any case it was difficult to know how to reach the boy. A creak overhead came to her rescue and she glanced up. "I am never sure whether it is safe to sit here, I don't know how it has all held together for so long."

"It won't for much longer," said Kolya hopefully. "Next year's snow at the latest, I expect. I shall sit up all night in the first blizzard just to see it go."

She laughed. "You will not be so happy with the front of the house pulled out and the snow coming in."

"It won't come down like that, Grandmamma," explained Kolya seriously. "Can't you see? The ends are solid, it's the middle which will fold down and the house will be like living in a cave." He ran his hands over the slanting poles, anxious for her to understand a problem which was perfectly clear to him.

"I didn't know you were so practical," she said, amused. "Your papa said music was the one thing you liked above all."

Kolya nodded. Music was so fundamental he did not think of it as something he merely liked. Music was not just the old piano at the back of the hall, it was all around, in the trees and the howl of the wind, in the off-key shouting of his friends and the ripple of water dripping off the eaves. He did not talk about it, though, it would be like letting cattle into the house, a soiling of feelings he had to keep locked away until he understood himself better.

Ilena sighed. She felt very old this morning and she had long since learned that nothing supremely precious comes without great effort. Kolya, however loved, was unknown as only a complex human being can be unknown, and the thought of setting out now to win his confidence and bridge the chasm of years between them was daunting.

"Ah, Mamma, Kolya, I'm glad you two have made friends again already. I expect your grandmamma has told you of your good fortune, of her plan to take you back to Petersburg with her and attend school there?" Aleksandr Berdeyev was living evidence that the uncomplicated desire to benefit one's fellow men is one of the most destructive forces on earth. He had never had a selfish or ignoble thought, yet the consequences of his idealism varied from the disastrous to the merely irritating.

Today was no exception and as his mother saw Kolya retreat again into his shell it was a real effort to reply pleasantly, "Why, yes, although I left it to you to discuss schooling with him. He was just telling me of his fears for the balcony."

Aleksandr tried not to be offended. He knew his actions had brought great sorrow to his mother as well as disgrace to his family, but liked no more than most men to be reminded of the inadequacies of his home. "It will last for years yet. If Kolya feels like it he can prop it up before he leaves."

"When will I be leaving?" Kolya asked, his expression still sullen.

"When your grandmother is rested, if she still feels like taking such an ill-mannered urchin to Petersburg with her. You should realize the sacrifice she has made, coming all this way to collect you and Lena. Lena will have two members of the family at her betrothal party so will not be shamed in Moscow, and you will have as much opportunity as you care to make use of."

"Why don't you and Mamma go to Lena's bethrothal, if some of the family have to be there?" muttered Kolya rudely.

There was an awkward silence.

"Your father will come . . ." began Ilena.

"No," interrupted her son. "If he is going to live in Petersburg it is time he knew, Mamma." He turned to Kolya. "You will not remember the year we left Petersburg, but there were riots and petitions to the Tsar which led in the end to an attempt at revolution. I was one of those who tried to lead the people to ask for what it was their right to have. You will learn more about these things as you grow up, but a man has to do what he thinks is right. I do not regret anything except that we failed."

"What happened?" Kolya had never thought of his dreamy father as a dangerous revolutionary. Everyone whispered about the atrocities of the revolution six years ago, and he was already visualizing his father wading through blood and turmoil, a pitchfork in one hand, perhaps a saber in the other. His eyes glistened with excitement. "What happened, Papa?" he repeated.

Aleksandr grimaced, not entirely averse to being a figure to reckon with in his son's life for once. He glanced at his mother and then looked away quickly. She had forgiven, so many times, oh God, why could neither of them forget? He answered Kolya brusquely. "Nothing. We lost and I was lucky to be allowed to live here instead of Siberia because my father, your grandfather, was still remembered for his . . . his services as a minister of an earlier Tsar."

"I will tell him about his grandfather," interposed Ilena firmly, "but we will have plenty of time together. Your father has nothing of which to be ashamed, but he is not allowed to leave here without His Majesty's permission. Only the house is left, the rest was forfeited to the state nearly a hundred years ago. The men of your family have always gone their own way, serving Russia as seemed to them best and not necessarily as opinion of the time thought she should be served. You must do the same when you are older and can understand things better."

Aleksandr looked at her gratefully. I never truly believed she understood before, he thought. He could not speak and Kolya looked from one to the other suspiciously: it was like a jangled piece of music, and he knew that whatever they spoke of, their thoughts were on something quite different.

He was angry suddenly, grownups were all the same,

they never explained things properly. Suppose his father couldn't go to Petersburg, why not be satisfied to stay together at Obeschino? Lena was excited enough about her stupid betrothal, let her go to Moscow and leave him alone. He wandered off in disgust to find Luka, kicking clods of earth across the rutted track until they disintegrated in satisfactory puffs of dust.

Chapter Two

Ilena Berdeyeva was exhausted. Not just tired or overtired, but drained beyond the point where reserves of strength could reach into the fragile jointing of old age; she felt on the edge of the grave itself. She had seldom known illness in her life but did not need a doctor to tell her that the crazy journey to Obeschino could still kill her if she allowed it.

She lay on the pillared bed in her apartment on the Sadovskaya in St. Petersburg, watching reflections dancing on the ceiling as the sun beat down on the Catherine Canal outside, conscious only of thankfulness she was back. The alleyways of memory were shrouded, then darkening with metallic edging to remembered scenes, suffocation drifted into thought until she could not struggle free of it . . . She woke shuddering and gasping, a sharp pain in her breast, breath clotted in her lungs. Somehow she pulled herself upright, grasping at bedclothes, the side table, anything to keep hold on reality, and after a while her vision strengthened; somewhere there was an easy breath again. She relaxed and lay back, smiling to herself. Not this time.

But soon, my love, soon, she thought, eyes going to

the portrait opposite her bed. A short while I must now give to our grandson if I can, and then, God willing, I will come; and it seemed as if the tight, stern lines of the canvas face relaxed in the way they always had, just for her.

How long it had been. Thirty years this spring since Nicolai had died and now, when she knew her sentence nearly over, she must fight to stay a little longer for Kolya's sake.

Ilena knew she should not have waited so long to go to Obeschino, but the distance, the old hurts to be reopened, a weariness with it all had made her recoil from involving herself yet again. Had it not been for word of Lena's proposed marriage she would never have gone, recognizing at last that she had no more of herself to give to the living. But when Aleksandr had written of the contract agreed for Lena with some unknown banker's son, white-hot anger had proved her resignation premature.

On the instant she had resolved to go, had written back to Aleksandr demanding the banker's address and announcing the date of her arrival. Aleksandr had sent it, knowing his mother well enough to be convinced that if he did not she was quite capable of tramping around the banks of Moscow until she found out for herself, but she was further incensed when his reply revealed that he had never met his daughter's affianced husband or his family.

"As you know," he wrote, *"I cannot leave Obeschino but when Katya was in Moscow last she had in mind the possibility of a suitable match for Lena. She is young, but too pretty to stay buried in the country much longer. Katya was very clever to find the Kobrin family looking for a girl of good birth for their son, as few in court circles would care to risk His Majesty's wrath by alliance with a proscribed family, and without*

a dowry or the opportunity to make Lena's acquaintance there is no incentive for them to do so."

Ilena had left for Moscow two days later, upset to realize how blind she had been to the needs of her grandchildren. Aleksandr and Katya were tragic, but at least they had plunged into their troubles knowing the consequences, had no one but themselves to blame for their isolation. Now the children were about to pay an undeserved reckoning as well: Lena to be sold off to a boy probably only one generation from the bazaar, and Kolya, who his father said was intelligent but for his head being filled with music, to grow up without ever sparking his wits and ideas on those of others.

She had been surprised by the size and style of the Kobrin house on the Znamenka, a fine, wide street running into the Aleksandr Gardens by the Moscow Kremlin. Her welcome had been warm, the Kobrins insisting on her staying with them and giving a reception in her honor. Old Kobrin was certainly an extremely able and at times disconcerting man, capable of saying harsh things in the heat of the moment which reduced his clerks and servants to occasional tears. But it did not take Ilena long to realize that neither his wife nor his family were in fear of him and when his immediate anger cooled he was both tolerant and affectionate. She was used to men who guarded their closest feelings, and was soon aware that Nicolai (to whose judgment she still subconsciously submitted all things) would have liked him.

"Terrible thing that, madame, of your husband's death," Kobrin said abruptly one evening when they were waiting for the rest of the family before going out. "I was a clerk in Petersburg at the time, learning my trade from a back-street usurer, and I remember the shock still. We all thought he and Loris were going to find an answer to some of our problems."

"I still don't like to talk about it." She had not been

able to talk of it for thirty years, carefully built-up control crumbling even now with words. Then suddenly she knew it was not true: with this tough, brusque banker, a stranger to the family and its problems, yet already not a true stranger any longer, with him she could talk, was almost compelled to talk after so long.

There was a long pause as she sat there, small in her stiffly braided black silk, plaiting and unplaiting her fingers. Suddenly he smiled. "Come, madame, let us go into my counting room, no one will disturb us there."

"But the reception . . ." protested Ilena feebly.

"Pho! Receptions are twenty a kopeck in Moscow and I think perhaps you do not wish to go tonight. Vanya shall take his mother." He bellowed up the stairs, servants scuttled in every direction, an oil lamp was dropped and it was Vanya who actually settled her in the counting room with a tray of coffee. He was a tall, handsome boy, with more gaiety than his father but with signs of the same shrewdness: Ilena already knew that her journey had been wasted, her granddaughter was going to be a very lucky young woman. She had not previously encountered the new commercial and industrial Russia springing up on every side, but she had found more life and enterprise with the Kobrins than anywhere in official St. Petersburg.

But when the bustle had died down and Kobrin was seated opposite her, she did not know how to begin, the moment gone cold again.

"It is strange how every Muscovite feels he must keep open house every few days, simply because the rest of the time he is visiting elsewhere and must not be the debtor in hospitality," said Kobrin with a chuckle. "One evening at home is what we all want and never get."

She smiled back at him. "I used to feel the same with all those dreadful official receptions in Petersburg. You probably know I was English and I had never been used to anything like it."

"But you must have been in Russia a long time now?"

"Yes indeed, nearly sixty years, and it has become truly my home. Although my elder son Gregor is settled in England and has married an English wife."

"And you did not feel like going back with him?"

She shook her head. "I don't know quite why I stayed. I love Russia, but then, just after Nicolai was killed, I hated it. Gregor went because of the way his father died."

"Perhaps you felt that all there was left to you of your husband would be lost if you left Russia," Kobrin suggested gently.

She was astonished by his perception; how could this man she scarcely knew see at once something which had eluded her own calculation at the time? She turned to him eagerly and he was able to see how she must have looked fifty years before: the speaking eloquence of eyes, the fine bones, every man's fancy caught by the unusual sweep of eyebrow, above all a steadfastness of character few could miss. Old General Berdeyev had good taste in women as well as politics, he thought.

"At the time it was just instinct but I never regretted it, the years have passed faster here than they would in England. There is always so much needing to be done, and now Kolya—I am taking him back to Petersburg with me, he should not stay in the country any longer."

"That alone will justify your decision. A life for a life. Those backwoods villages are the very devil. I know, I came from one." He scowled suddenly.

"You will look after Lena for me, will you not?"

He laughed. "I think you are looking us over to satisfy yourself on that point."

"Yes, I am," said Ilena honestly. "Wouldn't you? But I have liked what I've seen and I like your Vanya, too. I would wish to take Lena to Petersburg for a season and then let her choose for herself, but I am too old to chaperone her and I cannot think she'll do better than she will here. If she could come and stay the summer with you and is willing to be wed in the autumn, so be it. Vanya, like you, has enough address to fix his interest with a woman in that time."

A deep belly laugh shook him, an old villager's pure enjoyment breaking through sophistication. "God's life, madame, your husband would have had to watch out if I had been around when you first came to Russia!"

"I daresay you were scarcely breeched then," retorted Ilena tartly, but there was something very pleasant about genuine flattery at the age of seventy-nine. "It is a bargain, then?"

He kissed her fingers. "It is a bargain. We will not seek to persuade her but will leave all to Vanya."

He would be as good as his word, she knew, and now, lying in her bed in Petersburg, she was well satisfied. It was done, and she prayed God it was done right, all her judgment told her it was. But Kolya was still a problem and in the three weeks since they had left Obeschino she had made no progress with him at all. He was polite, carefully mannered as Lena was, grave and withdrawn for his age. But he would not allow himself to be trapped into wonder by the strangeness of Moscow, into friendliness by the gaiety of the Kobrins, or into affection by Ilena's attempts to establish contact with him.

The devil fly away with the boy! she thought sleepily, and then smiled at the unladylike phrase echoed from Kobrin. Strange what relief had come from telling at last the way Nicolai had died. I forgave, she thought, but I could not forget and it has poisoned us all these thirty years. How wrong I was, yet how indeed could one forget? But it will be easier now to tell Kolya in a way which will not diminish him, as it has diminished Aleksandr and me.

She slept.

Chapter Three

Kolya liked St. Petersburg immensely, and now the bruised rib which Luka had given him as routine retribution for deceit was almost sound again, he was able to relax and enjoy himself. From the moment of his farewell to Obeschino, with his father gravely blessing him before the icon, his mother rousing from her interminable slumbers to weep and the village people coming to offer Lena and himself tiny charms, tight little bunches of flowers or colored cream cheeses, he had been living what he privately called an inside-out existence.

The jolting carriage to Yakovka had tried his endurance to the limit, his rib throbbing until the only relief was to stand up and take his weight on the roof struts while pretending to watch the endless trees jerk past. His own misery had helped him realize what his grandmother must be suffering, and made it easier not to add to her burdens by concealing his own, especially when Lena spent much of the time in tears of apprehension. In Moscow he had been alarmed by the size of the Kobrin house, horribly ashamed of the rush basket which contained all his possessions, resentful as he watched Lena's tears turn to laughter with the whirl and gaiety he found so overwhelming.

Once in St. Petersburg, though, everything was different. His grandmother had to stay in bed for several days, so he was free to wander at will, to gape and get lost, to stare at the uniforms worn by nearly all the men and dodge flying carriages without fearing to be thought a country bumpkin.

He was fascinated by the piles of merchandise, a wealth unimaginable heaped on stalls, on the cobbles, in boats plying up the Neva. Cheeses, fringed scarves, fish, hot pies and live chickens in the bazaars; fifty different kinds of bread at Filippov's bakery on the Nevsky Prospekt, tubs of dark yellow Siberian butter and earthenware pots of cream at the Christiakov dairy on Gogol Street; rambling rooms full of toys and books at Peto's children's shop. The prices were incredibly cheap, a few kopecks would buy a dozen steaming patties or a trip down the Neva in a steamer with a clanging brass bell, but Kolya had no money at all, everyone appparently forgetting to supply him with this necessary commodity, and to him a kopeck cup of soup was as remote as the fabulous diamond-studded treasures of Fabergé or Alexandre.

He was cuffed and pushed, moved on by the police for loitering outside the Winter Palace, and even tossed a few kopecks for holding an officer's horse. He was guiltily proud of this, his first earnings, and expended it triumphantly on a highly colored confection of candy, studded with raisins and cumin seeds, arriving home in such a desperate state of stickiness that Marfa, the maid, hauled him into his grandmother's room by the scruff of his neck.

"Observe, Barina, the wicked little one, he has been stealing off the stalls!"

"I haven't!" said Kolya indignantly.

"Then how is it you return home covered thus, when your pockets were empty, shameless one?" She shook him.

"Enough, Marfa," interposed Ilena quickly. "If

Kolya says he has not stolen then he has not stolen. What reason have we not to believe what he says?"

Marfa threw out her arms expressively. "Look at him, Barina!"

Ilena smiled. "Yes, I think he could do with a wash. Come back, Kolya, in a few minutes and have your lunch on a tray with me and afterward I will get up."

Kolya loved her from that moment, and when later he told her how he got the money, she laughed. "Never be ashamed of earning an honest kopeck! I have been remiss not to give you pocket money, but I am well again now and there are many things we should think about. You mustn't mind Marfa, although sometimes she is very disagreeable. I picked her off the street when she was starving and have had to put up with her ever since. One always imagines the objects of one's charity must be delightful, yet it is often quite the reverse! And there you are with the burden of them forever. I have had many opportunities to engage a good maid but cannot do so because I could never turn Marfa away."

His grandmother's astringent realism constantly delighted Kolya. Now she was somewhat recovered from the strains of the journey, her tiny apartment was filled with visitors, although those who came invariably remarked on how everyone else had left town for the summer.

"Nobody has such good evenings as your grandmother," confided Micha Traskine, an immensely fat general commanding the cavalry school, to Kolya one evening. "I came once and found some drosky drivers dancing the gopak in the passage until the chandelier fell down into the cream cheese. Your grandmother had thought they must be cold waiting outside and asked them up just at the moment that tiresome woman who sings the leads at the Opera arrived. God, I never laughed so much in all my life!" His belly shook at the memory of it.

"Micha!" commanded Ilena. "Stop filling the boy's ears with nonsense and tell me about schools. We shall have to choose soon which he is to go to when they open again."

"Lord, Ilena, I don't know about schools. Send him to the Cadet College."

"No!" she said sharply. "Kolya is not going into the army. Every Berdeyev goes into the army as if it were the only career in the Empire, and none of them has come to any good in it."

"What's wrong with being a general, a governor, a minister as Nicolai was?" demanded Traskine. "Did a damned sight better for him than anything else, and for me too." He squinted down at his glittering medals and jellified body complacently.

"It got him shot and Aleksandr sent into exile. Even Gregor walked out to settle in England," retorted Ilena. She relaxed slightly. "It is the British in me, I suppose. I cannot feel it right for so much to be run by people in uniform. If Kolya chooses to go into the army when he is older, it is for him to decide, but I will not have him educated for it before he knows his own mind. Nicolai struggled always to do what was right and he succeeded more than most men would have done, but it changed nothing—nothing! It was all waste: the trying, the dying, all waste." Her voice died away, passion and anger burning up her strength until she looked gray and wizened.

Within minutes she was dozing uneasily by the fire and Traskine wheezed breathily in Kolya's ear, "You mustn't take any notice of her. I've know her nigh on sixty years and she never did give a damn what she said, or allow anything to stand in the way of what she thought she should do. Old Berdeyev was the only man who could handle her; since he died she's done her best to set society by the ears. Years ago she even told the Tsar his Guards' overcoats let in the cold where the extra gold braid was sewn on." He chuckled. "She nearly had him trying one on to see if she was right, but he remembered who he was just in time and she was banished from court instead."

Kolya soon found that his grandmother meant what she said. He was allowed to take advantage of Traskine's offer to let him join one of the cavalry riding courses during the summer break, but she would not consider any of the special schools set aside for the use of the aristocracy, although to his surprise Kolya discovered that he was probably a count.

"It is silly really," she explained. "Your grandfather was so high in the government that in the end we were Supreme Excellencies and I don't know what else besides. Your father was deprived of his rank in all the fuss over his part in the revolution six years ago, so I'm sure I don't know whether you, who were born a count since your father was deprived then, can still call yourself so or not."

Eventually he was settled in an unfashionable school hidden behind the Tauride Palace, which specialized in despised subjects like mathematics, and he soon became immersed in his new life, making friends and visiting areas of the capital he would normally never have seen. His special friend was Innokenty Rogov, whose father was a wholesale dealer in skins, obviously prosperous but still living in a wooden shed attached to his warehouse. The smell of putrefaction was overpowering, and as the yard was always full of ragged workers scraping and curing skins, the only time Kolya could enter it without a shudder was in winter after a fresh snowfall.

Subconsciously he spun out the time walking to the Rogovs', he and Innokenty burrowing into nearly every side street in the district, Kolya encountering for the first time the abyss of wretchedness into which the city poor could fall. There was poverty at Obeschino, the village huts were dark, wet and smoky, but nothing had prepared him for the crowded tenements of St. Petersburg.

In many cases the buildings were fairly substantial, put up by factory owners as barracks for housing their workers, but they were crammed from entrance to eaves, men and women together. Once, for a dare, he and Innokenty pushed their way past huddled sleepers on the stairs and penetrated the upper floors of one of these warrens of violence and misery. Bodies lay on bare slats and piles of rags in every attitude of sleep, coupling and despair, women were cooking over a handful of chippings on tin trays, children sitting apathetically searching for bugs in each other's clothes. Hideous faces floated in the half light like bloated corpses in the murk of a canal, while the stench sank into the skin and could not be scrubbed out for days.

Afterward Kolya and Innokenty sat on the steps of a tumbledown church at the end of the ally and wept. Both were used to lurching drunks and scabrous beggars in the darker streets, to occasional frozen corpses on a winter's morning and ragged families of destitute crowding around stoves kept alight for them in the churches, but the shock of such merciless degradation was too great.

Innokenty was the first to recover; older than Kolya, he had lived close to a very rough life for all his years. "Do you think the government knows what it's like inside those places?"

Kolya shook his head, his throat still tight with nausea. Innokenty slipped an arm around his shoulders, quoting in a thick Petersburg accent: "*Do Boga vysoko, do Tsaraya daleko!* God is too high and the Tsar far away!"

"The Tsar is not very far away, though." Kolya ignored the first part of this age-old saying of the poor. Instinctively, he felt that his grandmother would disapprove of blaming the Khersonskaya tenements on the Almighty. "He is at Tsarskoye Selo just twenty versts away, why can't he tell his people to do something about such things?"

Innokenty laughed and swept his hand around. "Look at it all! How many do you think altogether in Piter?" *

"I don't care," said Kolya obstinately. "Something ought to be done. When I'm older I'll write a symphony so sad everyone will want to know what inspired it. In music I'll be able to tell them better than in any speech."

Innokenty gave him a friendly push. "Trust you! The first thing you think of is music. How will you find notes for all the things you keep telling me music will explain? I think you'd find it easier in plain Russian."

"Oh no!" Kolya said earnestly, "You see—" He broke off as he saw Innokenty laughing. "You swine, you always catch me like that. You just wait until I invite you to the first performance of Konstantin Berdeyev's Symphonic Poem 'To the New Century,' then you'll understand how music can say more than words—if only I'm good enough," he added, suddenly smitten by doubt.

"Don't worry, anyone who thinks, sleeps and eats music as you do must be good enough or God has mixed up His blueprints. I'll come and cheer at your concert, then you will be famous enough to open all the marvels perpetrated by Innokenty Rogov, the miracle engineer of the twentieth century." Innokenty had not dared tell his father, still earnestly instructing him on the different qualities of wolf and fox fur, but he intended to study civil engineering and dreamed of throwing indescribably elegant bridges across the Neva,

* Affectionate nickname for St. Petersburg, used by nearly all its permanent inhabitants.

the Oka, the Volga and as many other of the innumerable rivers of Russia as he could. "At least my bridges will give work to these people, which is perhaps the best we can hope for now."

"There must be a quicker way," insisted Kolya, but his mind was sidetracked. Already his inner senses were fumbling among the sounds which might one day express a little of what he had felt and seen in the Khersonskaya tenements. Strangely, it was not the muffled drumbeat of defeat and despair which stayed with him as he walked home, his thought lost in polyphony; it was a high thin call like a trumpet note echoing above the rest. The call to hope, to the future, the call which he and Innokenty had both felt on the dirty steps of Trinity Church.

Chapter Four

Above everything, St. Petersburg came to mean music to Kolya: concerts and operas at the Aleksandrinsky or Mariinsky Theaters, four- or five-piece ensembles at private soirees, individual instrumentalists in stuffy students' rooms with an intent audience cross-legged on the floor following every twining melody and fiercely debating the interpretation afterward. The gay beat of military bands on parade square and in nobles' gardens, open to the public on Sundays; gypsy violins in restaurants and bars, or a muzhik strolling casually down a busy street playing his accordion as if he were alone in a forest.

Then there was the intense controversy surrounding new composers, seemingly springing up from every corner of the Empire and coming to Petersburg to electrify or disgust audiences with their primitive rhythms: Stravinsky and his *Firebird,* Rachmaninov, Scriabin, Prokofiev, all rippling the pool of accepted thought. Whenever Kolya could squeeze the money for a ticket, there were performances by Chaliapin, ballets with Pavlova or Nijinsky, the astonishing sets of Meyerhold to gape at in the Imperial Theater.

As a backdrop there were the sounds of Petersburg itself. Its seven hundred churches with their bells, icy arctic blasts keening off gilded dome and stone balustrade, yells of drivers clattering over loose cobbles at full speed, the wheeze of the ancient lift to his grandmother's apartment and quick cadences of drawing-room wit which contrasted so sharply with the slower intonations of Oryol. There was a special Petersburg silence too, as intense as sound itself. I will have a pause in my symphony, thought Kolya, so complete it highlights the rest. He was kneeling, looking out of his window as the sun rose; it was spring again and he could scarcely believe he had been in Petersburg nearly three years, yet life at Obeschino had so faded it was curling up in his memory like an old photograph.

He went three times a week to the Imperial Conservatoire to study music under Professor Weber, a very bad-tempered German from whom Kolya picked up a wider variety of oaths in three languages than from his school friends. When he first began his studies he had not even decided which instrument he wished to play, as already the idea of composing had taken entire possession of him: he desired only to acquire sufficient technique to communicate the images which music constantly focused in his mind.

Weber soon settled his doubts, calling him an arrogant boor and exposing his slightest shortcoming of skill or ear with brutal obscenities and, frequently, kicks and shaking. First the piano, then two years later the violin, at which Kolya himself knew he was only a moderate performer while Professor Weber stopped his ears and stamped with rage. By then Kolya was indifferent to these scenes; having survived the first onslaught there was nothing worse to be feared, and however much he hated Weber, hated him above all for not making the longed-for music joyous, he was undoubtedly very gifted musically. Kolya benefited from Weber in an unexpected way too: only real dedication could survive such treatment, and any intending composer needed to temper his dedication in the fires of adversity as early as possible.

Sometimes he would borrow an accordion and take it home so his grandmother might hear him play. He had at first been astounded to learn that his Olympian grandmother, with all her grand Petersburg connections, was unable to afford a piano for their apartment once she had paid for his schooling and music tuition.

"I have no money of my own and your grandfather had only his army pay, which was very little since every normal official is expected to live by bribes and he never did," she explained. "The family estates were sequestered as you know, when your great-grandfather was involved in the 1825 plot." She sighed, "The Berdeyevs are always throwing their hearts into some unwise scheme or other."

Kolya grinned. "I don't think you can be accused of excessive prudence, Grandmamma. A good few strange people come here to enlist your sympathy for their needs, and I heard how much the Tsar disliked being told his soldiers' greatcoats were too thin."

"Well, they were too thin!" she retorted indignantly. "So much fancy braid which the wind blew right through!"

Kolya hugged her. "I wish I had been there, I would have loved to see everyone's faces."

"Even Nicolai said it was worth all the fuss," she admitted with a twinkle. "Though he was furious with me, because, of course, so long as I was banned he refused to go to court either, except for duty. But it turned out well, we were sent down to the Caucasus in disgrace and had the happiest time I ever remember there. You would be surprised how things often work out in the most unexpected ways! As I was saying, though, I have to be very careful with money if I'm to be sure of managing; there will be very little for you or Lena when I am gone. It is such a joy to know she is provided for and happy."

"I don't mind, musicians are never rich," Kolya assured her. "When I write my *Petersburg Symphony* I will dedicate it to you and put in a very solemn cross-sounding march for you being expelled from court." He played a few exaggerated notes and stamped across the room.

"Dear Kolya, what happiness you have given me these last three years." Ilena smiled at him, eyes suddenly filling with tears. "I want you to know what great happiness, it is not many old ladies who enjoy their eighties as I am doing. All the nice young people you bring here make me forget how old I am. But you will have a girl of your own then. I shall be very content for you to dedicate your symphony to her."

"No." Kolya shook his head. "All my first impressions of Petersburg are tied up with you. Whatever else I dedicate to others, that will be yours. I expect I'll write lots," he added naïvely.

"Oh, I do hope so. I hope so much you will be the first Berdeyev to be able to do what he truly wished for Russia, now things are changing at last."

"They are not changing fast enough," said Kolya somberly. "You haven't seen the terrible things I have in some of the back streets . . . My God, you should see the way Rogov drives those poor wretches who work for him. There seems to be a strike or murder nearly every day somewhere in the city, but it astonishes me there aren't more."

"I may not be able to go out very often, but I'm not quite in my dotage yet," retorted Ilena tartly. "Neither am I a fool. I know things are still bad, but they are not so—so twisted any more! I used to despair because anything attempted seemed only to make matters worse. Now . . . there are new factories which mean work, better wages. The peasants are beginning to own their own land and once they do, nothing and no one will turn them into revolutionaries. They might even farm it properly."

"I wonder," said Kolya thoughtfully, remembering his father's struggles even to get the peasants to lift a plowshare at the end of a furrow instead of making the horses drag it around by main force.

Ilena laughed. "All right, you go out and do something about it, you have not the right selfishly to grasp at your music only. But I do see how different things are. I started to teach some peasant children to read soon after I was married and two years later your grandfather, as governor, had to enforce the Tsar's edict against me—the peasants were not to be educated." She smiled reminiscently. "We hardly spoke for days I was so angry. Now, many of the poor are going to school and you do not think it strange to mix with all kinds there. Although I could wish, my dear, that you would watch your language and your accent more carefully."

Kolya grinned. "That's old Weber, he still manages to shock even me sometimes. Grandmamma . . ." he hesitated, "do you think you could tell me more about my father? When I went home last summer he asked about you in such a way as if . . ." His voice trailed away.

"As if what, Kolya?"

"I—I don't know. It was a fancy perhaps, but we

went shooting together one day and I seemed to come to know him for the first time. He spoke of you as if he wished to find out whether he had been forgiven." The difficult words he had rehearsed for months were out. "Your grandmother is old," his father had said as they sat amid the hum of insects in patchwork shadows during the heat of midday. "Ask her for me one day if I am forgiven. I would like her to bless me before she dies if she can."

There was a long silence. Kolya examined his knuckles intently, not wishing to look at his grandmother's face. At last she sighed deeply and unclipped the rimless pince-nez she sometimes wore, purplish dents either side of her nose enhancing her frailty, the fine lines of her face, usually quickened with laughter or affection, sagging briefly. "I hadn't realized he was still not sure . . . I have been very wrong." She lapsed into silence again which Kolya did not dare interrupt although he was filled with impatience. There was some mystery, half glimpsed several times over the past three years. He felt he had a right to know, the thought almost unbearable that, now he had brought himself to ask at last, his grandmother might escape into some reverie of the past which would shut him out again.

He need not have worried. Abruptly she roused, fully alert in the way he loved best, when he never quite knew what she would say next and she was more like a newly sophisticated elder sister than a venerable eighty-two. "Poor Kolya! Fancy being consumed with curiosity all this while and finding me too formidable to ask."

"Oh no! It was just my father wanting—"

"But you were glad of the excuse to ask," she said shrewdly. "This tedious old age of mine, you will find it hard to imagine, but I had forgotten you did not know. Of course you should ask whatever you wish. You were told of his disgrace for supporting the 1905 revolution?" Kolya nodded. "That was not the beginning of it. He was a very sensitive child and I was at fault for encouraging him. I too always wanted to put everything right at once. Nicolai tried to warn me several times: 'The boy has to live in Russia' he said, 'you will break his heart if you let him think much can be changed by good intentions.' But I would not listen, how can things be changed if someone will not take a risk, believe it can be done? But Russia is like an overladen country cart to which everyone is harnessed. If one tries to stop, the others go on pulling just the same and if they did not, it would roll by itself."

"But you have just told me how much has changed, how I mustn't be content!" exclaimed Kolya. knitting his brows.

"I still haven't learned resignation," she replied dryly, "and I hope you never will. Nicolai did not either, although I may have made him sound so. But he knew the dangers as I did not and believed more was attained by pulling faithfully than by putting a chock under the wheels. We were sent to the Caucasus when I was in disgrace, as I told you, and Nicolai was in charge of supply and transport there. During the Crimean War he had gained a fine reputation as about the only general who did not steal the army's stores. It was beautiful there, and peaceful. We were very happy with our children and ourselves. I think it was the loveliest time of my marriage, although there is not a day of it I regret; even when we disagreed, it was with love. I so hope, my dear, one day you will know such happiness." She smiled at him.

Kolya muttered something indistinguishable. At fourteen he found girls a bore and wished she would simply tell him what had happened.

Ilena read his thoughts and continued after a moment: "The Turkish War broke out after we had been there five years, and then it was the same terrible nightmare we had known in Kharkov during the Crimean War. Shortages, disease, wounds which made you faint just to look at them, everywhere the dying. I pray God you will never know war, Kolya, in this fine new century of yours."

"There will be no more war," said Kolya confidently. "Russia at least needs her peace, whatever the rest do."

"I hope you're right, affairs do seem a little quieter." She sipped some tea. "General Loris-Melikov was one of our commanders against the Turks, the only successful one, and he appreciated the way his army was somehow kept supplied, although by then Nicolai was over sixty and not in good health. Often I feared for his life, he was so exhausted. He and Loris liked each other at once and two years later, when Loris was appointed by the Tsar to take control of the government, he asked for Nicolai to join him."

She stared unseeingly out of the window, plaiting papery fingers on her lap. "Nicolai had served the Tsar faithfully, but not unthinkingly. This was a chance to change things from above; he had always been sure conspiracy from below could bring nothing but misery in a country like Russia, although I often berated him for his caution. So we came back to Petersburg and Loris started work on a draft constitution. I was terribly disappointed when Nicolai told me what it contained, it was not really a constitution at all, the Tsar wouldn't hear of such a thing. But Nicolai insisted it was a beginning and certainly life improved while Loris was in power." She laughed. "Between them they threw out literally hundreds of police spies and Loris closed down the political police. The night they came back from the Gendarmerie after simply telling everyone the secret police was finished was only the second time I ever saw Nicolai take too much vodka. What a celebration we had! We knew it was too good to last but it was certainly something to have done. I would like to believe that you will live to see the day when political police are truly no more in Russia. If you do, make sure you celebrate it with a toast to your grandfather."

"I will," said Kolya firmly, liking the idea.

"Don't have too many toasts, though, vodka gives a terrible head the day after." She smiled at him teasingly and he looked at her with renewed respect; there was a certain firsthand knowledge in her voice. He and Innokenty had already discovered the distressing aftereffects of vodka and Kolya had had to spend an unexpected night at the Rogovs', where such a happening was not thought unusual.

"Within a few days of taking office Loris was shot at, but he wasn't hurt," she resumed. "I never knew an easy moment, though I tried to push it to the back of my mind."

"Why should anyone shoot at him, if he was trying to improve things?" interrupted Kolya.

"Because the really fanatical revolutionaries did not want improvement in case it should make the chance of revolution more remote," she replied promptly.

Kolya thought it over carefully. "I can see that. They would think it just a patch here and there and not really any change at all."

"They preferred people miserable and oppressed to content, and felt those who tried to help to be worse enemies than those who opposed them." There was real anger in her voice. "But who is to say matters would not be worse still with such people in control, should their revolution take place?"

Kolya tried not to feel impatient; his grandmother was, after all, very old. I expect I shall be set in my ideas at eighty, he thought, but could not imagine himself at such a great age. "I think things must be better if there were revolution," he said politely. "Have you read what some of the parties want, parties His

Majesty has banned and exiled though they have higher ideals than he will ever know?"

She leaned forward and took his hand. "Kolya, I cannot argue with you, there are things you will have to find out for yourself. I am sure no one of fourteen ever listens to their grandmother's politics. May I just give you one piece of advice which you will promise to try and remember?" He nodded. "There is an old Turkish saying I learned in the Caucasus: *Turn thine eyes from his face and thine ears from his words. Watch his hands.*"

Kolya looked completely blank, it seemed nonsense to him. "What does it mean?"

She shook her head. "You may never know, I hope you will not, but remember it. It is a wise saying and one day may help you make a choice. Your father learned the hard way. I was too preoccupied with my fears for Nicolai to notice enough of what he was doing . . ."

"What was he doing?" Kolya prompted her eagerly.

"He joined a revolutionary group, like me he wanted results in a hurry, he hadn't the patience to see how things must grow. His exile now is just because he, an officer, joined a peaceful demonstration in the 1905 revolution, but at the time of which I'm speaking, in 1881, the group he joined was very violent. Liberty Through Blood they called themselves, and the police were naturally active in searching for them." She wondered at her own cool tone; however many times she relived the moment, detachment, even now, would not come. She glanced at Kolya's intent face and glowing eyes: it would break her heart if he thought Aleksandr justified, yet it would be wicked to destroy his respect for his father.

He has a right to know, he must judge, she told herself firmly. "The group wanted new recruits but at the same time feared they might be police spies. Every new member had to undergo a test of loyalty, a task which would commit them forever, since after it they would not dare go to the police."

Kolya paled. "You mean—"

"Sometimes it was robbery, usually it was murder. Perhaps of an official, but often of a suspected traitor to the group so a double lesson was learned. They knew who Aleksandr was, he hadn't tried to hide it and they told him that before he could be fully trusted he must help them plan his father's murder, then there could be no going back for him, ever. Aleksandr knew he would be doomed too of course, but the sheer infamy of it would publicize their cause as never before."

Kolya said nothing. He dropped his eyes and started to fiddle with a loose button, she could not tell what he was thinking. The averted head, with its line of cheekbone and jaw, was suddenly agonizingly like Nicolai. She could not often see it, for the likeness was of mannerism and bone structure rather than looks, but at this moment it was almost more than she could bear.

"He refused, they insisted. They even quoted the Bible to him in mockery: 'to whom much is given, much is expected.' He truly believed in revolution and could not bear to feel he was too weak to do what was necessary, just because it was his own father. After all, anyone you kill is probably someone's father. So he finally agreed."

Kolya looked up at last. "He did it?" he asked in a flat voice.

"By God's mercy no! He planned it, he thought he could do it, but when the time came he could not. I didn't understand what was wrong with him, he seemed distraught yet would tell me nothing, and in my folly I thought it a girl he yearned for. He went to see Nicolai in his office and told him, it was my failure he did not feel able to breathe at home. Nicolai had him transferred away at once so he would be safe, no official knew he had been involved. Even when he was dying Nicolai made me promise I wouldn't tell the police what I knew by then, or allow Aleksandr to do so. Of course Liberty Through Blood knew what Aleksandr had done: he had not only failed but betrayed them too. They knew the police would arrest them within days and felt their faith at stake, so they killed Nicolai in his place. He took two days to die." She drew a deep breath. "It was not your father, Kolya, he was caught in an impossible situation and was still very young, but in my heart I blamed him bitterly. Had it not been for him it is unlikely such a small group would have picked on Nicolai as a victim. A month later the Tsar was assassinated and any change Loris and Nicolai thought they had achieved was swept away, it was all to do again."

Kolya blundered up and went over to the window, laying his forehead on the cold glass. He is too young to hear such a story, thought Ilena with a pang, but I have not now long to go and he must know.

There was no more to say and she did not try, needing all her strength to reach her bedroom door. She was surprised when Kolya put a hand under her elbow and steered her to the safety of her bed, his face still averted, still saying nothing.

"Shall I send for Marfa?" he asked gruffly at last.

She shook her head. "I think I prefer to be alone, especially from Marfa."

He smiled faintly. "Is there anything I can do for you?"

"Bless you, my dear. I have all I need for the moment."

On his way out he hesitated and then walked over to look at his grandfather's portrait. "Is it a good likeness?"

Ilena's lips curved. "Yes, very," she said softly.

He studied the face carefully. He had seen it often

but never really looked before, dismissing him casually as a fierce-looking old fellow. Now he knew that no one who had held his grandmother's love undimmed for thirty years after he was dead could be so dismissed. But even with close scrutiny the face gave little away: deep, tightly held lines, tough, watchful, unusually clean-shaven for a man of his generation.

Watching him, Ilena said unexpectedly, "I am glad you are known as Kolya. Has it never seemed strange to you?" *

He flushed. "I asked my father once, he said you didn't want me named after my grandfather."

"I couldn't bear it," she said simply. "But it had never occurred to Aleksandr you would be anything else. He could scarcely refuse me when I begged for you to have another name, but by then you were Kolya to him. Now I am glad."

Kolya ran his fingers along the brass rail at the foot of her bed. "Do you forgive my father now?"

"I forgave him years ago. He was the last person to intend harm to anyone, he only did what he thought was right," said Ilena gently. "Unfortunately forgiveness is not enough. None of it was his fault, but it happened nevertheless and has lain between us ever since. I tried to tell him when I came to fetch you and Lena that it was truly finished now, but for him I don't think it ever will be. The victim can forgive, it is not so easy for the forgiven."

Long after he had left the room she lay sleepless, eyes on the portrait, listening to him picking out odd notes on the accordion. Sad, reflective notes in tune with his thoughts, but as had been the case with Nicolai, it was not easy to tell where those thoughts were taking him.

* Kolya is the usual shortening for Nicolai, Kostya that for Konstantin.

Everything, whether good or bad, turns to music for him, she thought; whatever happens he will at least have that.

Chapter Five

Kolya only began to realize there was anything wrong when Professor Weber told him the Summer Orchestral School was to be canceled.

"I am leaving for Germany tomorrow and so are Professor Szentzler and the guest conductor. They may hold the school without us but I doubt it, I very much doubt it." He snorted contemptuously, his views on Russian inefficiency well known.

Kolya flushed; as he grew up he resented Weber's arrogant and disagreeable habits more. "Why are you all leaving, sir? Surely you can't go now, only two days before the school opens?" The intensive three weeks of orchestral work, open to exceptionally promising students from all over Russia and held after the end of the term in July, was the highlight of Kolya's year, when he could watch the shaping of individual talents into a splendid whole and feel himself an apprentice at his true trade at last.

"I have no wish to be imprisoned here for the duration of a war. In a week or two's time we may all be enemies and trying to kill each other, I think." Weber leveled an imaginary rifle and pulled the trigger, giving a faint hoot of laughter.

Kolya looked down at his fingers spread on the keyboard and was surprised by his own surge of anger. And I would like to kill you, you swine, he thought. He looked up and as their eyes met Weber's expression altered. After a moment he said quietly, "It is not a joke, is it, Kolya? I shall regret leaving St. Petersburg." He jerked a quick little bow and left the room. Kolya never saw him again.

Walking home in the hot sunshine, Kolya bought a newspaper and sat in the shade of Kazan Cathedral colonnade to read it. After a while he frowned, turned back to the front sheet and began to read again, more carefully. There was a risk of war between Habsburg Austria-Hungary and Serbia following the assassination of the Austrian archduke. It did not seem to Kolya a very serious risk, though, read as he might. The assassination was a month old, dispatches printed from Serbia appeared conciliatory and the confusions which everyone expected of Viennese politics as much in evidence as ever. What could there be to panic Weber, forty years a resident of Petersburg, on to the next train for Germany?

Kolya looked up and stared absently at the quiet buildings along the Nevsky, toward the graceful outline of the Admiralty and then all around him at spire and dome, at decorated façade and ponderous stonework, silent in the way the whole of Petersburg was silent, its people dozing or seeking the fresher air of countryside or sea. Even the sentry at the foot of the Kutuzov Memorial only shifted his position to keep pace with its thin, slowly moving shadow.

Comforted by normality, Kolya stood up, folding his newspaper into his belt. Only then did he see a small paragraph tucked into the back page announcing that His Excellency Foreign Minister Sazonov had given audience the previous evening to His Excellency the Imperial German Ambassador. His Excellency Minister Sazonov assured His Excellency the Ambassador of the Imperial Russian Government's intention to take only such measures as would secure His Majesty's interests in the present crisis.

On impulse, Kolya walked the short distance to the Foreign Ministry building but there was nothing to be seen; an air of complete somnolence lay over it too. Kolya himself was due to leave on his summer's visit to Obeschino at the close of the Orchestral School, and few Petersburgers seemed to have had similarly important reasons for lingering in the city.

He said nothing to his grandmother, knowing how even the faintest suspicion of war would upset her, but he sorely wanted to discuss the rumors with someone and next day walked across the city to the Rogovs'. He did not see so much of Innokenty now; he was a full year older and was frequently kept at home by his father to help in the business, while privately he struggled to keep up with his studies, hoping to seek entry to the Technological Institute in a year's time.

There was no doubt, though, about the way his face lit up at the sight of Kolya. "Kolya, my friend, welcome indeed. I thought you would be slaving with your orchestra in a sea of sweat."

"It is canceled," said Kolya briefly. "The German professors and guest conductor have left and some of the German students too."

"Why on earth? Is there trouble with the police or has Weber sworn at the director of studies once too often?"

Kolya laughed. "It would never have surprised me! But no, they are leaving for Germany through fear of a war."

It sounded absurd, like a practical joke, but Innokenty looked thoughtful. "The Bourse is badly down today and so are those of Berlin and London, the telegrams of prices always arrive in the afternoon."

"Oh, share prices!" said Kolya impatiently. "What have they to do with anything? Those stupid bankers are always pushing prices up or down just to make a profit."

"You and your student cafes," said Innokenty derisively. "If you had any knowledge of business at all, you'd know money is much too delicate to push around like that. I pity you if you can't earn your living by music, for surely to God trade is an utter mystery to you."

"In an ideal world there wouldn't be any money," said Kolya stiffly. "Who wants to harness his life to a profit?" In truth he was not much interested in politics, but he occasionally joined red-flagged student demonstrations out of sympathy for the slum poor thronging the city.

"Who wants to starve, which is what you and your like will do unless you come whining to the profit mongers for a handout," Innokenty flashed back. "You stay with the music you understand, Kolyushka."

Kolya swung around and out of the yard without speaking; Innokenty's use of his nickname inexpressibly sad with the sudden rift opened between them. As he walked home he noticed the growing numbers of people on the streets: at nearly every corner there were little knots of people talking, a group of students was eddying without purpose on the steps of the Imperial Library, the usual dignified calm of the State Bank disturbed by scurrying clerks and messengers. Share prices, he thought bitterly.

"Kolya, what is the matter?" his grandmother asked him, after they had sat in almost complete silence during the evening. "Shouldn't you be studying for the orchestra tomorrow?"

He shook his head. "Some of the important people have withdrawn and it is canceled." He could hardly lie about something they usually discussed at great length.

Ilena thought she understood his depression and did not probe further, it was a great shock therefore when Marfa came in wailing three days later, a smudged, black-printed paper in her hand. She did not need to be told what it was, three times before she had seen similar broadsheets, headed by the Imperial double eagle and signed by the Minister of War. The order for General Mobilization had gone out, the date Thursday, July 30, 1914.

"Why didn't you warn me?" she asked Kolya that night. "Such a thing, before I even knew there was serious trouble!" War again, this time with Germany and Austria, not distant Japan or feeble Turkey or the long-ago bungled affair in the Crimea. She could feel the strokes of her heart in every fiber of her body, like doom bells for Russia: half-awake, half-developed, half-changing Russia emerging from her chrysalis into a world which overnight had changed into a harshness unimaginable.

"I hoped nothing would come of it," Kolya said, worried by the look on her face. With the optimism of youth he had recovered from his depression of earlier in the week—his grandmother had not been so very wrong to put it down to the cancellation of the Orchestral School—and was now excited by the drama of events. Every day the capital filled up a little more, the barracks which littered the city bustling with men and horses, raucous with commands and gay with Imperial flags. The ministries too looked more businesslike, and groups of people gathered to cheer or boo the various arrivals without much knowledge of who the personages were. The Tsar was still away at Peterhof, but the windows of the Winter Palace were open to give glimpses of activity within and, most unexpected of all, when the guard changed at midday the new sentries were in service uniform, the last sight of white, gold and black disappearing with the heavy tramp of boots.

Saturday, August 1. At five in the evening the bell of Kazan Cathedral began to boom, then came St. Isaac's, then Our Lady of the Snows, then Trinity, St. Sergius, the Holy St. Vladimir, the Nevsky Monastery, St. Saviour-on-the-Blood . . . the German Ambassador had left the Foreign Ministry in tears, the declaration of war delivered. Kolya wandered for hours through the streets, fascinated. The atmosphere was incredibly gay, with parties out in the street, heads at every window, giggles in the shadows. It was only briefly dark, the northern night hesitating, then drawing out into another scorching day full of church bells and kneeling congregations overflowing down steps and alleyways.

It was midmorning by the time he returned home exhausted, to find his grandmother up and dressed, a hired drosky at the door, the depression of the day before sternly banished, her figure stiffly upright in black silk and lace.

"You—you are going out, Grandmamma?" stammered Kolya, suddenly aware that he should not have left her alone last night, knowing how she felt. Yet perhaps because of it he had not been able to forgo the gaiety of the streets.

"I am going out," she said flatly. "I am going to the English Church and you are coming with me. Go and wash, Kolya, you have fifteen minutes."

In such a mood she was formidable indeed and made him feel about five years old. She had not left the apartment since May, when Micha Traskine had taken her driving, but she was brisk and steady, scarcely needing Kolya's supporting arm.

Once in the English Church she looked around her, flooded with memories. The image of her old home far away in Sussex was brought back by the distinctive Anglican smell of wax, dust and brass polish, memories too of her first night in St. Petersburg sixty-two years before when she had entered this church as a last sanctuary in an alien wilderness. For this, she thought, is my long farewell. I shall not come here or stand on English soil again.

Kolya thought the service drab compared to the glories of the Orthodox service, but he enjoyed the fine, marching hymns and listened afterward to his grandmother anxiously questioning her acquaintance on whether Britain too would join in the war. The general opinion was against it and she was almost cheerful when they emerged into the oppressive heat outside.

"Gregor's boy Nicholas is three years older than you, so if England were to come in he would be at risk," she confided. "Although I must be lucky with Gregor and Aleksandr both too old and you too young to fight."

"I wish I wasn't," said Kolya wistfully. "Now it has started it seems tame to stay at home."

"You little fool," she said coldly. "If you go to war you die of dysentery so terrible you are half your weight in thirty-six hours, or you have your musician's hands run over by a drunken lout in charge of an ammunition wagon. I am not some card-room madame, I know war. Do not think you will have the privilege of dying for your country at the head of some glorious charge."

Kolya did not answer. For the first time he was angry with his grandmother, at the way her memories from an irrelevant past stained the excitement of the day, and they sat in a silence so intense that for a while they scarcely noticed when their drosky was hemmed in by crowds at the edge of Palace Square. A rumbling cheer went up, starting in the far spaces by the palace and rolling toward them until they were submerged in sound.

Kolya stood on the seat and in the far distance, a faint speck against the bulk of the Winter Palace, he saw, he was sure he saw, His Majesty. Another rumbling roar, changing cadence and transmuting into a

Te Deum and then the national anthem as it came. The crowd was so vast that the edge where Kolya stood was half a dozen beats behind the thrusting center, enthusiasm and singing alike reflected off dome and wall, the ground shaking with it, people weeping. Only the skies remained untouched, implacable, baking hot.

Another surge swayed over the surface of the concourse, like wind over steppe grass, as all knelt, holding aloft icons to be blessed while the distant speck made signs in the name of the Father, and of the Son and of the Holy Ghost, may He bless, keep and watch over you, my children.

Then the cheers rolled over their heads again, and few cheered louder than Konstantin Berdeyev, his century taking over control of events at last.

By his side, unnoticed, his grandmother wept.

Chapter Six

It was typical Petersburg weather—raw, bitterly cold, gray, yet in apparent defiance of the thermometer it was thawing. Every winter since Kolya had come to Petersburg—only he must remember to call it Petrograd now—January had had this exasperating wet thaw, feeling colder and more miserable than ever yet turning everything to slush, sometimes for a week or more, before freezing again to an unequaled rocky slitheriness.

This first winter of the war had already frozen away all enthusiasm from the streets, instead a grim despondency could be felt, touched here and there by anger at the lack of response from the government to the crowding disasters of the past six months. The first heady Russian advances into East Prussia were long since over, instead a deadly succession of defeats had brought a million dead by Christmas: Tannenburg, Masurian Lakes, Poland, Galicia, the regular Russian army was already almost destroyed. Countless millions of peasant conscripts could still defend Russia, but it was a barrier made of little but flesh, packed tight and offered to the butcher month after month, hoping he would become tired at last.

Kolya continued to attend the Conservatoire, practicing faithfully when there was no one available to teach him. The rest of the time he was occupied searching for food and fuel and he went less and less often to the Tauride Modern School. He stood for hours in line for bread, for thin blue milk, for a handful of fish or a few cucumbers. Old wooden buildings began to disappear as people chopped at them by night for firewood, and he often found it necessary to tramp across the frozen Neva to buy green timber from canny Finnish lumbermen making enormous profits sledging it across the Baltic. With time and effort it was still possible to find food, but prices were rising fast and nearly every week he had to ask for some trinket to sell if he was to pay for even the little he could find.

At last he swallowed his pride and went to the Rogovs to ask for work. The fur business was booming with so much demand for the army and old Rogov gladly took him on, ticketing, packing and invoicing skins. Innokenty was delighted. "I meant so often to come and see you. I hated to part with such a stupid quarrel; who would have thought we could fall out over stocks and shares of all things!"

"And you were quite wrong," observed Kolya. "Here I am earning my living by trade not music." He slung a half-cured, stinking skin into a corner. "I am grateful but I don't know how to be rid of the smell before I go home; my grandmother thinks I am still at school."

Whatever the horrors of curing putrefying skins and then having to scrub himself clean in the Rogovs' icy yard, the benefit to their diet was immediate, joints of beaver, fox and arctic hare providing almost prewar luxury. Not even this could help his grandmother, though; she weakened steadily through the winter, bedridden now and constantly chilled since Kolya had not the time to search for good fuel and the green timber gave out little heat. Marfa stoked and grumbled incessantly but nothing did any good, even the warm spring weather came too late to do more than give her one extra week of life.

Kolya took out the double windows toward the end of April, opening the casements to a flood of sunshine. Spring in Petersburg always came with dramatic speed, ice on the Neva melting like a volcano in eruption, hall porters scrambling onto roofs and shoveling snow into the street in one grand yearly avalanche so the view over the rooftops changed abruptly from white to red-painted iron or wood, the streets one day an ice-rock obstacle course, the next a morass.

"Kolya!" The voice was faint but clear. Ilena Vassilievna Berdeyeva would remain in full possession of her faculties to the last.

He turned back to the bed and sat down, taking her hand gently. "Yes, Grandmamma?"

"I had a letter from your father yesterday."

He nodded. "I did too."

"I have prayed for him . . . above all that he would know I prayed for him. I was a fool to think him too old to fight. If a reservist . . . cashiered ten years ago, is called up so soon . . ." She closed her eyes.

Kolya held her hand and said nothing. He too had been shaken by his father's letter announcing that he had been ordered to report for active service.

". . . I leave for the Polish front next week," he wrote, *"as a junior lieutenant in a line regiment since I forfeited my rank years ago. I must surely be the oldest subaltern in the army! As you may realize, I am not sorry to be going, to do something with my life again. Think kindly of me, Kolyushka, serve your country, do what is right, so that you at least will be able one day to look back on your life without regret.*

Bless you, my son. Your loving father,

Aleksandr Nicolayevitch Berdeyev."

He came out of his reverie to find her eyes open again. "When I am dead you must go back to look after your mother. She is alone at Obeschino now, she will need you."

Kolya nodded, his heart heavy, the thought of losing his grandmother and his life in Petersburg unbearable. No music today, no music tomorrow, no music any bloody day, he thought bitterly. "I will go," he said at last.

"The war will be over sometime; you'll come back to your music then," she said gently, and he felt ashamed for the way she had read his thoughts.

He gripped her hand. "I will miss you, Grandmamma; it isn't just the music."

She smiled faintly. "Do not regret me. It is the happy years I remember now, but had it not been for you, I wouldn't have wished to live so long and now . . . the end . . . is welcome. You are young, but you are strong enough to manage on your own. Feel me with you sometimes."

There was a long silence. Outside the birds sang and a gentle breeze fingered through the branches of a tree, already a faint green haze was showing on the twigs. Ilena stirred and muttered something, and Kolya bent his head to listen. "You remember the English book we read last year?" She did not open her eyes but the words were still clear.

"Do you mean the *Pilgrim's Progress?*" He had had terrible difficulty with the old-fashioned English and tangled imagery, and had ended by disliking it heartily.

The lines of her face deepened into the unmistakable shadow of a smile. "Poor Kolya, I will not ask you to . . . read it again. Your name . . . there is a passage . . . always made me hope it would be true of you. Konstantin . . . in English constant is the word . . . Mr. Valiant-for-Truth, I thought . . . look at it one day." She paused, exhausted. Indeed her exhaustion was painful to watch, if only she would stop talking, thought Kolya distractedly.

A deep shudder shook her, then another.

"She goes, Barin," said Marfa, and crossed herself, the lines of discontent on her face smoothed by feeling for the first time.

"No," said Kolya. "She cannot . . . not yet." He was seized by a terrible desire to hold onto her, to pull open by force the door closing on his youth, on love and security.

Almost as if halted by the turmoil in his mind, her breathing steadied again and Marfa opened her eyes in amazement. "Never have I heard the death breathing stop once it begins!"

He wanted to tell her to go away but the thought of such a scene over his grandmother's deathbed deterred him. Horrible ghoul, he thought resentfully, precious little you did to repay the kindness you received.

"Sell what you will, Kolya," the threadlike whisper came again. "It is all yours. Burn the portrait if you don't want it . . . not sell . . . burn it . . . promise?"

"I promise," he said, his throat tight. "I would like

to keep it, though, and the one of you." He could well understand her being unable to bear the thought of her beloved casually discarded to the indignities of a junk dealer's yard.

Soon the terrible breathing started again, until the edge of grief was dulled by a longing for it to be over. Her hand was slack in his and to pass the time he went across and searched for the *Pilgram's Progress*, flicking through the pages, trying to identify the passage she had meant.

At last he found it. *"And Valiant-for-Truth replied to the thieves who set upon him: I have stood firm and been a true man a long season, and it could not be expected I should now throw in my lot with thieves . . . My stand for the truth has cost too dear that I should ever lightly give it away."*

When he looked up her eyes were open; had it not been impossible he would have said she was smiling. "Good luck, Kolya," she said clearly.

He stopped Marfa closing the shutters and pulling the blinds. The sunshine seemed more fitting than ever the dark could be.

Chapter Seven

Kolya lingered in Petrograd far longer than he should have done, keeping his conscience quiet with various excuses as the summer passed. He gave up his job at the Rogovs' and devoted himself entirely to such music as remained in the city, practicing fervently, hardly letting a concert or a solo performance pass without attempting to gain admittance.

He paid the rent on the apartment by selling off his

grandmother's possessions one by one: he hated doing it, especially the things he knew had been precious to her, but soon he must leave for Obeschino and even last year's visit had been difficult enough, so chaotic had the railways become within days of the declaration of war. There was no chance of taking more than hand baggage with him, the future at Obeschino looked bleak enough with no likelihood of resuming his studies for years, so he was determined to make the most of the little time remaining.

Marfa continued to live in the apartment too and he was taken aback, one evening in late summer when little but bare boards remained, to find her curled up on the pile of rugs he was using as a bed. "What are you doing there?" he said sharply. He did not pay her wages, had scarcely seen her for weeks.

She giggled and he was amazed at the change in her. Gone was the old glowering Marfa, stiffly buttoned into high-necked blouses and rustling skirts, instead her hair was loosed, her face ingratiating. She seized his hand and he saw she was naked under the covers, his eyes held by the unexpected warm curves her movement revealed. He licked suddenly dry lips and knelt beside her. He had seen and heard most of the things an unsheltered student usually sees and hears in a great city, but his loins had never stirred before, his preoccupation with music leaving little emotion over to urge him out of his detachment.

Now he quivered to the feel of her, fumbling and reaching, unbuckling his trousers, but gently also running his hand along her face, wishing without being aware of the wish for more than just a coupling, for a contact, a word of endearment in a bleak world. It was this which stopped him cold, turning new-found need in a moment agonizingly to no need at all.

Marfa. My God, Marfa! He looked, in the transparency of summer dusk at her arched body, her closed eyes, her slack, stupid mouth parted to receive his, uncaring whether it was he or another of the many who no doubt helped keep her so well fleshed in this city of the undernourished. He made an inarticulate sound and pushed her away, ashamed at having felt desire but then abruptly humiliated, also, to find he was not yet sufficiently grown to do what he would without such quibbling affecting him. He put out his hand again and then knew the moment was gone. Even if he wished to, because he did not truly wish to, his body would do nothing that night.

Marfa stared at him with hatred as he stood up again. "At fifteen any boy in my village would be man enough to bed a woman as she wished."

Kolya remembered his grandmother had told him she had found Marfa an orphan in the streets, but decided argument was pointless. He glanced uneasily at the corner where her's and his grandfather's portraits were stacked against the wall, those at least were going with him.

Marfa followed his glance. "Even on canvas you're afeared of the old bitch. Perhaps you didn't like the thought of rolling on the floor with her maid, for all there isn't a carpet any longer."

"No, perhaps I didn't," said Kolya quietly, after a pause. "I think you had better take your things and go now, I am leaving at the end of the week." He was suddenly glad to have made the decision. He had not said he would go to Obeschino at once, but he knew he had already broken the spirit of his promise by staying so long.

"You're going?" she echoed. "For good?"

"Of course not. I will be back after the war, I still have years of study before I can start composing properly." I might just try something simple, if I get the time at Obeschino, he thought suddenly. I wonder if the old piano is completely ruined by moths yet.

She pushed back the rugs and stretched before beginning to dress, mocking provocation in every movement. He watched, enjoying the watching but otherwise quite unmoved. He reached out and ran a hand down her back. "You're pretty, Marfa." He held her a moment, and then unexpectedly kissed her. He realized then that she had felt some loyalty to her benefactor, had served his grandmother for years through obligation, but all the time resenting the confined lifc, her unrequited body. The service had been a duty but not a joy either to Marfa or to his grandmother. "I'll give you the spare key of the apartment and if you are careful you may not be noticed for a while."

She nodded, surprised by his change of mood, softened in spite of herself, and when he made the long tramp to the Petrograd Station four days later, she came with him, helping to carry the bundles of belongings he hoped to take as far as Lena in Moscow.

The station was jammed with people, pushing, shrieking, weeping, sitting apathetically on bundles as if they had grown to the dusty cement platforms. Soldiers sprawled asleep on every flat surface, rubbish blowing over their faces, people stepping clumsily over heaped bodies.

Kolya looked around resignedly. "You had better leave me, Marfa. I shall just have to sit it out, perhaps for days."

She put up her face quite naturally to be kissed. "Good-by, Barinushka."

He laughed. "It is just as well we are here, or this time things might be different. It is not only in your village that boys of fifteen can bed a wench with pleasure to both."

She blew him a kiss, waving until he lost sight of her in the crowd. He felt strangely forlorn after she had gone, as he clung to the few remaining pieces of wreckage from the past four years of his life amid the vast flotsam of war.

He sat on his baggage at the station for two days before finally heaving himself into a Moscow train, almost everything except some food and the rolled canvas portraits abandoned in the struggle. As the long, packed coaches clanked slowly over the points, he poked his head between two burly, rank-smelling soldiers and watched the warehouses and slums of Petrograd sliding past. It was evening but the sun was still well above the horizon and far in the distance he could see the gleam of gold which was Admiralty spire, a flash of silver marking the line of the Neva, the wide-shadowed trough of the Nevsky slicing past palace and church, shop and concert hall. As if to bid him farewell he could just hear the distinctive jangle of the Boris Church close by the Rogovs'. Innokenty, he thought, will I ever see him again?

"Write!" he had said to Innokenty at their difficult farewell earlier in the week.

"I will try," replied Innokenty soberly. "But I don't think the mail is going through. Even the harvest can't be shifted with the railways in such a shocking state, the cities will starve this winter."

"Write just the same," urged Kolya. "I will."

Innokenty smiled at him. "I promise. But I'm seventeen next year and into the army then—I'll see you at the front in 1918."

Kolya looked across toward the Rogov house; Innokenty had sounded as though he knew he had less than a year to live. And I have perhaps two, thought Kolya in sudden panic, staring at the fast-vanishing city. The mellow gold of buildings still showed here and there but otherwise Piter—beautiful, sad, exciting, squalid Piter—had withdrawn already into its own lavender and blue shades of distance.

He took a deep breath, rancid with packed soldiery. Somehow, one day I will be back, he resolved.

Chapter Eight

It was over a week before their train drew into Moscow, and by that time most of the passengers were on the edge of starvation. They had seldom traveled more than a few versts at a time and were often stopped for hours before inexplicably jolting on again. Food was sold by peasants appearing at wayside stations or out of the woods with a few eggs or wicker baskets of bread and honey, but Kolya had little money to spare and it seemed as if many of the other passengers were in the same state.

He had never been so glad to see flambeaux still burning in front of the Kobrin mansion, the effort of dragging his few remaining possessions through Moscow's streets almost beyond him. Had the Kobrins lived on the other side of town, he would have curled up to sleep where he stood and probably been robbed of everything he had left.

It took all his determination to force his way past the porter, which was scarcely surprising since he was crawling with bugs from the soldiers, haggard with hunger, his face filthy and showing the straggling beginnings of beard. In the end Kobrin himself came out to see what was going on and immediately welcomed him, tears running unashamedly down his cheeks.

"It is such a pleasure to see you, Konstantin, my boy," he explained, wiping his eyes. "So many knocks on the door are to tell us another of the family or of our friends will come this way no more. This God-rotted war." He crossed himself and then said simply, "Your grandmother, I prayed for her soul."

"Thank you, sir," stammered Kolya. Between excitement, emotion and hunger he was close to collapse, finally falling asleep among the remnants of the feast the Kobrins attempted to make him eat.

When he awoke he was in bed, washed, his hair shaven down to stubble, but blessedly free of bugs, total exhaustion replaced by a pleasant disinclination to move. He scarcely dared show himself downstairs with a head like a horse brush, but the Kobrins laughed at him, accustomed as they were by now to dealing with vermin-ridden soldiers on leave. Lena threw her arms around his neck in a way he found surprisingly pleasant; in spite of her love for him, his grandmother had never been demonstrative.

He kissed her heartily back. "You look very fine, upon my word. How many little nieces and nephews is it I have now?"

"Don't you dare tell me you didn't know, when Grandmamma made you write a polite letter each time one was born! Three!" She pouted prettily.

Kolya affected amazement. "Three? Er . . . let me see . . . that is Katya the second, little Sanka and . . . He pretended to scratch his head then whipped his hand away, embarrassed by the repulsive, bristly feel of it.

"Serves you right," giggled Lena. "Horrible boy. There is Maryushka, just ten months old. Vanya hasn't seen her yet." Unexpectedly she burst into tears and ran from the room.

"We haven't heard anything from Vanya for several weeks," explained Kobrin heavily. "One of his fellow officers told us he disappeared during an attack, we pray he may be a prisoner." He sat bolt upright scorning weakness, thick hands flat on the table, but all the while tears were running down his cheeks apparently without his knowledge, and his beard, which Kolya remembered as thickly black and curling, was limp and streaked with gray. "He is the last of my sons, God rest them. Ygor fell at Tannenburg, Leo near Lublin, Anatoli died here a few weeks ago from his wounds."

Kolya did not know what to say and wisely said nothing. In the three weeks he stayed with the Kobrins the old man never once referred to his sorrow again; much later Kolya came to realize it was the wild hope aroused by his arrival which had temporarily broken down his defenses, the hope that one of his sons had somehow survived to come home again. Madame Kobrina was completely crushed by the successive blows which had swept her four sons away, and drifted around the house, scarcely aware of the squalling litters of children underfoot, the sole evidence remaining of a vanished generation.

Everywhere in Moscow it was the same. In Petersburg, Kolya had so concentrated on his music, while most of his friends were not yet of army age, that the huge numbers of Russia's war dead had been a distant horror, not a poignant personal tragedy. Here, living with a family again and meeting their friends, he realized there was not a mansion, house, apartment or hut in Moscow which was not mourning its dead and mutilated loved ones. Food shortages were less acute than in Petersburg, the long *khvosty*, or waiting lines, outside every food shop not quite so long or so ill-tempered, grief rather than discontent the hallmark of Moscow in 1915 with its booming wartime production and spiraling wages.

Kolya would have liked to stay; he knew his presence cheered the household slightly and the second day after his arrival Kobrin bought him a magnificent grand piano. Thereafter Kolya played to the family on the evenings they were home, uncomfortable and awkward with the knowledge that he was not a performer of outstanding skill: his talent, if he truly had one, lay rather with sound and composition. But the Kobrins knew him as a musician, to them that meant playing the piano, and Kolya was only too willing to do anything he could to ease their unhappiness.

At last he sought out Kobrin in his counting room, where he was peering at columns of figures and rattling away at an abacus. "Ah, Kolya." He pushed his spectacles down his nose. "You see I still use an abacus like the Volga peasant I am."

"You are incredibly quick at it, sir." Kolya wondered whether he should have offered to help in the bank during his visit. "I think it would take me far longer to do the same work on paper."

"No need to flatter me, my boy," said Kobrin sharply. "I'm not ashamed of where I came from."

"No, sir, of course not. I come from a swamp village in Oryol Province but I hope to take my chances as you have yours," Kolya replied stiffly.

Kobrin threw back his head and bellowed with laughter. "You insolent young pup! You keep out of the bloody army. Russia will need a few like you after the war."

Kolya swallowed, unable to see what he had said which was so funny. "I am afraid I must leave for Obeschino at the end of the week, sir. I should be with my mother before the heavy frosts. I'm sorry to have to leave you all so soon."

Kobrin nodded, his face somber. "It is hard for you, it is hard for all of us. I am sixty-six years old and here I am back with a houseful of women and babies to support, and whatever I do the bank is sliding away from me. Another year of this devil-spawned war and we will all be sweeping the streets."

Kolya looked around at the polished mahogany,

marble, bronze, malachite and porphyry gleaming on every side. "It all looks firmly held at present, sir."

"It is not. The ruble, the foreign exchanges, trade, everything a sound bank is founded on are crumbling away, so how can it stand? That bloody stupid Tsar and his German wife, with their insane ministers and stinking Rasputin, have ruined us all."

Kolya knew a profound sense of shock. His talk was interlaced with vague revolutionary sentiments culled from his fellow students, but such bitter condemnation coming from a respected, solid banker like Kobrin made the ground itself shake under his feet.

"I have shocked you, eh?" Kobrin looked at him keenly. "I see I have, one forgets how young you are. But I was very fond of your grandmother and I am going to give you some advice. Stay at Obeschino; you will have enough to eat and the cities are not going to be fit to live in soon. The troubles which are coming may pass you by there. As soon as we're sure there is no hope for Vanya I am sending Lena and her children to England; your Uncle Gregor will do something for her there."

"To England!"

"Yes. I have money enough at present, so I may as well spend it on something worthwhile before it all vanishes. My wife and I are too old to start afresh, but the widows and children of my other boys are all going to stay in Finland for a while. Lena can travel with them before going on to England."

"But why? She can't wish to leave Russia, her children—" Kolya paused, confused, and then plunged on: "Their father has probably died for Russia; they should stay here and one day help build it up again."

For a moment he thought Kobrin would strike him; instead he spat into the solid brass cuspidor beside his desk. "I promised your grandmother I would look after Lena and I am doing so. Another year like this last one and travel will become too dangerous for a pack of women and children. As it is I shall send them in winter by sledge rather than attempt using the railways. It will not be long before money is meaningless; every bank in Moscow will close its doors and the power money still gives me will be gone forever. I shall be back among the rabble with everyone else, and starvation will make it a rabble to be reckoned with. In the past the army could be trusted to put down revolution but now they are all dead—the whole bloody regular army is under the snow and mud of the frontier. The army we have left is no different from the rabble itself. Now do you understand?"

Kolya fiddled with some pens on the desk and then said slowly, "I still think true Russians shouldn't run away. A real change is needed here and everyone left should help build something better after the war." He looked up and met Kobrin's eyes, then spat defiantly into the cuspidor.

Kobrin jumped up and hit him, openhanded with all his force, slamming his head against the carved mantel. "You stupid little sod! That's rough village talk and you'd better get used to it with your new friends, marching under your red banners and stringing up me and my like by our guts. You enjoy your revolution and at the end of it all you may be glad your fine idealists didn't rape your sister along the way."

Kolya heard him through swinging strokes of pain, but the words made no sense. Somehow he mumbled an incoherent excuse and staggered out of the room, as much upset by a quarrel with a man he respected as by the effects of Kobrin's blow.

Back in the counting room Kobrin wiped his spectacles carefully, then reached for the abacus again. His eyes fell on the cuspidor and suddenly he laughed. Well, good God Almighty, he thought, it is lucky I didn't promise his grandmother to look after that one.

Part Two
CONSUMING FLAMES
1917-21

Chapter Nine

The column of soldiers stretched forever. Heads down, hunched deep into coats, packs, old blankets, anything giving protection from the cold, tightly bunched in the forlorn hope that the man in front would take the brunt of the piercing wind, keeping moving because to stop meant death, frozen almost in the act of stumbling aside. Wavering lines of dead trees along the track marked their passage, where the bark had been torn off to chew, thawed out against their starveling bodies as they marched.

Trooper Berdeyev was beyond thought, putting one deadened leg in front of the other, the only spark of human feeling his resolve not to fall behind, not to burrow into the comfort of the deep snowdrifts along the way and relinquish forever his hold on his century. Officially he was a member of the 103rd Saratovsky Cavalry, but they had no horses: after two and a half years of war it was beginning to dawn on the generals that the thousands of horses littering their rear areas were almost useless, even though they had forgotten to make the necessary requisitions for extra infantry weapons. In common with most of his fellows, Trooper Berdeyev had only a knife with which to fight the invaders of his country.

The war had borne down on Obeschino as it had

on Moscow and Petersburg, the setting different but the miseries as hard to bear. He had arrived in late autumn, the woods mellow with sunshine by day, branches cracking sharply as frosts exploded late-flowing sap at night. The weathered log huts were unchanged, reed thatched or roofed with layers of silvery shingles, lurching slightly at the corners and strapped together by twining creepers. The slope of the fields, the bottomless mud of tracks just rimed by ice welcomed him with their ancient familiarity, even the balcony incredibly not yet fallen, only sagging a little lower to rest on fragile layers of undercarving.

But as he walked around the village he realized that there, in the place which was bone of his bone as even Petersburg could never be, the changes were cruellest of all. As the first hard frosts opened the humblest forest track to the insatiable demands of the army, the few remaining men and draft oxen were swept away, the pigs killed either for easier hiding or to be salted for the hungry soldiers. Such fodder as the quartermasters could find, the potatoes, the scrawny fowls and fattened calves, all disappeared into the unimaginable limbo to the west.

Stepan Ivan'itch, Vasili Ivan'itch, Ygor Dimt'ritch, Vanya Pyotr'itch . . . the long toll of village names gone forever was almost unbearable. Kolya's mind was unable to grasp the loss of every one of the boys and young men who had peopled his childhood. Many had tramped to the factories and wages of a new life rather than to war, but they too would never return to Obeschino. Of them all only Petya had so far returned, with a leg blown off and an agony in the stump which made him sweat every time the wind changed. Then Luka sidled home, a hole in his hand which everyone knew he had done himself but which they regarded as nothing but evidence of his good sense.

"What shall we do, Barin?" the village women asked

him if he walked past their huts. "Barin, what shall we do?" Everywhere the chorus was the same until only shame kept him from shouting at them; he knew no more than they how they could survive another year of war without their men or their animals, with only pieces of paper to show for their seized crops.

The summer of 1916 was incredibly beautiful. Calm, warm air strong with the scent of pine and hedgerow lay gently over the land, faint with hot shadows. Grass and birch rustled under a curved, starlit sky and then were etched to stillness by the bright haze of morning and pale blue flowing of light across the meadows at sunset. The harvest was good too, gathered laboriously by hand with only two oxen hidden from requisition to help with the work, but the army and the cities would see little of it, for the peasants had become skilled at hiding what they had left and no longer trusted the money they were offered in the markets of Yakovka or Oryol.

Kolya worked a sixteen-hour day in the fields and in the clotted little garden behind the house, any thought of music deadened by fatigue while his hands roughened and thickened like those of any peasant. In the few peaceful hours of dusk he had neither energy nor inclination to play the moth-eaten piano, but he never became used to the tedium of endless evenings without conversation or interest in anything beyond the immediate. The Petersburg wits and students had often been cruel or fanatical, shallow or malicious, but they had never been so utterly devoid of interest as he found his life at Obeschino with his mother.

He remembered vaguely that as a child he had found her fun; pretty and tender, quick to comfort scrapes and bruises, sweet-smelling and happy to see him when he prattled of adventures by the river or of monsters in the woods. She was still pretty, still tender and affectionate, but the years of idleness and isolation had so rotted her mind that after the evening kiss, the exclamations at his sweat and filth, the eager laughter over any little anecdote of the day which he recounted, she had nothing to say.

Firm news, beyond generalized rumors of disaster, was hard to come by, but news or the lack of news made little difference to the household. In autumn his mother bewailed the shortening days, in the spring she was surprised and happy to find them drawing out again, but when Kolya suggested that the longer hours of daylight might tempt her into more activity, she was doubtful and unhappy at the thought, summer drifting by without her making up her mind on so important a subject.

In September came news, so long awaited as to cause hardly any surprise, that Aleksandr Nicolayevitch Berdeyev was dead, destroyed not by wounds but by the sheer exertion and discomfort of war. Kolya refused to mourn him, certain his father had been thankful for release from a life which had long been insupportable, and only with difficulty hid his exasperation at the weeks of tears in which his mother indulged.

When he left Obeschino immediately after his birthday in January 1917 to walk the fifty versts to Yakovka and offer himself to the draftmasters, he was not being heroic or romantic or stupid; indeed words could not have described his reasons even to himself. It was the hypnotic, insatiable, bloody monster war itself which drew him, which was devouring everything and could not be allowed to leave him behind. He had slaved ever since the news of his father's death to lay in enough food and fuel to keep his mother safely through the coming year: stacks of split logs were piled in the cellar, corn hidden underground, fish, rabbits and even foxes frozen in layers of snow behind the shed, more fish and game salted for the spring. The night before he left he went out into the forest and chopped four long poles and hauled them back to the house. A harsh wind was blowing, the snow blinding, deafening. A lamp hanging under the balcony reflected flakes dancing in every direction like startled birds, fluttering and falling and fluttering up again. Golden light lay on the trampled snow as he heaved the poles into position, supporting the weight of the balcony as he did so on muscles toughened by the past sixteen months of labor.

"Whatever have you been doing?" demanded his mother when he came in at last. "The whole house was creaking."

"I expect it was, it has become used to a state of near-collapse," retorted Kolya. "I was determined to have the balcony shored up properly before I left; it is ten years now I can remember it needing to be done."

"Oh, the balcony! It has stayed ten years, I daresay it will last a few more."

"Perhaps I wanted to feel it would still be there when I come back," he suggested, looking around at the shabby furniture, the pale sheen of their one lamp, oil for the winter another worry.

She gave a faint shriek. "You are never going in this blizzard!" Although they spoke of it often and he had told her weeks ago of his intention to leave in January, she would never believe tomorrow could be the appointed day.

"It will blow itself out by morning," he replied indifferently. "And then be a good day for traveling while the snow is fresh. Taras Pyotrovitch goes part of the way to deliver our quota of timber to the army and I'll walk the rest easily enough."

"Oh, Kolya," her face puckered. "What will I do without you?"

He put his arm around her awkwardly. "You have fuel for this winter and next, food until well into the summer."

She looked alarmed. She had known he was going,

but beyond feeling regret and fear she had not considered the implications. "But next winter, Kolya! The war goes on forever, what will I do next winter?"

"The army would take me long before next winter anyway," he pointed out.

"Well, why not wait until they do?" she asked reasonably.

"I don't wish to go as a sheep to the slaughter. I go because—now—I want to."

"I think it's nothing but selfishness," she said sharply. "You are tired of it here. What about me, marooned in this mudhole eleven years when less than two has been enough for you?"

Kolya thought about it carefully. He had a trick of withdrawing from a conversation to think something through, and by the time he spoke again he saw to his astonishment that his mother was almost asleep. Yes, he thought, my God, eleven years at Obeschino would destroy me. But I do not want to go to war, if I had my choice I would go back to Petersburg, it is just that I must go.

He was so incensed with his mother for not staying awake on his last evening that anger alone stiffened his resolve to leave. She had stung him by her accusation of selfishness: he remembered Kobrin and thought of his promise to his grandmother. Well, I did go to Obeschino, he thought resentfully. Sixteen blasted months as a peasant by day and watching my mother sleep in the evening, it is enough. If she does not rouse this summer . . . she will know she must rouse, it may be the saving of her to have something she must do to live.

This lingering feeling of guilt was no comfort for a freezing trooper slogging across the endless plain. Southwest, ever southwest, the endless numbed footsteps. At Yakovka he had been pushed into a newly arrived draft from the steppelands of Saratov, their speech echoing Kobrin's blurred vowels retained from his Volga boyhood . . . he thought of Lena, by now in England. There had been a brief message from Kobrin to say the family had arrived in Finland nearly a year ago.

Night descended and everyone who could crowded into some wretched huts. Kolya, as one of the youngest recruits, was left outside as usual but by now he was used to it, almost welcomed the break in monotony provided by wood gathering, building snowbreaks, the glow of fire on the shrouded figures of his companions —usually it was the same members of the company who were left outside.

Although very cold there was no wind and in the calm air songs and boastings, tales of the old steppe and fears for families left at home soon snatched backward and forward. Kolya was astonished anew at the range of feeling these simple men put into a few words: much of his vocabulary was unknown to them and already he was finding obscure satisfaction in expressing himself as they did, in the scanty words of farm and field and church. His accent no one thought strange, they knew him for an Oryolsky, his hands and muscled shoulders proclaimed him a peasant as themselves, and in his two months in the army he had come to slur his vowels and scoop his consonants as they did.

"May God be praised we reach the end of our road before spring." Poliarnyi was a squat elderly man, twice passed over for the army but now finally included in the draft.

They all nodded agreement; the cold of winter was not so much feared as the icy mud and wet of spring. "How much further do you think?" Zakhar looked perpetually overwhelmed by fear, not of the war but of those around him. The tough scroungers of the column instantly recognized him as the natural butt for their malice, sending him scurrying after pieces of bark to mend their boots, dry timber for their fires or on extra fatigues in their place.

"A week, surely less than a week now." Poliarnyi nodded wisely.

"How do you know?" asked Kolya. The road was the same as it had been six weeks before: tramping men, hulked snow over vast dumps of equipment rotting into uselessness while they had nothing with which to fight except their bare hands, a few carts and trucks, the occasional hospital wagon.

"Ah." Poliarnyi winked. "I can smell it."

Kolya inhaled a lungful of smoke and spluttered. The others laughed. "The poor little one! Kolyushka, my boy, you should return home to your cradle."

Kolya slid a hand through the layers of blanket and uniform he was wearing into the pocket of his tunic. It was quite a feat to find what he wanted and his companions watched with the attention of those who have endless hours on their hands. At last he found it, a small screw of *makhorka,* a cheap and universal tobacco substitute. Poliarnyi's eyes glistened.

"I bet you so much," Kolya put a small pile on his palm, "that in a week we are still marching."

"You have lost already, Kolyushka. Give it to me now." Poliarnyi sucked his lips.

Kolya laughed and folded it away. "Not likely. Just think how the days will pass for you now, wondering whether you'll win or not."

In exactly three days Poliarnyi claimed his prize, as they all felt the earth trembling under their feet from the guns. It was as if he had extra senses tuned to the land around him. Two days after that they were turned aside from the march into a wood, runners in smart armbands greeting them as if the war depended on their arrival. A field kitchen appeared with the luxury of hot *kasha* gruel and fresh baked bread: they wondered why they had dreaded war so much. There were even some nurses just across a field from the wood, impossibly feminine in white starched gowns under their furs, and several of the men went to watch in wonder as they bustled about "like priests at Easter," as Zakhar said.

But then they were left alone. There were no tents, the kitchen and then the nurses disappeared, the snow and frost began to thaw, even gunfire became intermittent. For much of the day they scattered in search of food while the worried lieutenant in charge of them tried to find someone to give him orders, but the rest of the time they just stayed there—hour after hour, day after day, becoming wetter and colder and hungrier.

March. The rains began and they discovered that the whole countryside around them was a morass; in every direction pools of water were only prevented from becoming lakes by a haphazard overstitching of tussocks. Kolya barely recognized his companions; he knew he would not have recognized himself. They were all filthy and bearded, either skeletal with dysentery or puff-bellied from their laboring digestions.

They watched enviously as columns of men passed along the road. By night isolated groups tramped stolidly toward the front; by day much larger numbers (it seemed to Kolya) pressed eagerly back toward the rear. Occasionally their wood trembled to the sound of shelling; often the world was mysteriously silent but for the birds, the sucking of boots on the road or the occasional single shot which marked a deserter caught.

They heard rumors of units refusing to advance, of a government crisis in faraway Petrograd: it was difficult for raw troops to make sense of it all, the misery of wet and hunger more immediate than jumbled whispers of distant events.

"I didn't come all this way to rot in a bog," grumbled Poliarnyi. "Defend Mother Russia, they said; God go with you, my son, they said; your father the Tsar needs you, they said." He spat expressively. "This war does not know I am here, but my little farm in Saratov knows I am not there."

"My friend, you speak sense." Boiko was a black-browed giant of a man. If anyone in the company needed help he went to Boiko; he would carry a pack or a comrade, do a duty, give up his food to a fever-stricken youth who would be dead by morning. "Another month and I go home. My woman can sow but she cannot reap and salt and chop wood for herself and all the little ones. It will take me two months to walk home, but I can give the Tsar my father one more month in his wood if he wishes it."

"How can you walk home? You'll be caught, other soldiers will shoot you." Zakhar cringed as if he could feel the bullets strike his defenseless body.

Boiko looked scornful. "I have walked all the way here, as God is my witness I will walk all the way back. The land is large, officers and sergeants few nowadays. The soldiers are like us, they will look the other way."

There was a sudden blast of air, a flat crash. They all jumped up in alarm. "It was as if the devil himself opened his oven door and slammed it shut," muttered Zakhar, crossing himself. All over the wood men were on their feet, looking at each other, knowing nothing of battles. It was the first shell to come within a couple of versts of them in three weeks at the front.

The holocaust hit the wood with no more warning. German heavy batteries followed up their ranging shot with everything they had: from their vantage point the dark pool of woodland punctuating bright green enameled marsh looked an obvious strong point, straddling the road east and masking approach to drier ground beyond.

Kolya was blinded, deafened, thrown off his feet and agonizingly impaled on the hacked roots of an up-ended tree. He could not breathe. He was not aware of explosions, only of air being viciously pumped out of his lungs, his ribs collapsing on his heart, before a vomiting inrush of breath kicked his body into action again, only to be terrifyingly withdrawn in an instant.

As quickly as the tornado came, so it went. Had they known anything of war they might have realized that only the bog had thrown out the enemy's timing long enough to give them minutes to live before the assault came in.

But they knew nothing. Here and there in the wood men picked themselves up, mud-splattered specters gestured and grimaced, unable to make each other hear. Mouths gaped in screams but the survivors were too stunned to notice, many had simply disappeared, drowned in churned mud where even brief unconsciousness was enough for lungs and nose to fill forever.

Boiko pulled Kolya out of his tree roots; it seemed natural that Boiko at least should be unharmed, his uniform completely blown off, but so caked in mud his nakedness was scarcely noticeable. Kolya staggered over to the nearest clump of bodies, consciousness wavering as his tormented lungs sought recovery; they were all dead, every one neatly disemboweled by suction. He fell on his knees retching, but everything within him was already voided without his being aware of it.

Boiko shook him again, pointing. Others were pointing, he saw Zakhar with his mouth open, Poliarnyi standing on one leg, staring. Down the road and jumping from tussock to tussock toward them was a long line of gray figures. Kolya was still deaf, but he became aware of men falling again, saw branches flicking as if struck by invisible hailstones as the Germans fired.

It was the lieutenant who pushed his way through the dazed men: a boy not much older than Kolya. Few had taken much notice of him on the march, and during the weary time they had waited in the wood he had been as bewildered as they. Now he knew his duty. Drawing his sword he motioned the men forward: he was deaf too, the blood running out of his ears and from a long flap of skin hanging from his jaw.

Boiko pushed forward suddenly, stirred by the boy's courage, and some of the other men followed him, seizing pieces of broken branch and grubbing for stones as they went.

Faintly, through the thick stuffing in his head, Kolya began to hear sounds, very distant and indistinct. He clutched a heavy club of timber; it was curved and fitted with comforting solidity into his hand. He was still too dazed to think it odd to face machine guns and rifles with stones and clubs: not one of their company had yet been issued with a rifle.

The enemy, encouraged by the lack of return fire, came forward almost casually, beginning to call to each other, satisfied there was no enemy waiting for them.

"*Zhivo! Vperiyod!* Look alive! Forward!" The lieutenant leaped to his feet as the first enemy reached the edge of the wood, his words a tinny squeak in the distance.

"*Ura! Ura!*" Kolya heard, and shouted himself. "*Ura!*" Everywhere men jumped to their feet, battering at the gray figures, sometimes seizing a rifle and firing back along the road, more often simply knocking down and trampling astonished Germans into the mud with their patched boots. Just for a moment the Germans wavered, shocked by the semicrazed, mudstained figures lurching out at them, but it was only for an instant. The second line of attackers fired almost at once and plunged forward. Some of their comrades fell but the Russians were smashed back into the bushes whence they had sprung. The lieutenant was almost cut in two by a hail of bullets, Kolya tripped over Boiko and fell heavily, only to find Boiko was dead before he even struck the ground.

He stayed pressed to the earth, too terrified to move. He had swung his club at a German; he still remembered the man's look of amusement as he sidestepped, changing to bewilderment as he caught one of his own comrades' bullets in the back.

The Germans on the road kept up a steady fire and Kolya could now hear bullets ricochetting and tumbling end over end among the trees. He heard shouts from the Germans immediately in front of him as they yelled at their fellows to stop firing so they could advance, and a terrible high-pitched screaming from Zakhar as he crouched on his haunches, hands over his ears, a few paces away.

Kolya took a deep breath and began to crawl; it did not require much knowledge of war to understand that he had only seconds to get clear. He shook Zakhar's knee. "Come on!" He was whispering, for all the world as though the Germans could hear. "*Skoreye!* Quick! Can you crawl?"

Zakhar took no notice, continuing to scream and rock himself backward and forward. Kolya threw a desperate glance around, he dared not get up, the whole wood was alive with bullets, flipping just above his head. God alone knew how Zakhar so far remained unhit.

He jerked at Zakhar's leg to get him flat, to try and pull him clear somehow. Before his eyes, as Zakhar went on his knees, his stomach poured out in slippery grayish coils, his hands scrabbling among the unspeakable mess, trying to thrust it back, cursing Kolya for what he had done. Heedless of danger, Kolya staggered to his feet, lurching among the massacred trees and bodies, away from the carnage, above all away from the terrible sound of Zakhar's curses.

Chapter Ten

The 103rd Saratovsky re-formed in the village of Nosov, nearly thirty versts behind the front. Kolya was surprised to find over a hundred men had survived the cataclysm in the wood; somehow he had imagined he must be the only one to do so.

Nosov was dreary enough, even without sullen, unkempt men scattered everywhere. Thatch from the huts had been fed to the army's horses, walls pulled down for firewood, the few women so bundled up in rags that soldiers in search of sport stripped even the old in search of those young enough to satisfy them—and then often enough took the old anyway.

Kolya watched it all with indifference. He did not want a woman, indeed his shocked body and lacerated back could not have taken one, but Zakhar had cured him of any desire to interfere in the affairs of others.

"He would have died anyway," argued Poliarnyi. "He must have been holding in his guts with his knees and what kind of life is that for a man?"

"I know." Kolya was sitting on a bench, torn tunic open to the waist, battered cap shading his eyes, soaking up the spring sun gratefully. "It is the way he cursed me. I can't get it out of my mind."

Poliarnyi shook his head vigorously. "Every soldier curses his comrades without meaning it. You tried to help, forget it. You could easily have crawled by and left him." A bug dropped from his hair and he cracked it idly with his thumbnail. "Did you hear the latest talk?"

Kolya nodded. "I don't think it can be true, do you?"

"Of course it is true! The Tsar—*gotovo!* Finished!" He drew a finger across his throat. "The cook at the dressing station told me, it is well known all over the army, only our Godforsaken wood was left to die for a little father who had already left us."

Kolya stirred uneasily. His father might have cherished revolutionary ideas but he had also been an officer in the Imperial Guards, his grandfather a minister of state. There were too many generations of service to the Romanovs bred into him for his thoughts to settle. He felt disinclined for any kind of mental effort, his back desperately sore where the roots had stripped it down to bone in places.

"You see, Kolyushka," persisted Poliarnyi. "It is our Russia now; there was an order which said so while we were in the wood."

"Too damned much went on while we were in that wood," muttered Kolya. "Why the hell were we left there anyway if the whole army was retreating?"

Poliarnyi shrugged. "We are like old coats, always left behind somewhere. Can you read, Kolyushka?"

"Of course." Kolya was too relaxed for thought, although he had always been careful not to discuss his home or family, knowing life as an ordinary trooper would become intolerable if he were revealed as an aspiring musician, a possible count four years educated at a Petersburg Modern School.

Poliarnyi looked at him thoughtfully. "You're a queer one and no mistake. Here, I picked these up yesterday, you read them to me if you can."

Kolya flushed. "Over half the boys in my village can read, the priest teaches them." That at least was true; his reforming father had insisted on it and sometimes taught them himself, flushing boys out of hovel and field for lessons.

"Oh well, see what you make of these, then." Poliarnyi handed over a scuffed pile of smudged paper.

Kolya leafed through them idly, then sat bolt upright, the unexpected movement wrenching a grunt of pain from him. "My bloody back! I swear I never want to see another upended tree as long as I live." He chuckled suddenly. "We needn't worry about this one anyway. '*Instructions to all ranks concerning the use of delousing equipment.*' If they would only produce some delousing equipment, all ranks would no doubt be delighted."

"By the holy St. Andrew, Kolyushka, you're enough to make the saints in their heaven fight!" Poliarnyi pawed at him impatiently. "What do the rest say?"

"Yes, Konstantin Aleksandr'itch, what do they say?" Several soldiers were gathered around now, some fingering the papers hopefully as if touch would give them knowledge, one or two carefully spelling them out for themselves. The younger city poor could now nearly always read but in the countryside it was a rarer skill, laboriously acquired and easily forgotten, and the 103rd Saratovsky were mostly from the far steppe.

" 'Soldiers of the Motherland!' " read Kolya. " 'Russia is now a free country and you, Russian soldiers, are free men! As free men you will defend your homeland, throw out the enemy, build a new age for Russia, for yourselves and for your children. Fight truly! Guard your freedom!' " He looked up from the crumpled sheet and stared unseeingly over the squalid village. Far in the distance, caught by the setting sun, a single tall pine was shining brilliantly gold. "Well, by God," he said slowly. "*Svoboda.* Freedom."

Poliarnyi scratched his head. "*Slaboda.* What would that mean, Kolyushka?"

"Well . . ." Kolya hesitated. Just what did it mean to soldiers a handful of versts behind the front line? "I suppose it means we are all our own men now, the government will divide the land among us, we will not have to seek permission to do so many things."

There was an excited murmur, everyone nodding wisely, holding on to his neighbor as if contact would make the change more real, telling of the piece of land he coveted back in his village. Laughter spurted in one or two groups at suggestions of the retribution awaiting hitherto all-mighty officials. *"Slaboda! Slavoda! da! da!"* They smiled, punched each other in the ribs, shouting down the street to comrades, often just shouting.

"It is *svoboda*," began Kolya apologetically, and then thought better of it; it was the idea, not the new, unknown word which was important. He sat on through the noise, flicking over the sheets, a weird mixture of army orders, information posters and official proclamations; whatever else was being forgotten the official printing presses were working at full stretch. Right at the bottom he came on a small, unimpressive poster, blotched letters uneven, ink already turning brown. "The Council of Ministers of the Provisional Government of the Russian Republic proclaims that Nicolai Aleksandrevitch Romanov has been conveyed to his residence at Tsarskoye Selo following his renunciation of the throne. Dated . . ."

"My God," exclaimed Kolya, "it is nearly three weeks ago surely?" He added up as best he could in his head, his recollection of recent time being somewhat hazy. "And he had already abdicated then." He shook Poliarnyi by the shoulder. "Look, Polyushka! The Tsar has gone, there is a Committee of Ministers issuing all this stuff. Russia is a republic!"

There was a baffled silence. "Tell me, Konstantin Aleksandr'itch," one of the soldiers asked earnestly, "now I am free can I walk home to my village?"

Kolya hesitated. "No," he said finally. "I'm sure it doesn't mean that. The Germans are too close for us to go back to our villages yet. The officers would shoot you if you tried."

"But it says we are free," the man insisted. "And if

we are to choose our leaders, we can choose our officers and tell them to order us home."

"Da! da!" shouted several more. "Come on, Poliarnyi, you be our officer and order us home!"

Poliarnyi went a curious bright pink. "An officer? Me?" He turned to Kolya. "Could I truly do that, little one?"

Kolya shook his head. "Look, it says we must still fight."

"How can we fight! We are free men, free to say we cannot fight. We have done our best. Poliarnyi, tell us to go home now." Their mood was changing from happy rejoicing to anger, but the arrival of a field kitchen diverted attention for the moment. With the better weather food had improved slightly: rye bread most days, hot millet *kasha*, even the occasional tub of vegetable soup made an appearance. The countryside around Nosov was relatively unspoiled and as the long, idle weeks passed some of the men helped the village women in the fields or set traps for game. The German guns became a little louder, but not disturbingly so, as if they too were waiting on events.

The only excitement which punctuated this time of waiting was the arrival of a new captain and lieutenant, visibly disconcerted by the unkempt rabble they were meant to be taking over, the perfection of their tailoring only marred by the pale space on their caps where the Imperial eagle had been removed. They called the men into the street and began to read the new oath of allegiance issued by Prince Lvov, now president of the Council of Ministers. ". . . I swear obedience to the Provisional Government until . . . a system of government is established by the will of the people . . . I swear obedience—"

"Why should we swear?" yelled a voice. "We are free, why should we obey a pair of snotty-faced rabbits?"

The Lieutenant looked frightened, but the Captain continued to read steadily. The man next to Kolya threw a lump of mud, which missed, but the jeers redoubled. "We have our own officer! We choose now!"

The Captain finished his reading in spite of the noise and then stood staring at them; he did not seem afraid as his Lieutenant did, only scornful and angry. Finally, as the noise showed no signs of abating, he unbuckled his holster and fired a shot into the air. The unexpected flat crack chopped off the uproar and he spoke into the silence, his Petersburg drawl bringing a quick wave of nostalgia to Kolya but angering the men still further. They pretended not to understand him and began shouting back his words with bitter exaggeration and obscene mockery.

There was another crack, a silence, an abrupt, concerted howl from the front of the gathering, an undertone growl from the back as everyone who could not see asked his neighbor what had happened. A surge, a heave, an oppressive silence as the men started drifting away, some arguing but most silent, slipping among the huts as if they wished they had not been there.

The crowd evaporated from the front, leaving those behind to stare and in their turn to go. Within minutes the street was empty except for the bodies of the Captain, the Lieutenant and a soldier. The soldier was shot cleanly between the eyes, the other two flattened by a hundred feet, almost indistinguishable from the drying mud already.

Poliarnyi took his new responsibilities seriously; he was the only one unable to pretend it had not happened. He stood by the squalid huddle of bodies while everyone looked, then grabbed a couple of the most docile soldiers and ordered them to dig a grave. While they worked, a few men reappeared and gathered around them, at first in silence and then chattering excitedly. The meaning of revolution, if not of freedom, had begun to dawn on Nosov and the 103rd Saratovsky.

Kolya walked moodily back to the fields, where he and some of his friends were planting potatoes, each precious one cut into slivers so every eye was planted separately. Konstantin Berdeyev, he thought, the great onlooker. Four years in Petersburg, where I observed the misery but also the happiness, and did nothing but pursue my own concerns. The humblest trooper in the humblest dismounted cavalry regiment in the army, and my total war service is sitting in a wood and taking a swipe at a German with a branch. Even then I missed. A couple of inoffensive officers murdered, the Captain for certain the Petersburg son of a friend of my grandmother's and I stand at the back not even sure what is going on. A great new age is dawning for Russia and I am planting potato eyes God knows where in Galicia. He kicked a stone angrily and almost tripped over his flapping boot sole. He stood still and swore, the stored obscenity of five months in the army added to everything gleaned from Weber and his far-off student days. As he ran out of breath he began to laugh, the shapeless bundles of women around him glancing sideways in alarm.

"What ails you, Konstantin Aleksandr'itch?" demanded Mitya, one of the potato planters.

"Nothing." Kolya wiped his eyes on his sleeve; at seventeen and a half events of the past few weeks had been almost too much for him and hysteria was not far away. "I was just thinking that when my grandchildren ask me what I did in the war, I'll be able to say I missed a German with a piece of wood, and when they ask what I did in the Revolution I'll tell them I planted potatoes."

"Hark at the little one, thinking of grandchildren already," scoffed the oldest of the group. He had been a sergeant but, taking the dawn of liberty literally, had torn off his tabs and thereafter worked in the fields so as to leave Poliarnyi his new authority unfettered by the past. Small, slight and with a carrot-orange beard, even as a sergeant he had been known as Ruska, or Ginger.

"I hope thy daughter had an easy passage with the twins thy grandchildren?" inquired Mitya in mock anxiety.

Kolya looked at them with a half smile. I am sorry about the officers, he thought. I could not have saved them, but I am sorry. But so much blood has been spilt, these men are surely worth a little more. This must be where Russia's future lies, with these and the millions like them; this is my future too. He aimed a blow at Mitya. "Sons of pigs," he said, and they all laughed.

Chapter Eleven

Whatever Trooper Berdeyev's private decisions, the situation along the front remained uncertain. Officially no one dared notice the disappearance of two officers at Nosov. A few staff cars passed through, usually heavily escorted; a load of fresh uniforms at last arrived and food was regularly forthcoming, as if the High Command hoped that better conditions would change the mood of their men. If this was so, then it proved a serious misjudgment. Half starved, wet semi-clothed troops had energy only for survival; with warm weather and regular feeding most developed a driving urge to take advantage of the unprecedented conditions.

The return to health and warmth enabled many to

start the long tramp home, sped by rumors sweeping the army of land seizures in the villages from which they would be excluded if they did not hurry. Others turned to theft and murder until travel was safe only in company; still more plunged into endless arguments and speculation about events few understood.

One name on everyone's lips was Kerensky. A true socialist, said Ruska approvingly, who would give the peasants land and everyone their rights. Kolya thought more than once about joining the groups tramping eastward, of returning to Obeschino, Moscow or Petrograd, but something in his blood recoiled from desertion in the field whatever the conditions. He had a sudden vision of his grandfather's portrait: he might one day be able to face the searching painted stare of an imperial general as a mere trooper of the Russian Republic, but never as a deserter.

He was glad he had stayed when Poliarnyi came into their hut one evening and announced that Kerensky was coming.

"Here? To Nosov?" demanded a dozen voices.

He shook his head. "Half a dozen versts off, to the hill by the crossroads, sometime toward midday tomorrow."

Everyone went. All the winding tracks leading to the crossroads were blocked with soldiers wanting to see the man who was now attempting to rule Russia, the mass so great that most would only see a speck, few hear what he said. This time Kolya was determined not to be a mere onlooker, for once actually to know what was going on, and he energetically squirmed his way into the front of the crowd.

When Kerensky's car arrived an echoing roar of welcome arose, slatting back in flat waves from surrounding meadows and trees. At first sight Kolya was disappointed; he was still young enough to think that leaders should physically dominate those around them.

Kerensky wore a darker uniform than the sandy brown of the soldiers; slight and pale, he was also clean-shaven and this had the effect of making him look boyishly young to men accustomed to full-bearded generals and senior sergeants.

The feeling of disappointment did not last once he began to speak. He spoke slowly and clearly, only quickening as emotion was sparked in those around him. He spoke simply but somehow hypnotically, frequently interrupted by bursts of applause or the echo of his words thrown back by kindling enthusiasm.

You are free, he said.

"We are free men!" they shouted.

You will build a new Russia, he said.

"We will build a new Russia!" came the mighty response, rolling around the hills.

I have to ask one last sacrifice of you, he said.

"Anything!" Kolya joined with the rest.

The war must go on, we must continue to victory. You will drive the enemy from Russian soil, he said.

The great shouts in reply were without end. "Let us go now! We will win for you!"

You will win for Russia, not for me, he said.

They wept; many prayed, and when he left them they bore him on their shoulders to his car.

*

Had orders come within a measurable time of Kerensky's visits to the front, the Germans and Austrians would have faced a crisis of unknown dimensions, sheer fighting spirit could be hard to check in the huge spaces of the east, and with organization there was plenty of stockpiled equipment. But Kerensky was only one man, he had to travel the length of a two-thousand-verst front, he had to return to Petrograd, where in July an almost unknown Bolshevik party was launching its first attempt at power, he had to try and establish his government with promises, when in the midst of war promises could not be carried out.

The same old sitting about soon sapped enthusiasm and, like the rest of the 103rd, Kolya was depressed and apprehensive by the time they were at last ordered out of Nosov. It was like leaving home all over again, the bug-ridden huts, the paddle-footed women, the dark green lines of potatoes they had planted all set in the precious mold of familiarity.

"This is a bloody mixup and no mistake," growled Poliarnyi, strapping his rolled blanket over his shoulder. "Defending free Russia and still only our bloody fists to do it with. By holy St. Andrew, that fellow Kerensky was tricking us like those fat slobs of generals did."

In one respect he was proved wrong. By the time the 103rd took up their positions behind the front line they had been issued with enough rifles for one between two, although Kolya was still one of those left to carry ammunition. When their attack went in he would have to rely on picking one up from the fallen and he felt helpless anger welling through the chinks of his fear.

The front seemed quiet. A little whitewashed church stood about two versts ahead of them, its dome shining in the sun. The village around it was shattered but the church looked undamaged, surrounded by tranquil, sloping meadows, the lilac shadow of the Carpathians faintly brushed into the sky beyond. There were strange scrawling lines across the landscape and it took the 103rd some time to grasp that these must be enemy trenches. A buzz of alarm spread through the waiting men, sprawled in the open without cover, as they realized how near they were to the front line, which subconsciously they had expected to be like a chasm drawn across the earth.

More endless waiting, although the artillery barrage

had long since ceased; someone had blundered again. They played knucklebones with rounded stones in the dust, creeping away to drink from a nearby brook, chatting nervously with the unit on their left—on the right were some wild Kirghiz whom no one could make understand anything.

Suddenly, apparently without any signal, rifle and machine-gun fire spurted and spluttered, whether from friend or enemy it was difficult to tell, although a hard knocking from the Kirghiz proclaimed at least one machine gun in action there. Some high, sharp cracks from a battery behind them, shouting, an officer galloping down the road and telling them to advance.

Obediently they scrambled to their feet, straightening jackets, buckling slung blankets, exchanging sheepish glances as if to say, surely there ought to be something special about this, not just the usual routine of starting again after a halt?

The distant view of the church was deceptive. Close-to it could be seen as almost gutted, the dome tottering on crumbling bricks, showering dust as they passed. The village was deserted, with little left to burn, here and there a man falling from stray shots or shrapnel. Soon they were out the other side, scrambling in stifling heat over Austrian trenches, solidly made of revetted timber, in many cases with reinforced roofs, even tables and chairs. Again Kolya felt the dull burn of anger, tramping past weaponless, a cloth cap on his head, kicking aside the deep, padded helmets of the enemy scattered on every side.

It was anger which took him forward, for the desire to burrow into the safety of the Austrian trenches was almost irresistible; instead he began to run, fearing to stop and knowing that if he did he would never have the courage to get to his feet again. Around him others began to run too, and then they were over the meadow and into the trees beyond, the blessed shade and safety of the trees.

They could not wait there long, though; on either side they saw figures pressing on. Someone gasped, "Can't have those Kirghiz bastards ahead of us!" and they were off again.

"My God, we've done it!" crowed Poliarnyi. "Through the *kolbassniki** and out the other side!"

By then Mitya was gasping heavily, bowed down by rifle, pack and ammunition belt. He was older than the other men and after the long idling of past months already found the half run, half march of advance hard to sustain.

"Here, Kolya," ordered Poliarnyi. "You take his belt and rifle."

Kolya was only too eager to get his hands on a weapon at last but Mitya clung to it obstinately. A year in the army and only four hours in possession of his first rifle, he was not going to part with it.

"Come on, Mitya," said Poliarnyi impatiently. "You'll hold us all up. The sooner we finish this, the sooner we are home."

Ruska the ex-sergeant hardly ever spoke, but as the only one with any knowledge of warfare he could stay silent no longer. "Fifty days like this and you might go home, we've hardly begun yet."

"Fifty days!" Poliarnyi snatched off his cap and scratched his head. "Truly, Ruska?"

"Of course. At least that. *Vperyod, Tovarischi!* Forward, comrades!" He gave Mitya a slap on the back, forgetting he was not a sergeant.

They struggled onward, dusty plowland stretching before them, then a meadow ready for mowing, some of the men exclaiming at the waste of trampling it down, then out onto a corduroy log road across some

* Sausage eaters, i.e., Germans.

marshes, thick with troops, carts and guns pressing forward in excitement at victory.

Poliarnyi threw himself down beside the road. "Let us wait until it clears; to force our way across now would be to offer ourselves as dogs among wolves."

"No!" Ruska shouted at them urgently. "Up, you bastards! You can't wait here!"

"Who the hell do you think you are? Poliarnyi is our leader now; you shut up or go and rot with your Tsar!"

"No! No! We stay here!"

But Ruska stood his ground. "Listen, you fools. I am not your sergeant any longer but I don't want to die and neither do you. This road, just this one road across a marsh, look at it."

They looked. It was ordinary enough, a field track thickened with logs across wet ground, a village and fields at the far end, the sunlit slope of hills beyond.

"What of it?" growled Poliarnyi at last.

"If you were *kolbassniki* retreating, wanting time to dig fresh trenches and site your guns, wouldn't this road be the very place to hold an advance? Every man and cart just here crowded by marsh onto one track?"

They looked at each other uneasily, Poliarnyi fiddling with his straps, wise enough to see Ruska's point but also aware that the men would not obey an order to move off at once. "Listen, Poliarnyi," said Ruska urgently, drawing him aside. "You must get them away from here. Load your rifle if you must, but for God's sake don't pull the trigger."

"Of course I couldn't shoot one of my comrades," said Poliarnyi indignantly.

"You wouldn't," replied Ruska dryly. "You would blow your hand off. This ammunition doesn't fit but it seemed better to keep quiet as long as I could."

Poliarnyi stared down at his rifle in horror. "Do you mean the swine have tricked us again?"

"I don't suppose so," said Ruska cheerfully. "I doubt if they knew either." He shot the bolt of his rifle and leveled it at Mitya, since Poliarnyi was still staring mesmerized at his own. "On your feet, Grandpa. Do you wish to kill your comrades? Kolya, take his rifle and pack."

"No," said Mitya obstinately. "I will wait a few minutes and then I will take them myself."

"I told you to come now," said Ruska quietly. "Before God I will not tell you again."

Grumbling, Mitya lurched to his feet, allowing Kolya to take his pack but clinging to the rifle. The rest followed, secretly thankful to be away from a place which, now Ruska had pointed it out, seemed full of menace to them too.

The road was a nightmare of horses, vehicles and men, shouted commands, fierce oaths, the occasional scream as man or beast was crushed in the maelstrom. Where the rest of the 103rd had gone no one knew, but eventually their own little group struggled free of the throng and Ruska led them across to a shallow depression almost concealed by bushes.

At first no one spoke, thirst and exhaustion blocking their throats, but Kolya, being young, was one of the first to recover. He glanced sideways at Poliarnyi's heavy, sullen expression and felt uneasy. There were a few stray bullets from no very obvious direction and he kept his head well down as, without speaking, he crawled along a shallow ditch to the edge of the marsh to drink, filling his mess tin and offering it to Poliarnyi.

He pushed it away angrily. "I can get my own."

"Keep well down," Ruska warned.

Poliarnyi's face flushed a deep crimson, his hands opening and closing, breath whistling in his nostrils. "You son of a pig," he said at last, almost conversationally. "We have finished with sergeants, do you hear, we have finished with them! We are free men with our own leaders, not tied to sergeants' pack strings any longer."

Ruska nodded. "As you will, and I am happy to have it so. But war is a skilled business and the place for a quarrel is not half a verst from the enemy."

"And the place for free Russians is not half a verst from the enemy either, when their leaders give them bullets which blow their own hands off and not those of the enemy!" screamed Poliarnyi, hurling his rifle at Ruska, splitting his nose and sending him staggering back over the edge of their cover.

As if at a signal, the enemy guns opened fire, sweeping down the road in a great, destructive breaker of metal, blasting men and animals into the marsh, scattering limbers and ammunition wagons, then lifting with almost contemptuous ease to the crammed concourse of troops gathered at the far end of the causeway.

They were deafened by noise, nostrils and lungs clogged with dust, eyes assaulted by the sights of mass-acre, brains stunned by the amphitheater of destruction laid out before them. Counterattacking waves of Germans loped past, working down the flanks of the hills while the flail of bullets kept Kolya and his companions pressed to the ground, thankful for the uselessness of their weapons which ensured that no shred of foolhardiness would bid them attempt to stand.

They stayed huddled in their haven until dark and a slackening of fire. No one protested or felt anything except relief when Ruska took charge and led them out at last, thick blood congealed across his face, useless rifles and ammunition left behind. He took them away from the shambles of the causeway, back toward the enemy lines, then north and finally east, one minute fragment of Kerensky's shattered offensive, while behind them Germans and Austrians poured forward again through the Russian positions.

Nothing except space could now stop the enemy's triumphant advance. Nothing at all could stop the disintegration of the Russian army and of Kerensky's infant Russian Republic.

Chapter Twelve

Moscow was astonishingly quiet, gray, silent blocks huddled under snow-covered roofs, the streets treacherous with slush refrozen a dozen times into ridges running in every direction. Kolya, Poliarnyi and Mitya had traveled huddled in the corner of a cattle truck as far as Vinnitsa, then tramped and hitchhiked to Bryansk, where they had finally managed to cram themselves into a train after a week's wait in miserable wet and cold. While at Bryansk they heard how Kerensky had fled, his power toppled by the Bolsheviks in a scatter of shots and a great deal of confusion.

No one knew much about the Bolsheviks or their leader, Lenin, or indeed whether they really were in control, but once in Moscow, although the nature of this new ruling party might still be a mystery, it was clear enough who they were. As Kolya and his friends emerged from the station, crumpled, cold and hungry from their interminable journey, they were halted by a group of soldiers wearing red armbands and instantly distinguishable by their alert bearing. The unkempt slouch which had become the only acceptable attitude over past months at the front was completely absent, and Kolya stared at them in admiration. Something deep inside him had been offended by the disorganization and insolence which had been inseparable from his experience of the army: he had felt genuine regret when Ruska, and with him the last shred of authority, had left them without a word in Vinnitsa.

"Your papers, Comrades," one of the patrol said gruffly. "Where are you from?"

They fumbled for paybooks and army discs, alarmed by the thought of unknown papers which they should possess for safety.

"We're from the Galician front, it's very confused down there," ventured Poliarnyi. "Who are you?"

"Bolsheviki," the man replied briefly. "The party of the people. Where do you intend to go?"

"In the name of God, brother, how should we know? Our homes are near Saratov, except for Konstantin Aleksandr'itch here. We came to see the Revolution."

The leader did not smile, although his men exchanged covert grins. "There is no God now. Which is Konstantin Aleksandr'itch?"

"Here," Kolya stepped forward. "My village is near Oryol and I came to see the Revolution too." Let them think him a fool, there was safety in laughter and in a way it was true. It had seemed unbearably tame just to walk back to isolation at Obeschino when so much was happening.

The leader looked at him keenly and then gave them back their paybooks. "You are young, the Party needs men like you. You must all report to the Kamenny Barracks, where you will find food and somewhere to sleep. It is not permitted to wander the streets without papers, you will be in trouble if you try. See, I've put the date of your arrival in your books. You must go to the barracks today; tomorrow if you are picked up by patrols they will think you have spent your time in looting or anti-Party activity. The barracks are straight down to the river and on the right." The patrol moved off briskly.

Poliarnyi spat resentfully. "That son of cow gut. 'There is no God now,' " he mimicked. "The Lord of

Heaven strike him dead for his blasphemy; how will the sun rise tomorrow if God turns His face from Russia?"

Mitya shook his head and crossed himself. "We were fools to come, we should have gone home at once. It is all your fault, Kolya."

Kolya flushed guiltily. It was true he had been determined to go to Moscow but he had not sought to persuade the others, they had been eager enough to take personal possession of their revolution. "It is strange to see soldiers so well ordered," he said, changing the subject. "I should like to know more of these Bolsheviki."

"Don't be a fool. God will curse them all." Nevertheless Poliarnyi was the first to agree that they must go to the barracks, frightened by the discipline of the Bolsheviks, the first signs of order in a wasteland of confusion.

Kamenny Barracks were crammed with soldiers swept in by the Bolshevik patrols, their old paybooks confiscated but new papers withheld. Rumors abounded of the summary fate meted out to those found outside without the new, vital Bolshevik papers; consequently there was little choice but to remain, huddled into stinking heaps in every corner of the old building, the weaker left to freeze in the courtyard outside.

Every day red-armletted Bolsheviks came around, talking and explaining, then finally selecting a few to receive the precious papers. Poliarnyi and Mitya became worried and fretful, openly bewailing their stupidity in not going straight home, berating Kolya for his supposed persuasion of them.

"If you don't want to stay why don't you put in for a travel permit?" asked Kolya reasonably.

Poliarnyi brightened. "Do you truly think we could, Kolyushka?" He was finding the new complication of living almost insupportable, the decisions forced on him bewildering in their complexity.

It was Kolya who forced a way through the stagnant throng, who found a stuffy office where shabby, clean Bolsheviks were tapping out lists on typewriters, who summoned up courage to approach the tall, handsome boy who seemed to be in charge. "Comrade Commander . . ." Already he had picked up some of the necessary jargon from the Bolsheviks.

Poliarnyi nudged him sharply in the ribs. "Your Excellency."

The young man's eyes flashed. "There are no more excellencies."

Poliarnyi backed away, mumbling. "No more God, no more excellencies, what is the world coming to?" He approved of revolution whatever it was, but found it too elusive and worrying to grasp.

Kolya took a deep breath. The blasted boy was only two or three years older than he was and he hated to see poor old Poliarnyi, so uplifted by the first manifestations of change, now so diminished. "Comrade, we are troopers of the Saratovsky Cavalry, home from the front. My two friends here wish to apply for travel permits to go home." The typewriters stopped as two girls and an elderly man paused in their work to eye him derisively, before clattering on again.

"Oh?" said the young man, with feigned interest. "What makes you think I should waste valuable Party time on travel papers for Saratovsky troopers?"

"They are doing no good here and want to go home. Russia needs the food they can produce in their village." Such experience as Kolya had of the Bolsheviks showed them to be practical people, and it was to this practicality he appealed now.

"You do not consider it selfish to burden the Revolution with your trivial desires?" inquired the young man sweetly.

Poliarnyi plucked at Kolya's sleeve. "We'd better go."

Kolya shook his arm free. "No! If he would just give you the papers it would have been done now. It is not us wasting the Revolution's time."

They glared at each other, but it was the older man who came from behind his typewriter and pushed between them. "You do not want papers for yourself?"

Kolya shook his head, taken aback by this intervention. "I want to help in the Revolution, I am not quite sure how. I'm tired of watching from the back of a crowd." He had not known he would say it, but felt profound satisfaction at his decision.

The man snapped his fingers. "Make out papers for these two, Sacha, and give them back their paybooks. You come with me." He pushed Kolya out of the door and then rushed off down a long passage, so Kolya's boots flapped and clattered in an effort to keep up.

"In here." He bobbed into a cluttered cubbyhole, sweeping aside a mass of papers, books and old boxes to make room for them both. "Your name?"

"Konstantin Aleksandr'itch Berdeyev," replied Kolya, quite bewildered by the kaleidoscopic quality of life under the Revolution.

"You wish to help in the Revolution?"

"Yes, of course."

"You have military service?"

"Yes . . . well, I have been in the army nearly a year."

"But not on active service?" He spoke too fast, as though frightened of not having enough time in his life to finish all the affairs crowding into it, but there was humor as well as wisdom in the eyes peering over gold pince-nez, sensitivity in the long hands.

"I have been at the front, but received no training before I went. I faced one German attack with a branch in my hands and took part in an attack myself with nothing more damaging than a blanket over my shoulder." He made no effort to keep the bitterness from his voice.

"H'm." The man studied him with interest. "You say you are a trooper with the—"

"Saratovsky Cavalry. But we hadn't any horses, either."

"You do not have a Saratov accent."

"My village is about a hundred versts from Oryol," explained Kolya. "I was recruited into the Saratovsky as they passed through the province." At all costs he must keep away from questions about his family and background; he knew enough about the Bolsheviks to be certain that any member of the aristocracy was anathema, whatever his sympathies. But he had grown up rapidly in the past year and he was damned if he would cringe as a typical peasant probably would, faced with what was obviously real authority.

"You say you are a peasant?" The tone was distinctly suspicious.

"No. We own our own land." Kolya injected a note of slightly spurious pride into his voice. He must keep to the truth; lies were too dangerous with these people. Yet the truth must also hide many things.

"A *bourzhuis*." There was disappointment in the flat tone.

Kolya looked puzzled. This corruption of the French *bourgeois* was not, he felt, a word an honest peasant lad would know, revolution or no revolution. "We are landowners," he insisted aggressively. "We have a whole half-dessyatin of our own." He thought of their tumble-down house with its scrap of paddock and orchard; in strict truth it was all they did own.

"Oh!" The other looked amused and relieved. "I see. Are you planning to add to your family holding now, with the opportunities of the Revolution?"

"No!" Kolya felt he had had enough of farm work

to last him a lifetime. He flexed his thickened, chipped fingers longingly; oh, music! he thought.

"You said you wished to help the Revolution. What is it you wish to do? Tell me what you know of our Party."

"It is the Party of the people and of the future," said Kolya glibly, then saw he had made a serious mistake.

"Listen to me, Berdeyev. We have no time for flippancy and idleness now, there is a new world, not just a new Russia to build." He glanced at his watch. "I have wasted half an hour with you, in the hope it would not be wasted. You are the sort of material the Revolution needs: a son of the soil but uprooted by war and revolution, still young enough to be transplanted into our new way of thinking. If you had had a spark of real interest or initiative you would somehow have found a true Bolshevik here in the barracks to teach you our ideals. We offer you neither privileges nor advantages; not land, not a house, probably not even a life of your own. Everything we have is dedicated to rescuing those whose world this has never been. If we lose, we sell our lives dearly and absolutely; if we win . . ." He drew a breath and then said quietly, "The world has never seen the like of what we will build if we win. Poverty, injustice, war, all finished forever."

There was a long silence in the tiny, crowded room. "I am with you," said Kolya with conviction. "If that is what you want, I want it too."

The other stood up and held out his hand. "I thought I wasn't wasting my time. I am Comrade Rychagov of the Moscow Committee of the Party. You have a long way to go before you achieve full Party membership; it is something made precious by the difficult striving to attain it. Then you will still strive all your life to live up to your Party ideals. The Party will be your conscience, your companion, your mentor. Sometimes you will fail, but together we will succeed."

Kolya left the room in a daze, was shunted through offices, given papers, received his first Party orders from a remarkably pretty girl, whom he belatedly recognized as one of those who had been typing in the outer office. He fingered the piece of paper she gave him.

"Can you read?" she asked.

He spelled out the words obligingly, feeling he had faced rather too many questions recently.

She looked at him doubtfully, but he met her eyes with a guileless gray stare. Comrade Rychagov with his bayonet-sharp glance and staccato of words he took very seriously, but this delicately graceful girl was quite a different matter. She was small and in some indefinable way elegant, despite earnestly drab clothes. An edging of tip-tilted bone and provocative shaping of eyes showed a faint echo from the far lands to the east even while fair coloring and hair like the polished hazelnuts of Obeschino contradicted it.

She handed him his papers. "They are stamped, look. There is your name, your unit, where you should go." He took pleasure in the cleanliness of her nail as it underlined these vital parts of his smeared documents. It was not surprising the semiliterate should be baffled by all these papers, he decided critically; the typesetters must have been drunk, the printers insane. He felt a little lightheaded himself, with emotion and also the first entirely instinctive reaction of his life to a woman, a sharp, unexpected flick of the senses along uncharted channels, nerves stripped and aware with pleasure.

"Where is it?" He pointed at the smudged destination.

She took his arm and led him over to a map hanging on the wall. "We are here, Comrade. You report to the patrol point there and your section leader will tell you what to do and where to go for political instruction."

My God, they've certainly got themselves organized,

he thought, impressed again and suddenly proud to be part of something which was so obviously functioning in a disintegrating world. Her hand was still on his arm and he bent and kissed it, wondering how he could make her believe that he was sufficiently unfamiliar with Moscow to need her personal escort for at least part of the way.

She slapped him full across the face. "I shall tell Comrade Rychagov he was mistaken about you! You are not serious!"

His nose began to bleed, and, uniforms being more important than floors, he leaned as far out as he could and dripped onto the bare boards. No one had a handkerchief. There was a great flurry and several suppressed giggles before someone thrust a piece of towel into his hand.

He tipped his head back and mopped up conscientiously, catching an inverted glance of the girl as he did so, waiting quite unmoved for him to recover. There was no doubt about it, she was intriguing. The contrast of dark eyes and bronze fairness was scarcely more unusual than the way in which unwavering seriousness was clamped by an effort of will over an obviously passionate nature.

He tossed the bloodstained scrap into a wastebasket. "Under the new people's law, I'm sure every wounded soldier has a right to know the name of his attacker."

"Anna Dmitreyevna Vatutina, at your service, Comrade," she replied sarcastically. "And don't think that just because you've bled all over my floor we're linked in friendship through combat experience together."

He laughed. "Your combat, my pleasure, Comrade. It is probably the only blood I will shed in my life which I shan't regret." He blew her a kiss as he marched out of the room. The disadvantages of the moment were too obvious to linger, but no doubt even Bolshevik patrols obtained leave sometimes.

Before he left for his new post he went in search of Poliarnyi and Mitya, anxious to see whether they had been as successful as he in the settlement of their affairs. They were nowhere to be found; he stumbled over bodies, slipped in refuse, warded off blows from those he disturbed in his increasingly worried search. At last he found a wizened corporal with whom they had shared a corner and a mess tin for the past week.

"Have you seen Polinarnyi and Mitya, Papasha?"

"*Da! da!* They have gone." He nodded wisely.

"Gone? Gone where?"

"To their homes, they had papers, stamps, passes, many . . ." he gestured widely, "like that. So they went before any could change toward them."

"Did they leave a message for me?"

He shook his head. "They are gone, my son. They have gone home."

It was a shock. He had become used to Poliarnyi's constant grousing, to Mitya's defenselessness, the atmosphere of the 103rd Saratovsky they still carried with them, with which he had spent the most harrowing year of his life. It required conscious effort to realize that they had joined the many others in his short life whom he would never see again. He had gone down a passage while they stayed in an office to argue over a few papers and now their lives would never cross again.

"Thank you, Papasha." He gave him a screw of *makhorka*, the last of a supply scrounged on Bryansk station. "God go with you."

The old man cackled and touched the red armband Kolya had been given. "God is no more, they say, God is no more! Great Lord above, what will they be a-sayin' next?"

Kolya shouldered his blanket, presented his newly won papers at the gate and strode out into the streets of revolutionary Moscow.

Chapter Thirteen

Kolya did not like his new duties. He saw the need for them, but the first bright enthusiasm kindled by Rychagov soon staled with the day to day distastefulness of patrol duty as 1917 gave way to a bleak 1918. He was issued with better boots and entrusted with a rifle at last, although the cold penetration every shabby layer he wound around himself under his ill-fitting, bulky coat. But it was not the bodily discomfort of policing street corners in the harshness of winter which depressed him; it was the nature of much of the policing. Sometimes the patrol was friendly and helpful, working extra hours to bring wood for the old or spelling out mysterious forms for the bewildered, and then he felt again the hopeful pride with which he had left Kamenny Barracks. Too often, though, their orders seemed pointless or vicious, the vision Rychagov had made him see fading under the humiliation of behaving like a bully, his courage undermined by uncertainty.

When he went to his section center for political lectures, however, all was different again. The calm confidence of the speakers, the certainty of every answer, the dedication with which the Bolsheviks worked, many looking on the edge of collapse from cold and undernourishment, all combined to reaffirm his own commitment, to justify everything by the magnitude of the achievement for which they strove.

One night he could no longer keep silent and he challenged the speaker, a Comrade Abramannikov from Petrograd headquarters. "Comrade." He fumbled for the words he wanted and Abramannikov helped him at once.

Used to explaining to the humble and simple, he felt no impatience, showed no discourtesy to those who found thoughts difficult to articulate, only pride that he should be the means of awakening so many deprived minds. "Comrade soldier, you have a difficulty you wish the meeting to consider with you?"

"Yes." Emboldened, Kolya plunged on: "I believe in everything you have been saying, in the rule of the people for the good of all, the way we must work for each other. But I am with a patrol in the streets here and it often seems to me as if we behave with malice rather than justice."

There was a shocked silence and then muttered protests, but Abramannikov gave him the same grave attention Kolya had encountered from all the higher Bolshevik officials; it was one of the qualities which made them so impressive. "In what way, Comrade?"

"Well . . ." He looked at the hostile faces around him and then back at Abramannikov. "Yesterday we were ordered to a district near here, and told to turn out every citizen to scrape the streets."

"What is wrong? It seems a public duty to me."

"Yes, but . . . some of them were old ladies, girls, people who had never done such labor in their lives. They were not told to scrape the streets of ice because they could do it properly, but to humiliate them. They had no shovels or picks or knowledge how to carry out such a task; they had to do it so others could jeer at them doing it. That is not my idea of socialist labor for the good of the people." He still had not assimilated the experience of having to stand with a fixed bayonet, watching people of the age and bearing of his grandmother turn blue from the rasping effort of prizing ice sheets off the pavement outside their solid burgher houses. He was purging his shame in protest, but too late to assist those he had helped to terrorize.

"What is your name, soldier?" He did not call him comrade any more.

"Does it matter?" Kolya retorted, the misery of yesterday preventing prudence. "It is my question I want answered, what difference does a name make? I am not disloyal, I am true to the Party, but I feel the Party debases itself by such methods."

"Sit down! Be quiet! Shame!" Angry shouts echoed around the hall, but Abramannikov held up his hand. "Very well, I will answer you, but do not think in your arrogance that you can call the Party into question. The aim of a truly Marxist Party is justice, equality, the end of oppression. Agreed?"

"Yes," said Kolya firmly. "Yes! Yes!" shouted everybody.

"This means we must remove the source of these ills, otherwise we remove one injustice and another appears. Agreed?"

There could be no doubt of it. They all agreed.

"The source of these troubles of mankind is money, not wealth, for the wealth of a nation is something all can share. But money, coins, property, these are all ways of dividing up wealth so one receives and multiplies his gift and another gets nothing. From money flow inequality, greed, oppression, hatred, envy. All of us are pledged to be rid of it forever; no Party member will take more pay than an ordinary worker. Agreed?"

They all agreed. It was to be a truly new world.

"Very well. If this is so—and it is—then workers and peasants have no difficulty. They have been excluded, oppressed, treated with injustice; their acquaintance with money is slight and will wither away with the comradeship of the new order. The *bourzhuis* are different. They are corrupted, they are useless citizens because of their corruption. Those people you allowed yourself to pity yesterday, Comrade, are the enemies of the people, who will seize your revolution if they can, corrupt it if you let them. They must be destroyed. It is not pretty but it must be so."

"It must be so!" A great shout went up.

Kolya felt his face grow hot. He agreed with every word, but he could not forget the old ladies on their knees on the icy flagstones.

The meeting broke up in disorder soon after, but Kolya was not quite as isolated as he expected. Not many thought the old ladies of Rybnaya Street worth a protest, but Marxist conviction struck few responses from the peasants among the soldiers, whose main ambition was to turn workers' rule into possession of their own land.

Kolya left the meeting alone. Abramannikov might not know his name but his section chief certainly would. He would have to face reprimand, Party officials would be displeased, perhaps even cancel the first tentative steps he had taken toward Party membership. First, however, he had a duty to perform. A duty too long neglected and which the sights of Rybnaya Street and the arguments of the evening had pushed at last to the forefront of his mind.

He was going to call on the Kobrins.

Chapter Fourteen

There was no difficulty in thinking of reasons to justify his failure to go earlier. He had been swept into Kamenny Barracks without even an hour to call his own; from there he had been sent straight on duty with the Bolshevik street pickets, based on a section well away from the Znamenka, where the Kobrins lived. Nevertheless, he knew in his heart that, had he truly wished to go, he could somehow have snatched the time to do so.

His boots, one newly hobnailed and the other tied up in rags, rang unevenly on the wide spaces of Red Square where the cobbles were swept clear, but elsewhere the sound was muffled by shoveled banks of snow, in some places almost head high in the absence of municipal carts to carry it away. It gave an eerie feeling to the sleeping city, as if he were back in some giants' trench warfare; the blank, shuttered houses and absence of any lights added to the strangeness.

He slipped into the gardens below the Kremlin walls and made his way warily toward the corner opposite the Znamenka. Once there he stood several minutes in the shadows, probing as far as he could the darkened streets around him: this was a part of the city where, above all, he must expect to find Bolshevik vigilance. He crossed as far as possible under cover of snowbanks, but made no real attempt at concealment: if he were seen it would be fatal indeed to seem furtive.

He had a shock when he saw the Kobrins' house. Although the door was closed, the shutters were hanging loose and he knew from experience elsewhere in the city what that meant: the squatters were in. Looters often enjoyed destruction for its own sake, but squatters were careful to avoid damage to doors or windows which would render a house uninhabitable in bitter weather. Premises marked down for occupation had their shutters carefully prized off and window latches picked, often while the People's Police watched. He scaled the high wooden wall at the rear of the house and crept across the cluttered yard, still hearing nothing. Even rats were rare after four winters of scarcity.

The back door was only latched and he knew now for certain that something was very wrong; if he had not the smell of the house would have warned him. There were people sprawled in every corner of the hall, some snoring, a child whimpering, a group of men playing cards by the light of an oil lamp.

They looked up at his entry. "Wanting something, Comrade?"

Kolya was almost too knocked off balance by the extraordinary sight of Kobrin's elegant porphyry pillars supporting clothes lines, his squared marble hall caked with dirt and pocked with scars of old fires, to reply, but he was learning the arts of survival fast. "My sister, Comrades. Her home was burned down a week ago and her street committee told her to find shelter in one of the *bourzhuis* houses taken over by the people." Fires in Moscow, where many of the poor still lived in wooden huts, were too frequent for comment.

The man waved his hand. "Look for yourself, though no man's sister would be here alone."

"She is wed, her husband killed. She lived with his family but I don't know what has become of them." Kolya stuck firmly to the truth, however misleading.

"Ask Ygor, he is our chairman of committee and knows everyone here." He jerked his thumb toward the familiar counting-room door and turned back to his cards.

There was nothing else for it. It would look odd to refuse and if indeed he wished to find out whether the Kobrins were still here, huddled into some attic of their own house, then the committee chairman was certainly the man to approach.

He pushed open the counting-room door, swept by an emotion he could not name as he saw the high mahogany desks neatly chopped and piled for firewood. There were huddles of bedding on the raised dais where Kobrin had sat in state, descending to greet clients of importance, rattling his abacus like a back-street trader, or covering parchment agreements with beautiful copperplate characters learned in a Petersburg night school when he was over thirty.

"There's no room," growled a voice at his feet. "We've half the homeless of Moscow squeezed in here already."

"I'm not looking for a space, Comrade, but for my sister, who may be here." Kolya peered into the debris at his feet.

There were a few subdued suggestions as to what he might profitably do with his sister, but a woman's voice cut in authoritatively: "Shame on you, Comrades. You are behaving as if the new Russia did not exist. Why shouldn't we help a soldier of the Revolution in search of his family?"

"Thank you," said Kolya gratefully. "She may not be here but she is young and dark, small . . . er, like so." He shaped his hands in the air. "She has three children but her husband was killed."

The man at his feet, Ygor surely, rolled out of his rugs and stooped to lift a samovar onto the table. "There are none like that. Three children, no father, they would be known to all. Besides, the girl sounds pretty." He chuckled, but without offense. "No one forgets such, they are scarce enough. Tea, Comrade?"

Kolya nodded, eyes mesmerized by the samovar: listing slightly on twisted legs but undoubtedly the one he had seen fat, comfortable Madame Kobrina preside over on countless occasions. "What beautiful workmanship, Comrade." He ran his fingers over the tracery of wired gilt leaves, as if in admiration.

"It came with the house as you might say." Ygor laughed mockingly.

Kolya nodded, feeling sick. He took several sips of the boiling water which passed for tea before he replied, but his voice was steady enough and he wondered at himself a little. "I am with a patrol on the other side of the city and there too the *bourzhuis* are having to share their riches with the people at last."

"You could call it sharing," said Ygor dryly. "We hanged the old sod from his own lamp bracket." He pointed to the crystal chandelier, still beautiful but with some glittering drops hanging loose as if dripping in a sudden thaw.

Kolya gripped his hands together, watching his whitened knuckles and the betraying pulse across the surface of his glass. "All of them? Or just the old man?"

Ygor peered at him, suddenly suspicious. "You are not wasting thought on scum like that are you? A Bolshevik soldier should be in the forefront of the fight, not white like a girl at the thought of blood."

"I'm not afraid of blood! I've been at the front a year, which is more than you, O skulker in back alleys and hangman of old men!" Kolya threw discretion aside, swept by rage he no longer troubled to conceal. "I am not afraid, but I am sick to my throat of it. The Revolution is a revolution of justice, it does not need to be fed with the victims of scavengers who understand nothing of the new Russia we are going to build."

"Well said, little one." The woman's voice came out of the gloom again. "He was brave, we did not need to kill him."

"You were here . . . Comrade?" His voice almost stuck on the word.

"Aye. It didn't please me but it seemed to need doing at the time. He had killed his wife before we broke in, he knew what was coming to him." Her voice was indifferent rather than remorseful. "He was a banker, an enemy of the people, he knew."

Yes, thought Kolya, he knew. You enjoy your revolution, he had said, when they hang me up by my guts. Praise God the old man had been wiser than he and had sent Lena and the other women to safety while there was still time. He looked at the glass in his hand as if he did not know how it had got there; suddenly he could not bear to accept even water in this place.

He threw it down and watched with sour satisfaction as it rolled off the edge of the table and smashed on the marble. He looked at Ygor's puzzled and resentful face, at the woman who was able to feel detachment without remorse, and somehow was ashamed of himself too.

They cannot understand, he thought, they cannot yet sense the true nature of this revolution of ours. They can only lash out at what they see, I must not hate what has been stunted, I must not blame those who have no sense of guilt. He said gently, "We are all beginning anew, Comrades; let us look to the building and not to the smashing." He glanced at the shattered glass. "I'm sorry for my clumsiness. Good night, Comrades."

At the corner of the Znamenka he walked straight into a patrol. He had looked carefully enough but, preoccupied by his thoughts, he had failed to exercise the same minute care as on his outward journey.

"Hold there, Comrade! What are you doing in this part so late?" The patrol crowded around him in delight at finding something to break the monotony of the long night.

His brain was utterly cold, seized up and congealed with painful thought. For a moment he could think of nothing to say, staring at the muffled faces around him in stupid astonishment.

"Come on now, your papers, Comrade. Where have you come from?" The voice, which had shown nothing but friendly interest was now quick with suspicion.

Kolya unbuttoned his tattered felt overjacket slowly, fumbling for papers while desperately trying to gain time to frame a plausible reason for his presence in the heart of *bourzhuis* Moscow.

"You are with Section Eighteen over in the Basmannaya, what are you doing here?" The section leader tilted his papers to the moonlight, brilliantly reflected off banked snow.

"I came to visit a friend," said Kolya reluctantly, still unable to think of a more likely excuse.

One of the men said something and the rest laughed; knowing him for one of themselves, they were not hostile, only curious. The leader cursed them and turned back to Kolya: "Whatever these dolts say I shall need a deal of convincing you were visiting a girl in this neighborhood. It still needs a bayonet to have your way with them around here."

Kolya flushed, recollection again leaping at him out of the past. "Be thankful your sister will not be raped along the way," Kobrin had said brutally. Another subconscious memory of which he was not even aware made him spit in the snow. "Mind your own business." His voice was harsh and angry.

The patrol exchanged startled glances but the leader replied reasonably enough. "I can hardly accept that, Comrade. It is our business to know who moves in this area at night. Come, don't be foolish, account for yourself so we can all stop freezing here." He stamped his feet at the thought; it was indeed bitterly cold, although spring was not far away.

"Well, it was a girl . . ." Kolya stopped, changing his mind in midsentence. It would be too dangerous to claim a sister in the Znamenka; the story he had told Ygor would not survive even a casual check.

"Where does she live?"

He had a brilliant idea. "At the Bolshevik barracks by the Kamenny Bridge, she works for Comrade Rychagov." He was not sure of Rychagov's position but felt it must be fairly important.

"Very well, we can go down that way. We'll see whether your Bolshevik friends will vouch for you or not." The patrol leader's tone was skeptical.

Kolya felt a moment's panic, which he was sure the other had noticed. "B-but it is very late, you can't wake up someone like Rychagov now!"

"You were going to wake up your girl," he pointed out. "What is her name?"

"Anna Dmitreyevna . . . I can't remember her other name." He was not at all sure she would be willing to speak for him anyway. He rubbed his nose reminiscently and in spite of everything felt a choke of laughter.

There was a guffaw from the patrol; they were having an unexpectedly entertaining night. "He can't remember her name! A five-verst tramp to see a wench and he can't remember who she is!" The atmosphere began to change to the mildly hilarious.

The barrack gates were closed and guarded as usual and there was a long altercation before they were allowed to enter. Once in, the guardroom also became convivial, everyone plying Kolya with bawdy questions about the appearance and shape of his girl, since he could not name her.

Nearly an hour passed before she swept in, accompanied by a grinning soldier who had been dispatched to roust around the female workers, armed with such description as Kolya had been able to give.

"What the devil . . . ?" Her eyes fell on Kolya "Oh!"

"He says he was in this part of the city to call on you, Comrade," explained the patrol leader. "It didn't seem likely to us, knowing how you Bolsheviki are always so keen on the job in hand." He looked at her blandly: the fiercely earnest Bolsheviks, who had just ejected all the other elected delegates from the Workers' Constituent Assembly in Petrograd, were not particularly popular with rank and file revolutionaries.

"You insolent swine!" She looked as if she would gladly have struck him.

"Now, now," said Kolya soothingly, beginning to

enjoy himself. "As a faithful supporter of the Revolution, he has a right to express himself as he wishes. There are no Tsars here now."

"No indeed," everyone murmured. One man crossed himself, then looked around anxiously to see whether he had been noticed.

She rounded on him in fury and he had a fleeting impression of every separate part of her crackling with rage: taut, defiant body, every strand of hair, an intensity of dark eyes. Who touched her politics touched her, he reflected ruefully. "As for you, Konstantin Aleksandr'itch, you have been nothing but trouble from the day of your arrival here! I wish I had hit you harder." Even to herself it sounded feeble, like a child scolding a disobedient wolfhound.

Kolya turned to the soldiers helpfully. "She seems to know me, Comrades, don't you agree? Last time we met she made my nose bleed, so perhaps you might consider staying a little longer to lend me support?"

She flung out of the room, slamming the door as they all laughed, and Kolya encountered no further difficulty in extracting his papers from them, submitting to having his shoulders thumped encouragingly and sustaining with perfect good humor all the varied suggestions for a successful wooing. It was nearly two o'clock in the morning by the time he had shaken them loose and was able to start searching the building for Anna Dmitreyevna . . . Vatutina, he recalled somewhat belatedly.

The block smelled as appalling as he remembered and was even more crowded, but his daily life had consisted for so long of being jostled by multitudes of people in unwashed surroundings that he no longer took much notice. He knew he smelled fairly rank himself, the maddening, fiery itch of lice inescapable.

It took nearly half an hour of mistaken turnings before he identified the right passage, but after that it was easy—he could hear Anna's indignant, upraised voice at once.

He pushed open a door cautiously; Anna and two other girls were sitting and talking on a mattress on the floor. "Hello."

The other two jumped and gave little screams; Anna merely stared at him and looked furious.

"I came to apologize," said Kolya untruthfully. "I didn't mean to drag you into that scene in the guard-room, but the patrol wouldn't believe I was in this district just for the pleasure of seeing you."

"And I don't believe it either!" she snapped back at him. "You made the Party ridiculous with your *bourzhuis* talk about me."

He looked shocked. "Surely poor soldiers have a right to romance now as well as the *bourzhuis?* I never thought to see you defending privilege, Comrade."

One of the girls gave a snort and turned to her friend. "I don't think we are wanted here, Mariya. Nothing less than his blood on the floor again will satisfy Annochka now."

Kolya bowed and held the door for them. "Thank you, Comrades. If I call for help, I hope you'll come quickly."

When he turned to Anna again, he saw her rage had subsided; instead she was regarding him with acute suspicion. "You looked just like one of those stupid aristocrats who used to come to my father's shop, bowing like that."

Kolya cursed himself for his carelessness. With his fellow soldiers he had adapted himself completely and naturally, the life so different his old habits withered without effort. With Anna his Petersburg manners and courtesies had surfaced at once, without his even being aware of it. "Well, that's nice," he said, with a cheerfulness he did not feel. "Aristocrat Berdeyev, it just shows what the Revolution can do for a simple soldier."

"I don't believe it," she said again. "There is something odd about you. What were you doing in this part of the city in the middle of the night?"

"It wasn't the middle of the night when I left my post," Kolya pointed out. "I've been arguing for hours with that patrol. Why shouldn't I come and see you if I want to?"

"Don't be ridiculous," she said harshly. "We exchanged a few words and a slap on the face as you well know, Konstantin Aleksandr'itch, whatever you told those fools on patrol. There's nothing to attract you to someone like me. I've nothing to give except to the Party and you are clever enough to know it and not waste your time."

He stared at her, taken aback by the intensity of her tone. She was not looking at him any longer. Her hands were clenched and her face tightened with some emotion he could not grasp, as if it was an effort not to bolt out of the room to the safety of papers and files. She is like a piece of overstretched violin string, he thought, with all her emotions tied up in red Bolshevik bunting. He grinned at his mixed metaphors; it was suddenly very pleasant to be in this warm little office talking to a girl instead of Bolshevik propagandists, to forget the brutality and complications of life for a short time. It would be agreeable to attempt untying that red bunting; whatever she said, there was something very appealing about anyone so small and young bristling with such earnest determination on every subject.

"I didn't know your father kept a shop," he said casually.

"What is wrong in that? We renounced the profit motive and gave most of our takings to the Party."

"For heaven's sake! I bet you had bombs in the cellar and Bolshevik literature under the counter. What sort of shop was it?"

"It was a pharmacy," she said grudgingly. "Over on the south bank. I'm going to be a doctor when I can finish here."

"And what does the Party think of that?"

"Naturally it is with the approval of the Party. We will need Party members in medicine just the same as everywhere else."

"Oh, naturally," he agreed sarcastically.

She flushed with a return of anger. "Konstantin Aleksandr'itch . . ."

"Yes?"

"You are hoping to be a Party member. You don't sound like one at the moment—you don't behave like one, either."

"Don't I? Perhaps I find it difficult to be deadly serious all the time." He took her hand and kissed it lightly. "You will have to educate me."

She snatched it away. "Why do you have to make a joke of everything? There is too much to do, we all have too much to do, now we have a chance at last."

He stared at her somberly. "I know. But we will not build anything worth having if we can't laugh at ourselves sometimes. I believe in the Party, I want what it wants, but I don't like some of the things we are doing along the way. What do you think of a Party which turns elected representatives of the people out of their seats in the Constituent Assembly with bayonets?"

"I think that with elected representatives you have nothing but argument! We need to get things done."

"Not so very different from what the Tsar said," he pointed out dryly.

"But we are not like the Tsar, we want the good of the people! What a ridiculous argument!"

"Is it? I don't know." He stretched and yawned. "What a day I've had. I think I'm going back to my village for a while, to sort out my ideas and see how my mother is managing. I should have gone long ago."

Ever since he had left Kobrin's house he had known he must go back to Obeschino at once. "Could you have my papers stamped for me?"

She nodded. "I'll speak to Comrade Rychagov. There's no shortage of volunteers for the patrols just for the bread. I don't suppose there will be any difficulty."

He put his hands on her shoulders, feeling thin bones through the rough cloth, his flesh charged with sudden desire. He shifted his grip slightly, holding down her upper arms. "You won't be able to try for my nose this time." His voice quivered, denying his attempt at lightness.

He kissed her, clumsily at first, then with instinctive skill, inexperience swamped by an unexpected strength of emotion. So much lost, so much swept away; he longed to possess, to lose himself in something which was his, to belong somewhere again in the torrent engulfing them all.

"My love . . ." he whispered, mouth closing over hers, every sensation in his body searching for her, never wishing to leave her, so shaken out of normal control that even when he dimly knew she was weeping and tasted the salt of her tears he was at first only further exalted. It was a mist of half-forgotten attitudes and newforged willpower which drew him back at last, then he was stricken with remorse at her sobs, but unable to command his voice at first.

"Annushka, sweet . . ." the words cracked, then he had himself under control again, running his hand gently over her hair. It was fine and silky, smelling clean and faintly herbal; God, he would like to kiss her again. "What have I done to make you weep, Annushka?"

She could not answer at first, instead screwing her fingers into his back, where she had been holding him, until he winced involuntarily.

"I'm sorry, I didn't mean to hurt you." She wiped her nose desolately on her sleeve while he searched the room for some scrap of material. There was little left now of the dedicated Party worker and he did not know whether to feel remorse or delight at the way he had unknowingly swept away a guard which was maintained with such obvious effort.

"Here." He offered her a minute rag. "I expect it's off the same towel I used for my nose. It wasn't you hurting me, I speared my back on a tree root months ago when I was in some shelling at the front."

She blew her nose carefully; the rag was scarcely large enough to hold. "What a lot one doesn't know about people. I didn't realize you had been at the front." She sniffed thickly. "I'm sorry to be so stupid."

He sat quietly on the edge of the desk, folding his still trembling arms and making no further attempt to touch her. He no longer wished to take anything she did not want to offer. "I think there is quite a lot I don't know about you too. Do you want to tell me about it?"

She shook her head. "No, not really. It was just . . . just I couldn't bear it like that. I've seen enough of men with their bodies on women they wouldn't recognize an hour later."

Kolya was about to protest but, young as he was, instinct held him back: she had not only seen but endured men with their grasping bodies. He had witnessed quite enough of the drunken ferocity awaiting women in the dirty passages and unlit streets of revolutionary Moscow to know the probable horror of some of Anna's experiences. She was too proudly dedicated to admit any fear or refuse errands into the slums; no wonder she was grasping her Party faith like a saint at the stake.

He felt suddenly dizzy, his sight blurred for an instant. He was almost asleep on his feet, exhausted by shock on clanging shock. He stood up and the room steadied; instead his back began to throb as it still occasionally did. He picked up his battered cap; it would be the last gut-rotting straw if he passed out now, in front of this strange, difficult, but also pathetic and endearing girl. His girl; already strands of understanding and misunderstanding, contact and recoil forming a pattern between them. He could afford to wait. He turned his mind from the knowledge that he would certainly have to wait and guard himself with endless patience if he were to find the Anna he wanted, the passionate Anna given without reserve which the Party had already found.

"I think we should both have a couple of hours' sleep before we are back at the grind tomorrow." He thought dully that he would not have even a minute's rest after the long tramp back to quarters, and then the inevitable, savage discipline he would face both for his absence and for his temerity of the evening before. "Perhaps when I call again after you have spoken to Comrade Rychagov about my travel papers you could come out with me for a while. If you'd like it, we could go for a walk along the river. I find the barrack atmosphere is beginning to make me retch."

"Me too." She smiled at him shakily. "Thank you, Konstantin Aleksandr'itch, I would like to come, just—just for a walk." She looked at him anxiously to make sure he understood what she was saying, while all the time the tilt of her eyes, the expressive curve of her lips, promised so much more. He nodded wordlessly and she laughed suddenly: "It isn't easy to get time off, but I'll tell Comrade Rychagov how urgent it is for someone to attend to his recruit's Party education!"

He smiled back at her, a shift of relief in his heart. Without even noticing it she had been betrayed into her first act of levity at the Party's expense.

Chapter Fifteen

Obeschino. Asleep under the brilliant stars of spring, the village looked so unchanged that war, revolution and violence might have been a dream.

Kolya stood under cover of the forest edge. Not far from here he had sat with his father after shooting snipe in the summer of 1913, hearing him speak of his grandmother's forgiveness. Today his father was just one of the vast legion of Russian dead, pushed casually under the sod in Poland, now declaring itself newly free of Russia. All the same, there was something satisfying in looking at such an unchanged scene, giving a sense of home to a place for which, in truth, Kolya had only tepid affection.

At last, satisfied the village slept, he stepped from the trees and made his way around the fields toward the ridge on which the old Berdeyev house stood. I wonder if the balcony has held up, he thought, with a strange stirring of anticipation.

It had not. He stood, still hidden by straggling bushes, and looked up at the house silhouetted against the sky, roof shingles gleaming faintly in the starlight. He could see at once how the balcony had fallen, sagging inward on itself so it blocked the door with a tangle of supports and brittle creeper. He frowned, remembering how he had wedged it; short of force he did not think it would have fallen like that. He stooped into the tangle and tried the door without success, but the familiar window was fairly clear. With the memory of a hundred boyhood entrances crowding his mind he pushed the prong of his belt buckle down the side of the frame and pressed hard.

The wood creaked and bent as it always had. Slipping over the catch, he pushed the double frame aside and climbed into nostalgic parlor smells, recognizable even through the damp and must of long disuse. For it was disused, it did not need investigation to prove it, although he went through all eight rooms just the same, those in the front of the house slanting alarmingly with the pull of the balcony.

He stood helplessly at last, hands hanging and feeling the chill of sweat, colder than the uninhabited damp of the house. It must be because she feared to stay after the balcony fell, he thought suddenly. She could not stay through the winter once that happened. He sat on a sagging chair and put his head in his hands; he was very tired.

He awoke with a start and stared about him. He could not remember where he was: the strange, cramped, sloping hallway, everywhere dust and clinging mold. Even as he wondered, memory returned and he scrambled stiffly to his feet, caked boots weighing him down even as his spirit was weighted by the desolation of the house. He went through every room again but found nothing which would give a clue as to what had happened. Clothes, bedding and furniture were mostly in place; his own room looked as if it had not been touched since the last night he had slept there. But nearly everything from the kitchen was gone although he made a better breakfast than he had in months from remembered caches of honey, mildewed biscuit, rubbery dried fruit and pickled cucumbers.

He did not know how long he sat at the familiar kitchen table but eventually he rose briskly, a whole set of decisions made without conscious thought. He wound up several buckets of water from the well and scrubbed himself down, gasping at the icy shock. He washed his tattered uniform, dipping his hand automatically into the crock where soap was always to be found and unsurprised to find hardened pieces still there. He hesitated over some of his father's old field service uniforms, the unpiped breeches at least should be safe to wear, but finally decided against it, the cloth was too good. So he wrapped himself in an old curtain and waited stoically for his clothes to dry. He did at least take one of his own old shirts, some new foot bandages from a winter set of his father's, and wrapped the best of the food in his blanket pack.

Then, late in the afternoon, he let himself cautiously out of the house and made his way to the river, keeping well away from the village. In the distance he could hear women's voices, for the fine weather had brought them out into the fields after winter's hibernation, but by the river all was quiet and dim. Achingly familiar patterns stippled water and bank until shade and deep merged into one and the whole setting might have been carelessly smudged on canvas by a child with a paintbox containing nothing but greens and browns.

Luka was there. He had known he would be; poor Petya might stagger around on his one leg trying to help, but Luka was certain to be found well away from the fields on such a day as this.

Kolya left his blanket in the undergrowth and sauntered casually down the path along the riverbank.

Luka looked up, calling a careless greeting which died on his lips. "Kolya," he said stupidly, then again, "Kolya."

Kolya put his hands in his pockets and looked down at him, at the massive chest and thick muscles which had bruised his ribs so many years ago, at already sagging folds of flesh along neck and jaw. "What happened to my mother?"

Luka came out of his stupor and reeled in his line. "Dead."

In his heart he had known it, but it was a shock nevertheless. A fish plopped, widening ripples set the trailing grasses undulating and the bitter familiarity of it caught Kolya by the throat. He could not speak and Luka glanced at him in derision. "She was a useless bitch anyway."

Kolya kicked out hard, toppling him off his tree stump, and they both went down in a tangle of fishing line. He saw the slack-lipped satisfaction on Luka's face and a moment later they were fighting in deadly earnest, complete silence, except for an occasional grunt, a token of their intensity. Luka was fighting to kill, secure in the knowledge that such pleasure was now safe, no awkward police inquiry would result from the death of a former barin these days.

Kolya too was animated by a fierce lust to destroy, to batter this sneering face, somehow typifying everything which had already smirched the high hopes and noble aspirations of the Revolution, had destroyed or scattered his friends and family one by one. Luka lurched forward, his head striking into Kolya's, and he felt the terrible, remembered grip fasten around his ribs, knotted thumbs grating agonizingly into the vulnerable place on his back. Somehow he brought up his knees, braced on the ground between Luka's legs, dug his head into layers of rubbery fat and groped for Luka's face, breath almost gone in the intolerable pressure.

Luka grunted contemptuously, swung bodily sideways and smashed him against the ground, the movement momentarily breaking his own grip. With all his ebbing strength Kolya jerked both knees into Luka's crotch and he gave a sharp cry of pain and rage. Kolya lashed out again, then twisted his leg through Luka's, tight-braced against his other knee. He was no longer a carefully mannered boy, he had had to hold his own among men sometimes brought beyond the edge of savagery by the intolerable conditions of war and revolution. The leg lock shown him by Ruska one night in the Galician woods would tear Luka's hip out of joint if he struggled, every movement only increasing the leverage.

Kolya felt his trap of sinew and bone close, his leg a living fulcrum, and Luka began to arch to the strain, mouth open, head back, breath snatching on the ratchet of his throat. "How did she die?" Kolya spoke harshly, his own consciousness scarcely held.

Luka thrashed his head from side to side, mumbling incoherently, and Kolya bent forward, increasing the pressure. "Stop!" Luka screamed. "In the name of God!"

"There is no God," said Kolya coldly, and meant it. There could be no God in this bitter valley of earth. "How did she die?"

"She froze to death." The voice came from just behind him. Fat Masha stood, arms folded in her shawl, unmoving, watching the fight with the casual interest of an onlooker: it was one of the few exciting things to happen in Obeschino for generations.

It took almost more strength than Kolya possessed to break his hold, to step free. The circulation in his leg was cut off by the pressure he had put on Luka, and it doubled under him.

Masha steadied him. "I thought you would be back." She looked down at Luka with satisfaction; he was moaning gently, his whole body curved against the agony in his thigh. "He will at least have an excuse for not helping with the spring sowing."

Kolya passed his hand shakily over his forehead and sank down on a tree stump. "Tell me what happened."

Masha nodded matter-of-factly. "I will tell you, Barin, then you must go. We did not mean harm and you only bring danger on yourself if you seek revenge."

She paused as if expecting his agreement but he said nothing.

She sighed. "I remember how it was with three, Konstantin Aleksandr'itch, thou and thy silences." She checked with her fingers; "It was after Christmas but before Epiphany, I remember. Vasya was back from the army when all had thought him dead, and in his hut there was *kvass** for all. He brought tidings of the town, how we are all equal now and should have what is ours."

"We have owned nothing but our house here for nearly a hundred years." Kolya did not look up.

"The Barina did nothing yet she fed well. We heard our new masters say it is right to share, so we went to ask the Barina to give us our due."

"Drunk," said Kolya in the same expressionless voice. "The food I had trapped and sweated for, to leave her enough when I went into the army."

She massaged her elbows thoughtfully, unabashed. "She was foolish, Barin. All we asked was a share and when she began to weep and shout, some lost patience and thrust her out to cool while we decided what it was right to take. We left her enough to live as we do."

"How did she die?"

"We saw her tapping at the window, then she went away again. There are sheds, we thought she had gone in one of those, she had a coat. When we left in the morning we found her frozen on the step; she was sitting as if she thought it a summer's day. As God is my witness, Barin, we touched nothing in the house but our share." Kolya made a smothered movement and she added, old face crinkled with innocent amusement, "One family thought they would live there, for the house is better than anything in the village, but they came back whey-faced, crossing themselves and swear-

* A kind of beer made from fermented black bread.

ing it was haunted when the balcony fell in the middle of the night. No one will go there now, but I think it was someone jealous of their good fortune."

Kolya stirred at last and stood up slowly, leg and back settled into a dull, angry ache. Luka rolled away from his glance, burying his face like a child in some leaves. For the life of him he could think of nothing to say to Masha, thoughtlessly cruel as she was usually thoughtlessly kind, her only emotion mild resentment that the Barina had been silly enough not to go into the woodshed on a cold night.

"God go with you, Barin," she said now. "I will tell Luka to say he was set on by bandits; there are so many now, drifting home and enjoying robbery on the way. He will not want to admit himself bested by the little Barin, half his size and"—she counted on her fingers—"but eighteen summers old."

"Don't call me Barin," he said irritably, strapping on his rolled blanket. "We have finished with that nonsense at least, even if there was no need to murder the innocent to get it."

"It was not murder," she insisted. "We gave her a coat, we took nothing but our right."

He gave up, let her murmur a blessing over him, even while the rest of his mind recoiled from the thought of her—Fat Masha of all people!—seated at his kitchen table, wide mouth agape with laughter at his mother's face frantically pressed against the window. In his disordered thoughts it was as if her solid, weather-beaten figure were Obeschino itself bidding him farewell, even while his fingers twitched to meet around her throat.

He went a half-day's journey before fatigue forced him to halt, his mind filled with a turmoil of hate and guilt. For was he not to blame as well, when he could have been home by the time of his mother's death? He was lying on a bed of pine needles, staring up at the sky, when he remembered another distant promise, then he lay the rest of the night tussling reluctantly with the knowledge that he must go back.

Oh well, what is a day? he thought resignedly. There is nothing to hurry for, in fact I think I might not return to Moscow yet awhile. Anna needs time to find herself again. I told her I would be away until autumn. As he tramped the weary versts back to Obeschino he turned this thought over in his mind and decided it was good. He was tired of revolutions however ideal, of guard duty however necessary: he would scarcely admit even to himself that he was tired too of the self-control and difficulty of his relationship with Anna. Although he had never been close to his mother he was now truly alone and in his loneliness he thought of Anna with a longing tinged with despair. He had been delighted by the warmth and welcome she now showed him, by the way she turned to him sometimes with unself-conscious pleasure. When he had kissed her again on Kamenny Bridge the day before he left Moscow, she had come to him gladly without shrinking, forgetful for an instant of haunting past and Party priorities alike. But never for long, he thought sourly, whatever I do she cannot forget, and I am tired of patience. Patience for what, after all?

Suddenly he could not wait to get back to his music. He discarded the idea of Petrograd regretfully; if music survived there then too many musicians would know him. He decided instead to try Kiev, the cradle of Russian civilization. If he could only get started again, perhaps the Moscow Academy of Music would be open by winter, the first wave of hate against the past settled enough for his birth no longer to be such a deadly danger.

It was dark when he reached Obeschino once more and climbed in through the familiar window he had thought never to see again, which he bloody well never would see again, he swore savagely to himself. He went directly to the cupboard in his old room and pulled out two stiffly rolled canvases.

Straight out through the hallway again, avoiding the kitchen, no flicker, no concession to memory allowed. He pushed his way through the wilderness of the garden, gathering wood shavings and dry leaves from the shed on his way.

He took a flint and steel from his pocket and lit the shavings carefully, blowing on unevenly sputtering coils until they caught, a small flame creeping up, then flaring briefly as it touched the leaves. He picked up the canvases, then, almost reluctantly, unrolled them—he had not meant to look. His grandfather's face stared up at him, all hollows and dark, harsh lines until the flames flickered in a puff of wind, abruptly warming painted flesh to life, eyes glinting straight at him.

He threw it from him on the fire and at once the flames caught, bursting greedily upward, frying the oil, curling canvas into ash within seconds. He could not bear to look at his grandmother's likeness as he laid it gently on the flames, tears running down his cheeks, for her, for his mother, for the past and his aloneness, he did not know which.

He could still see the glow of fire when he regained the shelter of the trees. That at least was one promise kept.

Good luck, Kolya, he remembered bitterly.

Chapter Sixteen

By the time he reached Kiev it was June and the Germans were there before him. He had heard talk on the journey south of the infamous peace made at Brest Litovsk, indeed he felt his route must be clearly marked by blobs of spittle, every peasant he spoke to reacting in the time-honored way to the terms of the peace.

"We've been betrayed. Those devil's spawn Bolsheviks have given away half Russia to the *kolbassniki*," an old boatman told him, as he finished his journey to Kiev in comparative ease, floating down the Dnieper. "You will find many here who rejoice, fluttering their flags of Ukrainian freedom, it is Rus like us who weep to see our land chopped in pieces."

It was true enough, as Kolya found. Flags in the unfamiliar blue and yellow of Ukrainian independence flapped from windows or hung motionless in the heavy, dusty heat of the city. Ukrainian national dress was all the fashion and German troops, if not popular, were at least able to take safety for granted, strolling in the Kzeshchátik, the main street of the city, laughing at the dozing watchmen still clad in shaggy sheepskin in the stifling heat of summer.

In spite of the Germans, Kolya rapidly came to feel the spell of Kiev, with its wide streets, dark chestnut trees and elegant, unlooted houses. He loved the cascades of lilac spilling out from behind every wall, so thick with scent you could feel drunk on it, was fascinated by the liquid light tipped over everything by lumpy, milk-white lamps hung on crusted chains along the Nikolaevskaya. Above all, the lighthearted happiness of Kiev was so different from Moscow or the gray misery of the front. No one seemed to have much to do; even the Germans walked slower and slower until they spent most of their time at cafe tables flirting with dark-eyed Ukrainian girls, gay dresses and bright colors making up for the emptiness of shop-windows.

He worked unloading timber on the Dnieper mud

flats: filthy, exhausting labor but unless he was prepared to work for the Germans there was little else. When he had saved up a pocketful of gaudy new Ukrainian notes he walked up the twisting streets one evening in search of a music teacher and was astonished to see the Opera House open. A performance of *Russlan and Ludmila* was about to begin and on impulse he parted with a handful of notes and bought a ticket.

The familiarity of it took him by surprise, and he sat gaping like any peasant soldier from the backlands. Brilliant light sprayed over gilt plasterwork and crimson velvet from massive chandeliers, the chattering women gaily dressed in elegant prewar dresses. Only a sprinkling of soldiers and peasants like himself in the better seats, the extravagant national dress of Ukrainian officers and field gray of the Germans were reminders that he was not back in the Petersburg of what already seemed another age.

Then, the music. He was not particularly fond of Glinka and the nationalist oratory thrust into the score annoyed him, but just to be listening to music, to allow his mind to dwell critically on the performance, to begin laboriously unraveling the twined threads of point and counterpoint, was like easing open a door to the promised land after long wandering in the wilderness.

He staggered out into the warm darkness hours later, dazed with happiness. Recklessly he bought a flask of vodka and perched on a stone balustrade overlooking the Dnieper. He wanted company; it was a celebration, a return to life after serving sentence in the charnel house, his body so alive he knew certainly that this night he wanted a woman.

He offered his flask to a girl selling hot pies to the strolling crowds and she accepted with alacrity, taking a swig which made him blink a little. "Here, soldier, have a pie in exchange!"

He took out the rest of his notes, the huge denominations meaningless. He could earn some more, tonight was special. "I'll buy the lot, then you can keep me company."

Under her thin muslin blouse her bosom shook as she laughed. "It's your money, soldier!" She was quite unsurprised and he could not take his eyes off the curve of her breast as she pressed against him, tray discarded. "You've found an uncomfortable wall if it is company you want." She looked at him with open invitation.

Kolya swallowed. "Where would you like to go?" He drank some more vodka and put his arm around her waist. "God, you feel nice."

No tears or reluctance here, nor the necessity to chain down desire with pity and understanding. Instead she playfully counted his ribs through his ragged tunic and the image of Anna was lost. "You're nice too."

He couldn't wait, unfamiliar longing and need suddenly so great he feared he could not contain it another heartbeat. He reached for her blindly.

"Here." She thrust the tray of pies at him. "You take these. I'll be beaten if I lose the tray." They ran together, gasping with laughter and scattering pies underfoot, to a secluded corner of some gardens, thick with the heavy scent of lilacs.

She was as eager as he, no finesse about it, but instead a mutual slaking and afterward an unexpected tenderness as they lay in each other's arms through the short summer night. She was lighthearted, entirely natural and exactly fitted his mood, teasing him, stirring him quickly again as he discovered both his own body and hers. They felt no dawn chill, still drowsily loving as the birds began to sing, the sky flushing faintly in the east. He stretched luxuriously, everything in the world different; a delightful weariness weighted him yet his blood seemed to circulate at twice its usual rate. She jumped to her feet, she was all leaps and dives even in their lovemaking, he could not imagine her in repose. He watched her rise on tiptoe, blowing a kiss to the sun like a woodland naiad from mythology, quite unconscious of her nakedness.

He laughed, their whole relationship had been laced with laughter, and threw her clothes at her. "You'd better put something on; it is not only the birds waking up."

She dimpled mischievously and trickled a handful of earth over his bare chest. "Speak for yourself, soldier."

He yelped and tried to grab her but she ran off, dodging in and out of bushes until they both collapsed, breathless with laughter, into each other's arms again. "It is lucky there are no park keepers any longer," gasped Kolya, giving a snort as the picture they must present struck him.

They went down to the Dnieper and bathed as the sun rose above the domes of Kiev, a holiday of irresponsibility flooding them both. They met nearly every evening after that and often he helped her sell pies to hasten the moment they could search for a place to make love. Avdotya, for that was her name, lived under a table in the bakery where she bought her pies, he on some planks under a bridge by the wharf, but in the heat of summer it hardly mattered: she had already told him that when autumn came she must travel back to her village to help in the harvest. Ever since she was fifteen she had come to Kiev in the summer to find work and, he suspected, excitement, and then had returned placidly to the routine of her village for the rest of the year.

One evening, far earlier than he had expected, she told him she must leave. "Everyone speaks of how the new government has decreed the land to be ours, even if our Ukrainian leaders keep silent. It is this which will wed us to the Rus again, for the landowners here already fear for their lives if they try to hold what is theirs."

Kolya grunted lazily; between Avdotya and his music he had scarcely given the Revolution a thought for weeks. "The Bolsheviks are not interested in peasants having their own land whatever they may say."

She laughed. "They'll never get it away from us once we have it. I saw one of the carters from my village yesterday; my family already have double the land they had. There will be much more work to be done by us all; I must go back."

"I will go with you." Kolya was shaken by the casual way she regarded her departure, alarmed by another whole relationship sliding away from him.

She laid her fingers across his mouth. "No, Kolyushka. You have your life, I have mine. We have given each other much happiness, is it not so?"

He smiled lopsidedly. "You know it is."

"That is how it must be, a summer to remember. I know how it is with you; your music could not flourish in a village."

"You could come back with me to Moscow." He had worked doggedly to regain his skills under an old professor in Kiev, but his fingers were too clumsy to play as he wished and anything short of excellence jarred him. He was more set than ever on composing and had begun to crave the stimulus of other musicians, of orchestras, of hammering out techniques on the anvil of criticism. He needed to return to Moscow, now again the capital of Russia as Petrograd was threatened by anti-Bolshevik armies, yet could not bear to accept the end of his holiday from harsh reality.

Avdotya shook her head. "I would be lost in your world, Kolyushka, and you would hate mine. It is over, can't you accept it?" There was little of regret in her manner, or of the passionate creature he had known during the summer, only the brisk practicality of a peasant going about the hard business of living.

He stared at her, feeling cold. What had seemed to him a miraculous dawning of pleasure and happiness was not a miracle at all, but something which happened all the time all through the world. It was over.

Music, the rock, remained.

Chapter Seventeen

Once Avdotya had gone, Kiev seemed bleak and more alien than before. Kolya found he had no heart for practicing; his performing talents, never outstanding, he knew to be forever lost. His clumsy, thickened fingers simply would not give his raging brain the sensitivity it demanded.

He determined to leave for Moscow as soon as frost made travel possible; the rains had already begun and roads would be a quagmire until they hardened with the onset of winter. Trains were running, but very uncertainly through a countryside infested with Ukrainian nationalists, the Red Bolshevik army, anti-Bolsheviks (who were beginning to be called Whites,) peasant revolutionaries and heaven knew who else. Kolya intended to start by train but was sure he would have to be able to walk if necessary.

The frosts came late that year of 1918 or he would have already left before the incredible news came through of German defeat. They had asked for an armistice and one of the conditions imposed was withdrawal of their troops from Russia, including the

Ukraine, whether the nationalists wanted them to stay or not.

There never was such a rapid disintegration of order. One day German troops were saluting their officers, polishing buttons and sitting idling in cafes; the next came the news of defeat accompanied by rumors of unrest and mutiny in Germany itself. Within hours the smart Germans became slovenly, officers disappeared into their mess for protection and vociferous groups of soldiers appeared demanding repatriation and a swiftly changing list of rights.

Kolya had no choice but to stay on awhile. All available trains and wheeled transport were commandeered by the Germans, and Germans moreover in a dangerously unpredictable mood. Atrocity, reprisal and counterreprisal spread, murder even in the streets of Kiev became common, prices soared and riots broke out in the bread lines patiently waiting, sometimes for days, outside the bakeries.

Quite by accident Kolya heard from the baker for whom Avdotya had worked, and from whom he occasionally obtained casual work in exchange for bread, that the Bolsheviks were beginning to emerge from hiding as the Germans withdrew, and had already set up a skeleton administration in the old city.

"They have to be careful, though. Party organization is weak with so many Red workers murdered by nationalists last winter. Even when the Germans have gone it may be months before the Red Army can fight its way here." The baker gave his dough some irritable thumps, it was dark gray and filled with coarse granules of everything from dirt to sawdust, rye husk to pea haulm.

"Where can I find them?" asked Kolya eagerly, he was rail-thin, already finding half the weight he had carried easily during the summer too much for him.

The baker shot him a cautious look. "Those who support the Reds know where to find them."

Kolya fumbled in his tattered pocket; the remnants of his uniform were torn and patched and torn again. "Here, this is my recommendation form for Party membership signed by Comrade Rychagov of the Moscow committee. I served on the Bolshevik patrols for a while but then I had to go back to my village as I told you."

"You don't seem to have done anything to help when the Party here needed any support it could find."

"No." It seemed incredible now that he had loitered the whole summer away, hating the Germans and the nationalists who would destroy Russia, yet doing nothing about it, assuming others were equally passive. After a moment he added honestly, "I'm afraid I had become weary of politics. I came here to find peace for my music and . . . and then Avdotya came along."

The baker laughed. "The Avdotyas of this life have a habit of coming along." He sighed reminiscently. "Ah well, you should be like me, take her one moment and the next back to your work. No need to follow 'em around like a bitch in heat."

Kolya picked up a sack slowly, staggering under its weight, unable to trust himself to speak. Of course. A girl like Avdotya coming in from the villages for a summer in Kiev would use her body to pay for her place under the bakery table, as no doubt she had similarly paid the carter and the meat vendor. He had known it but foolishly thought that for this summer she had been his alone.

He went down to the old city the same evening; for a shabby ex-soldier like himself there was no real difficulty over finding Bolshevik headquarters. It was a hive of activity, blazing red posters on the walls and red cloth flung over tables, a blessed breath of familiarity after Ukrainian blue and yellow.

"What do you want?" They all looked exhausted and underfed as he did, but there was the same brusque concern for the obscure he remembered among the overworked officials in Moscow.

Comfort and a sense of belonging spread over him. "I am a comrade from Moscow. I wanted to help."

"Good, go over there and wait for Comrade Kyuchenko." There was no hesitation, instead welcome, the immediate sense of purpose which struck a fresh response from his mind.

He had to wait for hours, but as he sat watching young men and women chasing in and out, the stream of people coming to this dusty, crowded room as to a haven whence some miraculous framework of order might emerge, some hand of help be offered, he was fascinated rather than restless.

Kyuchenko was a small, dark Ukrainian who had once been very fat. Now flesh hung in folds and pouches, making him look as if his body was in the act of dissolution. "You say you are a comrade from Moscow?" His Ukrainian accent was so thick Kolya had to struggle to understand him, but he welcomed it nevertheless; not all Ukrainians were nationalists then.

"Not a full Party member." He produced his papers again. "I am only on probation, not even a candidate yet."

"Hm." He flicked them over rapidly, but he did not look as though he missed much. "Where have you been all summer?"

"In my village in Oryol province and then here. I had leave."

"Why here?"

Kolya hesitated. "I thought music meant more to me than anything else and I wanted to come here to study."

Kyuchenko looked at him blankly. "Music?"

Kolya flushed and nodded. "I want to be a composer

above all else, but I have spent most of my time humping timber."

For a moment he thought Kyuchenko was going to laugh and somehow that would have been unbearable, but he did not. "Well, why not after all? The Revolution will open fresh fields to all." He slapped the papers together. "Very well, Comrade, I will admit you as a candidate member. We don't have time to go through all the usual steps to membership in the crisis we have here now." Kolya stammered his thanks, overwhelmed with relief and pride, while Kyuchenko filled in and signed various endorsements on his papers and issued his first Party card.

The next few days were a whirlwind of activity. It soon emerged that Kolya could ride, whereas most of the other Bolsheviks were city workers or intellectuals and therefore incapable of the cavalry policing urgently needed around Kiev. Within weeks, so outnumbered were the Bolsheviks and so confused the situation, he was commanding his own squad, sent out eastward to test the truth of rumors about the approach of a Bolshevik force from "Red Kharkov," where the workers had long since seized power.

It was a splendid feeling to be trotting along at the head of his own command, even if it was only half a dozen men. Deep snow fields reflected a million refractions of light and from time to time they passed bundled groups of marchers carrying fluttering banners of red, occasional blues and yellows almost swamped by what was now a peasant revolution on the march.

They were a mixed bunch, thought Kolya, considering his patrol. Two boys, Vanya and Seriozha, even younger than himself; Totúshka, an old Tsarist cavalryman who seemed willing enough but extremely dull-witted; and three Kiev workmen who until a week ago had never sat on a horse but whose enthusiasm allowed them somehow to ignore the agony of burned thighs and aching backs. None of them were Party members, which was why he was in command, but all were alight with enthusiasm for the Revolution, including presumably Totúshka, from whom scarcely a word could be prized.

By the afternoon of the second day snow was falling thickly and Kolya had to call Vanya in from his duty of scouting ahead, the dangers of losing him greater than the slight risk of surprise. He wondered uneasily whether they should keep going and risk losing the track, or camp under conditions which almost guaranteed death if they had to stay long. Not for the first time he became aware of his own inadequacy, his sheer lack of military knowledge. He was not even confident he would be able to reload his carbine in such conditions.

A flurry of snow drove under the collar of his German cape, which had seemed very splendid but was now obviously inadequate. Vainly he tried to peer into the murk to distinguish some object, but one moment the horizon appeared immeasurably distant, the next as if his horse's hoofs were tipping over the edge of the world. Snow plastered his eyebrows and nostrils, icicles forming painfully around mouth and nose even under the cloth wound around his face.

If only they could find somewhere to shelter, thought Kolya despairingly. The sky was darkening, snow slanting in streaks like prison bars, so it was some while before he grasped the significance of hardening outlines to bush and shrouded scrub around them.

"It's clearing!" he exclaimed in relief. "Look, we can see ahead now." He shook the nearest slumped figure, having to rouse them one by one and then start with the first again; one advantage of responsibility was that it did at least keep you awake when the lack of it invited resignation.

The wind howled and whined, whirling snow thickened, slackened, thickened again. "I heard a dog," said old Totúshka suddenly, the first time he had spoken since morning.

They listened intently, unaware how their eyes strained with effort until they felt the first crackle of frost edging the eyeball. "There it is again!" several exclaimed at once, but direction was another matter, the deadening walls of snow sifted sound aside, their numbed senses unable to make clear judgments.

Only Totúshka seemed certain and Kolya decided to follow him. The horses were floundering badly now, snow frozen hard in some places, swept into belly-deep traps in others.

"*Posmotrite!* Look!" Totúshka pointed. At first they could see nothing, then glimpsed the squared edge of a verst post; they were back on some kind of track. The smothering drowsiness of cold was banished by hope as they pushed on, able here and there to recognize layered snow instead of powdery masses, the only indication that others had passed this way before.

The looming shape was a surprise when it came, dark and tilting, half hidden by drifts, but unmistakably a posthouse and identical with a thousand others on every main road of Russia. Framed Imperial regulations and a list of hire charges still hung by the signboard, the only change from normal the unpolished state of the brass bell upon which impatient clients had formerly rung for service.

They were too numb to dismount, sitting on splay-legged horses like ghosts out of the dark, the distance to the ground impossible to contemplate. Vanya solved the problem first, leaning forward and tipping headfirst into a drift, the crack of his anklebone terrible in the silence: he had been unaware of his foot frozen solidly into the stirrup. He did not cry out; indeed he felt nothing, lying half into a drift staring stupidly at his cocked-up, right-angled leg.

Warned by his example, the others dislodged their feet somehow before slumping out of the saddle, but once out it was blissful to lie back, bodies so deadened the snow seemed comfort itself, and it needed the most savage effort of will to attempt massaging agonizing feeling back into loins and legs.

The posthouse remained shrouded in darkness, shutters closed, any sound they made lost in the howl of the storm. Kolya was about to thump on the door with the butt of his carbine when a thought forced its way through the lumped ice floes of his mind. The Imperial regulations. He peered again and the Romanov double eagle stared back at him; he had not seen one undefaced in over a year.

He glanced at the others. Apart from impervious old Totúshka they were far gone, and Vanya at least must be found shelter at once. So must the horses, yet they were beyond responding to any danger save the overriding menace of the cold. "Come," he said quietly. "We will go with the horses into a shed. Totúshka, you go ahead and see what you can find while we carry Vanya. Be as quiet as you can," he added privately to Totúshka. He attempted to work the bolt of his carbine but it was completely frozen; if they were attacked there was nothing they could do.

Within a few minutes Totúshka's bulk loomed out of the snow again, leading them one by one over a drift spanning the log palisade around the posthouse, past obscured buildings until they reached a sod byre wedged with drifts, hidden entrance discovered by his countryman's eye. Inside it was unbelievably warm, there were a few cows and a closed stove to keep them from freezing, hens roosted in the shadows and a couple of pigs contributed to the fearful stench as their dung roasted gently next to the stove.

"Marvelous!" exclaimed Kolya. "Totúshka, however did you find it?"

The old man said nothing but laid his finger along his nose and winked heavily, as if to say, this is not the first peasant byre I and my fellows have looted.

At first the cows and hens set up a great furor, but their horses were too cold to join in and the men too would have lain where they fell had not Kolya staggered to each one ordering his cloak off, handing him trusses of straw to scrub himself and his horse, insisting they kept going until the blood circulated properly again. Vanya was by then in great pain, his ankle not just broken but every muscle so torn and swollen that he begged them to cut off his *veliki*, felt boots which were normally so loose that half a dozen wrappings would fit inside.

"No." Kolya tried not to look at Vanya's pleading eyes. "He must keep it on. Once it is off we'll never get it on again and he'll lose his leg with the cold."

"I could stay here with him while you ride for help," suggested Seriozha, tears in his eyes. "For God's sake, Kolya, we can't leave him like this."

Kolya shook his head, wondering whether he should explain his fears about the posthouse. "He must be able to ride."

Illyrion, one of the workmen, snatched at his arm. "To hell with riding! You kill him if you make him ride like that!"

"He dies if we leave him behind. This posthouse, we won't find friends here. We don't know which road we're on or how near our Red armies, but one thing is certain, they've not been this way and left the Imperial eagle untouched. This must be White country."

"The eagle?" repeated Seriozha blankly.

Kolya nodded impatiently. "Even Ukrainian nationalists throw things at it, yet this one is untouched. We must be gone by dawn; someone will be here to tend the cattle. Get what sleep you can. I'll take first watch."

It was agony to stay awake; he had to walk up and down on legs which felt like fence posts, his sight wavering with fatigue. He laid his head against some wood framing to hold himself steady, to prevent himself vomiting with dissolving balance, and then started awake again on his face in the muck, in a sweat of panic and unable to distinguish whether he had been asleep seconds or hours. He rose unsteadily and went over to the door, hoping to judge the time from the darkness, but on the way was stopped by Seriozha, trying to hold Vanya still as he tossed on the straw, semiconscious and moaning.

"He can't ride." It was a flat, accusatory statement.

Kolya stared down at him, cold foreboding gripping his stomach; his first command was turning into a disaster. "No," he said finally. "We shall have to take it in turns to strap him behind us. We'll splint his leg as best we can outside the boot."

"You utter swine," Seriozha spat at him, the hatred of his tone all the worse for the whisper in which he spoke. "Why not leave him with me in the warm here, what difference will it make to your precious patrol if it is two short instead of one? We're bloody lost and you know it."

Kolya paled. "I would leave him, and you too, but if I'm right and there is no sympathy for us Reds here then—"

"But this is Russia, not some conquered country! Who would harm one of our own wounded soldiers? If that is all you fear then I stay."

"No! You obey orders, we all ride." Kolya woke Totúshka to keep his watch, but even when he lay down sleep would not come. Vanya's moans, the confusion in his own mind, the cramps which twisted his muscles unmercifully as blood struggled back to full circulation, all combined to toss him in blurred wakefulness throughout the remaining hours of darkness.

Chapter Eighteen

Aris, another of the Kiev workmen, roused them in the surly gray of early dawn. In spite of the fetid warmth of the byre everyone was aching with damp and stiffness, while stove and animal fumes combined to produce vicious headaches and grit-hard throats.

"God," Kolya whispered, rolling over and burying his head in his arms. He wanted nothing so much as to give up, to lie forever and let the dark wash over him. Had he been alone the effort of rising might well have been too much but he knew he must somehow force the others into movement. Stifling a groan, he rose to his knees, pulled himself upright and staggered to the door. The snow had stopped and a few stars were showing in the changing sheen of the sky. He took a deep breath and scrubbed his face with a handful of snow, spitting and gasping at the sting of it but feeling the command of his mind locking again into the gear of his muscles.

Aris had woken the others, except Vanya, whose face was already that of an old man, fleshless and sharply pointed with suffering.

"I'm not going," said Seriozha positively. "Do what you like, I stay with him here."

"Strap him up in front of me, Aris," ordered Kolya, ignoring him. He had oiled the bolt of his carbine the night before and he slid it back with a faint click.

Aris hesitated. "Why not leave them both here?"

Seriozha scrambled to his feet. "Shoot me if you like, Comrade Commander. I won't go, and you do not take Vanya unless you kill me first."

The little group stood motionless, all eyes on Kolya as he fingered the stock of his carbine. He remembered how Ruska had forced the 103rd Saratovsky on their feet somehow: I wonder whether he really would have killed Mitya if he had not moved, if he had had a rifle capable of firing? he thought despairingly.

He could not do it. He turned away abruptly and thrust the carbine back into its saddle holster, unable to speak against the unsteadiness in his throat. It was utter failure.

They led their horses back over the snow bridge and out on the track, Totúshka nosing ahead to look for verst posts. It snowed intermittently all day, but not with the viciousness of the day before. They saw nothing and as far as they knew were seen by no one, the country deserted, the occasional hut blank of the life it must once have sheltered. Kolya flogged himself into carrying out his duties, each man watching a different sector, the scout riding with carbine ready cocked until his gloved hands and the mechanism froze and he had to be relieved. No one spoke except for necessity; comradeship destroyed, command a charade, his orders obeyed perfunctorily, lip service to a nervous kid playing soldiers.

The attack came with no warning at all. They were riding through the same endless plain as light drained away into another depressing dusk, fence posts showing above drifts to the right, faint shadow to the left where scrub was drowned in snow. Kolya himself was riding scout, carbine at the ready but his finger so frozen he would already have asked for relief had he not feared the derision of the others.

He heard a shout from Aris; by the time he wrenched his chilled body around to look, flying shapes were on them out of the dusk. Whites? Nationalists? Brigands? Fellow Reds believing them to be one of these things? There was no means of knowing and in complete confusion they hacked and swore, lurching as numbed bodies would not answer to the screaming emergency of the brain. Kolya managed to fire once and thought he hit someone, but there was no time to reload and he attempted to hack his way back to the others. Shots sounded flatly against deadening snow, shouts encouraged enemy and friend alike, horses whinnied, a man screamed and went on screaming, a pitch of agony so terrible the combatants hesitated a moment and looked in horror at such a sound.

It was only a flicker of hesitation, then the lunging and hacking began again. Kolya was half unbalanced from the saddle before a fierce blow on the shoulder thrust him back, then his carbine splintered as he instinctively used it to guard his head. He thrust the jagged end into a face and heard a cry of pain, saw upflung hands and spurting blood. More shots and cries, a fleeting glimpse of Aris and Totúshka on foot and back to back, slashing with their sabers before they disappeared in a melee of hoofs. He shouted and plunged forward, felt a blow under the ear which sprawled him from the saddle, but the pain was divided from him by an immense distance. He could hear fighting all around and dimly wondered whether the enemy were fighting each other, shots, shouts and clashing steel eddying away down the road.

He was not sure whether it was truly dark or it was only darkness within his head, but he groped his way to Totúshka and Aris like a blind man, fumbling at their bodies for a sign of life, calling for the others as if he were alone at a picnic.

"Here's another," he heard a voice say. "Robbing the dead already by the looks of him."

He opened his mouth to protest, but feeling himself seized it seemed unimportant. He was pushed down the road, shambling and stumbling, hands twisted into his back. He could feel the stickiness of blood on his neck and its warmth running down inside his clothes, but no pain; the other shoulder where he dimly remembered an earlier blow, throbbed fiercely.

More shots ahead, but isolated, not haphazard as in battle. Crops of four or six, a pause, then another group. Bunches of flowers, arpeggios and cadenzas, he thought dazedly.

"Put him over there, Comrade," he heard. "Another couple of dozen and we'll be off." He was shoved roughly down in the snow with a huddle of others.

Comrade.

His brain struggled desperately but it was slipping under its load like a greased wheel on ice. Think. Think quickly. Another punctuation of shots; he knew what was happening now, prisoners were being shot and he was in the next batch.

Who were all these prisoners? His mind attempted to take up connected thought again but any pattern eluded him. They had been attacked—by how many? Not more than ten, he thought; they would have been overwhelmed at once otherwise.

Another pattern of shots. At least twenty or thirty must by now have been shot. Not his men. His attackers? Yes perhaps, if they had been a small party ahead of the main body.

Comrade.

"Comrade?" He spoke aloud, voice cracking. He moved his head slightly and now he did feel a stab of pain.

"What's the matter, bandit?" asked a voice mockingly. "Want to turn Communist to save your skin?"

Communist? It was unfamiliar, yet also familiar. "Bolshevik," he said clearly. He hadn't many words, they must be clear. Important. "Bolshevik from Kiev."

A hand reached out of the dark, slapped him sharply across the face. "Stop blubbering, you can't save your skin that way now."

The pain in his neck sharpened with the jerk of the blow, but it somehow reminded him of Anna. Oh, Anna. He plunged in the murk of his mind toward a refuge which was no refuge and then savagely thrust thought away. "Take me to your commander. I have a message from the Bolsheviks of Kiev, you can always shoot me after."

"Shoot you? If you waste the Comrade Commander's time he'll burn your guts before your eyes." But there was doubt in the man's voice, the sound of mumbling, boots on the road. He was hauled to his feet, hustled urgently forward, twice tripping and sprawling full length.

The second time rage came to his rescue and he turned on them savagely. "Help me up, you goat-got bastards. If I am a Bolshevik messenger I will not help you dead, if I am not you have only minutes to wait before doing your will. Either way you disgrace your cause and shame yourselves." He wavered onto his knees. "Help me up."

One drew back a leg to kick but changed his mind and heaved him up sullenly. Somewhere, very cold, very remote, Kolya felt a slight ripple of satisfaction.

The Commander looked grotesquely squat in a heavy fleece coat, the red cloth star on his cap confirmation of Kolya's hopes. His guards thrust him forward, a rabbit punch in the kidney nearly winding him even while prudence made them hold him upright, just in case he was what he claimed. He sagged in their grasp, unable to speak while the Commander shot a volley of questions at his guards and then at himself. At last, exasperated by his inability to answer, they dumped him among some corpses at the side of the road and thrust a flask of vodka at him.

He gagged at the first sip. "No . . . just winded . . . couldn't drink . . ."

The Commander crouched on his heels in front of him. "You claim to be a Communist?"

Kolya shook his head and then wished he had not as the movement tore at the crusts of blood welding his collar to his neck. "Bolshevik . . . from Kiev."

"Well, what the hell difference does it make? Bolshevik, Marxist, we are all the Communist Party now." He looked at Kolya thoughtfully. "You say you come from Kiev?"

"Yes," said Kolya baldly, keeping his head rock-still this time. He indicated the red patches sewn to his collar wordlessly.

"Do you have any papers?"

He handed them over and ventured a gulp of vodka. It was atrocious: raw and corrosive on the tongue. He began to feel sick and became aware of his body trembling, a deep shudder spreading with his awareness of it into every muscle and sinew, until he clamped his teeth on the collar of his cloak and jammed his hands between his knees in an effort to control it.

He heard another shot and stammered: "Please, there are four of my men somewhere. Two—two are dead, I don't know about the others." Without thinking, he turned his head again and almost blacked out with the pain. He groped at his neck, fingers stumbling on a long slash, not deep but gaping from ear to throat; it was a miracle the artery was untouched.

The Commander returned his papers. "These seem to be in order. I am Skobolev, commanding 72nd Red Cavalry, do you have a message for me?"

"No. Comrade Kyuchenko of the Kiev Committee sent me to find out how long they had to hold before the Kharkov army arrives. Conditions are very bad in the city." He began to describe them but broke off in a panic, hearing more single shots. "My men, Comrade Skobolev, please, could we—"

"If they lived you are probably too late; we have

nearly finished." Skobolev turned to one of his former guards: "Go and see if there are any others dressed as this man is among those to be shot." He turned to Kolya. "We have to be quick; it isn't safe to stay long. The whole country is alive with bandits and Whites."

"You shoot your prisoners, then?" Kolya did not attempt to keep the disgust out of his voice.

"What do you think? How could a small group like ours take them with us?"

"But can't you tell them of our cause? When they understand about the new Russia many would want to join us!"

"Oh yes, certainly," Skobolev agreed sarcastically. "Let us all sit down in the middle of a freezing plain and discuss Marxism, persuade them with the speeches of Comrade Lenin! Are you out of your mind? This is war, not a political parlor game; we kill the enemy first and then there is no doubt about those who survive being on our side. Besides, have you seen what the swine do to our men?"

Kolya stood up carefully. He felt desperately weak and chilled right through to the deep, continuing shudder in his guts, but he could stay upright and the bleeding from his neck had stopped. He had no strength for argument, though, his mind grasping only what was essential, and Skobolev's words triggered another recollection. "I had to leave two men a day's march back, one was injured. Are you heading west? May I come with you?"

"Only if you can keep up; we shoot our own stragglers too. You should have done the same; if you left them you will not find them alive." The soldier returned. "Well?"

"No one alive, Comrade Commander."

Another figure loomed out of the darkness. "All prisoners shot, all wounded unable to ride shot, the riding wounded ready to be escorted to the rear." The shadowy shape was ramrod-straight, restraining himself with difficulty from saluting. Obviously an ex-tsarist n.c.o., thought Kolya hazily. He pulled himself together. "May I go to make sure, Comrade Commander?"

"No." Skobolev shouted for his horse. "If Rykov here says everyone is dead or accounted for, then everyone is dead or accounted for. I can't waste more time on you, although at least it was the easy meat your little squad offered which tempted those pigs out of cover and let us kill them. You either ride with us and keep up, or you go back to our lines with the wounded. It is your choice, but I will shoot you myself if you drop behind."

"I'll come with you." Perhaps one of the others survived among the wounded; he would never know. His duty now was to Vanya and Seriozha, to insist on a search being made for them. He must find the strength to stay in the saddle, to avoid giving that filth Skobolev the satisfaction of shooting him if he failed to keep up.

It was his loathing for Skobolev, rather than fear for himself, which kept him going until bivouac, and then through the following day. He dared not move his right arm for fear of starting the bleeding again, and the blow he had taken on his left meant he could scarcely hold the reins, could not possibly defend himself in action. Rykov slashed a sheepskin saddlecloth into strips and wound it around his neck to keep the frost from the wound. "It will freeze else, and never heal," he said curtly as Kolya protested at the monstrous bundle on his shoulders, and the comfort from it was undeniable.

Mercifully his horse was as exhausted as he, and the hours passed without incident. However much he might detest him, he soon recognized Skobolev as a very competent commander, swift and assured in handling his men, alert to danger without allowing it to divert him from his primary aim of scouting ahead of the main advance. Twice during the day Kolya heard a single shot and saw a dark bundle left behind to mark their line of march; the second time another terrible bout of shivering seized him, panic loosening every muscle: many more days like this and it would be him.

During a halt to breathe the horses Skobolev came cantering back. "Come with me, Berdeyev, there is something I want to show you."

Kolya followed him to a group of scouts gathered by a verst post and stared numbly at the object in their midst: the body of what had once been a Bolshevik soldier, limbs neatly split and gutted, bones removed and tidily placed beside the untouched torso. The terrible rictus of agony frozen on the man's face, eyeballs solidified by ice in nightmare protrusion, lips and tongue chewed to shreds, testified to the inconceivable prolongation of his death. Skobolev was quite expressionless. "You should have shot your men as I do. Is this one of yours?"

"No." There were no words, no thoughts, no emotions left. When they moved on again the creaking of the horses' hoofs on snow tore at nerves laid open and gutted as that wretched soldier had been, his agony prolonged yet again in the mind of every man, branded into every consciousness.

Dusk was not far off when the posthouse and its huddle of buildings at last broke the immensity of white, at first so small it might have been a verst post, then unnaturally large in a landscape without perspective.

"Don't go in," Skobolev ordered curtly. His hand closed over Kolya's bridle and at his nod a dozen or so men scattered among the outbuildings while others broke into the posthouse itself. There were some distant shouts, a couple of shots. Kolya licked his lips fearfully.

Rykov reappeared through the posthouse. "No

bandits, although they've been here. Four prisoners. Postkeeper, wife, two drovers." Skobolev must have looked an inquiry, for he nodded imperceptibly.

The prisoners were dragged out into the roadway, the drovers scuffling on their knees begging for mercy, the postkeeper and his wife standing in silence. They knew their lives to be horribly forfeit, no possible pleading could offer them a way of escape.

"My two men—" Kolya could not ask the question.

"We will bury them, Comrade." There was rough sympathy in Rykov's voice.

"How—" Another question he could not frame.

"Don't ask," said Skobolev harshly. "It is better not to know."

Kolya nodded but then dismounted clumsily. "I will see them buried, they were mine."

Rykov came with him, bringing a couple of troopers, and when it was over they avoided each other's eyes as if ashamed to belong to the same race as those who inflicted such obscenity on their fellow men.

The posthouse was well alight by the time they left the byre, but Kolya stopped one of the men when he would have tossed a blazing billet into that too. "Leave it be; at least let animals live when men have forfeited the right." The soldiers looked at him in astonishment but Rykov swore at them and they followed without argument.

It was quite dark now and by some mysterious alchemy brilliant orange flame turned the snow blood-red. A greedy, roaring crackle almost drowned the screams of the postkeeper and drovers, speared by fencing stakes through the crotch to the sod roof, writhing hideously as its damp solidity mercilessly preserved them from the flames.

"The woman?" croaked Kolya. There was no more vomit left in him and abruptly he was racked almost double by stomach cramps. Rykov jerked his head.

"They will kill her when all who want her are finished."

There was a crash and the scene immediately darkened as the roof fell into the flames. The screams stopped, the tearing shock to staked bodies at last enough, even when the flames would not yet have killed.

"Give me your rifle." Kolya was still hunched over the terrible spasm of his stomach muscles and Rykov handed it to him, thinking he wanted it for support.

Indeed it did help. He pushed through clustered figures, relaxed and chattering now, the tensions and horrors of the day released by violence. The woman was lying stretched across a discarded saddle, hands pulled aside and frozen into buckets of water melted in the flames and frozen again within minutes.

The men around her made room for him good-naturedly enough, the savagery and speed of their rapes gave time for all. He shot her between the eyes before anyone realized what he was about.

Chapter Nineteen

The horror of that first patrol of the Civil War came later to typify for Konstantin Berdeyev all the degradation of the apparently endless fighting which followed. The postkeeper's wife was the first human being he positively knew he had killed, but she was the first of many: he never again left behind a wounded man, never let his men keep a prisoner alive. He would offer recruitment into the Red forces, sometimes arguing all night with those he might possibly persuade, but if the man was obdurate then he was shot. Occasionally rumbles of discontent would drift back to him from the higher command, pointing out that valuable information was being lost by overhasty execution of prisoners, but on the whole he gained a reputation for cold-blooded devotion to duty and the Communist Party. Whenever he was free he attended lectures and discussions on Marxist theory and Communist ideology, observing debating skills, the use of rhetoric and ways of silencing or persuading the doubtful.

Rather surprisingly, considering he had had to rescue him from his incensed men after the killing of the postkeeper's wife, Skobolev recommended Kolya to the Red Army command and by the summer of 1919 he was commanding a half squadron of cavalry. In July he received his card as a full Party member and was almost at once transferred to the 66th Red Infantry as commissar, where, such is the immemorial habit of armies, all his hard-earned experience of irregular cavalry warfare was completely wasted.

The regiment was mostly locally recruited, which meant its loyalty might well be in doubt if it had to face Ukrainian Nationalists in battle, and was commanded by an ex-tsarist Major Kottbus. The Red Army was so short of men with any technical knowledge of soldiering that there was no choice but to employ tsarist officers, where these had survived and were willing to serve. But naturally enough they were not trusted, even though some served with great devotion and loyalty. The normal practice was to attach a Party member as commissar to those commanders whose political loyalty was felt to be doubtful (which meant virtually all commanders) to discharge the duty of indoctrinating the troops with Communist principles, to acquire by observation such military skill as he could and to take over at once if the military commander appeared to be failing his duty.

This dual command, which in fact put ultimate authority in the hands of commissars who were usually young, brash and militarily illiterate, gave rise to endless trouble and indecision. If anything was to be achieved the relationship between commander and commissar had to be close and sympathetic, each willing to step down when a particular matter exceeded his own competence. Fortunately for Kolya, Kottbus possessed a dry sense of humor, which was probably the best possible lubricant in such a situation, and was also extremely competent, having served with the Mikhailovsky Guards throughout the war. It seemed best not to inquire how he had survived to command a regiment in the Red Army and Kolya did not enlighten him on his own origins, either.

Sometimes the temptation to talk without reticence was almost overwhelming. Summer nights camping along the Dnieper, long yellow flames from driftwood campfires flickering over relaxed hands and faces, the plaintive sounds of soldiers' choruses, all invited confidences. Kottbus knew old Petersburg intimately and spoke often of people whom Kolya had met or seen in gatherings around the city. He had heard Chaliapin sing and attended performances of opera, plays and ballet at every theater in the city. He had been to Imperial receptions in Tsarskoye Selo, where fat old General Traskine had once taken Kolya, and made no attempt to hide his nostalgia for what was so irremediably gone.

"To hear you speak, I would expect to find you with Petlyura or Denikin,"* said Kolya idly one night. "I can't imagine any combination of circumstances which would make someone like you a Red Army commander."

"A similar combination of circumstance no doubt as brought you to be a commissar. The only difference being that you have a future here and I have not."

* Ukrainian Nationalist and White commanders respectively.

Kolya sat up abruptly. "There can be no similarity between us."

"Between the good Party man with his political lectures to the troops and the ex-tsarist who will face a firing squad once the Reds win?" Kottbus had a laugh like a hacksaw. "Don't you believe it, my boy. I serve the Reds now because they are going to win and I believe the sooner they do so the better, for the sake of this suffering country of ours. You serve them because you are convinced it is right; when eventually that conviction fails they will get you too. There will not be much difference between us then."

"No!" said Kolya violently. "My God, I haven't been through this past year of unspeakableness just to see it thrown away. True Party members will see it is not."

"Of course," said Kottbus sarcastically. "True Party members like you will move the earth. I'm glad I shan't be around to see it."

After this exchange Kolya threw himself with redoubled vigor into the task of rousing the soldiers to political awareness, but however hard he tried he seemed to make little progress. The men had a way of listening with detached apathy, lost in a kind of gloomy boredom, resigned to the inevitable as they might be to a shower of rain but gaining nothing from it. Occasionally there was the odd recruit, perhaps even a group of recruits, who listened avidly, and he had to take what comfort he could from them, although vaguely uneasy to find that enthusiasm often drove these prospective members of the Party to denounce others not similarly moved, with all the inevitable feuds and hatreds this stirred up in the regiment.

Kottbus was philosophical about the strains this imposed on discipline, taking the view that comic opera amateurishness was only to be expected from a bunch of Reds, while Kolya was thankful enough to abdicate military responsibility and shelter behind his commander's ability. Since his nightmare first patrol he had striven desperately to hide his lack of confidence, his fear of sending men unnecessarily to their deaths because of his own incompetence, but his transfer as commissar had come only just in time to save him from nervous collapse.

"What do you want me to do with Semonov?" asked Kottbus one day. They were marching across undulating plains to the east of the Dnieper, hurrying to reinforce Kiev, unexpectedly threatened by Petlyura's advancing forces. "It's your department, I think, Comrade Commissar."

Kolya trudged some distance before replying. The heat and dust were suffocating, his pack dragging at scarcely healed shoulder muscles. "Nothing," he said eventually. "He's a reliable soldier, he will not desert or be a traitor, which is what counts."

Kottbus shook his head in mock reproof. "Comrade Lenin would not approve. 'All class enemies are enemies of the state and hostages to the Revolution.' You can't have been listening to the divisional commissar the other night."

"I don't think Comrade Lenin was referring to someone like Semonov," said Kolya carefully. "Hostages are hostages anyway, kept safe so long as they behave themselves."

Kottbus rasped out his sawmill laugh. "In all this Civil War have you ever seen a hostage returned safely?"

"I've never taken one," Kolya replied briefly. "If I did he would be safe so long as the terms of his captivity were observed."

Kottbus looked at him thoughtfully. "The nineteen-year-old commissar who always shoots his prisoners. Before you came to us I heard whispers about you and wondered what sort of monster you were. Now I just wonder what you are."

"Well, I'll tell you what I am." Kolya's voice and hands were trembling; he was suddenly consumed by an anguish which destroyed in an instant his carefully maintained guard. "I'm someone who wants to be a musician and has become a murderer, a commander who lost every one of his men on his first patrol, who thinks death cleaner than the foulness which otherwise happens to prisoners." He passed his hand over his eyes but it was shaking so badly he crushed his fingers under his pack straps in an attempt to steady them. "Do you think I can't still remember every man I've shot when I try to sleep at night? How many more do you suppose before we all go mad and Russia bleeds to death?"

There was a long silence. "You poor bastard," said Kottbus at last. "God help us all when people like you turn into butchers."

Kiev fell again to Petlyura's forces at the end of August, thc Red Army retreating as the first frosts of yet another winter put a gossamer of white on leaf and puddle and curled chill mist into the slightest break of ground. With the early dawn and in the clear starlight of perfect autumn nights the countryside was beautiful, the play of curve and shape an infinitely changing refreshment to the eye. But in the full light of day the bareness of space was revealed: for verst on hundred verst the land was bleak and devastated with no crops being harvested, no animal to be seen, no bustle to thresh and plant and preserve before winter came.

Every village was burned, every hut and cottage reduced to a few blackened timbers or pile of sods. The towns were silent, people only by the slow-moving old, by huddles of gaunt women and big-bellied children watching the passing armies in voiceless hatred; which army it was made no difference.

By the end of October, the 66th was holding a line of trenches guarding the road north from Kiev to Chernigov, where the Red Army's Southern Command was situated. There was no enemy in sight; indeed this seemed to be the kind of war where one very rarely did see the enemy, only his obscene destruction, while you tried not to look at your own. A few women were moving northward up the road, somehow carrying their children and passing the line of trenches as if they did not exist. Swollen children, children with parchment skin hanging in flaccid folds, coughing children, weeping children, silent children too weak to respond to anything any more: there seemed no end to the terrible sights of the road.

"The mothers will live as long as the children do," said Kottbus softly. "Then, when the children die, they die too. The men go first: into the army or killed because they cannot bear it any longer and attack the first soldier they see, unable to endure the knowledge they can do nothing to save their family."

Snow was sifting down, very slowly. The men in the trenches watched silently as a woman sank to her knees a quarter verst away and did not rise again.

Kolya started to his feet but Kottbus held him back. "Leave her. The death by cold is merciful compared to watching your child starve. You shoot your prisoners, I let the women freeze." He swore suddenly, savagely, his face twisted with anguish.

Further down their line one of the soldiers scrambled out of his sodden trench and ran down the road to bend over the woman. He heaved her over his shoulders and walked back through their line to the village behind, where a few tattered figures still moved among shattered huts. Two other soldiers ran out to stop him but he brushed past them unseeingly and one of them shouted, hand snicking back his rifle bolt.

"Stop!" Kolya threw off Kottbus' hand and slid down the rough bank to the road. "You bloody fools, what do you think you are doing?"

"It is Semonov again!" Zhavin, one of Kolya's keenest Marxist converts, turned to him eagerly. "He's deserting this time!"

"Nonsense," said Kolya irritably. "Can't you see he's only taking that wretched woman to shelter? He'll be back."

"A true Communist should obey orders and he was told to stay in the trench," said Zhavin stubbornly. "He is always making trouble and you have done nothing about our cell's complaint when he refused to burn down that barn on detached patrol in the summer." He stared at Kolya accusingly and added, "We are ordered to burn anything which could give the enemy shelter."

"A whole village was living there; even a single enemy soldier could not have squeezed in." Kolya attempted a lightness he did not feel.

The man looked contemptuous. "They would soon turn the people out into the cold and use the barn themselves."

"And when this war is over, any villagers who survive will remember it was the Reds who spared them and the Whites who did not," retorted Kolya with sudden rage. "It is not for us to destroy Russia, to win a corpse! Semonov with his mercy reflects more credit on the Party than you do."

"He disobeyed orders. I reported it and he should have been punished. See how he disobeys again now."

"I am Commissar, you reported to me, it is my responsibility. He is a faithful soldier, leave him alone and go back to your post." Kolya was consumed by cold fury to find it was one of those he had so proudly won for the Party who should fall short of true idealism already.

Zhavin shuffled his feet and exchanged a covert look with his companion. "It is a Party matter, we should have a cell meeting to discuss it."

Kolya nearly shot him, then and there. Almost blind with anger, he pulled out his revolver, watched the men's expressions change from insolence to stubbornness, from stubbornness to fear, from fear to terror with recognition of the deadly purpose in their commissar's eyes. Kolya heard a distant shout from Kottbus but it was not that which stopped him, it was the shock of knowing how much he wanted to kill, for his own satisfaction to take what had become the easy way to obliterate an enemy, to save those no longer enemies. He holstered his revolver again with trembling fingers. "Get back to your post," he said thickly, and this time they went.

Kottbus was standing at the top of the trench looking down at him inscrutably. "Why didn't you shoot him?"

Kolya blinked and pulled out his revolver again, carefully ejecting the bullets and putting them in his pocket. "Because I wanted to kill him too much. That one I would have killed for myself and enjoyed the doing of it. I think I will not carry a loaded gun again."

The snow was coming down more thickly now and he shuddered suddenly, with cold and sick reaction. Another winter, dear God, would it never end?

Chapter Twenty

For Kolya the winter was surprisingly and suddenly cut short. Sheer lack of supplies forced a lull in operations and as the armies lapsed into semistarved passivity he was posted to a military school for Red officers at Gomel.

The Red Army had become painfully aware of the dangers arising from divided command and wished to train its own military commanders as quickly as possible, selecting likely candidates from among the younger commissars for intensive training. Kottbus came with him to the little wayside station of Bragin, whence he could get a train to Gomel, and together they embarked on a truly fearful drinking bout, drinking first gloomily, then hilariously, then tearfully and finally with a kind of desperate resolution to outdrink recollection, memory, horror, even comradeship.

Kolya awoke the next day with a head like Vulcan's forge, a mouth and throat which felt rasped down to bare sinew. He was on the train; he could feel its uneven jerking through every raw nerve of his body; Kottbus had gone. He remembered nothing but the dark little cabin where they had drunk the night away, but through the pounding in his head recognized the compassion with which Kottbus had given him temporary release from the foulness drowning his thoughts, had eased a parting with oblivion. "It will be victory next year," he had said. "All the foreigners except the Poles have gone, and them alone we can beat. The Whites won't promise the peasants their land but Comrade Lenin tells them it is theirs. They will fight for whoever gives them the land."

"If there's any land left." Kolya's words were slurred.

"The land remains, whatever happens the land remains. I will be gone by then if I survive."

Kolya wept at that, to think his friend would be gone; he sniveled a little now in his sleep but did not truly rouse.

Gomel was less than a hundred versts from Bragin but the journey took four days, the train panting quietly at rest for hours, then equally inexplicably rollling on again. For the whole time Kolya slept and woke and slept again, faces and feet, dark bodies and piercing light coming and going before his blurred vision and staggering brain. It was the first time in nearly a year, except when granted the oblivion of exhaustion, in which he had rested without waking almost immediately in a sweat of panic and guilt.

By the time the train reached Gomel he was reeling with hunger, but feeling steadier in himself than he had in months. He had no baggage, no money, no boots, not even a spare shirt. Just a scrap of paper authorizing him to enter the School for Infantry Officers of the Red Army of Workers and Peasants, an unloaded revolver, a filthy sheepskin coat, ragged breeches and foot bandages so thickly swathed that he tripped when he tried to step out briskly.

The school was lodged in an ex-theological seminary and he was staggered by the order and cleanliness everywhere. Beds with real sheets. Baths, heads shaved. Delousing. New, smart uniform, peaked cap with red star. Textbooks on topography, tactics and gunnery. Thick military overcoat. Boots. It was like a dream with its smells of polish and hot food; he lay awake all night just with the joy of being in a bed again, of being warm and dry.

The appearance of normality was deceptive of course. Gomel was menaced by Denikin and his cossacks to the south and by the Poles to the west, but meanwhile four hundred students had a breathing space in which to master the arts of war before fighting both of them.

Their instructors, apart from long-standing Bolshevik's charged with their political education, were all ex-tsarist officers who regarded their students with a skeptical eye but whose professional pride was nevertheless engaged by the task in hand. The students were not all Party members, but soon became snared by the excitement and ambition generated by the opportunity which was theirs. There were husky peasant boys from the surrounding country, politically enthusiastic industrial workers from Gomel and Chernigov, picked candidates, like Kolya, from the army itself. Very few could have expected to rise above the rank of sergeant in the old Imperial army while here they were told daily in their political indoctrination classes that they were not just future generals but future managers, administrators and engineers as well.

The course was incredibly mixed. The cadets had to fell and drag in all their own fuel, yet even so the buildings were nearly always freezing and everyone slept in all their clothes. They had to learn about weapons, commissariat, tactics, movement of large bodies of troops, Marxism, siege warfare, Russian military history, the speeches of Comrade Lenin, drilling and target practice, dialectics and debating, mathematics and topography, the aims of the Communist Party . . . The list was endless, the day sixteen or seventeen hours long, the food hot but very inadequate. At least nightmares were impossible, sleep descending like a shutter the moment they lay down.

Sometimes they would turn out to help in a local catastrophe, a fire or a cossack raid, and the town soon adopted them as its own. After the long procession of tattered, dispirited, thieving men back from the front, the freshly uniformed, tightly disciplined cadets from the school improved the morale of the whole district and in turn gave the cadets an overweening pride in themselves. They suffered their first casualties before the course was even finished: a quick Polish raid made the school the only defense for Gomel, the mutiny of a Red brigade to the south brought them the terrible duty of firing on their own troops. Forty of the original four hundred did not graduate for academic or political reasons, but nearly double that number were killed before their six-month course was finished.

The most lasting memory Kolya took away from the cadet school was of War Commissar Trotsky, the civilian who had taken over the task of forging the new Red Army on the anvil of war. The Polish raid on Gomel caused utter panic, fleeing soldiers looting and raping as in the worst days of 1917, civilians piling belongings into carts and blocking the roads. Trotsky arrived out of nowhere, slight, frail, wearing a badgeless uniform and the pince-nez of a lawyer, and within hours the chaos was straightened out. When the cadets marched out to meet the Poles he was standing in the square, not saluting like a general, but watching them silently, sadly, proudly, like a father sure of the worth of his sons both in life and in death. They gave him a cheer as they passed and he unclipped his pince-nez and bowed awkwardly, a man without the gift of physical presence but who held, without a word spoken, the respect of every cadet as they went out to war again.

Kolya, as one of the few with any proper education, found little difficulty in passing out among the first half-dozen of his course. He was sent to command a cavalry unit operating out of Chernigov and within a short time he realized that Kottbus had spoken truly, it was the time for winning. One day he happened to call on a friend from the School for Infantry who was serving as divisional commissar, and saw their lists of deserters. With victory coming they were very few but his commissar friend was particularly indignant over the defection of one of his regimental commanders. Ex-Major Kottbus had chosen his moment to depart and thereafter the almost continual advances of the Red Army did not surprise Kolya; he understood his former commander well enough to know he would not go until his men were able to do without him.

Only the Poles continued to fight fiercely, now allied with Petlyura and his Nationalists, their cavalry scouring far and wide until it seemed that not only people but every growing thing must disappear from the face of the earth. No planting was done, no animals grazed, there was no value in the dozens of currencies circulating, and in the cities, where there were at least buildings left, even the rats had disappeared. Farther north peasants hid in woods, secreted a few animals in ravine and copse, but down on the open plain there was no cover: it was impossible to imagine such desolation.

Suddenly the Poles disappeared too. Tukhachevsky, the Red Army's commander in the west, was attacking toward Warsaw and the Poles returned to defend their homeland, leaving behind such of Petlyura's troops as remained, roaming like beasts in a land where even banditry was impossible.

Kolya's last action of the war was fought on the heels of the Polish retreat, where the familiar Ukraine country gave way to the dispiriting slop of the Pripyat Marshes. He had been sent with a double squadron of cavalry to harry the Poles and deny them time to dig in, even supposing they wished to. The sky was stained dark with smoke and everywhere there was the smell of burning. In the whole summer's campaigning Kolya had not seen even a distant twist of smoke, there were no stacks or byres or crops left to burn, but here was another whole area to be scoured and ruined. He felt helpless, torn with rage and despair in almost equal proportion, and he shouted at his men to hurry.

It was a mistake. The horses were tired and long underfed, and when they spotted a group of huts surrounded by lazily grazing Polish horses they could not respond to his instant order to charge. Instead the Poles spilled out of the huts, scattering into stunted undergrowth and the moment was gone; a minute later the unexpected stammer of a machine gun began to slice men off the saddle. It was a fierce little engagement, fought with deadly, killing lust on both sides. In the end the Poles pulled out, which was what they intended to do anyway, but there were fifty dead in the squalid little hamlet by evening.

Kolya sat all night, wrapped in his greatcoat, silent by the smoldering warmth of burned huts. He could hear the excited calls of his men, the groans of the wounded, a scream as an orderly probed for a bullet without anesthetic while his own insides cringed in sympathy. He felt utterly exhausted.

He himself was unscathed except for a long, burning graze up one arm but he knew at last he could take no more. Fifty more dead, his own men, Poles, what did it matter? For a burned-out huddle of huts in a swamp, where the fields had already gone back to marsh grass and briar. He resolved at that moment to resign from the army at the first opportunity.

Slight as it was, the graze on his arm refused to heal. Four years of near-starvation rations almost totally without fats seemed to have destroyed the capacity of flesh to draw together. It was stitched by a Polish doctor but pus gathered in the stitches and he refused to stay in the hospital with its infernos of wounded, their limbs swollen into blue and green masses of putrefaction crawling with maggots.

With the drawing out of autumn the cavalry was ordered to fall back on Gomel and he went to report to his area commander, Yakir, hero of the Red breakout from Odessa. He found his headquarters in the Town Hall not far from his old military school; he felt almost nostalgic toward Gomel, as if he were coming home at last.

Yakir was only a few years older than he was, with an ascetic, rather remote face, drawn with weariness as they all were. "Sit down, let's have your report after you've warmed up, eh?" He passed over a tumbler of vodka and Kolya drank gratefully. "You say you've just over two hundred men but only about sixty fit horses?" he asked thoughtfully, later.

"Yes, Comrade Commander. The men are not very fit either but they can ride, while the horses will die if they are pushed again before spring."

"You don't look fit yourself." Yakir stabbed a finger toward Kolya's arm; he had had to put it in a sling the past few days as every moment tore it further open.

"It was very slight," replied Kolya ruefully, "but it won't heal, although every time we halt my runner is boiling water and following me around with steaming cloths. If I had two whole arms I would wrap them around his throat." The hot fomentations on the open wound were agonizingly painful, sometimes he was almost too faint to ride, but at least the deadly signs of infection had been kept at bay.

"Pity. I have some work for your command."

"Yes, Comrade Commander?" He tried to keep the dismay out of his voice.

Yakir looked at him keenly. "There are too few of us left for personal feelings to come into it any longer. When you see what we have to do you wonder how we will ever manage to build—not rebuild, but build something far better than ever before."

"I wonder too," said Kolya soberly, rubbing his

glass between fingers and thumb. He added impulsively, "I should like to leave the army as soon as I can."

Yakir frowned. "This is no time for leaving the army."

"But I want to build," explained Kolya eagerly; in some ways he was old already, in others betrayed the fact he was not yet twenty-one. "I can't bear the thought of one more man killed under my command, stand the sight of another prisoner with his guts torn out or his epaulets nailed through his shoulders—"

Yakir held up his hand. "You are a Red Army commander, a full Party member, you will do as you are told. But we all believe the destroying is nearly done, the time for construction here at last. You will be part of it, the Red Army is part of it. I want you to go to Gorodnya here." He drew a map toward him. "From there you will organize such help as you can for the area round about, put down banditry, try to reassure the peasants so they will plant again once spring comes." He walked restlessly across the room. "There must be some animals hidden; once the peasants feel trust again, they will reappear from somewhere. I am sending small units to each of the larger villages in my area to spend the winter, to get to know the people, live and work with them. Some places have no men left at all and they will need your help, but above all we must start building trust, so discipline is all-important. Can you do it?"

"Yes, Comrade Commander," said Kolya eagerly. "It is just what I would like; the men will be pleased to get back to the land too."

"Some of them," said Yakir cynically. "You will see. It will not be easy to keep them in hand when they have become so used to murder and robbery. Have that arm of yours seen to before you go, and rest yourself when you reach Gorodnya until it is well;

that's an order." He came to the door with him and Kolya noticed the painfully inflamed patches of eczema on his hands: the burden of command in the past desperate two years had been even harsher than the burden of combat.

Two days later he left for Gorodnya, but the night before he did so a package came for him from headquarters. On opening it he discovered a small crock of yellowish fat and a scrawled note from Army Commander Yakir: "Eat it yourself."

In an obscure way Kolya felt that Yakir's simple humanity had shown him, at a time when he desperately needed reassurance and faith, something of the true meaning of the Revolution again, distantly felt but so nearly lost in the everyday brutality of living.

Part Three
THE WHITE HEAT OF HOPE
1923-24

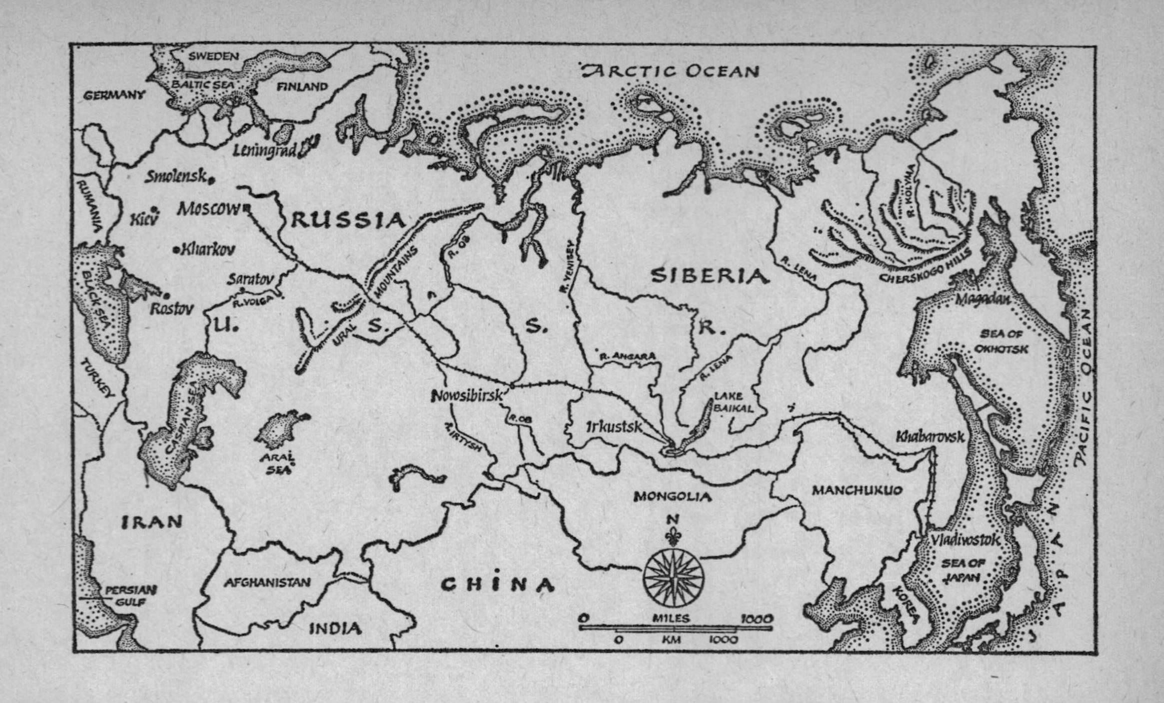

ARCTIC OCEAN
SWEDEN
BALTIC SEA
FINLAND
GERMANY
Leningrad
Smolensk
RUMANIA
Kiev
Moscow
RUSSIA
Kharkov
BLACK SEA
Saratov
R. VOLGA
Rostov
U.
S.
S.
R.
URAL
MOUNTAINS
R. OB
R. YENISEY
SIBERIA
R. LENA
CHERSKOGO HILLS
R. KOLYMA
Magadan
SEA OF OKHOTSK
PACIFIC OCEAN
TURKEY
CASPIAN SEA
ARAL SEA
Nowsibirsk
R. OB
R. IRTYSH
R. ANGARA
R. LENA
LAKE BAIKAL
Irkustsk
Khabarovsk
MONGOLIA
MANCHUKUO
Vladivostok
SEA OF JAPAN
JAPAN
KOREA
IRAN
AFGHANISTAN
CHINA
INDIA
PERSIAN GULF
N
0
MILES
1000
0
KM
1000

Chapter Twenty-one

Anna Vatutina was lying full length on her bed in the room she shared with twenty others, fingers firmly in her ears, attempting to learn the chemistry of the nervous system. On one side of her, two girls were washing their hair; on the other her neighbor was kneeling in tears, a drab brown skirt spread on the floor in front of her.

Anna looked at her uneasily once or twice, then with growing irritation as her tears showed no signs of abating. It was really too bad, there was nowhere to study now she had her chance to become a doctor. Laboratories worked a shift system, libraries were mostly shut while the Party made up its mind which books were politically undesirable. She unplugged her ears resignedly. "What is the matter, Ekaterina Vasilievna?"

The girl raised a blotched face. "My skirt, Anna Dmitreyevna. I have burned it with the iron, see." She pointed to an indistinct puckering of the worn material. "Arkady has asked me out, whatever shall I do?"

"You can borrow mine," said Anna indifferently. "I shan't want it tonight."

"You would truly lend me yours, Annochka?"

"I want to work," retorted Anna brusquely. The chance to have a whole corner of the room to herself was well worth the risk that Katya would be careless with her skirt. It was hardly a risk anyway; in the Moscow of 1923 everyone was used to taking care of their slightest possession. Everything one did not value greatly had gone already and the little that was left was both vital and irreplaceable.

"You are sure, Anna?" Katya kept repeating as she dressed with finicking care for her evening out. Young men were scarce after nearly nine years of war. "You are truly sure?"

In the end Anna would not answer, hunching her shoulders and pretending an interest in her studies which was impossible under the circumstances. Three hours, she thought exultantly, when at last Katya had gone, at least three hours before she is back again with tears of happiness or tears of shock and astonishment. Katya swam through life on a rainbow of tears, and as with a rainbow, however often it happened it was impossible not to look, either with wonder or foreboding.

"Go away," said Anna crossly, when someone put a hand across her page. Communal living was ideologically correct and in practical terms inescapable, but it was a bore all the same in the winter when there was nowhere else to go. "I've paid with my skirt to have this time to study."

The girl pulled the book away and Anna had to take her fingers out of her ears to grab it back. "You didn't hear what I said. You're wanted downstairs."

Anna blinked. "Why?"

She shrugged. "Party member Vatutina, he said. That's you isn't it? There's not so many full Party members here."

Anna swung off the bed, instantly alert. Party business could never wait on a member's convenience. She did three evenings a week of Party work besides her medical studies, helping with political education classes and typing for Comrade Rychagov; it was an endless problem to fit in all the equally important demands of medicine and the Party. Not equally important, she reminded herself sternly, the Party gives meaning to all the rest.

She bundled into her old cotton padded trousers, it was bitterly cold in the passages, and unless they scrounged wood constantly for the old boiler in the dormitory, ice formed on the blankets while they slept.

She saw a shadowy figure under the single dim bulb of the hostel hallway. "You wanted me, Comrade? Party member Vatutina."

He looked at her carefully, then gave a strange lop-sided smile which was almost a grimace. "I think perhaps I do."

She flushed, puzzled and angry at his stare, a little frightened too. The hall was deserted, with empty concrete corners full of darkness, and the man looked very strange, a face all hollows and lines, rough clothes casting a monstrous shadow on the wall. "I thought you wanted me on Party business, Comrade. Otherwise I'm busy studying."

He reached for her hand. "Anna—" and then broke off as she snatched it away and turned to flee back up the stairs. He took off his cap and held it in both hands, palms flat against the wall behind him. "Anna," he said again.

She turned, hesitating, part way up the stairs. He had not moved and his stillness reassured her. "What do you want?"

"Anna, don't you remember me? Konstantin Berdeyev, five years ago at the Kamenny Barracks and then—" He smiled but the effect was grotesque with the sharp planes of light and shade thrown on his face by the naked overhead bulb. "Then we walked out a couple of evenings and I kissed you on Kamenny Bridge."

She came back down the stairs slowly. "Konstantin?

Kolya?" She peered at his face uncertainly; there was nothing about him she recognized. The tousle-headed boy with dreamy gray eyes and a passion for music, who had refused to take anything seriously, even the Party, had vanished. Here she saw a man with military shaven hair, eyes sunk behind cheekbones like those of a corpse, a thin beak of a nose set over a tightly drawn mouth it was impossible to imagine lighthearted.

"You don't recognize me?" The tone was flat but she saw the slight tremor of his jaw, and suddenly the face was so familiar its unfamiliarity was erased as if it had never been. The high outward flare of eyebrow and narrow profile so untypical of the central Russian peasant he said he was, above all the quietness with which he had waited for her to make her decision: she remembered still the patience he had shown toward her years ago. Once he had gone she had never thought it worthwhile to dare another approach to the world beyond the Party and medicine.

"Kolya!" she said gladly, hugging him. "I thought you were dead."

"Oh, Anna," he said huskily, holding her tightly. "It is good to see you again." He laughed unsteadily. "What a stupid thing to say when I've been thinking about this for months, wondering whether I would be able to trace you and if you would remember me at all." Who else in the world knew him as Kolya, a person, any more? In the fearful time since the end of the war, he had found himself grasping at the knowledge that Anna at least would not have changed. She feared men and loved the Party enough to be doing exactly what she had said she would do; although he had known he should not come, he had been unable to resist coming.

"I thought about you often for the first year after you went," she said frankly. "I was angry at first you did not write, but as the months passed I became sure you would not be coming back."

"I meant to—" He broke off and shook his head as if to clear it. "It's no good, Anna. I'm so confused at seeing you again, at—" at holding a woman who is not a staring mass of bones, at trying somehow to begin picking up the threads of civilized life again, he meant to say, but the words would not come. His mind would not respond to a set of circumstances so at variance with everything he had endured in the looming crater of the past. He was behaving like a boor and could do nothing about it. He wanted to take her here and now on the grimy concrete, his control trembling away from him with the feel of her body. No, by God, he did not want to do that. "I had better go," he said abruptly.

"B-but—" she was disconcerted afresh; no sooner had she grasped a part of him she knew than it changed and became something quite alien again.

He shook her off roughly and pushed out of the door, leaving her staring at the black rectangle where he had been, relief struggling with concern and alarm. Without thinking, she ran out into the darkness, her face stung by blowing ice crystals. She saw him pause in the smudged light of a single street lamp and put out a hand as if to feel its steadiness and she called out, running down the rutted path.

"Kolya . . ." She did not know what to say, knew only he must not go away like this. "Will you come and see me again?"

He stared at her, still holding onto the lamp post. "Would you like me to?"

She laughed shakily. "Of course, why else would I be standing in the snow"—she looked down at her feet suddenly—"with only felt socks on!"

He unbuttoned his coat and picked her up, wrapping her feet in the flap of his jacket and carrying her back down the road to the hostel. "You will lose your feet like that." He did not put her down again.

She slid an arm around his neck. "Perhaps it wasn't quite as silly as it seems." They kissed, but almost at once his terrible hunger frightened her, it was a blinding, driving, consuming need to seek—what? Possession? Oblivion? Sanity? His physical weakness made him set her down almost at once and as he did so he glimpsed her white face, sensed the resolution she needed not to flinch from him. He rested his forehead against her shoulder, ashamed and utterly spent. After a while her arms went around him again and they stood together, not speaking, not kissing, but in some measure at rest.

"Would you meet me tomorrow evening?" he said at last. "You do not have to."

She was taken aback by the humility in his voice; whatever had happened to him these last years it must have been very terrible. "I want to, why else do you think I ran after you like some shameless hussy?"

"You need not fear me, I promise." She started to protest but he laid his fingers across her lips. "I don't blame you, I fear myself sometimes. Where shall we meet?"

"I have to go to a Party meeting," she said reluctantly. "It will be late by the time it is over."

She half expected one of his remembered flippancies about the Party, but it did not come. She could just see red collar patches under his coat. "Would you be too tired after?"

She almost smiled at the contrast between such old-fashioned solicitude and what she knew had nearly happaned, here in this squalid hall open to every passer-by. "No, I shan't be tired; no one has time to be tired nowadays. I would like you to meet me." She was startled when he bent and kissed her fingers. Just like one of those stuffy old aristocrats in my father's shop, she thought confusedly, her Party hackles rising and assailed afresh by misgivings.

He really was very odd.

Chapter Twenty-two

Anna's life was immensely complicated by the fresh dimension Kolya brought to it. She was uncertain of her feelings yet unable to resist seeing him, desperately busy with Party work as well as her studies but guiltily aware that she wasted a great deal of time thinking and worrying about him. Without her noticing the change, her instinctive attitudes of withdrawal and indifference were being remorselessly flaked away under the hammer of her concern for him.

In many ways their first meeting might have been a dream. The following night he was polite, almost distant in his manner, and she never again saw him with his control so obviously cracked apart. Occasionally he would leave her abruptly and she came to wonder whether it was because he could trust himself no longer; other times he would be almost relaxed, strolling with his arm around her waist like any other young man with his best girl on a fine evening.

They did not sleep together. She was ashamed of the way he accepted her tacit resistance when his need was so great and so obvious, but the scarred fear from the rapes she had suffered in the disorders of 1917 revived under the intensity of emotion she sensed waiting to be released in him, which he could scarcely hold down much longer.

From occasional remarks she could piece together something of the horror of the Civil War years, but she knew there was much about which he felt unable to speak. One fine spring day they took a tram to the outskirts of the city and as they walked through some straggling woods she asked idly about his mother, remembering he had left Moscow originally to see her.

His face tightened in the way she had come to dread. "She is dead."

She slipped her hand into his. "I am sorry, Kolyushka."

He did not respond and would not tell her how she had died, until eventually she became exasperated. "Kolya, for heaven's sake, you like me to come out with you, don't you?" He nodded but said nothing. "I can't go on like this, you want my body but not me and I can't give myself like that. You hold me away and tell me nothing! Nothing about you, about your hopes, what you have done, what you want to do! It is like going out with a ghost!" She was nearly weeping, a weakness she despised.

He stood very still. "That is what I am, Annochka, a ghost from the past although you don't know it, and ghosts have no future. I have always known I should keep right away from you." Every time they met he swore to himself it would be the last.

"Rubbish!" She was angry suddenly. "We have won a revolution; how dare you stand there and say you have no future, you a Party member!"

"The Party will not let me do what I want. A staff course for commanding officers! I ask you, what nonsense is that for a civilian at heart now the fighting is over?"

"Of course, your music," she said, wondering how she could have forgotten it, realizing it was because he had not once spoken of it.

"No!" he almost shouted. "I am finished with music."

"Finished with music?" she echoed in astonishment. "You told me once—"

"Everything has changed," he broke in harshly. "These past two years of so-called peace in the Ukraine . . . after those I knew I could not turn my back on what needed to be done for my own selfish ambitions. If my mind has nearly burst apart with so much misery, what sounds could I put on paper to express a fraction of it?"

"Kolya—" She was alarmed by the anguish twisting his face but he swept on, the dam of reticence broken at last.

"Down there men take the newborn babies and bury them alive while the mother sleeps; they dare not keep them for the horror of watching them die, cannot endure to kill their own with their bare hands. I have ridden into a dozen villages and seen only a few bloated dogs, crept out to feast on the dead. The first place I saw a family well and healthy I could have wept with joy. Then when I left some poor wretch plucked my sleeve and begging me to save them, for the healthy family fed on the living, and being the only ones fit to plow and reap they handed out just enough to keep a few alive so they might have fresh meat for the winter."

"Stop! Please, Kolya—" She sat on a fallen tree and put her hands over her ears.

He dragged them away. "You wanted to know, and now you are going to listen. Here in Moscow all you are told is how our Red Army is everywhere victorious, of the fine new world to be built. No one speaks of how the land is so destroyed, life so brutal, the people so exhausted we cannot even begin. All those theories, even honor and mercy, mean nothing to the starving. All Lenin can do with his new Policy is let the strongest peasants grab the land, the toughest muzhik sell at a profit again, start printing money like a pack of capitalists. Otherwise we shall all starve and a hell of a joke Marx and his new world will be then. What do you suppose our millions died for after all?"

She listened quietly, not flinching as his fingers bit into her wrists. "Kolya, it is not like that. We are all tired but we are trying. Can anyone do more than give the very best and most precious thing they have? You have given, of your own free will, your music. You have turned your back on something which to you was your life. I understand now a little of what you have been feeling. But you have given it, it has not been taken. A gift is a very precious thing, the Party and the people are enriched by such gifts from ordinary men and women every day and only they know the price of them. From such sacrifices can spring only what is fine and true, none of it is wasted. Nothing given with love is ever wasted."

He sank down beside her and put his head in his hands. She could see the roughly puckered scar running across his neck; it must have nearly cut his throat, and her unexpected, retrospective fear at the thought made her realize at last how inescapably she loved him. When he had gone before she had been left desolate, but astonished and disconcerted by her desolation. Now he was existence itself; if he went again she could not contemplate her loss. She could be in no doubt either about his love for her, although he had never spoken of it. While every meeting between them had imperceptibly solidified her own feelings, they had exacted a fearful toll on him as he floundered in the deep pool of his desire and disillusion, a price no man could have continued to pay without love to ease the burden.

For the sake of their love she must herself break through the last barrier between them, she would destroy him if she denied him much longer, through her he must recover his hold on life and hope again. The very intensity of her gaze penetrated his consciousness and he looked up, staring at her without speaking. His face had filled out a good deal since he had returned to Moscow, but tense lines of strain and the forbidding remoteness remained.

Now, as she watched, it began to change. His eyebrows twitched into a kind of rueful interrogation, the steeply flaring line of them turning almost to caricature, a glint of real amusement came into his eyes, the mouth curved to tenderness. "Oh, Anna, I do love you so," he said simply, and when he kissed her it was as if life had begun afresh, as if desperation had never been.

"I love you too." What simple words to sweep them into a new world, she thought hazily, so I come to him whole and not split in pieces..

With the change of everything between them the need for fierce-clenched control had gone too. He no longer feared he would be unwanted, only that the filth he could not escape in his mind would ride his body into degrading or terrifying her if he allowed the urgency of his need free rein. It was Anna now who stripped his guard, silenced doubts, would not let him think, deliberately blocked out thought with glad willingness to give herself utterly, in love and generosity, if not yet in full pleasure.

They lay in the brown and gold and green of a hollow beside a little stream all afternoon. Birds sang with the total abandon only found during the brief warmth of a normally cold climate, there were faint rustles under the leaves as other creatures pursued their busy lives; occasionally they heard voices or a distant laugh, but no one came near.

"I'm sorry," said Kolya, much later, still holding her.

She did not pretend to misunderstand him. For all his love she knew she had, the first taking had shaken her by its ferocity. The joy of her spirit and tentative responses of her body had not been enough to purge the outraged recoil of memory, a shaming tinge of revulsion and fear banished only by an effort of will. She held his hand over her heart. "I think it will not be that way again."

He buried his face in her breast. "Never. I have outrun my ghosts. Your love has led me out of the past but you needn't fear I do not know the price you paid for it." He caressed her gently, hands holding and lips rousing her this time with the restraint of love, passion a gift of delight and graced with laughter, striking aside the shackles of the past.

They walked back to the center of Moscow, hand in hand all the way like children. "We must get married," said Kolya as they leaned over the parapet of Kamenny Bridge, peering into the dark water as if they expected to see their own selves of five years before. "I have half a room which I should have thought sheer hell a few years back, but is luxury now." Neither of them noticed the slip, to a true peasant half a room had always been a luxury. "We'll search for another mattress."

"Why a mattress, why not a table or a chair?" she teased him. "But there's no need to get married, you sound like a real old *bourzhuis*. The Party does not encourage members to be married, it implies inequality."

"Perhaps I feel like an old-fashioned *bourzhuis* with you. I want us to be married."

"Does it matter?"

"It matters to me. I hoped it mattered to you."

"No," she said thoughtfully. "I don't think it does. As the Party says, it seems outdated, it makes no difference to my feelings."

"It makes no difference to mine either, but every member of my family is dead or disappeared, every friend I have is swept away the moment I take my eyes off them. I want you for always, I want to be tied down to something again, or rather to someone I can feel and hold no matter what happens." His arm tightened around her.

"There seems no difficulty about the feeling and holding." She laid her head on his shoulder and smiled at him. "Kolyushka love, the Party does not like marriage. Even if we did marry, we could go at any time to the Civil Registrar and sign a divorce; it isn't like one of those old church weddings."

Kolya gazed across the water at the Church of Our Saviour, where his sister Lena had been married, how many aeons ago in 1911. He still remembered his restlessness during the chanting monotony of the service, but now he craved for ceremony with which to enshrine his love, for permanence in a shifting world. He was being childish, he decided.

All the same, though both their Party cells disapproved, they went along to the Registrar and signed his book as a duly married Soviet couple, Kolya giving as his birthplace a hamlet near Yakovka which he remembered as completely burned out. It was a thoroughly unsatisfactory ceremony and Kolya felt diminished by it. He had thought his distant boyhood attitudes long since and willingly buried but he was plunged into gloom by the grudging bureaucratic mumbles and unable afterward to shake off his resentful feeling of having been cheated.

"If this is marriage then I was right and you were wrong, it has spoiled everything," said Anna fretfully at last, when he showed no signs of breaking the silence between them. She, too, felt resentful that she had for the first time gone against the Party to do something which seemed to her ridiculous, but was given meaning simply because he wanted it. Now apparently the ceremony had been as meaningless to him as to her: she had betrayed her Party loyalty for a chimera and her anger turned against him, kindling an unexpected desire to hurt. "If your Party obedience means so little to you, I wonder whether a stupid gabble of words between us would bind you any more."

Kolya walked on scowling, but said nothing. Infuriated by his silence, she shook his arm and shouted, "Well, would it?" Passers-by stopped and stared, then grinned at each other over what was so obviously a lovers' quarrel.

"Yes," he said briefly.

She could have cried. Whatever her misgivings over Kolya's determination to defy Party attitudes on marriage, her heart had been warmed by his desire to do so for her. Now the guilty happiness of the day was ruined.

She would not give him the satisfaction of seeing her tears; a true Soviet woman did not give in to such weakness. "I have to be back at the Medical School in an hour." Her voice was uncertain, her thoughts on the elaborate deceptions she had planned to cover her absence for the rest of the day. "I don't know when I will be finished."

"Anna—" He swallowed, he too could not quite see where things had gone wrong, but the change was clear enough. He looked at her directly for the first time since the Registrar's office and his expression softened. "I'm sorry. What a hell of a way to behave on our wedding day."

"We should never have done such a stupid thing." She regretted her rejection of his altered mood as soon as she spoke, for he turned away at once. She ran after him, tugging his arm. "Kolyushka, I'm sorry! I wasn't thinking what I said."

"I know, that's what makes it the truth." He shook her off.

"Oh, Kolyushka." She was weeping now. "What will you do this afternoon?"

He considered it carefully. "Get drunk, I should

think." He saluted her ironically. "I will see you in your own time, my love, at my—our—home."

She had never done such a terrible dissection as she did that afternoon, Kolya's face, tight with hurt, constantly bewteen her and her work. She knew the shocks of recent years had made him unpredictable in a way which could turn him into a stranger at times, his musical sensitivity giving him a range of feeling which made him more vulnerable than most men. Although he usually managed to maintain his composure and balance, she sensed the effort this often required. Now he had voluntarily forced a fissure in his guard so as to admit her, he was unexpectedly defenseless against the slightest thoughtlessness or lack of generosity on her part.

By evening she was beginning to feel frightened, deliberately delaying her departure from the laboratory from minute to minute, humiliated by the jokes and comments of her fellow students. She had never seen Kolya drunk but had encountered too often the blind violence induced by vodka, knew too well the difficulty this new, unknown husband of hers had in controlling his emotions even when sober, to be other than deeply apprehensive of its likely effect on him. As she mounted the stairs to Kolya's half-room in Stolovy Street, slippery with grease and smelling strongly of boiled cabbage, only the deep river of her love overcame eddies of fear and panic, the insistent tug of horrifying memory urging her to return to the known safety of her previous life before it was too late.

He was completely, coldly sober.

She lifted the blanket hung across the middle of what had once been a small bedroom and he stood up, pushing aside some books on the marble washstand which served as a table. "Welcome to your home," he said quietly. He was even dressed formally, in an almost new tunic with three gold rectangles of rank on the sleeve, and astonishing dark red breeches decorated with yellow braid.

She blinked at him stupidly, the difference from all she had feared or expected too great to grasp. "You look very smart."

"The War College of the Red Star for Party Officers," he replied in the same detached tone. "They can't feed us and they have to use Imperial generals to instruct us, but at least they can make us look like a pack of tsarist peacocks." He brought over some small packages. "Our food issue for the week."

"I must see the hostel committee about my rations," she said guiltily. "I forgot all about it." She looked around her; he had shown her his room a day or so before but she had not really taken it in. She saw the two mattresses eloquently separated by a packing case cupboard and flushed; they looked at each other, feeling a ridiculous embarrassment, imagining listening ears on the other side of the blanket.

Kolya laughed suddenly and buried his face in her neck, holding her tightly. "God, what fools we are."

It was going to be all right. She lay beside him much later, listening to his breathing and filled with a joy she had not known before. It was going to be all right.

Chapter Twenty-three

Kolya did not get over the shock of his wedding day for some time. He knew he had nearly lost Anna and was upset by his inability to express his feelings with the sensitivity she roused in him, by his driving need to find something solid on which to build in a shifting world deprived of music.

Strangely, his wife's serenity told him that she had gained all the confidence he had so unexpectedly lost. It mattered desperately to him that all should be right between them; she simply knew that it was. She was eagerly passionate, bubbling with enthusiasm over the Party, the future, her progress toward becoming a doctor, responding with glad intensity to his every approach. She never seemed tired or discouraged, neither did she have any reticences in the earnest simplicity of her beliefs. Everything about her, once given, was given without reservation. Her rages were swift and forthright, the atmosphere one moment electric with her scorn, often discharged the next by laughter.

Looking at her, Kolya did not know whether to be more surprised by the change in her or by the way she remained the same. The tense wariness he remembered from their first encounter at the Kamenny Barracks had completely disappeared. Her curiously curved eyelids, which appeared to smile even when her face was in repose, were no longer incongruous as her expression relaxed from its former prickly defensiveness. She did not keep her hair tightly coiled any more, its warmth almost extinguished by austerity, instead she stifled his protests and made him chop it short: within a day he could not imagine her any other way.

"It is surprise which makes it curl," he teased her. "Like a prisoner let out of solitary confinement."

"That's better," she said encouragingly. "Last time you remarked on my hair you likened it to pig food."

"I never did!" Just for a moment she caught him with the mock-seriousness of her expression.

"You said it was the color of hazelnuts, and they are used for pig food around the Baltic where my mother came from," she pointed out, eyes glinting at him.

He held her in his arms and ran his hands through it until every hair stood on end. "It's like a bear's ruff now and serves you right. Never let the Party sentence it back behind bars again."

She stiffened against him. "The Party has nothing to do with it."

He kissed her and the moment passed. In this she had not changed at all, she would joke about herself or medicine, ridicule the pompousness of officials, the fearful inefficiencies of everyday living, but the Party was completely set apart. It was a shine in her mind which added meaning to everything else, at once an endeavor beyond question and a framework within which everything else was set. Kolya found such a devotion a refreshment to his own convictions but its unquestioning intensity sometimes alarmed him. What would happen if one day he could not live up to such standards, or if she herself were set adrift by disillusion?

Kolya had somehow assumed that if he loved and was loved deeply in return then he would know tranquillity again, but it was not like that at all. His commitment was total, he had no doubts, but he had never attempted to forge a relationship of the nature he found he now wanted. His grandmother was the only person to whom he had ever been truly close and she had been wise enough to know that with the chasm of the generations between them she could hold him only by leaving him free.

Now he did not want to be free; he wished passionately to share and give of himself openly as she did, but was held back by the control which circumstances had clamped over his emotions, and also by the most fundamental deceit of all. If she knew he was not just one of the hated *bourzhuis* but a member of the aristocracy, outcast from humankind by all good Marxists, then she would recoil from him. Their love would not be sufficient to span the gulf which this would represent; too much of her was given to the Party for her to be able to reverse her thinking on such a subject.

Sometimes he felt a terrible desire to tell her, to test whether her love for him was greater than anything she could feel for the Party, but each time prudence held him back. He knew his own loyalty to the Party, that his being the son of a count in another age was meaningless. But it would be deeply unjust to put such a division of loyalties on someone so incapable of duplicity, for once she knew, as a Party member she would have the absolute duty of denouncing him as a class enemy.

He continued to have nightmares, comforted only when Anna brought him out of the deathly horror of his recollections. These became more horrific still when anxiety changed nameless, charred, screaming figures into Anna, her mouth wide and blackened, all the bones of her beautiful body laid open, and he struggled against the knowledge that it was somehow he who had delivered her to such torment by his selfishness in involving her in his life. On those nights she held his slippery, sweating body closely, whispering endearments, soothing him like a puppy with her hands.

"You will have to be a psychologist instead of a surgeon," he said ruefully one night, after a particularly bad attack had left him weak and shivering. "You didn't know what you were letting yourself in for with me."

She answered him obliquely. "I'm glad you insisted we married properly. I didn't know then what you meant, now I do."

He lay there quietly, treasuring the gift she had given him, hearing the angry mumblings of the disturbed Bibikov family on the other side of the blanket dividing the room. "Anna," he said softly at last, "this moment is perhaps our true wedding, when both of us know we cannot just sign a book and get a divorce. We are no longer the same apart."

"We're not the same in another way either. We're to

have a child." Anna took his hand and laid it between them. "Ours."

He shot up on his elbow. "Truly?"

"As a fledgling doctor there seems no doubt of it to me." He heard the laughter in her voice.

"Well." He lay back and looked at the ceiling. "Fancy having two of us screaming at night." Then, conscious she might be disappointed by his reaction, he hugged her. "I'm so pleased, love. The Bibikovs will be wild though," he added with a chuckle.

The timetable imposed by the baby made him think seriously about their future. Anna would have only about six months to go to her final medical examinations by the time of the birth and her faculty seemed confident she would be able to study at home for part of the time if she hurried to complete the necessary practical work. Later, the baby would be cared for in the hospital crèche while she took her examinations and the year of compulsory studies afterward.

"I'll have to wait for the extra years of surgical training," she said philosophically. "There will be no difficulty about returning later." She was lying back against the wall while Kolya prepared the supper. He enjoyed waiting on her and also the pleasure of watching her relax, lines of tiredness after a day at the hospital disappearing as they talked together. "I still can't help marveling that it is I, Anna Dmitreyevna the pharmacist's daughter, who is to be a Moscow surgeon. With everything open like this to all our people, what a nation we will be one day."

"The only thing open to me still is soldiering." Kolya looked at the four gold rectangles now on his sleeve, promotion had just come through for those in the last year of their staff studies. "I applied again last month to retire but nothing ever comes of it. I've been trying to get out for nearly three years."

"Perhaps you are too valuable to the country and the Party as a soldier."

"I should be useless." He looked at her soberly. "You at least know how I feel. I don't think my mind could support many more horrors."

She held his hand tightly. "The war is over."

"If I were a religious man I would cross myself to hear you say so. Comrade Lenin himself said the capitalists would never forgive us our revolution." They both fell silent, thinking of Lenin now on the edge of death; when he was gone nothing would be quite the same.

"Who—" Anna began, but he silenced her with a jerk of the head toward the curtain and the possibly listening Bibikovs.

"It is not for us to speculate on Party matters." He added in a whisper, "Uncertainty will bring fears for a while; don't even think about a successor to Lenin."

Anna laughed at him. "What a conspiracy! We are Party members, we all decide surely? It isn't something to be hushed up, as if the Tsar were still in his palace."

He refused to reply, making a great clatter with the plates, and next time they were out repeated his warning not to allow herself to be drawn into discussion on such a topic. "I am perhaps overcautious," he added, "but Party discipline can mean different things to different people. To you it means guidance while you serve something you have no desire not to serve, and you find it a support to lean on."

"And to you?" she asked, surprised.

He walked on slowly, one hand under her arm, the other in his pocket; he had a determinedly unmilitary attitude for one who, at the age of twenty-four, had reached a comparatively high rank. "I am already in dispute with the Party about leaving the army. I know it is not quite as simple as you think."

"I saw Comrade Rychagov yesterday." Anna glanced

at him. "I didn't exactly tell him you wanted to come out of the army, but you know how he is . . ."

Kolya grinned. "Never stops talking for an instant."

"Yes, but he is wise, too. He said you should use the army; the Red Star College was not just a military establishment; officers from there could be asked to do anything. He said you should pick what you wanted to achieve and you would be sure to find the army had a course which was something to do with it." Tell the boy to go and join the Red Guards Band, he had actually said, then he can get rid of that musical itch before it drives him crazy. She had laughed, but decided it would be better not to pass the comment on.

"I know what I want to do," he said irritably. "I want to go into the countryside and make it prosperous again. Every good Communist wants to build factories and power stations, but I don't. Food comes first and without it factories are so much scrap metal. I thought I had had enough farm work to last me a lifetime, but now I want to study agriculture properly and it is no good telling me the army has a course for that. They just send some illiterate general to the Caucasus, tell him to grow cotton and shoot him when he fails."

"Kolya—" She was alarmed by his bitterness.

"It's true, they've just done it to one of our lecturers in guerrilla warfare. What the hell did he know of cotton? So the army loses a specialist and the Caucasus is still not growing any cotton. It makes me want to spit."

"Yes, you are a long way from being a peasant now," she said caustically. "Otherwise you would not hesitate to spit."

His eyes widened with shock and then he laughed. "One civilizing result of eight years in the army. No wonder you are so good for me, you always find whatever cause there is for rejoicing."

Nevertheless he thought over Rychagov's advice, discovered a factory which made both military and agricultural equipment, and asked his director of studies if it would not be wise for future staff officers to have some technical knowledge of the vehicles under their command. After much discussion he obtained permission to attend the factory on detached duty to make the necessary studies, and spent nearly five months there while everyone forgot about him. He even attended the parade to mark Lenin's death with the factory workers rather than joining the serried crimson, green and gold of the Red Star College.

Anna had her baby in the autumn of 1924, a girl, lusty and bawling within a short time of birth. Fortunately the Bibikovs were almost as delighted as Kolya and Anna, poking their heads around the blanket at the first sign of a whimper and spoiling her shamelessly, while old Bibikov thieved milk in startling quantities from the Commissariat of Finance, where he worked as a stoker. They called her Sophie and it suited her dark, curved vitality exactly.

"She is just like you," remarked Kolya one day, watching critically while Sophie's smiles turned to yells and back to smiles again. He was thankful to think she would perhaps not be saddled with his infernal complications.

"How can you say so!" Anna demanded indignantly. "Look at those eyebrows, like swallow's wings." She traced the minute, flaring line lovingly. "I always meant to ask you where you inherited such extraordinary-looking things."

Kolya glanced in their scrap of mirror. He had not really looked at his face in years, accepting it when he shaved each morning as a matter of course. The appalling rations and sufferings of the Ukraine had swept all softness from it; only the dark, swooping eyebrows still gave him any look of youth at all. He grimaced at himself and turned away. "My grandmother. If Sophie grows up at all like her we'll have to watch ourselves;

she was still very much to be reckoned with when she was over eighty." For no reason he thought of the burning portraits and felt unexpectedly sick. I will not think of it, he told himself grimly.

"What is it?" Anna knew him too well by now.

"Nothing, just memories. You and Sophie will make me forget them, eh, Sophie?" He threw her up in the air.

Anna snatched her back, scolding. "She is too young for that!"

Sophie dribbled at him thoughtfully and he laughed. "A girl is never too young to be cuddled by a handsome fellow like me."

Happy as his life now was, he did not forget his determination to be free of the army, taking care to pass out well down the list at the end of the course and then applying yet again to go on the reserve. Again there was no reaction; instead he received curt orders to report to the Commissariat of War for assignment.

The anteroom to the Appointments Board was full of officers and there was a general atmosphere of strain. One by one they went into an inner room, one by one they came out, faces inscrutable or faces dejected, some obviously delighted, others abject at their fate. Whispers went around the room, starting over by the door: he is to command the air experimental station near Rostov! Poor devil, he is attached to geological research in Siberia! He is to be Colonel of the 271st! My God, he is to organize camel remounts in Uzbekistan! (*Camel* remounts? Nods and laughs, yes, camel remounts.) There was much restless shifting and Kolya felt an overwhelming urge for fresh air, but everything was tightly sealed. Instead he leaned his forehead against the icy glass and gazed at Moscow spread before him: the block of the Kremlin, the curl of the Moskva River, roads and spaces at last beginning to show some signs of returning hope and life, the people no longer haggard with want, merely exhausted by the struggle for existence. He sighed and turned back to the room: if only he could take part in work which really needed doing.

His name was called at last and a sentry ushered him into a room full of mirrors, so it was some seconds before he realized the Appointments Board consisted of only three men. In the middle was an immensely fat commissar, the sort of man who joined the Party for what he could get out of it, thought Kolya uncharitably. To his right a thin, gloomy brigade commander, to his left—Kolya stared with a shock of recognition, groping for the name.

"Konstantin Aleksandr'itch Berdeyev. Graduate in thirtieth place from the War College of the Red Star, full Party member," intoned the Brigade Commander, his voice matching his depressed appearance.

Kolya stood to attention. "Yes, Comrade Brigade Commander." He looked out of the corner of his eyes at the third man; what the devil was his name?

"You have been a Party member since 1919, peasant by birth." The Commissar spoke in a thick, unfinished kind of voice. "Your papers, Comrade."

Kolya handed them over, copies of his various applications for release firmly attached.

The third man spoke. "You attended a vehicle factory; this to us makes you suitable for transfer to tank experimental work." The voice jogged Kolya's memory.

"With respect, Comrade Skobolev, I should like to leave the army."

"Do you know me?"

Kolya nodded. "Yes, I—"

"Stand to attention, damn you," rasped the Brigade Commander unexpectedly. "What the hell do you think this is, a Tatar bazaar?"

Kolya flushed and stiffened to attention. "I had the

honor of meeting Comrade Skobolev on patrol out of Kiev in 1919."

"At ease," said Skobolev lazily. "Comrade, I really don't think we can carry on a sensible conversation with officers looking like statues of tsars two hundred years dead."

"As you wish, Comrade Senior Commander." He looked more gloomy than ever now.

Senior Commander. Military ranks were officially abolished, officers being referred to according to the nature of their command; generals especially were anathema, so infected with tsarism that, whatever the inconvenience, the term was never used. Nevertheless that was what Senior Commander meant. Kolya stood at ease and looked at Skobolev speculatively; surely it must be a chance.

"Yes, I do remember you now, I can see the scar on your neck. The boy who lost his patrol to the Whites, and then was so squeamish I had to pull him out from under my men when he shot the woman they were raping." Skobolev looked as if he thoroughly enjoyed the recollection and Kolya immediately remembered how much he had detested him five years before.

"It doesn't say any of that here." The Commissar pawed peevishly through the papers in front of him.

"Papers never do say the really important things, eh, Berdeyev?" Skobolev was examining him intently and Kolya felt suddenly afraid, as if this man could read his soul.

Attack was the only possible thing, discussion of what was or was not in his papers to be avoided at all costs. It would not be difficult to find out too much about him if anyone really tried. "I should like to have my applications to be placed on reserve considered now. I feel I can serve the Party best elsewhere."

"Where else?" inquired Skobolev blandly, unsurprised.

"The last months I was in the Ukraine I was sent with my squadron to Gorodnya, to help the people there. They were starving; in four years of war I had not seen greater misery. We did what we could, but I had not the knowledge to help them as I wished. I would like to study agriculture and help in our socialist program for the land."

"You want to be a farmer?" demanded Skobolev incredulously.

"Yes, Comrade Senior Commander. The memory has not faded, I still wish to do what I can for people like those of Gorodnya."

The three stared at him blankly, and Kolya had difficulty in choking back laughter, irresistibly reminded of the tasteless stone carvings on the building opposite his grandmother's apartment: ill-proportioned, with bulbous knobs like dead eyes.

"Well, Comrades," said Skobolev after a long pause. "I think we are all agreed that we do not want the Red Army commanded by lunatics, and I personally have experienced the lunacy of which this officer is capable." He glanced at the others and then barked, "Application approved. Unsuitable for tank command. Placed on reserve indefinitely." He scribbled on Kolya's papers; the other two added further official scrawls and stamps.

Kolya replaced his cap and marched from the room. He was out at last.

Part Four
STEEL FROM THE FORGE
1928-34

Chapter Twenty-four

The annual assessment and planning meeting of Klintsy Sovkhoz* was an important and formal affair, attended by representatives of the area Party committee from Smolensk, of the People's Commissariat of Agriculture, by local representatives, People's Police and, of course, the sovkhoz director and his deputies.

People's Sovkhoz Director Konstantin Berdeyev knew a spasm of annoyance as he opened the meeting, glancing around at all the prying, ignorant faces sweating over papers, resenting the way they sought answers to problems they did not understand among the mass of unintelligible figures in front of them. Outside, the passing of a massive thresher drowned his opening words and sifted fine dust over everything.

The Agriculture man slapped his file irritably. "What did you say?"

Kolya did not alter the rapid monotone in which he was flipping through the obligatory opening facts; they were well known to those present anyway. ". . . 6,240 dessyatins under grain for the past year, 3,836 dessyatins of permanent pasture . . . forest, swamp and scrub . . . 300 draft horses, 18 tractors . . . pigs . . . cows . . .

* State farm, i.e., state owned and run; a *kolkhoz* is an ordinary peasant collective.

regrettable outbreak of swine fever . . . mastitis . . . early frosts . . . late frosts . . . all my machinery frequently laid up for repair."

The meeting drowsed as the statistical hailstones fell; no one took any notice of complaints which were repeated with minor variations every year. The vital point was whether production targets had been met. As one of the few sovkhoz of any size in the Western Oblast† Klintsy's performance was vital, both to the prestige of the Party in an area where most land was still farmed by individual peasants, and to the oblast's ability to fulfill its food quotas. Annual delivery figures haunted every district official in the Soviet Union, for failure to reach target meant reprimand at the very least, at the worst accusations of fraud and profiteering, leading to prison or execution.

"Now, Comrades, for this year's figures." Kolya pulled out a series of typewritten sheets, no need to demand attention now. "As you know, these are estimates only, we cannot yet reach exact totals."

"Why we don't waste our time at meetings in the winter, when there is plenty to spare, I can't understand. Unless it is that the comrades from Moscow and Smolensk do not understand how much the figures in their notebooks depend on the amount of work we can do in five months of the year." Nothing ever stopped Vera Lesichina, head of Klintsky's livestock, from expressing her contempt for any slackness in the Party which, because it was the Party, she regarded as above fatigue, self-seeking and fear.

"We can hardly be unaware of it, when you tell us so every year," said the smaller of the two men from Moscow. Viktor Tulaikov, Kolya noted, glancing at the list of names before him. "However, it is necessary to

† Large administrative district based on Smolensk, a city about 200 miles west of Moscow.

plan as early as possible what your requirement will be for next year."

"Requirement!" exclaimed Vera indignantly, curls bobbing out of her kerchief with annoyance. "Who can say now what we will be able to grow next year?"

"The Party can say," replied Tulaikov dryly. "They are able to decide what deliveries will be necessary."

"And I say the Party cannot just decide! What if it freezes until May, as it did two years ago? The Party must not be drawn into capitalist error—"

"Capitalist error?" Tulaikov interrupted icily. "Comrade, you forget yourself. The Party cannot fall into capitalist error."

"No, that is what I am saying." She thumped the table in anxiety and astonishment that the Party could deviate for an instant from paths of which she could fully approve. "The idea that just more targets are enough is not Marxist, we must trust the workers to know what is best for the common good."

There was a chill silence. "I do not see your argument, Comrade Lesichina. You do yourself harm by asserting your own opinions against those of the Party, especially if you attempt to represent these as Marxist interpretations."

"I am a Party member, I have a right to point out error. It is my duty to do so!"

There were coughs and agreement from her fellow deputy directors, Venzher, Golikov and Chapeta. Kolya said nothing, staring bleakly down the table between the angry faces ranged on either side. A whole year of endeavor, of killingly hard work, and now everyone was involved in some petty wrangle without waiting to hear the results. Another backbreaking twelve months to come and what he was meant to produce from the vast estate under his control was, he had no doubt, already fixed in far-off Moscow without the slightest reference to him or to those who were meant to be the spearhead of the new order in the countryside. He was proud of what they had accomplished in the three years he had been at Klintsy, by genuine co-operation, by what he believed to be a true expression of Party idealism whereby, among other things, he and every Party member on the sovkhoz accepted no more than a skilled workman's wages. They had achieved something here and he could not bear to see it treated lightly. This was revolution, the Revolution he believed in, of equality and endeavor and not Party bickerings, the faint echoes of which reached them at Klintsy, assailing him with a deadly sense of loss, bitterly emphasized by the disgrace and exile of Trotsky. He remembered the slight figure bowing gravely to the cadets at Gomel as they marched out to battle, and he grieved privately for what was gone and what was lost.

At last he slammed the flat of his hand on the table. "Comrades, I think we should finish our report on this year's activities before starting an argument on targets for next year."

"The five-minute cat fight time is over," said Venzher, grinning.

"Is that what you think, Comrade Director?" Vera stared at him with great, hurt eyes. "Five minutes by the clock for Vera to shout her piece and then on with business again? I didn't think you had such attitudes to sincere Communist objections."

"I don't." Kolya cursed Venzher inwardly. "I endorse them. But I think we would do better to discuss the whole issue at one time, together with next year's program. Let us dispose of this year first."

"Yes indeed," she agreed at once, and they all sat forward, recalled to the really vital business of the day.

Kolya read through the figures before him in a carefully neutral tone, but there was no doubt about the achievement they represented. In every case targets had been exceeded, except for pigs which had suffered from epidemic swine fever. Vera, Venzher, Chapeta and Golikov were the only ones sitting relaxed, faint smiles on their faces, as they vainly tried to hide their pride.

"There was only one brigand raid," concluded Kolya. "We organized an expedition against them but they got away through the marshes. We recovered the stock stolen and this is the first year we have suffered no loss from this cause." He remembered the disillusion of his arrival, fresh from a one-year intensive course in agriculture and full of ideals, when the first thing he had had to do was start killing bandits all over again.

"All your deliveries in full?" demanded Tchichaev, the local Party man, as if unable to believe his good fortune.

"Except the pigs, but we have small extra deliveries of eggs and flax to counterbalance that," agreed Kolya "Vera Lesichina is in no way to blame for the shortage on the pigs, there has been fever throughout this area, but Comrade Golikov managing the tillage and Comrade Venzher representing the workers' collective deserve the highest praise. No director could wish for a more dedicated and hard-working team."

There was a flurry of congratulation and some little girls were brought in to present bouquets, as Kolya had arranged beforehand. Each year his deputies pretended not to notice the children waiting and giggling under the window as they came to the meeting.

After this the atmosphere changed as the Moscow contingent opened their briefcases and brought out the following year's targets. Kolya and his deputies were dumbfounded by the figures which were produced: every quota was up by between fifteen and twenty per cent, flax by nearly thirty per cent.

Even Vera said nothing, everyone looking at Kolya

to make the stand which must be made, for if they accepted such figures they were bound to face Party discipline in a year's time when failure would have to be admitted.

Kolya considered carefully, while the silence intensified around him. He had always habitually understated his production, although such a practice if detected could be dangerous. This gave him some margin for the yearly delivery crisis, but even allowing for this there was no hope of Klintsy meeting such norms under present conditions. "We are honored to be given so large a part to play," he said at last. "May we know the reasons for such increases?"

Tulaikov nodded. "The cities are short of food, deliveries have fallen sharply over the past two years. The new Five Year Plan is especially framed to rectify this."

"How will you rectify it simply be demanding more, if you didn't get the smaller amount asked for last year?" demanded Golikov angrily. "It is ridiculous to expect an increase when our machinery is more often broken down than not."

"Perhaps you could work harder, supervise your workers more carefully, so it does not break down?"

Golikov spat. He was a shaggy-haired peasant from the Don with just a smattering of education, and no consideration of what was due to the Director's office had prevented him from expressing his contempt in the traditional way. "What will make them work harder? They are not Party members building a paradise; to them it means nothing. They believe in the land, here and now. They like farming it well, I like farming it well, but they do not farm it just for the pleasure of seeing your Moscow trucks roll up to the door and take it all away for nothing."

"You are paid a proper price—" began Tchichaev, fearing a reflection on the local Party.

Golikov spat again, insultingly, straight between his feet. "Paid! A price which scarcely gives a man with all his labor-days fulfilled enough to live on. Ask Director Berdeyev here, how much money do we have to buy new equipment?"

"None," said Kolya. "Whatever we produce, prices are so low it is impossible to show a profit. Our machinery breaks down, Comrade Tulaikov, because it is badly made by men who care for nothing but meeting production schedules which are too high for their capacity."

"Who cares what price or what wages anyway?" interrupted Venzher. "My workers are dissatisfied because, whatever they earn, there is nothing to buy. We have had no delivery of goods in the past nine months to our sovkhoz store."

"I care what price," said Kolya. Venzher was a pest, a good cheerful worker but quite unable to grasp the complicated planning and management needed on a sovkhoz the size of Klintsy. This entailed hours of extra explanation before he would agree to some new idea: without persuasion he was as obstinate as a steppe ox and carried his workers with him. "Unless we are paid a fair price we can't equip or run the sovkhoz properly."

"Wages, prices, profits, what capitalist words are these?" demanded Tchichaev. "What sort of *bourzhuis* are you breeding here, Comrade Director?"

There was an indignant gasp from Vera, but Kolya answered quietly enough. "I think perhaps this is the same point Comrade Lesichina was making earlier. If the Party uses the method of imposing targets from above without consultation, then this contradicts the efforts of local comrades who wish to achieve an enthusiastic and understanding co-operation with their fellows. If arbitrary figures are imposed in a non-Party way, then non-Party forms of inducement will have to be used, like money and goods. We do not seek it, but if you cease to attempt co-operation and will not offer inducement, then you throw away enthusiasm and your production as well."

"And what is your solution, Comrade Berdeyev?" A square, burly man who had accompanied the Moscow group spoke for the first time, his clumsily shaped figure encased in a smartly tailored suit at variance with both his appearance and his country surroundings.

"I don't have one," replied Kolya stiffly. "It is for the Party to decide, but I should like to think it will be able to avoid such a choice. If it can't then the only thing left will be force."

"So you accept your target figures?"

"I think it is a matter for technical assessment in a Party spirit of realism and co-operation. I do not see what it has to do with the GPU."*

The meeting was completely still, his four deputies staring at him in alarm, the other delegates looking intently at the floor. Everyone had known who the observer was; everyone until now, as at every other meeting, had tacitly ignored his presence.

"Do you accept the figures?"

Kolya sighed. "Do I have any choice? If I am ordered to accept these figures, I will accept them, but both the Commissariat of Agriculture and I know that they cannot be achieved. If we had a greater reliability in our machinery, very much more fertilizer, a feeling our problems were understood and an effort made to supply our needs, then we could certainly surpass these targets in a few years. We can't do it immediately and certainly not as we are now."

"You will have a much greater work force supplied to you over the next few months."

"I don't want more men; the workers' collective has

* Political police. At different times known as Cheka, GPU, NKVD, KGB. A change of initials without significance.

the labor we need. More people would simply mean poverty for everyone." Venzher nodded agreement.

"You will have more people," the man repeated. "With them you will produce more." He was the sort of person to whom numbers are everything: limitations imposed by recalcitrance of soil or climate, feeling or ideas were nothing. Figures were the fulcrum to shift the world.

Venzher jumped to his feet. "Director Berdeyev has just told you we don't want more men! All they will do is consume our crops. We will deliver less and the wages we hardly see now will be gone altogether!"

The other shrugged disinterestedly. "There will be a large movement of peasants into the sovkhoz this autumn. I have a plan here showing additional lands to be added to Klintsy before next spring as a result of government action against the kulaks. Their delivery targets will of course be added to yours."

"The richer peasants of the area are coming here with their land?" Kolya could not hide his dismay. Kulak was a general term for any villager who was even slightly better off than his fellows, and included most of the enterprising peasants. If such men were forced into Klintsy, made to give up everything they had labored to create, then their resentment would destroy the willing, pioneering attitude they had built here.

"Certainly not! They are capitalists, not peasants. They would ruin a Soviet society like this. Neighboring peasant land will be added to the sovkhoz with the poorer peasants, the richer ones go."

"Where to?"

The corners of his mouth turned down. "Right away, where they will not trouble you, Comrade. There are projects in the east where they can forget their capitalism in socialist labor."

Rough, bearded Golikov was pale with anger. His

family were small farmers down on the Rostov steppe; he was always telling anyone who would listen about their snug twenty-dessyatin holding. "You can't turn farmers off their land, they would kill their beasts, set fire to their barns first!"

"Let them," he said indifferently.

"But—but . . ." Golikov spluttered incoherently. "In the name of God, man, we are short of food! Why destroy the best farmers we have? You talk as if they were landowners of the past, not working peasants who had their land from the Revolution!"

"I will tell you why, Deputy Director Golikov." He leaned across the table with sudden venom. "Because they and their kind would corrupt the Revolution—if they could, think of themselves and not the Party first. Because they are starving the towns when they will not deliver food at state prices; like you they squeal for shoes and coats and luxuries to buy with their precious money. If the soviet state is to be industrialized then we can't waste effort on clothes and trinkets for peasants, or time on vermin like the kulaks, either."

They never learned his name, nor did they see him again, but long after the meeting ended it was his presence which dominated them, his apparently new-born standards which could not be dismissed. If the battery of power which was the Party now spawned such as he then the future was imponderable indeed. The foundations of life, which had begun to solidify during the past handful of years, seemed to shift yet more fearfully again as they watched the delegates drive away down the dusty track.

Chapter Twenty-five

After the meeting Kolya walked the five kilometers to where the last of the flax crop was being pulled. He usually rode one of the solid sovkhoz horses, both to save scarce fuel and because most of the Klintsy land was only accessible from the roughest of tracks, but on this occasion he wanted time, a great deal of time, to think without interruption.

Nothing more had been said about target figures, no doubt Klintsy was already registered with those impossible norms for next year, but his mind refused to grapple with the necessary, indeed vital, practical problems. Instead it returned again and again to the atmosphere of the meeting: fear, resentment, determination, all these had been tangible, yet did not quite match the over-all sensation he still retained. Halfway to the fields he stopped, absently watching the pluck and bubble disturbing a wayside pool. He had it now, it was power. The Party was powerful and could be ruthless, but it had the dynamic of ideals and purpose to share the pedestal of power; today he had seen, obliquely and only the merest flash in passing, the pedestal itself, unadorned.

He heard the sovkhozniks before he met them, the younger boys and girls singing a bawdy song with lines chanted in sequence and invested with all kinds of cheerfully open suggestion. Across the open fields came also a sound of summer wind like violins tuning, the steady drumbeat of tired but docile hoofs, a distant obbligato of trickling water . . . With an effort Kolya wrenched his sensations free from the involuntary treachery of music which lay in wait for him still, the void of loss immediately fresh and raw again, as if the battle had never been won years before.

But when he greeted them it was as People's Director Berdeyev, with no trace in his manner of the forebodings aroused by the meeting or of his still-twitching musical nerves.

"The tractor has broken down again, Comrade Director." Valya the foreman pushed his cap to the back of his head. "As God is my witness, they must make them of cardboard."

"What is it this time?" asked Kolya resignedly.

"The camshaft, Comrade Director, the same as the other two."

This was serious; they had already waited since last summer for replacements for the others.

"Is there no chance of us making such a part ourselves, Comrade Director?" one of the girls asked, pleased to have the Director walking home with them and anxious to draw his attention to her rounded hips and broad, willing shoulders.

Kolya shook his head, frowning. "The metal needs special hardening, and casting too, not like the parts Valentin makes for us."

There was a general laugh. Valentin was an ex-goldsmith, much in demand for making all manner of unobtainable spares, as well as trinkets which the young men wanted for their girls. There had been a terrible fuss the previous year when Golikov had discovered him performing prodigies of skill to replace lost wiring in the harvesters, while simultaneously converting the same filched wire into filigree rings and brooches for sale.

"Kharkov is not too far, would it not be easier just to go to the works and fetch what we need?" The speaker was a woman with a deeply wrinkled face, although in the way of peasants it was difficult to tell whether she was forty or sixty. Most of the sovkhozniks were young but if the GPU man was right, and they were never wrong in such matters, they would soon be joined by many more like her.

Kolya hesitated. He had long watched what he said, but was uncomfortably aware that the future might demand a degree of care which no one had yet grasped. "Their program is set by the Party as ours is," he said at last. "It would be sabotaging their efforts if we attempted to advance our interests at their expense."

She sniffed. "We care too much for passes and paper these days. It is easier just to go."

God, don't I agree, thought Kolya. Instead he said aloud, "We must gather the rest of the flax over the next two days. I will borrow some oxen from Vera and arrange with Comrade Golikov to shift two of his tractors here. I have to go into Smolensk tomorrow. I will see what I can do about camshafts."

"Did you make the Moscow people promise us a delivery of goods for the store, Comrade Director?" asked Valya. "My wife gives me no peace for thinking of my credit of labor days."

"No promises. They will try to send us a delivery and I certainly hope for some winter clothes." He hoped it was not a lie.

"Produce, produce and then they take it all away," grumbled one of the men. "What has happened to all the good things we used to buy? We grow more flax every year but not one linen shirt have we seen on the sovkhoz since I came. What's the point of it, I ask you?"

"For the moment we have to build for the future; everything is going into industry." Kolya gave the correct reply, but he too remembered the goods piled in every market before 1914, the incredible cheapness of baskets of cherries and sweetmeats. People had been desperately poor, but when they had a few kopecks it had bought real bounty.

"Industry! Everything is industry these days! What are they making that every shop is empty? I ask you, I ask you," the man repeated angrily, and the others laughed, but Kolya knew he was voicing a real and dangerous grievance. If there was nothing to buy, eventually the peasants would refuse to produce.

He walked back part of the way with them, then turned to go across the fields to his own cottage at the far end of the village. A timid hand plucked his sleeve. "Comrade Director, will you be visiting Party headquarters in Smolensk?"

He nodded. "Yes, Adelina Andreyevna. Is there something you wish me to do for you?"

She wrung her fingers nervously. "It is my mother, Comrade Director. She is old and a widow."

He waited but she seemed unable to say more. "Do you want her to come and live with you? I can give permission if you wish."

"Oh no, Comrade Director! She lives with her grandson, but some men came and took him away. He is a good boy and hard-working. They have only two dessyatins, but they live well. Their hut has been boarded up but she sits on the step day and night to make sure there is no doubt it is hers. It will soon be cold but she will not leave and lose everything, there must be some mistake—" Her voice trailed away.

"You wanted me to make some inquiry about the case at Party headquarters?" His anger sounded in his voice.

"No. That is to say, yet—if you would be so good—would you, Comrade Director?" The courage required to ask such a favor of the Director ebbed before the harshness of his tone.

"I will try," he said briefly, brushing off her thanks and tears, striding across the field to get away from her, but too sick at heart to go home. So it had come to this; eleven years after the Revolution which had ushered in a new age, and an old woman was crouched on the doorstep of her boarded-up cottage, doomed by the industry of a grandson who had made them better off than their fellows.

"Daddy? What are you doing out here in the dark?" Sophie came trotting out of the dusk. "I saw you coming and then you didn't come."

"I was thinking, sweetheart." He swung her up on his shoulder. At four years old she was an imp of affection and mischief and had long since conquered him totally, their relationship uncomplicated in a way he sometimes felt was true of nothing else about him. Their son, Yuri, was eighteen months younger and with the endless work and worry of the sovkhoz he had really seen very little of him, while Sophie had been inescapable in their tiny Moscow lodging all the time he had been studying, planting herself squarely from the start wherever she thought his eye would rest on her.

"Why didn't you come in, Daddy?" She settled herself comfortably. "Can't you think with us there?"

He laughed. "I remember when you were two years old and I wanted to mend a window, you got between me and the screw."

She took it as a compliment. "I like doing what you do. What have you been doing today?"

"Nothing you would enjoy," he said grimly.

"Didn't you enjoy it either?"

"No, I certainly didn't."

"You are the Director, why didn't you come and pick mushrooms with me instead?"

"Whatever gave you the idea that directors do as they like? The bigger the job, the less you can do as you wish."

"Perhaps you need some help," she said wisely,

listening to his tone rather than the words. "Why don't you write to Comrade Stalin and ask him to help you? He has the biggest job of all and will help everyone."

"You have been to the Pioneer Storybook Circle, haven't you?" He set her on her feet and they walked through the dark, hand in hand, toward the lighted square of the cottage door.

"Oh yes!" She gave an excited skip. "Misha read us such an exciting story of how all the children of a village chased out the enemies of the people for the wolves to eat, then they went all the way to Moscow to be thanked by Comrade Stalin himself. He gave them a great banquet, with mountains of food as high as that!" She gave a jump and touched the branch above her head.

"Didn't you feel just a little bit sorry for those sent out into the dark to face the wolves?" He kept his voice steady with an effort.

"But they were enemies of the people!" she exclaimed, and then paused, head on one side, glancing at the dark depths of the wood bordering the field, where sometimes in winter they heard the distant howling of wolves. Involuntarily her hand tightened on his.

Later that night when he went to kiss her good night she almost suffocated him with her hug. "I think it was *horrid* to send them to the wolves!"

He held her tightly, almost in tears. What words could express the feelings of a father who, for her own safety, must coldly crush the flowering plant of human pity in his daughter?

"You know you must not question the stories you are read," he said gruffly at last. "It is kind of everyone to give up their time to you; it would be ungrateful if you seemed to criticize what they say."

"Couldn't you come with me to 'splain to them about the wolves, Daddy?" she asked in a small voice. She tried to twist around to see his face but he kept it tucked fiercely over her shoulder.

He shook his head. "Directors mustn't get above themselves and interfere in what is not their concern. I interfere with enough as it is."

She chuckled. "Like finding Ignat Fydr'itch and Agafa in the haystack together."

He laughed, in command of himself again. "Which is something else you should not speak of, Sophie Konstantinovna!" He put his finger to his lips. "Remember. It is our secret about the wolves."

She spat on a pink forefinger and made a cross on his forehead. "I promise. Agafa does promises like that."

He went out into the darkness of their tiny veranda and leaned against the creepered rail, staring unseeingly down the road and feeling the chill stickiness of his daughter's spit on his forehead. Sweet Christ above, he thought despairingly, what am I to do? He did not believe in God, had not thought of God except as a casual expletive for years, but was not aware of any incongruity.

"What is the matter, *vazlublenny?*"* Anna came out and kissed him. She shivered. "For heaven's sake come in, I can feel winter coming."

As he followed her inside he looked with fresh eyes at the comfort of their cottage. It was tiny, with barely space to cook, eat and live in the middle space they used for all these purposes. On either side were two cupboard-like rooms tucked under the sloping roof, one where the children slept on straw mattresses on top of their winter stores, the other where he and Anna had a real bed brought from Smolensk, with a square of space left over so small they had to take it in turns to dress. Nevertheless the cottage was snug and warm, it was not shared and at a time when most people were

*Beloved.

making do with corners of rooms and passages they were very fortunate. It had been a fierce struggle to make Klintsy productive, but even in the frantic rush to meet targets and work schedules, Kolya had never altered his view that adequate housing of his workers was a basic ingredient in the enthusiasm he sought to kindle. All had the same simple pattern of cottage which could be constructed from local materials, and new families were helped to build their own at the first slackening of effort in the fields. Some soon deteriorated into hovels but most were neatly and proudly kept, a major reason for the steady trickle of peasants seeking to join the sovkhoz.

"Tell me." Anna pushed aside the medical books she had been working on. She was long a qualified doctor, officially attached to Klintsy, but she had not given up her dream of surgery, studying at home and at Smolensk Hospital whenever possible.

"I don't know that I could," said Kolya slowly, edging restlessly around the room. "We had a bad meeting."

"But why? You were pleased with the figures; everyone knows we have done well at Klintsy this year."

He scowled. "We have done well, but for next year they have given us figures we cannot possibly reach. In my view we are going to produce less, not more, next year."

"Less?" she echoed blankly. "You can't produce less, surely? Everything is going ahead so fast, and now with the new Five Year Plan more will be produced each year."

"You sound like the Moscow planners," he said irritably. "We can't produce more just because the plan says so. We will have to keep back more seed for sowing new areas we are reclaiming; we will need more fertilizer and more tractors too if we are to make such land productive. There is no suggestion we can even keep back enough to feed ourselves if we fall short of the target."

"You will reach your target," she said serenely. "You've never fallen short yet, and the Party would not ask you to do the impossible."

He looked at her in exasperation, her faith in both the Party and himself merely reinforcing his own disquiet. "We can also expect a flood of surly peasants forced on us because the plan requires the seizure and collectivization of their land."

"There you are," she said triumphantly. "The Party has given you the means to produce more!"

"What makes you think so? These people will not be volunteers; they will do grudgingly what has previously been done gladly. When even our own people sometimes drop stones in the thresher for no better reason than they feel it is time to sit in the sun awhile, what do you think it will be like when our members regard Klintsy as a prison?"

She knitted her brows. "You know, Kolyushka, I think you are being unreasonable. I went to a Party meeting at the hospital a week ago, and we listened to a comrade from Moscow. He told us how the Party was strong enough now to go on the offensive again, how Comrade Stalin wishes to establish socialism in the country as well as in the towns. Why should the peasants work for profit when the rest of us work for the good of the Party and the people? We will produce far more once the money factor is gone from agriculture too."

"The factory worker has to work, however low his wages, if he wishes to eat. A peasant does not have to; he has the power to refuse to produce more than he needs for himself."

"But that would be wicked! He could be forced anyway."

"How? If you shoot him, all you have is a dead

peasant and still no food. If you seize the food he produces for himself, he starves and so do you, next year, when the land lies derelict."

He watched her with a touch of sadness as she grappled with the problem. "There must be some who would see our collectives are better, our sovkhozniks are happy after all."

"So what would you do with the rest?"

"Kolya," she looked at him squarely, "what has happened to you? You believe in socialism, you have given up so much, done so much, so you could help build a fragment of the future here, in the way we all wanted."

"In the way we all wanted," he repeated. "Can't you see, if this collectivization goes ahead by force instead of persuasion, it will not be like that at all? I don't know what has happened to me, but I am beginning to think a lot has happened to the Party without our realizing it."

"Don't be ridiculous," she snapped, all certainty again as the argument returned to familiar ground. "Collectivization has always been a Party aim. If Comrade Stalin thinks the time is ripe, then he is probably right, especially if Party members like you are changing to such *bourzhuis* attitudes. And for heaven's sake sit down," she added, coming down slightly from high ideology. "I can't stand you squeezing past me any longer, while I wait to catch the things you knock off the shelves."

He gave a snort of laughter and sat on the edge of the table. "You were the one who wanted me inside." He kissed her, almost savagely, the way he had kissed her during some of his worst times in Moscow and seldom since. "Come to bed, love. I can't stand much more of this argument; we are going to have to live with it long enough in the years to come. I want socialism, but I hadn't previously thought of it in terms of Adelina Andreyevna's mother sitting on her step to freeze while her hut is boarded up behind her." It was only afterward he remembered that he had not even mentioned Sophie's fairy story to Anna, which was the final cause of his distress.

Their lovemaking was harsh, unrelieved by tenderness or laughter, and afterward he dreamed of hideous pits of starving people being consumed by packs of wolves, their smoking huts sliding down into muddy slime on top of them, all the old fearsome memories riding him again after years of liberation from their grasp. He woke shuddering and sweating with shock, muscles limp with terror, and lay awake the rest of the night, not daring to sleep again.

He watched Anna as she slept beside him, eyelids curved in sleep, one hand under her cheek so her lips quirked almost into mockery. As dawn slowly lightened their tiny room her flesh warmed under his gaze; once she murmured something and shifted against him, but she did not wake. He listened to the strokes of his heart, triggered again the moment his mind returned to the horror of his dreams: it seemed part of the pain that she should sleep. He wanted the comfort of her arms but could not bear to ask for what had always been so freely given; he was shamed by his lack of tenderness the night before but remembered how she too had been devoid of softness.

In the past their arguments had been stifled by kisses, differences banished with the joy of loving and their marriage had been enriched by it. He sweated in another morass of panic as he faced the knowledge that this road was now closed to them. Love could not be used as a weapon to batter each other into submission, to stifle argument and sweep aside doubts once these drove into the core of belief each held inviolate. But if not to love, where then did they turn?

He went into Smolensk the following day feeling

tired and slightly dizzy. They were fortunate at Klintsy to have a wayside stop on the main line from Smolensk to Bryansk, and a small siding had been built for freighting out the sovkhoz produce. More remote collectives often had as much difficulty getting rid of their crops as they did in producing them.

Smolensk looked modestly prosperous compared to the time three years previously when Kolya had come in pride and trepidation to take charge at Klintsy, chosen as a long-standing Party member, but painfully aware of his lack of practical agricultural knowledge. Damage inflicted during the Civil War had been made good, the rutted streets were tidily swept and the people looked less driven than they had. The shabby buildings were brightened by flowing red flags and colorful Party posters, even if the shops mostly displayed empty shelves or a drab, secondhand clutter of trinkets.

After routine but difficult meetings with the Railway Freight Department and the Statistical Section of the Party, he managed to see Rumyantsev, First Secretary of the local Party and virtual ruler of the huge Western Oblast. Rumyantsev's membership of the Party dated back to 1905 and, although in many ways an unlikable man who had never lost the conspiratorial habits of his revolutionary youth, he did retain one great virtue. He was always willing to see anyone, to reply in his own handwriting to the humblest petitioner, to get drunk with an astonishingly representative cross-section of his oblast.

As director of the most efficient sovkhoz in the area, on whom depended a considerable portion of Rumyantsev's reputation for fulfilling his production quotas, Kolya was always likely to find admission to Smolensk Party counsels easy, and Rumyantsev was full of praise for his exceeded norms.

"Yes, it's all very well," said Kolya bluntly. "But

next year is a different matter. You have the new targets?"

"Of course." Rumyantsev nodded.

"Well, then?" Kolya was disconcerted by his calm.

"You will be wise to co-operate in reaching whatever figures Moscow feels are necessary for the people's good. The Party has decided that deviations from socialism in the countryside are no longer to be permitted. There are bound to be difficulties but they must be overcome; it is our attitude which is important."

Kolya had no difficulty in understanding him; the oblique reference was something at which all Communists had become adept over the years and no one more so that Rumyantsev with his rough bullying manner and subtle network of influence and control. Rumyantsev did not expect him to reach his targets, but then no one else would either. It would be zeal and co-operation in overcoming the inevitable chaos about to descend on them which would count in a man's favor. But under such circumstances this could only mean utter ruthlessness; every Russian who had lived through the past fourteen years knew that nothing except force had the power to cut through chaos. He stood up, unable to keep still, and began to pace the room before suddenly rounding on Rumyantsev. "Why? Why? Comrade Lenin always said we must take time. In his later writings Marx did not think human nature could change overnight—he did not expect peasants to be truly revolutionary. What benefit to the Revolution if everyone starves again?"

"It is not for you to decide." Rumyantsev's tone was not unkind. "You keep out of such matters, do your job and produce as much as you can. We're going to need it all and Moscow will not accept failure. Only success will allow the Party not to think too deeply about any doubts you may have."

Kolya stared at Rumyantsev's thick body and flabby, drinker's face, wondering suddenly what doubts he too might be hiding. After twenty-five years as a dedicated revolutionary, what disillusion could be there.

There was no point in persisting; Rumyantsev had no more power than he to change policy. Instead he turned to matters where the Secretary's power was real. "Ivan Pyotr'itch, my tractors have suffered a series of disasters this year, but the most serious concern is the camshafts. These seem faulty in manufacture. I already have three broken down within months of delivery."

"So?"

"Well, for—" Kolya gripped himself resolutely. Rumyantsev was merely needling him for his own purposes, to reassert his authority after a moment of relaxation. "If I am to chase some impossible target, I must at least have machinery which works. Have I your permission to approach the army workshops unit here to see if they can help us?"

"No. We can't look to our own petty advantage in this situation; such actions would carry a dangerous interpretation."

Blood rushed into Director Berdeyev's face. He saw the stuffy office and obligatory portrait of Comrade Lenin through a film of fury, had almost snatched the First Secretary by the collar before a vestige of prudence restrained him. "What the devil do you expect me to do, harvest next year's crops with our teeth? At the present rate of breakdowns, I'll have perhaps twelve tractors for ten thousand dessyatins of farmland. Not to mention the scrub I must somehow start reclaiming if these new targets are to mean anything at all."

"You will have plenty of people."

"People! Everyone keeps telling me I shall be overrun with people. What the hell will they achieve except eat their way through more of our crops?"

"You must not let them."

"How? They have to live. They cannot work unless they are not just fed, but well fed."

Rumyantsev shrugged and stared out of the window. "There will be many surplus to requirements with the new methods of collectivization."

Kolya looked at him disbelievingly and then said slowly. "There is an old woman, Tatyana Chibenko, the mother of one of my sovkhozniks. She has been turned out of her hut at Sartsevo, and her grandson who works their two dessyatins has been taken away. She sits all the time on her step, waiting at least for her hut to be given back to her."

"They were doubtless kulaks, denying their produce to the people. The new program is aimed at such as they."

"And you cannot—will not—even see she has her hut back? She is one of those surplus to requirements?"

Rumyantsev drew a pad toward him. "If she is old and sick I will see what I can do, but it is the land of such people the Soviet state needs. Without force they will not give it up."

"No," said Kolya bleakly. "I am sure they will not."

He left immediately afterward, there was nothing to be gained by staying and he felt too uncertain in his own mind to attempt argument. He had thought he would never recover from his experiences in the Ukraine, but his happiness with Anna and the task of bringing back prosperity to the countryside had somehow carried him through. However hard the work, however achingly, persistently lost his music, he had known a fierce satisfaction as he saw the land under his care grow fruitful again, had seen a measure of tranquillity return to the minute scrap of Russia for which he had become responsible. Surely, whatever the arguments, it could not be right to throw it all into ruin again?

He walked swiftly, tripping over loose stones, brushing past old women haggling over a single egg or squawking hen, without thought as he climbed the rough stone battlements surrounding part of the city. Smolensk lay on slight green hills on either side of the Dnieper, a patchwork of wood and stone and concrete dominated by the cathedral with its clustered domes: from this vantage point the city's sprawl was almost insignificant compared to the vastness all around.

He leaned against the crudely shaped stone blocks and gazed at his beautiful land, encompassing the melancholy of space and infinite patience, the inspiration of size with simplicity of spirit. The sky was brilliantly blue, darkening in the east but in so flat a land even the shadows were resplendent with reflected light. Clumps of woodland filled with sad and shining colors broke the monotony of ravine and rolling plain, a sharp-edged wind polished the air: Konstantin Berdeyev stood a long time listening to the faint pulse of the land, the never-ceasing rhythm of trees and river and grass. When at length he straightened stiffly and moved away, the anguish was still there but deadened slightly. Russia had offered her own refreshment and he had settled on at least some of the things he must do.

Protest would be useless. It was not just the danger which deterred him but the impossibility of abandoning every ideal which had ruled his life, of struggling against the mainstream of endeavor in his own land, the inevitable waste of such a gesture and the ruin it would bring on all he held dear: to Anna and the children, to Klintsy and the hundreds there who now depended on him. He must preserve what he could, fight where he had a chance of winning, hold to what he still believed.

Before he left Smolensk he went to a factory huddled outside Catherine the Great's Gate, which produced press metalwork for the railways and also a weird assortment of other items, from bolts to harness fittings.

"*Ayí,* Konstantin Aleksandr'itch, it will be a cold winter." Old Antonochka was employed by the factory to sweep rubbish and always gave the same greeting, regardless of season. He had only one leg and one eye, having been blown up at Tannenburg, so he was unable to shift the rubbish, only push it around as he leaned on the broom the keep upright. His hour of courage was past, but his poverty and pain went on and on, his work at the factory a last bastion of pride.

"*Ayí,* Antonochka. I didn't know I was coming here today or I would have brought you a bag of corn. I'll bring some next time I jump the train."

The old man chuckled; the flying leaps necessary from wayside stations were proverbial. Most of the trains were freight and even obliging drivers only slowed to a walking pace as they passed the smaller stations. Kolya stayed a few minutes talking to Antonochka, humbled by the burdens of his life and feeling the doubts of the afternoon slipping away again in comradeship. Lev David'itch, the factory manager, was a good man and his largeness of heart had welded his work force into a truly remarkable community.

"Lev," said Kolya, when he finally found him scrabbling under an immobile lathe, soaked in grease. "I have a favor to ask."

"Anything, Konstantin Aleksandr'itch, anything I can do. The devil rot this machinery," he added as they walked to his overflowing cubbyhole of an office, trailing grease and wads of cotton packing. "I'm not allowed to close even a section for maintenance in case we fall behind in our allocations."

"Would you be able to forge me half a dozen tractor camshafts?" It did not sound too hopeful.

Lev pulled at his lip thoughtfully. "I don't know. We do some work not too dissimilar but it would be quite outside our run, very wasteful. Why can't you send to the tractor works?"

"Why don't you have spares for your lathes?" retorted Kolya.

Lev shook his head. "Ah, my friend, what folly. If I could shut down for maintenance just occasionally, I would soon produce more than enough to make up."

"Then why don't you?" demanded Kolya brutally. "Like this you fall short of target anyway. It's better to gamble and try to produce some of the stuff we need so much."

"Is that what you are doing?" He poured vodka from a bottle marked Sulphuric Acid.

Kolya nodded. "You would be risking something if you did it for me."

Lev tossed back the drink and reached for another. "I will see. If I gamble here everyone in town knows about it within the hour; at Klintsy you may be luckier for a while, but not forever."

Kolya explained the new figures to him and he whistled thoughtfully. "I thought only industry was working twenty-five hours a day."

"Yet twenty-five hours a day produces less than would sixteen, sensibly organized. Next year I shall also have to feed far more workers than I can use, if rumor is correct."

Lev nodded. "I've heard things too. I give work where I can, the rest—" He looked at Kolya directly. "Some are to be driven into the marshes and left to starve, others sent to the east. Socially alien elements, they call them."

"We call them." Kolya stood up. "We are both Party members, we can't pretend it isn't us. You are trying to keep your part going, I am trying to keep mine, but it will be little enough against our share of the guilt for what is being done."

No more was said, but as Lev walked to the gate with him, he said suddenly, "Bring me one of your damaged shafts, Konstantin Aleksandr'itch. Such faulty design arouses my engineer's curiosity."

Kolya grinned. "I will. May good fortune, peace and plenty attend your path." The traditional phrase was dredged from memory as they clasped hands. Whatever was lost, comradeship remained.

Chapter Twenty-six

"Comrade! Comrade Director, open up!"

Kolya took confused seconds to realize the thumps and knockings were not part of more appalling dreams, but reality. He rolled out of bed and edged open the outside door. Yefím, who called himself station master but was in fact man of all work at Klintsy sidings, darted into the room on a blast of snow, babbling out some story of fire and disaster.

"Quietly, Yefím, quietly. Tell me what has happened." Kolya yawned irresistibly. God, he was tired.

"Comrade Director, there's a message for you from Party headquarters sent through Smolensk station. They tried to ring the sovkhoz but the line is down."

Kolya nodded. In blizzards it nearly always was down.

"They want you to take a convoy of tractors to help the village of Selnyi. They have a fire and the Chairman of the village soviet has been murdered." Yefím's popeyes stared at him in astonishment at such wickedness. He was pale and slender with soft, restless hands, and spent any spare time he had paying court to the middle-aged widows of the sovkhoz. Apparently nothing else interested him, since he despised the freight trains which never quite stopped at his station.

"I'll get dressed," said Kolya briefly. He was ashamed of his instinctive dislike of Yefím and gave him a tumbler of vodka to prove to himself that this dislike was not real.

Anna helped him dress in layers of felt and matted sheepskin; it was going to be a very tough journey if Smolensk did order him to reach Selnyi in this weather.

She clung to him. "Take care."

"I will." He held her tightly, suddenly overwhelmed by how much he loved her, by bitter knowledge of how circumstances had eroded his determination not to use love as a weapon. As events over the past few months had torn his mind apart again, consideration and tenderness alike had been thrown into a maelstrom of emotions he had failed to control. As doubts crumbled his idealism and bitterness sharpened his temper, only her apparently limitless generosity in giving herself had prevented their whole relationship from dissolving. He ran his hand gently over her face, smoothing back tumbled bronze-fair hair, feeling the smile trembling on her lips. "I have no words for what you are to me. I wish I had."

She laid her cheek against his. "Oh, my dear, you are mine again. These past weeks . . . I knew I was losing you."

"My hold on life, remember? That is what you have been to me again. When I lose you, I am lost too. But I have no excuse for how I have behaved."

"The excuse of scarcely ever an hour's sleep without nightmares," she suggested, smiling.

He shook his head. He knew her unshaken faith in the Party too well to be able to discuss his nightmares with her, even now.

Anna shook him lightly. "Kolyushka, love, there is no need for apologies or excuses. So long as it is you and not a stranger I scarcely know, all I have to give is yours to take."

"My love," he said huskily, "if I had not words before, what can I say now?" All I have to give . . . Without realizing it she had gone straight to the root of their dilemma, for the inmost core of her belief she was powerless to yield.

She laughed. "Nothing, with Yefím in the next room and you wearing smelly sheepskin! What words have we ever needed when all was well between us? She kissed the end of his nose. "Don't let it get frost-bite, it is just right how it is."

He knew she had added gift to gift, for his sake deliberately lowering a tension he was ill-equipped to bear, when few women could have foregone the requitement of stretching the moment out. Even so, he was too shaken to face Yefím with full composure.

To gain time he looked in on the children. Sophie bounced up at once. "Where are you going, Daddy? Can I come too?"

He tucked her into the front of his jacket, pretending to take her with him. "You would at least keep me warm, little one."

"You'll keep away from the wolves?"

"All sensible wolves are asleep on a night like this." He tucked her in scarcely able to reach into the tiny straw box where she and Yuri slept, laughing when she wrinkled her nose as Anna had done at the reek of his jacket.

Outside it was bitterly, fiercely cold, but he scarcely noticed the icebound, hostile world for the joy and warmth of his parting, the lingering memory of Anna's and Sophie's arms around his neck, the thought of them all snugged down in security whatever the world could do.

Yefím cranked the old station telephone proudly, excited to be part of an event which for once was not slowly hauling through his preserves without quite stopping for him to grasp at it. The line was bad, but after many crackles and cut connections, Kolya recognized Rumyantsev's voice with surprise. Affairs at Selnyi must be serious indeed if the First Secretary was in his office at such an hour.

He began to feel skeptical about a straightforward fire. "Ivan Pyotr'itch? Konstantin Aleksandr'itch here."

"Good. You must get through to Selnyi with as many men as you can. How long will it take?"

Kolya glanced out of the cobwebbed window. "In these conditions, eight hours or more. But our tractors are not built for such work, we will certainly lose some. What of my spring sowing?"

Rumyantsev said something indistinguishable in the crackle, then more clearly. "You must start at once,"

"I can't hear, Comrade," said Kolya cheerfully, his mind still on Anna. He had no intention of leading a tractor convoy in such weather, without some very pressing reason.

"You are to start at once."

Kolya waited until interference almost drowned speech and then bellowed back, "When do you want me to leave, Comrade? Is it urgent?"

"It is urgent," snapped Rumyantsev, suddenly sounding alarmingly close. "The line is blocked and two coaches of troop reinforcements are stranded. You are the nearest Party cadre."

His voice faded again but Kolya stared at the instrument reflectively. This sounded odder and odder.

"Can you hear me?"

Kolya rubbed the mouthpiece along the stubble on his cheek while shouting back "no!" away from the instrument. He met Yefím's astonished gaze, watching every move with the fascinated attention of the born bystander, and recollected himself hastily. He would have to be more subtle than that.

"Konstantin Aleksandr'itch," Rumyantsev was speaking very slowly and distinctly. "You are to leave with as many men as you can, as soon as possible, to render all aid to Selnyi."

"Yes, Comrade. How many people may have to come back with us?"

"I don't know. Do what you are told. Put yourself under the orders of the police you will find there."

"Not the Chairman of the village soviet?"

"No. He is dead. At once, Comrade." Rumyantsev rang off.

Kolya replaced the mouthpiece slowly, trying to sort through the scattered information he had received. He had been through Selnyi a couple of times and thought the population around forty families, say two hundred people. Certainly not a size to merit a police detachment, or rouse the First Secretary from his bed to deal with a crisis there. Or two coaches of troops, he remembered suddenly. He saw Yefím staring at him unblinkingly and swore aloud. Yefím was just the kind of greasy slob, skulking on the outskirts of the Party and looking for favors, who would delight in reporting any hesitation in the Director's actions.

"Thank you, Comrade, for the use of your phone." The words almost stuck in his throat. I am no comrade of Yefím's, he thought sourly, nor do I like the way the Yefíms of this world have their own sort of power in this new setting with the Party on the attack. He clamped his thoughts firmly on the grace that was Anna; he must not lose his moment of contentment so soon.

The first few kilometers of the journey went surprisingly well, the tracks around Klintsy were kept open and only the previous night's drifts barred their way. Progress slowed as it became necessary to winch over obstructions, and by midafternoon they had covered barely half the distance. Then they gained the cover of a curving edge of forest and the track was scoured almost clear; where it was not the trees provided quick winching points, although not free from danger. In such temperatures trees could explode from frost alone, without the added pressure of cables, but with the near-onset of night speed was vital.

"The devil's shit on this, Comrade Director," gasped Valya, the field foreman, manhandling yet another chain forward. "If there is no fuel at Selnyi we shall be stuck there for the winter."

Kolya had not dared burden his tractors with too heavy loads, knowing the conditions they were likely to encounter. "We have enough, but not if we have to take out two hundred people. The tractors won't take much more of this, though."

As if in answer the engine note of one of them changed to a high-pitched howl, a pulsing cloud of smoke hanging in the air above. Valya sprinted to shut the engine off but it was too late, there was an appalling groaning crack as it seized up.

"We shall have to push it off into a drift," said Kolya curtly. "It will be quicker than digging a track around."

"*Bozhe moy,* Comrade Director, what will we do in the spring?" Golikov plowed down the road toward him, reddened eyes gleaming above the icicles coating his wrapped facecloth. "There are two more which sound like scrap metal in a madman's guts."

"We have to do this first, Sergei, my friend." Kolya clapped him on the shoulder; it was not the time for voicing his own doubts. "The people of Selnyi will die if we cannot get through to them." As he spoke he felt ashamed; it was not concern for the people of Selnyi which had prompted Rumyantsev to send them off on this mad, destructive journey.

"I never yet heard of a fire in winter which swept

through a whole village," grumbled Golikov. The men were uneasy too; without being told they knew there could be no simple explanation for what they had been told to do.

The column jerked into slow motion again, broken abruptly by an explosion as the tree from which they were winching, weakened by frost, shattered into a timber shrapnel burst. The cable, suddenly released, recoiled quicker than the eye could track and hurled the nearest tractor on its side, opening it up like a gutted fish. The driver was thrown clear, catapulted into a drift with only a hole like a fox burrow to show where he had gone. The winchman was incredibly untouched, trapped by jagged pieces of ripped-up engine block, the weight held off him by the winch, sheared from its mounting by the unraveling shock of cable and smashed under the tractor to leave a precious, saving space in which he was imprisoned.

It all happened so unbelievably fast that no one had time to escape the hail of splinters, lethal with frost-rimed edges. Valya died where he stood, slashed into bloody fragments. Sergei Golikov was completely unharmed, standing out in the open yet without so much as a chip lodged in the sheepskin of his jacket. The driver of the second tractor was neatly decapitated as he leaned out to talk to his winchman, his blood freezing in long stalactites as it spurted out on the snow, the man he was speaking to speared a dozen times and dead before his body touched the ground. The rest of the column was mercifully protected by drifts and Kolya, who had been standing beside the leading tractor was saved by its bulk although showered with hot oil as it was flung over within a pace of him.

"Comrade Director! Comrade Director!" He became dimly aware of shock and whiteness, of ruthless hands scrubbing snow over his face as he thrashed weakly to escape them. His eyes hurt like hell.

"Help me up," he said thickly. He felt eager hands pushing and pulling, the uncertain reeling of the earth beneath his feet, but could see nothing. "What happened?" Panic was dense in his throat as he blinked frantically in search of sight.

"More snow, Comrade Director." The relief to his burning eyes was enormous as they packed snow on again. His senses reeled and then steadied; he remembered what had happened now. "Who is hurt?"

A gabble of voices. God, if only he could see. He shook of some of the hands supporting him and began to scrape the snow from his face, frightened now of frostbite.

"Go easy, Comrade Director. The snow will ease the pain." He recognized the voice of Pyotr, one of Vera's young stockmen. He seemed to be about the only one keeping his head.

"Quiet!" he rasped, senses swimming again. "Golikov?"

"Yes, Konstantin Aleksandr'itch. What a terrible thing to happen. I was standing right there and then—"

"Are you all right?" Kolya cut him short brutally.

"Yes, Comrade Director." He could hear the offense in his tone.

"Who is hurt?"

Another gabble of voices as they began to count. Others went away and came running back with tales of bodies. He found it hard to decide whether they were telling him about the same body several times, or about different ones.

"Valya is killed, also Ygor and Stepan of the second tractor," came Pyotr's voice in his ear.

"What about the leading tractor?" His face above the cloth wrapped around his mouth and nose felt crisp and numb.

"The driver has disappeared, Ilya is trapped underneath."

"Dead?"

"No, Comrade Director, untouched. It is like a miracle of heaven." He felt the movement as the boy crossed himself and grinned painfully. In moments of crisis the age-old peasant superstitions revived, and how could one say it was a miracle of Lenin that Ilya survived in a handbreadth of space with all the weight of an overturned tractor poised over him?

He struggled to assemble his thoughts. It was not easy while the bogey of his own sightlessness leered at him, fattening on fear and pain. "Get him out at once. He'll freeze to the road in minutes, be dead in half an hour. Sergei?"

"Yes, Comrade Director?" Golikov was stiff and correct, angry at having been made to look foolish in front of the men.

"Try to pull him clear. If you can't, get the men onto lifting the tractor. Use links of the chain perhaps to prop it up until he can crawl free. Anyone spare to look for the driver. He has disappeared, you say?" He turned to Pyotr. Was that a gleam of light he could see in his left eye?

"Yes, Comrade Director. No blood, though."

No blood; yes, Pyotr was a bright lad. "Look, Pyotr, leave me, I'm all right now. He must have been thrown clear into a drift somewhere. You have minutes to find him before he freezes; try to work out where he must be. Stand behind the driver's seat and follow the curve with your eyes if you can." He felt the boy fumbling with something and a moment later he put a strip of some kind of material in his hand.

"Tie it over your eyes, Comrade Director. You are not badly burned; the frost will do more harm than the oil once it is cleaned." Kolya clumsily did as he was bid; it was surprisingly difficult to hold his balance in a dark world. As the numbness receded slightly, his eyes began to hurt fiercely, but Pyotr was right, in such conditions snow the pain killer rapidly became frost the destroyer. He listened intently, forcing himself to stand still and not interfere with the few minutes available to save the lives of Ilya and his driver—Evgeni, he remembered, a middle-aged man with six children.

He heard grunts of effort, curt directions from Golikov, not the right man for such a delicate task; the dead Valya would have been far better. Pyotr shouted; nearby there was a concerted moan of frustration as the tractor sank back, the frantic, heaving men sliding on the ice. There was no sound from Ilya, fast lapsing into a coma of cold and shock.

"How many are helping Pyotr?" Kolya demanded, unable to stand by any longer. He took a step forward, was surprised to find it easy and took another until his hand rested on twisted metal, the tractor's radiator, he supposed.

"None, Comrade, we are all doing what we can for Ilya." The voice was breathless with effort.

"Two of you go. If Pyotr has found Evgeni, he has a better chance than Ilya now." He ran his hands over the wreckage, but it conveyed little to him; one glance was what he need. He snatched off the wool strip impatiently, exclaiming as frozen tears ripped the skin from his cheeks. Holding the strip half over his eyes, he looked sideways, where he had seen the glimmer of light before. He could have shouted with joy; there was something to be seen. He steadied himself with an effort, willing his sight to clear. Time was surely running out for Ilya.

Shading his eyes with the cloth, he struggled to identify the jumble of images floating in and out of his scrap of vision, to make sense of the appalling mass of ripped machinery. He knelt down, just able to see Ilya, grayish face untouched by the monstrous weight looming over it. "Pickaxes," he said briefly. "Chip a passage in the ice where there is no risk of disturbing the balance of the tractor, there, see? Then pull him out if you can."

"He may be trapped—" began Golikov, indignant at not having thought of such a simple solution.

"Yes." Kolya knew he must try to mollify Golikov, on whom much of the smooth running of the sovkhoz depended. He held the cloth across his eyes again, they seemed to be oozing a kind of slime, he could not make out whether it was oil or blood. "It was worth your effort to lift the tractor off him, but there is no more time. If he's trapped he is lost anyway."

Golikov grunted. "What a bitched-up mess." His tone was accusing.

Now there I agree with you, thought Kolya. He could hear picks chipping frantically, the minutes slipping away before they could fasten a rope to Ilya's belt and tear him free from the ice of the road. He was not trapped but he was already dead. Evgeni was hauled unhurt from six meters of snow, laughing in the aftermath of shock at his escape, and soon filled with vodka from smuggled flasks.

"Get them moving again, Sergei," said Kolya urgently. "We must leave the bodies unburied, we can't stay here with night coming on. We shall have to chance winching again, but get everyone clear first."

"The driver and winchman can't be clear."

"I will put the winch in gear as I can't see to drive." It was scarcely courage; he felt almost any risk worthwhile to bring this nightmare journey to an end.

"Who will drive, then?"

Kolya was silent, waiting for Golikov to accept that it must be him, but he did not.

"I will, Comrade Director, I've learned to drive a tractor," Pyotr offered.

"Very well," said Kolya, after waiting yet again for Golikov. "Sergei, you organize the cable laying, shout to us when you are ready and then take cover. Once we are winched forward we can act as anchor for the others."

There were no more disasters, and as if satisfied with the price exacted, the elements also relented slightly. A clear moon floated in a brilliantly lit night, frost hardening the most powdery drift so few more winchings were needed.

"I can see a glow, Comrade Director," said Pyotr as they waited beside the tractor for one of these. "And I think the track improves after this stretch."

Kolya unwrapped his facecloth, the night was completely still and did not convey an impression of intense cold, only a sluggishness in the blood set the alarm bells of the mind jangling even while reactions were almost too slowed by cold to respond. He too could see a glow of fire, but he did not know whether to be elated by what he could see or alarmed by what he could not.

Chapter Twenty-seven

If sleeping had been unpleasant, torn with pain and framed by uproar, waking was even worse. There was churning panic when gummed, swollen eyes refused to admit even a glimmer of daylight, the stiffness of filth and exhaustion, the reality of leaden silence replacing noise and containing the infinitely greater menace of utter desolation. Kolya lay a moment, straining to catch the slightest sound, chill with absurd fear that he had been abandoned, sightless and useless in a deserted village. After a while he realized he was wrong; there was sound. Boots creaked on snow, there was an occasional shuffle of passing clothes, but not a single voice was raised in fear, anger or lament, there was not so much as the whicker of a horse or moan of a stalled cow.

Gingerly he sat up, hands to his face easing off a stiffened cloth; only after it was free did he realize that someone had laid it over a layer of grease to prevent sticking. He licked his lips and grimaced, rancid fat by the taste of it. He must look the most repulsive sight, unshaven and raw, grimed with oil and slapped up with goose grease or something of the sort. He heard footsteps and then Pyotr's voice.

"Comrade Director! You are feeling recovered."

Well that was one way of describing it, he supposed. "Yes, thank you, Pyotr, much recovered. Did you put this stuff on my face?"

"Yes, Comrade Director. You are hardly burned; the oil must have cooled as it flew through the air toward you."

Kolya chuckled involuntarily, feeling the tug of crisp skin across his cheeks. "It sounds like a lovers' meeting. Can you find a clean cloth? If I'm not burned I ought to be able to see, if only I could bathe my eyes open."

"It's the oil, Comrade Director. They are very much inflamed, and of course I could not use vodka to clean them as I would have elsewhere."

Kolya winced. "God, no. Find me a cloth and some water, or milk perhaps, will you?" He had to know whether he could see or not, had to get some of this filthy oil out and shift the flame of pain a little so he could think again.

It was an agonizingly frustrating process, bathing and soaking at the oil, resisting the temptation to scrub it out by brute force.

"You can't hurry it, Comrade Director, you can't hurry it," Pyotr kept repeating, shifting from foot to foot in his anxiety.

Eventually Kolya had to admit he was right. He could now see reasonably well out of part of his left eye and his worst fears had subsided, for he thought the right fairly sound too, though so swollen he could only open it a fraction.

He threw the cloth back in the bowl. "What is happening here?" He was alarmed by the way his own preoccupations had prevented him from taking any notice of the unnatural atmosphere at Selnyi.

Pyotr shook his head. Kolya saw the movement and the weakening nausea of relief made him long for sleep again, this time with his senses let off the chain of suspense, pain reduced to the just supportable.

He stood up. "What is happening?" he repeated. "Where are the tractors and the rest of our Klintsy people?"

"Out there, Comrade Director," said Pyotr reluctantly, flickering a thumb. "Comrade Golikov is acting under orders of the police."

"Take me there, will you, Pyotr?"

Outside it was the gray light of dawn again. By rotating his head and squinting carefully from under his fur cap he could see a slithering kaleidoscope of images: burned-out huts, dark heaps of . . . ? He stumbled over hummocked snow and looked more carefully. Heaps and holocausts of slaughtered cattle. "How many piles like this?"

"There is not one animal left alive in the village." Pyotr's tone reminded Kolya that he was a stockman, more outraged by such a calamity than by occasional frost-stiff human bodies sprawled beside the track.

Then he saw the first huddle of live villagers, sitting in a circle and staring between their feet. Not a head moved or eye turned in their direction as they passed. Kolya had to keep his eyes down but he saw irregular lines of ragged boots, not even shifting weight or stamping against the cold; one with splayed, ancient

"We pull out with you to Klintsy."

Kolya stared at Pauker's boots, feet planted apart, confident, unyielding. The voice suggested to him someone very young, down on his cheeks, glowing with health and duty. Unbidden, his senses conjured up a gay dancing theme to a thin instrument like the piccolo, sound slipping into the void of sight as if never ruthlessly banished. Alarmed, he pushed it away again. "I lost several tractors coming over. It won't be easy to take all these people with us even if it doesn't snow again."

"There are only seven of us left," replied Pauker, astonished.

"But how many villagers?"

"They stay. The kulaks might as well die here as elsewhere now the huts are burned, and the others have left nothing worth taking into a kolkhoz. As the peasants themselves would say, 'The girl without a dowry doesn't get wed.'" He laughed happily at his joke. He did not sound cruel or vindictive; it was all too ordinary and matter of course. He did not like forcing peasants into the snow to die but it was a job like any other. One came, one did what one was told, one believed the fate of the Revolution to be staked on success and beside it the fate of unknown villagers was irrelevant.

Kolya stared at the old man, still kneeling in the snow. He had not picked up the cloth. "How many of them are there?"

"I don't know, about a hundred I suppose. There were a hundred and eighty, but we've killed forty or more, some have run off, others must be dead in the huts."

Kolya turned to Pyotr. "Go and find Comrade Golikov and ask him to start up the tractors; see if you can find any trailers or fuel here." He turned back to

Pauker. "We must leave as soon as possible; the track should be clear if we hurry."

"Konstantin Aleksandr'itch, you are well, then?" Golikov hurried up. He sounded distinctly disappointed.

"Thank you, Sergei, yes." Kolya had been pinned out in the open, unable to move for fear he would betray the limited extent of his sight; now he seized the opportunity to go with Golikov away from Pauker's certainties. Above all, he needed to keep the two apart if he was to have any chance of overbearing them.

The tractors had been put in the station building and started up surprisingly well, and Pyotr found two hay sleds which would be even better than trailers.

"Right." Kolya spoke with a briskness he did not feel. "Sergei, you take as many of our people as you need and start loading the villagers. The fittest will have to walk at least part of the way."

It was not long before Pauker arrived at the run. "What are you doing? I told you, the peasants stay here!"

"Listen, Comrade Lieutenant. These people are all citizens of the Soviet state. They may have been misguided, but those who actively opposed you have no doubt run off or been shot; these are merely bewildered. The Party has decided their selfishness must be changed to a new way of thinking so they have the right to make the best of the opportunity the Party offers them. If they fail it is for the Party, not us, to decide what is to be done with them. There are babies and children here too, Soviet citizens of the future; they have no fault and we need them."

"But we risk ourselves by taking them! They are counterrevolutionaries!" Pauker sounded baffled rather than hostile.

Kolya was very tired, his knees trembling with the effort of staying upright. He did not know whether he believed his own arguments, but dimly grasped that he must believe them, for Anna's sake, for the children's sake, if not his own. "Are you a Party member, Comrade?" he asked abruptly.

"A candidate and a Komsomolnik,"* Pauker answered proudly.

"Well, I have been a full Party member since 1919 and we did not hesitate to risk ourselves for our fellow workers then." He was almost sure a slur on his courage would sting Pauker more than any argument.

There was a long pause. "Yes," said Pauker slowly. "But I had not thought of these capitalist-infected vermin here as fellow workers. I still do not."

A blast of wind and snow swept down the desolate street, whirling blackened thatch and momentarily fanning smoldering embers into flame again. Kolya wondered whether any other race on earth would have a philosophical discussion under such circumstances. The Jews, he decided hazily, faint memory of his grandmother's Bible-reading stirring in his mind. He shook himself aware again. "So there is your task as well as theirs. It is not the Party's intention to wash its hands of any citizen anxious to reform." He hesitated and added in a softer tone, for this he did believe, "Never forget, Comrade, the Party is our conscience and seeks to become the conscience of all men. We may fail but the ideals of the Party cannot."

"Thank you, Comrade Director, I will not forget." Pauker sounded completely sincere. He had both the heedless cruelty and the unsophisticated generosity of extreme youth. "It is going to snow again soon; shall I help Comrade Golikov to load?"

Kolya nodded, weaker with relief than he had been in the tension of argument. This at least was a battle won not lost.

* Young Communist League.

Chapter Twenty-eight

It was only natural that the people from Selnyi should dislike Director Berdeyev intensely: Lieutenant Pauker and his men had long since departed, but the Director of the sovkhoz remained as a daily reminder of the torn fabric of their lives.

Klintsy too was profoundly changed, for the sovkhozniks themselves were mostly peasants or the children of peasants, the only difference being that they had, cheerfully and willingly, wanted to build something new and been encouraged to do so. It had not been easy, the idea of possession too deeply ingrained to be eradicated, but enthusiasm had blurred over many of the undoubted difficulties. Now, suddenly, the people of Klintsy began to wonder whether they too might be threatened by these inexplicable new Party attitudes. Carelessness grew to epidemic proportions, brigandage revived and in some cases the brigands were clearly dispossessed relatives of people now forced to live at Klintsy, and received their active assistance.

By the end of the summer it became obvious that Klintsy, in common with every other agricultural enterprise in Western Russia, would not only fail to meet its new targets, but would fall far short of the previous year's production. Director Berdeyev was officially reprimanded and only retained his position because of his previous success and the abysmal performance of every comparable sovkhoz. It was made clear, however, that repetition would not be tolerated. If he could not force a change of heart then the GPU would.

"You will have to make an example of the people

responsible," said Golikov one morning after he had presented the dismal tallies of the flax harvest. "Those stupid sods from Selnyi are infecting everyone; you have been too soft with them." Golikov no longer cared to remember his instinctive revulsion from the idea of forcible collectivization.

"Who is responsible? How the hell can we pick out one or two for what has become a general attitude?" Kolya felt a helpless anger, well aware that control of Klintsy was slipping away from him. Even open insolence was not unusual any more, while the old methods of easy comradeship no longer sufficed. Yet he did not dare discipline men as he had in the past, almost without thinking about it. With the GPU never far away and an angered Party demanding penal punishment for the slightest misdemeanor, a forfeited labor day could be instantly turned into a fifteen-year sentence for sabotage, a petty offender face a firing squad for treason. In the eyes of the Party inefficiency and counter-revolution were no longer distinguishable.

Golikov shrugged. "Does it matter? The whole lot of them and half our own. You could pick out anyone with your eyes shut." There was insolence in his tone, too. It had been impossible to hide the Director's troubles with his eyes during the summer and Golikov was increasingly hostile as his ambitions grew. He bitterly resented the stories which had grown out of the journey to Selnyi, sensed derision over the way he had crouched in a snowdrift while Pyotr and the Director winched the tractors clear. Generations of land-hungry farmers were in his blood and the thousands of dessyatins at Klintsy excited him with almost unbearable longing. He knew the multiplying difficulties facing the Director. One day he would show them all.

"I shall have to have names and specific accusations," said Kolya unwillingly, aware of the corner into which he was being driven. Quite apart from the danger of his own position, Klintsy under Golikov could scarcely prosper, would face the GPU squads within months and probably starvation as well, since food stocks for their own consumption would be taken if their targets went unfulfilled for long.

Golikov's eyes gleamed. "There's no difficulty about that, Comrade Director. I could give you a hundred names tomorrow and another hundred the day after."

Kolya walked home afterward a prey to black depression. "What can I do?" he asked Anna desperately. "We must produce. I can't give our new sovkhozniks any more time to accept our different ways here, when the towns are hungry and every extra sack of grain we sell abroad buys equipment we need so much. The only reliable tractors we have are American, bought by selling food and minerals when our people have nothing but a few slices of black bread for a fifteen-hour day."

She put her chin between her fists and scowled fiercely. She did not look any older than the day they had married and he was again swept by his love for her, the one unchanging element in a moon-scape world. Suddenly there was no difficulty in finding the words he needed, fresh-minted as if they had never been used before.

"Oh, Anna, I do love you so." He took her in his arms and kissed her as if he would lose himself in her forever, assuage the nightmare life had become with her passion and unfailing response to him. They came together in a kindling firebowl of emotion, their bodies striving as if they could not become sufficiently one, yet this time there was also a sweet yielding of spirit, the grace of tenderness.

Afterward they sat, with her cradled in his arms, neither speaking, both shaken and drained by the intensity of their emotions.

"You have never been more completely mine," she

said at last, with a queer sideways smile. "The stranger has truly gone at last."

He stirred and shook his head. "A stranger to myself sometimes. But you have always been the still center around which everything else revolves."

She looked slightly shocked. "You still come out with some very *bourzhuis* ideas." She smiled and kissed him again. "Any wife would like them, though."

He held her tightly. "I am failing everywhere else; tell me I am not failing with you."

She laughed. "You are certainly not failing with me!" She ran her finger across his eyes. "You're tired, love, that's all. I know this is a difficult year for you, but the Party cannot fail now and neither will you."

"No," he said bitterly. "In order to build you must destroy, how many times have I heard that. It is just that I had long since thought my time for destroying was over. I don't feel I can go through the whole miserable business again."

"You must," she said sternly. "You will never know peace if you don't. It is all falling on our generation. Sophie and Yuri and others like them will grow up fresh and untouched by the old possessiveness and envy."

"Do you know," he said slowly, "you look so frail and delicate, but you are much tougher than I am."

"Women have to be. We see the way ahead, not the scruples tripping up our feet." She even looked tough for a moment, but there was a glint of mockery in her eyes and he knew she was again trying to strengthen him in the only way she could.

He stood up, setting her on her feet, and stretched, yawning. "I see the way ahead, but I don't like the knowledge of how many we are going to crush to get there."

"How many?"

He looked at her in surprise. "How many?"

"Yes, you are talking as if Klintsy were going to be a slaughterhouse. How many?"

He shrugged. "Once you start, how can you tell?"

"Guess." She shook his arm. "Go on, Kolyushka, guess. Two, three shot, half a dozen exiled to restore discipline here?"

"I don't know," he said flatly, animosity suddenly kindled between them. Whatever they did, the world could not be shut out.

"I'll tell you then. I know the Selnyi people hate you. I've tried to explain that they would have been left to die but for you, but they don't care and will not listen. They have yielded only to force and you can't now try kindness. They spit between your feet and despise you as well. If you have to let the Party shoot a couple and discipline a few more so Klintsy produces what it should, then it is their choice, not yours. Otherwise five times that number die in Moscow or Kharkov because there is no bread for them, children grow deformed because there is no milk, while you go free, keeping your scruples clean. How would you feel if it was Sophie or Yuri screaming with a swollen belly and I had waited all day in line for bread which would not nourish them?"

He went out, banging the door behind him.

He had never been a match for Anna's logic and certainty, and the impact was all the more devastating when his body had so recently craved hers with such overwhelming, almost humbling completeness. He could not shake his mind free from her clear, accusing voice or his flesh from its dependence on hers. He walked slowly down the dusty lane, the chill dusk pleasant after the heat of the day, though winter was less than a month away.

He must make his own decision, with yet another thousand dessyatins of peasant land due to be added to Klintsy before the end of the year, he could delay no longer. The high-powered, mighty Director of Klintsy, he thought wryly, manager of the largest agricultural enterprise in the Western Oblast, wandering through the dark trying not to have his mind made up for him.

He sat on a fallen log and looked at his laced fingers. Anna, Anna. To him such a creature of contrasts with her softness and hardness, her love for him and for the Party in which she never saw contradiction, always giving herself without reservation. Sophie had screamed with fear when he had returned from Selnyi with his blackened face and inflamed eyes. It was not the child's fault, but he had been hurt nevertheless by the way she struggled against seeing him even weeks after. Yuri on the other hand had been matter of fact and curious; he had come truly to know his son for the first time in the ten days of blindness Anna had imposed on him, telling him stories and playing games in which he too, as well as the child, had had to rely totally on his imagination. He discovered that Yuri was already thirstily groping for facts about the world he lived in, wanted to know how airplanes flew, what made trains move or corn sprout. He was completely different from Sophie, ruthless with any attempt to put him off with less than a complete answer. He was serious where Sophie was gay, yet with a sudden spark of delight at anything which caught his sense of the ridiculous; painstaking in a way which made his sister scornful; undemonstrative yet responding with such wholehearted affection to his first experience of his father's undivided attention that Kolya had felt ashamed.

Fortunately, the extravagance of the blizzard which followed their return from Selnyi had kept everyone isolated in their own cottages and made rest relatively easy. Anna had cleaned out the oil, dressing and bathing his eyes every two hours in a month of devotion, but the inflammation had persisted, recurring every dusty day through the summer. It was aggravated by their inability to find any dark glasses in the whole of Smolensk and Rumyantsev eventually brought a pair back from Moscow. The damp autumn afforded additional relief, to Golikov's ill-concealed disappointment. His time will come, thought Kolya, and a fine mess he will make of it.

An hour later he walked home again, still undecided. It was simply not the sort of choice he felt able to make.

Running an enterprise the size of Klintsy involved an immense amount of paperwork; the old days when Kolya had spent much of his time out on the sovkhoz lands were long since gone although he still tried to visit every section at least once a month. Each of the eight villages, the forestry department, the graneries and barns, the sawmill with its production of stakes, gates and carts, the many maintenance squads—it was becoming an impossible task.

After a long morning in his office the following day, Kolya decided that the most pressing need was another visit to the workshops. Cultivation had been delayed throughout the year by shortage and unreliability of equipment and the position showed no sign of improvement. As he locked his office door, he thought how strange it was that someone like himself, whose inclinations were completely opposed to desk work, whose first choice had been music and second farming, should spend so much of his time stranded in a morass of paper. A trick of memory brought him the voice of Innokenty Rogov, telling him what a fool he would make of himself in business. Innokenty, with his ambitions to throw bridges across every river of Russia, dead in Brusilov's offensive of 1916. He slammed his mental door shut on memory at once; he had not thought of the past in years, must not on any account think of it again.

On his way through the village he heard chanting voices from the school and on impulse went in. The new school serving the sovkhoz was a great source of pride, one tangible result for all their labors. In class after class the teacher brought pupils to their feet as he walked in, exclaiming with pleasure and showing off drawings and exercises, poems to Lenin and mathematical problems which had him groping for forgotten calculus.

"They are all bitten with the idea of a scientific career," remarked Ivan Perichev, the head teacher, afterward. "In the top class all except two want to be scientists or doctors or agricultural chemists. It is wonderful the Party puts such opportunity in their way. When I was a lad only three in my village did more than learn their letters."

"What do the odd two wish to be?" asked Kolya curiously.

"One shows some talent for art, the other wants to explore the ancient history of the Smolensk region. You remember Valya the foreman who was killed? His boy."

"Yes," said Kolya slowly. "I remember Valya. I don't know how one gets to study the history of Smolensk but if any recommendation of mine will help, let me know. How is Sophie shaping?" Yuri attended junior school the other side of the village.

Perichev hesitated. "She does not concentrate enough, Comrade Director. She will dance and sing with passion and I think she has musical talent, but she will not see the need for anything else."

Kolya was astonished, how little after all one knew of one's own children. After a moment he realized he was immensely glad. "Can she be taught properly here?"

"Naturally, Comrade. If she really has ability she will have to go to Smolensk later, but I've told her she will have no recommendation from me until she settles to her other work."

"I'll tell her too," said Kolya grimly. "If she really cares for music, she will not mind what else she has to do to get it."

Perichev looked at him strangely. "As you say, Comrade Director."

Kolya came away from the school immensely cheered, feeling it had restored a sense of proportion, obscured by recent problems. The purpose, order and discipline of the children, above all the feeling of young minds finding fresh horizons, were stimulating. How much really we have achieved, he thought. They are our future and you can see already that they truly will be different.

The workshops too were a hive of activity, the atmosphere relaxed with some of the men whistling cheerfully and fresh flowers in the vase below Lenin's portrait.

"Good progress, Comrade Director," Evgeni called out. Newly promoted from mechanic to foreman soon after his brief experience with the snowdrift, he had proved an unexpectedly successful choice. "Two tractors will be ready by this evening, and we have started on six others." He reeled off a mass of further work in hand. Kolya had already decided that he was an optimist, but the workshops were one place where optimism was badly needed and he simply made due allowance on Evgeni's delivery dates. They walked around slowly, discussing ways in which parts could be improvised when spares were not forthcoming, as was often the case.

"What's this?" asked Kolya abruptly.

Evgeni looked uncomfortable. "It's one of the camshafts you obtained for us, Comrade Director."

"So I see. What has happened to it?"

"It's no good, Comrade Director."

"That is not what I asked. What has happened to it so it is now no good?"

Evgeni shrugged. "I don't know."

"Don't be a fool, man, of course you must know," said Kolya impatiently. "You also know the trouble we have had to obtain even a few of these." And the risks Lev has taken to make them, he thought to himself.

"I don't know, Comrade Director," repeated Evgeni obstinately.

Kolya stared at him, anger tight in his throat. "The Party would call this sabotage, Evgeni Mikhail'itch."

Evgeni wiped his forehead, suddenly pale. "No, Comrade Director, I swear it, there was no sabotage."

Kolya did not need to be told, but he was intent on shaking Evgeni into admission. He looked carefully at the shaft; it had great indentations bitten into it. Used carelessly as a lever or for thumping a bolt into place he guessed, because some stupid oaf could not be bothered to fetch the proper tools. The decision he had avoided last night was suddenly made. Klintsy could not possibly go on like this; the culprit would have to take his chance with police vengeance. "Who did this, Evgeni?"

Evgeni licked his lips, nervously wiping his palms on oily dungarees. "I don't know."

"Come with me," said Kolya curtly, leading the way to the tiny cubicle which served as a tool store. "Now, Evgeni, listen to me very carefully. You are foreman here, what happens in the workshops is your responsibility, just as the whole sovkhoz is mine. I can't possibly overlook such carelessness and neither can you. You have a duty to the Party and to your comrades here to carry out your duties properly, to discipline those who fail. I must do it with you, you must do it with your workmen."

"I can't say," said Evgeni miserably. "I will see he is punished privately."

"That's not the point," said Kolya patiently. "He must be subjected to the proper discipline of the sovkhoz so others may learn from his example. Some private fine of a few cigarettes will not do."

"I did it myself." Evgeni looked at him with bright blue accusing eyes.

Kolya wanted to shake him. "If you refuse to say, it puts a more serious complexion on something which otherwise I might be able to deal with myself. An attempt to conceal sabotage is conspiracy or worse; my punishments will be nothing compared to the Party's on such a charge." Conspiracy was counterrevolution, punishable only by death. Yet even as he strove to make the distinction between discipline and vengeance, Kolya knew he was being hypocritical. Whatever punishment he gave under present conditions was bound to be reported to the Party and to become a criminal matter, as Evgeni well knew. Why else would he lie but to save the true offender? He opened his mouth to retract, to give them both a line of escape, but the words passed unuttered. Anna was right, the choice was no longer his.

A terrible fear of what he might have to do seized him. "For God's sake, Evgeni, this is still between the two of us but I can't leave it there, with what we both know is open defiance. I must know which man here is too careless to be trusted with such a responsible job."

Evgeni spat, the immemorial gesture of a mind made up. "I did it myself."

Kolya stared at him appalled, his body chilling. Evgeni. No longer an abstract who must be sacrificed to restore discipline, a careless workman with five years' penal labor for a moment of stupidity. For a man in Evgeni's position to admit such wanton damage, with no reason given or attempt at defense, it was death. Death for the man dug out of a snowdrift, a Ukrainian with a mole on his cheek and the face of a sad, stripped monkey, who entertained them in winter with his native dances.

The father of six children.

Chapter Twenty-nine

"I thought the applause for Kirov almost as great as that for the *Khozyain*," observed Rumyantsev, lowering his voice.

"Not a doubt of it," agreed Kolya. He could never avoid a certain wry amusement at hearing this word, often used by officials to refer to Stalin, even though no one else appeared to find it strange. It was the old term a serf had used for his master and implied ownership as well as authority, and its bitter aptness made him add with sudden anger, "Perhaps there will soon be no need to lower your voice as you say so."

Both were Party delegates from the Western Oblast to the 1934 Party Congress in Moscow, and although Rumyantsev was familiar enough with the city, Kolya had found it hard to take in all the changes of the past eight years. It was still shabby and its citizens looked as strained and tired as ever, but massive warehouses covered the little wood where he and Anna had first made love and the train bringing them from Smolensk had pulled past factory after factory, a glow of sweating effort reflected from the dark February sky.

"He's going to have a job on his hands, though, if

there is to be any shift of power," said Rumyantsev suddenly. "He's a Leningrad man, the *Khozyain* has control of all the levers here."

"Now he's elected one of the secretaries of the Central Committee, he will have power here too." Kolya gazed about him as he spoke, recognizing some of the great names of the Revolution, prompted by Rumyantsev, who knew most of them. Kamenev, Zinoviev and Rykov; Bukharin, until recently in disgrace for opposing the headlong pace of collectivization; Tukhachevsky, the most brilliant fighting general of the Red Army. He glimpsed Yakir too and would have liked to greet him, but did not get the chance for Yakir was now among the Party greats, a full member of the Central Committee when even Tukhachevsky was only a candidate member.

"You can tell he's a Leningrad man by the cut of his suit." Rumyantsev gave one of his belly laughs.

You could indeed. Petersburg, thought Kolya nostalgically, with an almost vertiginous rush of memory. Dark, well-tailored Kirov stood out from the baggy-suited Muscovites and provincials around him, just as his views on the more conciliatory direction the Party's policies should take in the future had stood out in the preceding speeches.

As they filed into the Congress Hall, Kolya felt an unexpected sense of pride at being one of the delegates chosen by the Party, a small part of the framework around which achievement was at last being built. He had been taken aback, though, by the lack of discussion in this highest forum of the land, the almost casual way in which Stalin's lightest wish was instantly agreed to and issued as a decree. He studied some of the other delegates: they looked gray and careworn, with tight, anxious expressions and the nervous gestures of the overdriven.

As he did, he thought grimly.

The efforts of the past four years, following as they had on already superhuman efforts of reconstruction and re-education after the Revolution, had brought leaders of the Party everywhere beyond the edge of exhaustion. He wondered how many had an Evgeni on their conscience as he did: almost everyone, he guessed. For the accomplishment of even partial socialism, of collectivization, the creation of industrial discipline in a peasant country where the idea of regulating life by unknown clocks was an unacceptable novelty to many, could nowhere have been achieved without its sacrifices. It was still difficult to accept some of the things which had been done, and Kolya knew from his own experience what the haggard, guarded faces around him must hide. For when one is attempting to erect success as a defense against conscience, then the utmost ruthlessness with oneself and with others becomes the only acceptable standard.

Evgeni had been shot in Smolensk after months of imprisonment. Nearly two years later, when Anna told him how the boy, unbalanced by guilt, had had to be sent to a hospital for treatment, he learned that it had been Evgeni's youngest son who had used the camshaft as a Napoleonic cannon in war games with his friends. It was the final bitterness to know that Evgeni had died protecting someone whom Kolya himself would have immediately agreed was better punished privately.

He had resisted the exile order on Evgeni's family, their presence a living reproach, but at the same time a spur to sagging, exhausted effort. If he failed now at Klintsy, Evgeni's death became nothing but an unforgivable, sour farce.

In 1932 a full-time political officer was appointed to all sovkhoz, and Klintsy was sent one of the new generation of Party activists. Lieutenant Bezhov of the GPU was twenty-two years old and knew Marx and Lenin almost by heart, when some older Party members believed their message but found the words difficult to understand. He watched them all, and Kolya knew the boy was laughing at them behind their backs, biding his time and laying traps with the irrational joy of a child at play.

With Bezhov's arrival repression increased. Two sovkhozniks were shot the same year and another six the year after when harmless old Chapeta, the Party Organizer, was found with his throat cut. The culprit was probably one of the many with a new, personal grudge against the Party which had destroyed their lives but no serious criminal investigation was attempted.

Discipline was less and less Kolya's affair; neither could he decide any longer what food stocks were to be kept back on the sovkhoz. Targets became meaningless as nearly everything they produced was stripped from them the moment it was harvested, and malnutrition appeared even at Klintsy in the midst of plenty. Rumors of famine elsewhere were rife as the battle with the peasants went remorselessly forward; only Director Berdeyev's past success at Klintsy giving him any leverage against insatiable official demands. He no longer believed that there could be any justification for this Party-made disaster but it was too late; he could do nothing but labor to the limits of his strength to make it a success and save as many of those committed to his care as possible.

A decree allowing Party members full salaries rather than the wage of a skilled worker was another shock, although he and Anna continued to draw at the old rate. It was intolerable that after so much effort and sacrifice they could perhaps be thought to be doing it all for money. They also had the same rations as other sovkhozniks, knew the same anguish as Sophie and Yuri grew listless and whining on inadequate food. The only brightness of those years came from Anna, who through it all remained serenely confident and untroubled by doubt. A new world could not be won without supreme effort, and if one last struggle was needed to free man from the shackles of war, disease and want in which he had been fettered for so long by his own greed, so be it. In Kolya's arms at night she wept over the suffering around them, but each day she turned her back on despair, made even the children see their want as a gift they gave to a shining future.

Bezhov came into the Director's office one morning soon after the decree on Party members' salaries and tossed a packet on the desk. "Your pay. A bit old-fashioned, aren't you?"

Kolya flushed violently, possessed by a rage he could scarcely control as this insolent youth trampled casually over his private beliefs. "What I choose to draw is none of your business. Get out of my office before I kick you out."

"You are wrong, Comrade People's Director Berdeyev, you are wrong. It is my business. The Party has decreed proper salaries for its members, so you will draw what you are told, if I have to stuff it up your backside."

Kolya knocked him down and very little in his life had given him so much satisfaction. Rumyantsev saved him from Party reprimand, probably arrest, but Bezhov stayed on.

It was not just Rumyantsev who saved him; it was his own technical competence. With want and starvation everywhere shriveling the countryside, the massive production quotas from Klintsy were a gleam of hope, showing what could be done. The Party, for the moment, would forgive much for success.

Slowly, as 1933 drew on, the sullen mood had begun to lift. The sovkhozniks were stirred again by a sense of achievement as perfect weather ripened a full harvest, permission to keep anything surplus to quota at last restored. What had been sown in resentment was reaped in a rush of spontaneous happiness as sun and shower in exact sequence turned fullness to bounty and bounty into abundance. Kolya even managed to obtain a load of goods for the sovkhoz store, so wages were not just meaningless scraps of paper any more. Above all there was food again: the first eggs many children had been allowed to eat, cucumber in place of strips of bark, bread made of corn instead of the sweepings of barn and sawmill.

Pyotr the stockman married a Selnyi girl that autumn and the whole of Klintsy joined in the celebrations, with grain to spare for vodka and beer. It was the day when Klintsy rejoiced at the end of hard times and marked the reintegration of itself: fiddles scraped far into the night, accordions teased even ancient feet into rhythm and few remained sober for long. Kolya and Anna attended, but withdrew early to let everyone enjoy themselves without constraint.

Afterward they wandered, wordless, hand in hand over the quiet stripped fields, brilliant ocher in the setting sun. The children tumbled and shrieked ahead of them, half-starved lassitude of previous months already banished.

"It is done," said Anna at last, softly. "Oh, Kolyushka, my love, it is truly done at last."

He held her fingers to his lips. "And I still love you more and more each year. Do you realize we are ten years wed next month?"

"What a ten years they have been," she said reflectively. "In spite of all the suffering, it is something after all to have built a new world. We are lucky to have been a part of it."

Kolya thought of Evgeni and winced. He had become the symbol in his mind for all the splendid vision which the past four years had almost ground out of him and which Anna had so miraculously preserved intact.

"Perhaps, but now we have done our part, it might be better if we were swept aside to let those with clean hands take over."

"Sometimes I quite lose patience with you!" she snapped, in the quick way she occasionally did. "We have had to endure much, but Comrade Stalin was surely right not to let us rest and start counting kopecks like a pack of *bourzhuis!* You know you have done nothing of which to be ashamed."

"I don't look like a man with nothing to be ashamed of," he observed wryly.

She glanced at him and her expression softened. "I love you how you are. What you have achieved shows too."

He laughed and they strolled on. It was true he did not look like a man of only thirty-three. Apart from the old scar on his neck and still occasionally tiresome inflammation of the eyes, his face was unhealthily devoid of color, both from poor food and constant anxiety. Recently a nervous bunching of muscles in cheek and jaw had given his expression a curious, wary tension which degenerated into a recurrent flick under pressure—and Party members were never free from the terrible pressure of imperative instructions, resistant facts, nagging doubts and guilt-laden actions.

"Rumyantsev wants to put me on the list of regional Party candidates for the Congress next February," he remarked. "What do you think?"

"Well, of course! What an honor for you and Klintsy! You didn't think of refusing, did you?"

He shrugged. "I'm not sure it is right for people like me to go."

She stopped abruptly and forced him to face her, then slid her arms around his neck. "Kolyushka, you will destroy yourself like this. You must get away from this obsession with the past. Your strength has carried us all through this terrible time; you mustn't give up now."

He looked down at her pleading face, dark eyes intent on his. Although he was not particularly tall, she had to stand on tiptoe to reach him. "You haven't got a single gray hair yet," he said irrelevantly.

"Still like pig food," she agreed mischievously. She watched the lines of his face ease with laughter and then added gently, "You make a mistake, you know, love, if you think the young are pure and merciful. It is surely us who should have learned something from experience. Who knows better than you the cost of what we have achieved, will guard it so we do not have to pay again? It is you who know the horror of having to deal with an Evgeni, not some boy drunk with the excitement of power."

Kolya watched Sophie and Yuri playing leapfrog on the stubble, their clear young voices shrilling in the dusk. His arms tightened around her and they kissed, slowly and quietly, the time one of contentment rather than passion. She felt him smiling: "You may say it is my strength, but I think it is your vision which has sustained us. You are like one of those whalebone corsets women used to wear. No one can bend while you are around, but inside all is such grace and softness."

So here he was, a Western Oblast Party representative to the 1934 Party Congress, seated alongside fat, sweaty, hard-working Rumyantsev and listening to thunderous applause for Kirov after a speech which everyone considered to be an oblique appeal for moderation after the helterskelter ruthlessness of the Five Year Plan just finished. Few doubted that Kirov's election as a secretary of the Central Committee was a first step toward a possible change of leadership; equally, very few had any idea how such a change could be effected.

Kolya's eyes were drawn to the present leader of

the Party, Josef Vissarion'itch Stalin, sitting inscrutably on the platform, watchful, endlessly patient. Indeed it was this feeling of patience which had impressed itself on Kolya. He had seen a delegate go up to Stalin the day before and ask him something, at great length and with much gesticulation, a fussy, self-important little nobody from a back province. Stalin had stood, quite unhurried, listening, nodding, vital events and people eddying around him while he apparently gave full attention to whatever problem it was put before him. Here without doubt was a leader to be respected even if, for Kolya, hatred was not far away either. It was his unflinching determination which had demanded such sacrifices from them, his authority before which the delegates quailed so fearfully that every sentence he uttered was greeted by cheers, while his slightest suspicion made them physically ill. Already Kirov was looking uncomfortable at his eminence, his friends spreading rumors that he was sickening for influenza.

Looking at the closed faces around him, listening with distaste to frenzied applause and sycophantic speeches, Kolya could find few clues to the real feelings of the Congress, could scarcely clarify his own thoughts. He had voted for Kirov, hoping desperately that the overtones of conciliation and compromise in his speeches reflected his true feelings and were not just a charade concerted with the Khozyain to still the delegates' doubts. But who really knew what was truth any longer in this uncharted world they now inhabited?

At the giant rally marking the end of the Congress, it became clear that the Muscovites at least had few doubts. They greeted Kirov's fiery speech on behalf of all the delegates with almost hysterical delight, every reference to conciliation the signal for more waves of cheering.

The choice was surely made, and Kolya felt a deep if slightly guilty relief. The people had reasserted that they were human beings, not revolution fodder. Flesh and blood could not stand any more. After seventeen years of exhausting struggle, Kirov and conciliation were what they wanted, what they now demanded so unmistakably that the Party could scarcely batter through any more of its ideals without a cost too appalling to contemplate.

Kolya looked along the dais at Stalin. He was staring calmly at the crowds, quite relaxed, almost resigned.

Five months later the Central Committee announced that a drafting committee had been established to draw up a new constitution for the Soviet Union, a constitution which was to be a milestone along man's road to democracy, embodying all the rights to which a revolutionary people were entitled. Even those who had disagreed with Stalin in the past were included on the committee, men like Bukharin, who had attempted to defend the peasants against the assaults of the state, Radek and Rakovsky, whose names had scarcely been heard for years.

Conciliation had come at last.

Part Five
COLD ASH
1934-41

Chapter Thirty

"Kirov has been shot! I've just heard it on Radio Moscow." Anna met him halfway down the road home, the biting wind of December insufficient to deter her urgency. "He was killed instantly."

"Shot? Who by?" Kolya felt stunned. They had often discussed the events of the previous February Congress and he had given carefully noncommittal talks on it to various Party cells in the area. The reception of even the little he had to tell was so enthusiastic that it was hard to imagine anyone wanting to assassinate Kirov, on whom so many hopes rested.

Anna shrugged. "Some madman, I think. They say he was in the pay of foreign diplomats."

They listened to almost every news broadcast of the next few days, to the solemn music and heartfelt tributes. Kirov had been shot as he went into his office in Party headquarters in Leningrad, the assassin Nicolayev was already arrested and had confessed to receiving payments from a foreign fascist power. In retaliation 104 anti-Soviet plotters in prison in Leningrad had been executed.

"I don't see how that can help," said Anna, always scrupulously fair. "If they were already in prison they can't have been to blame."

Kolya shook his head. "They had probably not been

shot before because Kirov wished to be done with executions. It looks like the reversal of his ideas already." Perhaps it is also Stalin who wishes by instant retribution, to make sure the habit of assassination is not catching, he thought grimly.

Gradually shock and unease died down as nothing else happened, and it was early in the new year before Party members were summoned to a meeting in Smolensk to pay tribute to the dead leader.

"We'll leave the children with Agafa and have the night out," said Kolya cheerfully. "Lev was telling me there is quite a good little place opened up in Lenin Square." They had mourned sincerely for Kirov and neither felt it wrong to use such a rare opportunity for their own pleasure.

As they walked to the station together, Kolya put his arm around her waist and kissed her. "You are as beautiful as the day we married."

She laughed at him. "More beautiful, I hope. I spent most of the afternoon in tears."

As he looked at her, he realized it was true, she was more beautiful now. The love and generosity he had sensed in her then was now clear for all to see in the warmth of her expression and the soft curve of her lips. The contentment and certainty which the years had brought showed in the unshadowed contours of her face, while for him alone there was the light of her eyes, the instant spark of contact which a look alone could bring.

She had kept her slender figure, too, and the touch of elegance he had noticed even in the squalor of Kamenny Barracks. Her colored cotton kerchief was knotted casually around her throat instead of smothering her hair as the other women wore it; when he had brought some old harness home she spent hours polishing the links and buckles with brick dust and then wore them twisted with leather as a belt. Sometimes she and Sophie would tease out threads from some old scrap of material so she could use them to embroider little flowers on cuff or pocket and Kolya longed to be able to buy her something—anything—which would be gay and colorful, but there was nothing. Instead, there came to be perhaps the greater happiness of looking around him for some of the many things which gave her pleasure: a curiously shaped piece of bark for the mantelpiece, some drilled bone for buttons, the weeks of winter evenings he spent one year, chipping and polishing a flecked pebble they had found in a stream before getting Valentin, the ex-goldsmith, to set it as a brooch.

They jumped the train together, Kolya hauling her up at almost the last second as the six Party members going from Klintsy had the same half minute to scramble aboard. There was an almost festive atmosphere, relaxation still too strong a draught to take without intoxication. Anna smiled as she watched Kolya arguing with Venzher about the possible form of a new constitution; this time last year he would never have suggested turning a Party meeting into an excuse for a night out.

"The Director has forgotten the affair of Evgeni at last," said Vera's voice in her ear.

"He never will forget it," she replied seriously. "I think he does now accept it. I wish he had let the family be resettled elsewhere, though. With two of his children already working on the sovkhoz and another leaving school nearly every year, he can never get away from them."

"It is seeing the way he looks at them which has made the people forgive him," said Vera wisely. "And Evgeni was a fool, too. If he had told the Director that the little Sasha had done it then all would have been well. Even a workman would only have got five years for carelessness. Evgeni walked on his own fate. Our people know it was not the passing whim of a tyrant which made the Director do it."

"It was not right for him to be forced into such a choice. The Party should not turn every error into charges of sabotage and treason," said Anna slowly, surprised at her own words. "It was fear of what would happen to anyone he disciplined which allowed matters to reach the point where he could give way no longer."

Vera looked at her in surprise, the Comrade Doctor was known throughout the sovkhoz for her uncompromising Party ideals. "You have changed," she said bluntly.

Anna laughed. "Perhaps we all have a feeling that the worst is over. We have won and have nothing to fear if we relax a little."

"If you can relax, Comrade Anna, then we can certainly look for a change from the Party." Vera's eyes twinkled. "A six-legged calf will be an act of God again instead of a capitalist plot." A few months ago she would not have dared make such a joke, and the Comrade Doctor would not have laughed.

The meeting was crowded, dense with Party members from the whole district, but Rumyantsev on the platform sat silent and abstracted. Usually he shouted greetings and barbed cracks across the noisiest assembly, the guttural roar of his voice flaying latecomers unmercifully. When at length he rose to speak, his voice was strained and harsh, a perfunctory comment on Kirov occupying barely a minute. "Comrades," he went on, after a brief pause, "we are faced by a situation of great danger. Comrade Stalin personally investigated the assassination of Comrade Kirov, and has questioned the traitor Nicolayev at length. He discovered some terrible things, above all that the ranks of the Party are riddled with traitors."

There was a concerted sigh throughout the hall yet

nobody moved so much as a hand, all rigid with shock, foreboding and sheer astonishment.

Rumyantsev, wiped his forehead and continued rapidly: "Fifteen Komsomolniks were executed with Nicolayev, but before they died they made still more terrible disclosures. This was not the mad scheme of a few Leningraders corrupted by foreign imperialists, but a deep-laid counterrevolutionary plot. Comrades, some of the leaders of the Party placed the gun in Nicolayev's hand! Even before this they had showed themselves as class enemies by arguing against our great leader Stalin . . ." He paused for applause, but once it started no one wished to be observed as the first to stop, and Rumyantsev did not dare to check it.

The clapping went on and on, giving the meeting an air of almost hysterical force, dying down from sheer exhaustion at last as everyone continued the motions but sound gradually faded away. When Rumyantsev resumed he looked more harassed than ever. "The utmost vigilance is now necessary, for it is certain there are thousands of masked enemies within our ranks, who must be rooted out ruthlessly. These are to be found even in the highest places: the arch-traitors Zinoviev and Kamenev have already been arrested to face charges which will make every honest citizen howl with anger." He sat down suddenly and Kolya remembered that Rumyantsev was an old colleague of Zinoviev and in times past rather given to boasting about his connection with such an important man.

A delegate sprang to his feet in the front of the hall. "Comrades, may I at once set on record the horror of the Smolensk Party at such perfidy. We must all resolve to be ruthless and vigilant in seeking out and denouncing traitors."

There were shouts of agreement, as delegates rushed to show enthusiasm for the new line, to dissociate themselves from those now plainly doomed before it was too late. It was also resolved without a single dissenting voice, although Kolya was probably not alone in feeling shame at his silence, that the records of every member should be scrutinized and the Party urged to act immediately on any suspicion which was aroused.

As Kolya and Anna left the hall Lev passed them, saying softly, "It is the end of making those parts for you, Konstantin Aleksandr'itch."

"I will collect what you have tonight," Kolya replied swiftly, thinking of the vital replacements which should be waiting for him.

"No, I throw them back in the foundry the moment I return. Don't come near me for more."

"It has begun," said Kolya bitterly, looking after him. "Conciliation is over, even the trust between comrades is over."

"Don't be ridiculous." To Anna the carefree sensations of the journey into Smolensk still seemed more real than the meeting, which was too bizarre to assimilate. "Of course the Party has to seek out its enemies when such a terrible thing happens. True comrades have nothing to fear."

"Can't you see it is more than that? What motive did the more moderate members of the Party have for murdering Kirov? Rightly or wrongly he was their hope for the future. Kirov did not help his own murderer into Party headquarters, but someone did. The NKVD guard all entrances and answer only to the central control of the Party."

"What are you saying?" She stared at him, white-faced.

He shrugged. "I don't know. No one knows. But apparently every Party member is expected to regard all his comrades as potential traitors when we haven't the slightest idea what really happened. I do know who controls the NKVD, though, and who is likely to gain from Kirov's death even if it wasn't planned."

"Kolya, you must never suggest such things, not even in your heart! It is the most terrible treachery!"

He looked at her appraisingly; she was shocked at him for saying it, not for a moment concerned in case he might be right. Why should he argue, when her serene belief might save her, his suspicions put him at risk? He sighed. "We had better go straight back to Klintsy; the more we keep out of Smolensk for a while the better." The return to unshadowed loving, their new peace and tranquillity was crumbling almost as he watched.

Three weeks later Lev David'itch was expelled from the Party and dismissed as manager of the factory he had guided to such remarkable achievement. On his next visit to Smolensk, Kolya called at Lev's little apartment overlooking the factory, where previously he had enjoyed even the smuts and smoke which intruded on his few hours of leisure, joking that the red glow of the foundry sent him to sleep.

"Konstantin Aleksandr'itch, you should not have come." He was trembling at the unexpected knock on his door.

Kolya laughed. "It's a poor outlook for us all if we can't visit a comrade in trouble. The Party puts a duty on us to reclaim backsliders."

Lev's fingers, the precision instruments of a born engineer, fumbled helplessly with the samovar. "It is all over with me, with you too I expect. This is not like the old days when Party discipline was meant to help and support, none of us will escape. Did you know that poor old Antonochka with his one leg has lost his job?"

Kolya stared at him unbelievingly. "Antonochka? In God's name, why? He isn't even a Party member."

Lev laughed bitterly. "No doubt because I had

the common humanity to chat with him a moment each day. Why else?"

"I'll ask him if he would like to come and live at Klintsy." Kolya resented his feeling of fear as he said it, ashamed of the temptation not to say it.

Lev shook his head. "It would only help prove that he must have been part of an oppositionist group, if people like us bother about him." He put his head in his hands. "Comradeship, that was what the Revolution was all about, remember? Now it is a man's death warrant."

"What can we do?" Kolya spoke his thoughts aloud; it was scarcely a question.

"Nothing." Lev did not look up. "Why do you think the Party is being turned into a place of terror instead of honor, but to take the means of doing anything away from us? How can a man think of defiance when all his thoughts are on how to save himself, preserve his family from disaster?"

Kolya tried to divert his thoughts, thoughts which uncomfortably mirrored his own. "Why were you expelled?"

Lev gave a sharp bark of angry laughter. "They found deviations in my attitude to my work and in talks I've given to Party cells about industrialization. There was even a suggestion I had indulged in sabotage when I stopped machinery for maintenance. No one mentioned your spares which might have been a valid cause for complaint."

"Who manages the factory in your place?"

"A fellow called Ivanov. I believe he's quite competent, but the workers resent him and have already denounced him for counter-revolution. He won't last. Ridiculous, isn't it?"

Kolya fidgeted restlessly around the tiny, shabby room. Framed Party commendations, a bad photograph of a little girl about Sophie's age, an old yellowed group in tsarist uniforms waving a revolutionary flag; with difficulty he recognized a grinning Lev in the front row. "What will you do now?"

"What can I do? Wait for the knock on the door, I suppose."

"You should leave here," said Kolya suddenly. "Go as far away as possible, take an ordinary job in one of the new developments. Change jobs often and keep moving for a year or so; as you've been dismissed you must have your papers."

Lev rubbed his face slowly. "You may be right, but it looks like an admission of guilt. I've done nothing wrong. If I could believe I'd be given a trial, then I'd have nothing to fear. At least if they take me here like an innocent man my wife and daughter may be spared. My wife's family live here too; she will need support when I am gone. Without help a condemned traitor's family will starve, be hounded from job to job by those too terrified of contamination to employ them."

"Better try to stay together if you can." Kolya felt sad and helpless. "Is there anything I can do?"

Lev shook his head. "You keep away. It was good of you to come but don't do it again. Good-by, old friend." They embraced silently, it was like saying good-by to the Party they had known as well. Kolya never saw him again and never knew whether he had been arrested or had taken his advice and moved away. He telephoned once, to be told the line was disconnected, and when he walked past a few weeks later the apartment was occupied by a new official from Moscow.

Chapter Thirty-one

The following months were immensely confusing.

The harvest was again excellent and the food position improved rapidly. Bread cards were withdrawn and kolkhozniks encouraged to farm their own plots once their labor days on the collective were complete: still more amazing, they were allowed to sell their produce on the open market. Conciliation was apparently still the policy, with glowing reports of the new Stalin Constitution soon to come into force. Party newspapers were full of honors and awards to ordinary people, Orders of the Red Star, of Labor, and of Lenin following each other with bewildering rapidity. For millions life was obviously improving at last, binding them to the Party Leader and encouraging their resentment against local officials who had been the hated vanguard of the past upheaval in their lives.

Many younger people suddenly discovered an attractive new avenue of promotion. If you coveted a job or a higher position in the Party, then all that was necessary was criticism of your superior and, sometimes within days, he disappeared. Life for some became an exciting progress as the path to higher responsibilities was cleared by such simple methods; that they in their turn might become the target for such attacks occurred to very few. It took a little while for the full possibilities to be realized, rather longer for those who stood to gain so much to grasp that the exhaustion, tension and mistakes of those above them constituted counterrevolution, but, once started, the process was irreversible, slowly gaining momentum and swinging ever outward from its axis.

Although the great had most to fear from the intoxication of power in unaccustomed and frequently unidentifiable hands, the humble, like Antonochka, often suffered too in the wash of hysteria, resentment and fear sweeping the country.

Vera came hammering at their door one evening, breathless with laughter and haste so they could scarcely make sense of what she was saying.

"Bezhov?" said Anna, frowning. "What is he up to at this time of night?"

"It is Kiril. You know," she glanced fleetingly at Kolya, "Evgeni's second boy."

"What about him?" interrupted Anna hastily, frightened of seeing the look on Kolya's face which mention of Evgeni usually brought.

"He was bedding some girl in the piggery—"

Anna burst out laughing. "What a place! Couldn't he find anywhere better than that?"

Vera wiped her eyes and chuckled. "I don't think I should have been too pleased with the piggery in my day."

"Why have you come here with such a tale?" Kolya could not keep the coldness from his tone; the very name Evgeni stripped his nerves bare to the blast of conscience.

"I wouldn't come running like an old gossip to her hedge, you know that, Konstantin Aleksandri'tch." Vera could not hide her hurt. "But Bezhov says they disturbed the breeding sows . . ." She could not help giggling again. ". . . They must be very young and vigorous to have upset all the sows and Bezhov too!"

Anna glanced at her husband's set face. "What happened?"

"He had dragged Kiril off and is accusing him of sabotaging sovkhoz pig production targets. I ask you, does he think the boy lay with the sows by mistake?"

Anna laughed. "You can't be serious?"

"Since when did the Bezhovs of this world say anything they didn't mean?" Kolya pushed his chair back angrily.

Anna put a hand on his arm. "What are you going to do?"

"Get the boy out before a formal accusation is filed. Once the word sabotage is written down it is ten years in a labor camp at the very least."

"Ten years for making love in a piggery?" she echoed blankly.

"Ten years for sabotage. Who will worry or even listen to what the sabotage was?" He pulled on his coat with quick, fumbling jerks.

Anna looked at him anxiously. "Be careful, Kolyushka."

His eyes narrowed; normally rather pale, his face was thickly flushed. Anna had only once or twice seen him like this and it meant that his usually well-controlled temper was about to burst out of its cage. "Why? Why the hell should I stand by and see one of my workers, a boy of eighteen, sent for ten years to Siberia for finding a piggery the only warm place to bed his girl on an October night? We none of us bled or sweated our guts out for a Party which would do that." He went out, slamming the door behind him.

"I'm sorry," said Vera unhappily. "I didn't think."

"No," Anna smiled briefly. "He is right. The Party wouldn't expect us to suffer because a wrong choice was made for once, and a callow lout sent here dressed up in a uniform too big for him. We shouldn't have been patient so long."

Vera eyed her doubtfully. "Bezhov had the confidence of the Party. The Director knocked him down and he is still here."

"The Director is still here too," Anna pointed out.

"Don't worry, whatever Bezhov may be, we can rely on the justice of the Party. The Director could take the case to Comrade Rumyantsev if necessary; he may be harsh, but he is not spiteful."

*

Although gripped by violent anger, Kolya was thinking hard as he half ran toward the village. Speed was vital; if a formal charge were once made, nothing short of murder or arson would reverse police processes. Arrived at Bezhov's office, he waited a moment to control his breathing and then walked in.

Kiril and a girl he could not name were standing in front of the desk with Bezhov lounging behind it, his face alight with malicious laughter.

Kolya took in the blank ledger and triplicate police forms at a glance. "A good joke, I trust?"

"Comrade Director!" exclaimed Kiril with relief, forgetting he had never exchanged anything except formalities with his father's murderer before.

Kolya ignored him, staring at Bezhov. "Tell me your joke, Bezhov. I have an excellent sense of humor."

"It isn't a joke," snapped Bezhov. "Unless the Comrade Director thinks sabotage a joke?"

"No. Do you?" asked Kolya sweetly.

"Certainly not! What the devil do you mean?"

"I mean that anyone who pulls in a boy for questioning because a couple of sows squeal with envy, when he reminds them they have been too long off the boar, must have either the inclinations of a Peeping Tom or the sense of humor of a guttersnipe. You puling little swine, what made you think you could play practical jokes with the Party?"

"I am not playing jokes," Bezhov too was flushed with anger. "I have caught a pair of saboteurs in the act."

"Oh yes, certainly," said Kolya caustically. "In the act of what?"

For the first time Bezhov hesitated.

"Well?" Kolya pressed home his advantage. "Kiril did it, you watched it, I am a married man with two children. You tell me what they did."

"They disturbed the sows," said Bezhov sullenly.

"A boy takes his girl out and they run around disturbing a pack of sows?" Kolya gave a bark of laughter. "You miserable little sod. I asked you what they did."

"All right then, they . . . he took her and raped her. The struggle disturbed the sows."

Without taking his eyes off Bezhov, Kolya addressed the girl: "Do you prefer a charge of rape?"

"No," she whispered. "I wanted to go."

"You see?" said Kolya softly to Bezhov. "The Soviet state encourages its citizens to feel free to mate with whom they will, unhindered by the old ties of inequality. There is no charge of rape."

"I was not going to charge them with rape. It was sabotage."

"Very well, then. Write it down. 'A girl and her boy made love in the hay, the pigs squealed, it was sabotage.' Then you have the gut-rotting insolence to tell me you aren't holding the Party up to contempt in the interests of your private jokes? What's the matter, did you fancy the girl yourself?"

"No!" Bezhov lunged up from his desk.

Kolya stared at him in silence and then turned to Kiril and the girl. "Get out. Go home and don't speak of this to anyone."

"What the devil do you think you are doing? You can't interfere with a political officer and his duty!" Bezhov dipped his hand toward his holster, only to feel the Director's hand fasten paralyzingly on his arm.

"I can't interfere with your duty, but I can and will prevent you harming the Party through your spite and perversion. A charge of sabotage goes through without question, the charge you have to write here and now, while I watch, would get you expelled from the Party for moral delinquency. I tell them to keep their mouths shut for your sake and the sake of the Party, not theirs." He let go of Bezhov's arm. "Well?"

Bezhov looked him full in the eyes. "One day it will be you on your knees in front of me."

"Dear me," said Kolya mildly, anger suddenly spent. "Melodrama as well as practical jokes. Once boys are in uniform it is difficult to remember just how young they still are." He pushed Kiril and the girl out of the room in front of him. "If you come to me in the morning I will approve any application you make for papers, so you can move to town for a while. I think you would both be better away from Klintsy."

"God, yes," said Kiril fervently. "I have to thank you, Comrade Director, for helping us." He looked stiff and uncomfortable as he recollected what lay between them.

"No, this was one thing I was glad to be able to do." It was true: it was good to stand and fight and win again.

As 1936 drew on, though, this brief victory was revealed as illusion. Nothing except the weapon of terror in their midst had meaning any more. In Moscow, Kamenev and Zinoviev were put on trial charged with Kirov's murder, with spying and sabotage, these staunch leaders of the Party with thirty years of dedicated service to the Revolution.

"These are people we have long admired," said Anna, wrinkling her brows in puzzlement. "It is incredible that the Party has survived at all with so many of its leaders seeking to wreck it. You can tell from the evidence they are nearly all implicated."

"They have been in prison eighteen months," replied Kolya briefly. "They have families, children, belief in the Party they still cannot deny."

She paled. "The Party would not use such methods! Even the Tsar didn't threaten the families of revolutionaries! Surely you can't read such evidence and still believe them innocent?"

He turned away wearily; the bitterness of constant disagreement was corrosive, even their love no longer proof against it. "It is the fog of not knowing anything except what we are told which has killed the Party."

"The Party is not dead," said Anna confidently. "It can survive anything, even the treachery of its leaders. This trial proves it."

"I hope you're right." He spoke almost with resignation, but to his mind it was Stalin and the NKVD who had betrayed the Party, and it was not they who were on trial.

Shortly afterward an order came for a general reregistration of Party members. This had occurred at regular intervals in the past but this time it acquired an inquisitorial cutting edge which left no one safe. Old Party cards were called in and then, after a nerve-stretching interval, members faced individual interrogation before a special investigating commission. Those who failed to obtain new cards from this commission immediately lost their jobs and usually disappeared within days, to what fate no one knew.

With each day of waiting Kolya and Anna found it more difficult to struggle against the pressures driving them apart. Contentment and self-confidence were eroded by the impossibility of discussing even everyday events, Kolya fearing to endanger Anna by revealing the extent of his disillusion and horror, Anna alarmed lest any attempt on her part to overcome his doubts appeared to question his loyalty.

Inhibition spread from one area to another of their relationship, even the children watching them in constant anxiety to judge whether a chance word would shrivel chatter into silence again. They still found solace in each other's arms, but there too, subtly and against their will, there was a change. Had either been able to hide their thoughts, or in the past been less in harmony with the other, it might have been easier. As it was, there was infinite pain in knowing how each was striving to exclude more and more of themselves from a union which had once been so complete.

Because they tried so hard, because they had so much to save, they were successful, but success was a destroyer too. When so much of self was ruthlessly banished the sweet ease of spontaneity was lost, the cancerous growth of isolation and bitterness creeping even into the comfort of physical love. About this too, they could not speak.

Venzher was the first Party member from Klintsy to be summoned before the commission. He arrived back the same day, safe with his new card but unable to voice his obvious relief, which itself could cast doubts on the justice of the Party.

Anna belonged to the hospital cell in Smolensk and was reregistered without difficulty. She had never considered the possibility she might not be, but the day she came home with her new card Kolya drank a great deal too much vodka. The heads of the surgery, pathology and radiography departments in the hospital were all expelled and lost their positions, their places taken by their delighted deputies. Anna was upset and mystified to think such dangerous reactionaries should have been found in the hospital itself.

"Although I knew all of them graduated from the old University of St. Petersburg, I had never thought them disloyal," she said regretfully. "Being old, I suppose they could not forget the past. I hope they don't lose their pensions; they have served the hospital well even if the Party is perhaps right not to trust them."

Kolya did not reply, knowing how expulsion from the Party was almost invariably a prelude to arrest.

Then Vera went for investigation.

"A good journey, Comrade." Kolya could not let her go without even a word.

"To hell with them, Konstantin Aleksandr'itch. I was serving the Party when they were still in the egg, they can't accuse me of anything." She tightened her shawl with an angry tug. "I don't know what we've come to, wasting our time like a bunch of silly kids when there is proper work to be done. I'd like to have the lot of them shoveling out my cowshed."

"Don't tell them so. For your own sake keep your mouth shut, and for mine, don't tell them I said so."

Her mouth fell open. "Konstantin Aleksandr'itch, you of all men do not take this nonsense seriously? I am a good Communist and we're all workers here, what have we to fear?"

"What makes you call it nonsense, Comrade?"

"Well, it is!" she snapped. "Thousands of counter-revolutionaries waiting to be unmasked, I ask you, where would we find such people at Klintsy?"

"But you think they might be present elsewhere?"

"Well, I don't know. How could I?" She began to look alarmed.

"Yet you presume to call it nonsense when you admit you do not know? This could be called anti-Party activity, Comrade." He looked at her unblinkingly.

"For God's sake, Comrade Director . . ." Her lips began to shake.

"And the Party has always maintained that excessive calling on the name of God could show the survival of superstition. You should surely have overcome such a fault if you are a sincere Party member."

She stared at him speechlessly, slowly rubbing stained, cracked hands on her ugly, work-torn dress.

"You see, Vera," said Kolya at last, gently. "It will not matter what you say, if they wish they will trip you up. Answer exactly what they ask, not a word more."

He watched her go with a heavy heart; she was surely too outspoken and simple to survive. To his relief and surprise she did return the next day, but with an official reprimand inscribed on her card.

"They said my work for the Party showed evidence of bad thought." She had obviously been unable to retain the long words of the original condemnation. "A reprimand! Twenty years in the Party and now a reprimand!"

Kolya privately thought her lucky, but she was inconsolable, the humiliation of official reprimand all the more unbearable because her sincerity made her search endlessly for her fault, leafing over the difficult print of Marx and Lenin, unable to find anyone to help her for fear of contamination.

Vanka, the forestry head, went next and never returned. Three days later two of his foresters were arrested, their families driven away, their cottages boarded up. It was not easy for Kolya to find the courage to ask about the charge, and when he did he met only a blank stare from the officer in charge.

"Matters of state, Comrade Director." He showed his NKVD identity care. "No affair of yours, unless you're involved, of course." He stared at Kolya insolently. "Under investigation yourself at the moment, aren't you?"

Kolya felt the blood leave his face. "No."

He laughed and turned away. "Every little tin-pot boss is being cut down to size. We want no capitalist attitudes here, you'll see."

Bezhov, who was watching, laughed too.

That night Kolya lay a long time beside Anna, listening to her breathing and to the slight rustle as either Yuri or Sophie turned over in their straw. "Anna," he said at last, softly.

"Mm?" She turned over sleepily, feeling for him instinctively in the darkness.

"Anna, I think you should put in for that course of surgery you have always wanted to take."

The soft movements of her body against his ceased abruptly and her eyes flicked open. "Are you crazy? It would mean living in a hospital for two or three years, probably not even in Smolensk. Ever since I felt myself truly married to you I have never wanted it at that price."

He held her tightly. "I know, *vazlublenny*. But I think now you should put in for it."

"Why?" She pushed him away and sat up.

He hesitated. "There are many reasons. Sophie's music would benefit from better teaching in the city; Yuri too could go to a technical school." He smiled slightly, unseen in the dark. At eleven years old, solemn, steady little Yuri wanted to be a flier, his imagination caught by stories of pioneering Soviet airmen in the arctic.

"Kolyushka, you mustn't try to relive your lost music through Sophie; she has not the drive and spark you once had." Anna lay back stiffly beside him, staring unseeingly at the reflections on the ceiling, faint, like reversed negatives on the whitewashed surface. He could hear the hurt in her voice, rasping his own unhappiness. In the old days she would not have so quickly misinterpreted him, when the barriers of the mind had been against the outside world and never against each other.

"Perhaps she hasn't" His tone was deliberately offhand. "Who knows? I was just pointing out as tactfully as I could that the children at least might be better off if we parted awhile."

"Why should we?" The misery of past months congealed abruptly at his words.

"I haven't been summoned to Smolensk yet for my

new card. I don't know what will happen when I am."

"Oh, Kolya!" She kissed him. "What a fool you are! Of course you have nothing to fear."

Instinctively his arms went around her, longing for the comfort of her body, but it was no good, he could not thus accomplish the separation which might secure her survival and that of Sophie and Yuri. He rolled away and sat on the edge of the bed. "No one who has administered anything fails to leave grounds for complaint against him. What of the forestry department here under my control, where they seen to have found some fault? Or of my dealings with Lev, if he was arrested?" And what of the bitter enmity of Bezhov, he thought but did not say.

"I don't care," she said stubbornly. "We stay together. You are a sincere Party member; it isn't as if you were a class enemy with something to hide. There may have been mistakes here and there, I think there was with Lev, but you are speaking as if the Party were deliberately trying to destroy itself."

"Perhaps it is. As I keep saying, we don't know any longer what is happening."

"Oh, rubbish!" She could have shaken him. "The Party is only seeking out treason and crime—what is wrong in that? I've heard you say often enough that some Party members are unworthy of their trust or have been too harsh in their methods. What complaint have you if the commission takes them from behind their desks of power and makes them drive a tractor or a lathe again?"

He wanted to shout at her, make her see the truth of what happened to those the commission condemned, but such an argument would be futile. If he convinced her of his danger, she would never go. Staring at the wall, he said, "I don't think it is logical any more, or a question of innocence or guilt." Just power, he reflected bitterly, with Stalin in the middle of it. When this is finished he will preside over a desert stripped bare by the fear and lust and power he has created. "Everyone at the hospital knows of your desire to learn surgery; it wouldn't seem odd if you applied for a course." His brain would not supply the words he needed to make her go, only doggedly repeat what he knew must be done.

"No." She knelt beside him, her arm around his shoulders. "Kolyushka, if you should be in trouble for anything you have done, and I don't believe it for an instant, there would still be no risk for us. You would need us more than ever then. I have been reregistered; under the rules of the Party I could speak for you."

He threw her off roughly. "You don't know what I might be accused of, what strains an investigation might place on the Party loyalty you value so much."

"I know it couldn't be anything but an excess of idealism." He could not see her face, but sensed she was smiling. "I haven't lived with you for thirteen years without discovering how you think." She was upset by such brusque rejection but put her arms around him again, determined not to let him thrust her away.

"But if I had offended against the Party you would feel differently." His voice sounded thick in his own ears.

"Well, of course! Because then it would not be you, the man I love! Kolya, what is the matter with you? You are behaving as if you believed yourself a criminal already."

He sat rigid, he could scarcely bear this cold-blooded hacking at the numberless strands which surely bound them together forever, at the only mooring on which he could utterly rely in a quagmire world. But Anna had confirmed all his own fears: if she attempted to defend him to the Party when he was arrested, there would be no hope for her either. He must force her away before it was too late, and he knew now there was only one way of doing it. "You boast of how you know me," he said at last, harshly. "Of how you know my thoughts, my ideals, but you do not. I am a class enemy, willfully deceiving the state all these years. Through me the children too, and probably you."

"I hope you are not going to tell the investigating committee so," she said dryly, refusing to take him seriously but further dismayed by his deliberately wounding tone.

Kolya forced himself away from her arms and from the bed, standing in the minute space against the wall, hands behind him, the deep-drawn breaths with which he was struggling for control the only outward sign of his distress. "You do not know me," he repeated. "You may have lived thirteen years with me but I am still a stranger to you. I am not a peasant, born in Oryol Province and raised on half a dessyatin of mud. I am a count, born in Petersburg, one of those who can remember the past like the professors of Smolensk Hospital, and sometimes regret it. My father was an officer in the Tsar's own guards, my grandfather a general, a provincial governor, eventually a minister of state assassinated by revolutionaries. I am not even pure-blooded Russian; my grandmother was an Englishwoman and a devout Christian, with whom I lived for years. To the best of my knowledge I have a sister alive and living in England, no doubt an enemy of the Soviet state."

She stared at him aghast, now standing against the wall she could see him clearly, his face implacable. She could be in no doubt it was the truth she was hearing and with a rush of memory she recalled some of the questions he had roused in her mind from time to time by his unconscious attitudes, by his reticence, even by his very appearance. There was a long silence.

"You deceived me all these years," she said shakily at last.

His hands were driven hard into the wall behind him. She had thought first of the deceit between them, not of his fraud with the Party. He wanted to weep. "They will never believe you didn't know; you can't even denounce me safely. The children—"

She slapped his face. "Don't you dare bring the children into this! Of course I wouldn't denounce you, what a swine you must think I am! The same kind of swine you were, I daresay, when you didn't have the common honesty to tell me before we married instead of thirteen years and two children later. I expect you would have liked one of those fancy church weddings after all."

"I expect I would," he said bleakly. "We didn't get much joy from the Civil Registrar, did we? You can't help bringing the children into it, either. You are like the Party, what is fair for you is not fair for me." He had not moved, only his eye started to water where the blow had caught him. Both thought simultaneously of the other time she had slapped his face as a boy of seventeen; a move, a gesture, and neither could have resisted reconciliation. He steadied his voice with an effort. "See how I have corrupted even your Party loyalty without your realizing it, since you are no longer willing to denounce a class enemy."

The malice of the taunt was unbelievable and she sank back on the bed, hugging her arms around a body which felt scraped bare of self-respect. "Go away," she said dully. "Leave me alone and let me think."

"While you decide whether to betray the Party for the needs of the flesh? What a very feminine viewpoint. The Revolution didn't change so much after all." He felt sick hearing his own words.

"Go away," she repeated, hands over her face.

"So you can start learning about yourself in a way you never really troubled to learn about me? What a joke out of hell it is: all your fine Party loyalty, all that idealism of yours, and in the end it means nothing so long as you have a husband and a warm bed. What does it matter after all, if the Party is the sworn enemy of such as he?"

She did not look up. "It means something."

"But not enough to force you into acting against your own interests?"

She lifted her head and stared at him. "I would not act against you."

He felt the blood leave his face, the impossibility of what he was doing freezing the senses. He took a deep breath: "When we were first wed I thought my parentage might matter to you, so I didn't tell you for fear you might denounce me. Can you wonder that I'm sick to the teeth of your Party cant when tonight it took scarcely a minute for you to decide you wouldn't betray me? You needn't fear the commission, I can still lie to them, but before God I am tired of posturing at home and all the misery it has brought us. You know I believed in the Party, I did my best for it, but now I'm finished. I'll do what I must to survive, but in my own home I want comfort again."

She stared at him, dark eyes enormous in her pale face, tears trickling unnoticed down her cheeks. "What have I ever denied you?"

"What have you ever given me? Only what was left after the Party had taken its pick. So long as I shared the Party with you, it was enough and I remember it with pleasure . . ." His voice faltered on the stilted formality dismissing all their years together like a casual night's bedding, but he drove himself on immediately. "It isn't enough any more and you have to choose. Keep the Party as the center of your world and do your surgery, or stay with me knowing you have betrayed the Party by not denouncing me. I intended to use the commission to make you face what has been wrong between us; now I'm glad I've told you everything so you can't avoid the choice any longer." He knew it was not a choice, after such cruelty as this what of him was there left for her to keep? And as he also knew too well, the denial of belief could not kill belief itself.

"Why don't you say the one thing you haven't said, that after all these years you still remember it wasn't only the Party which had its pick of me, but half the revolutionary mob of Moscow too?" She had no tears now, her mouth stiff on words dry-rustling among the rubble of the past, revealing a long-festering wound he had not even suspected.

No hatred, no love, nothing vital left any more.

He gathered up his clothes with hands shaking so badly they slid to the floor again and he kicked them violently out of the door. He could not have spoken again, another minute and he would have vomited where he stood. Ideology forgotten, it was the personal body blow he had not foreseen, the unforgivable, which had accomplished his purpose for him.

Once in the kitchen, he lit the lamp and began automatically to strop his razor, although from the darkness outside it was still the middle of the night.

"Daddy?" Sophie crept out of her cupboard, dark hair wildly tumbled. She was tall now, all awkward movements and half-fledged shyness. "What's the matter with you and Mummy? I heard terrible arguing."

"Go back to bed," he said roughly, unable even to look at her. "You should be ashamed to listen at keyholes."

She flushed. "I didn't, I swear it. I could just hear you were upset, I couldn't help it."

"That's what all eavesdroppers say. Go back to bed."

Her lips trembled and he thought she was going to protest at the injustice, but instead she whisked away and he could hear her trying to stifle her tears under the bedclothes.

He stared at his face in the scrap of mirror over the pump handle: the face of a betrayer, the man who had delivered his family into misery, into the threat of deportation or worse. How well he had known that he ought never to involve others in the contradictions of his life. The nightmares of selfishness and guilt which had plagued the early months of his marriage reached up to him again in self-accusation.

He shaved with the quick strokes of habit, the cold pull of steel switching his thoughts suddenly to the way of escape it offered him. Several Party members had committed suicide rather than face investigation.

No. It might be escape for him, but it was an admission of guilt. The NKVD would never be satisfied until they knew what had frightened him so badly that he preferred death to interrogation. Once they searched through his past, really searched in the knowledge there was something to find, it would not be difficult to discover his parentage. Then their only answer to it would be the wiping out of those to whom he had given his love and his blood.

"Daddy, you've upset Sophie," said Yuri accusingly beside him.

Kolya started and cut himself. "You little fool, what do you mean by startling me like that?" He dabbed at the blood on his cheek. God, his nerves should not betray him at a child's voice.

Yuri did not move, standing straight and stiff beside him, thin legs sticking out of his coarse nightshirt. "I didn't mean to startle you, but you shouldn't have said cruel things to Sophie. She only wanted to help."

Kolya finished wiping his face, his eyes were swollen and uncomfortable again, but this time he did not think it was the oil. "There are a lot of things I should not have done which I have done. I hope you will manage better one day."

Yuri rubbed his nose. "You always told me that if I did something wrong I should put it right as soon as I knew, leaving things made them worse. Will you come and say sorry to Sophie now?"

An abyss of apology and explanation yawned in front of him, the butchery of emotions more self-perpetuating than any other form of violence. He shook his head, a feeling almost of paralysis spreading through his senses.

"Why not?" Yuri never let up halfway on anything.

He could not hear any more. He pushed past Yuri, clumsily stumbling into Sophie's tiny retreat as he forgot the narrowness of the entry. She was huddled face down in the dark and did not turn as he dropped a swift, wordless kiss on her hair.

Yuri jerked aside when he touched his shoulder, all he could manage on the vertiginous slope of his private hell which was only just beginning. Days, possibly weeks loomed ahead in which he must watch Anna in torment and seem indifferent, in which he must not seek to heal the wound her words had revealed.

He knew that if he had offered Anna the chance to save her life at the cost of poisoning all the love between them, she would never have taken it. If he had known the way it would be accomplished, he would not have had the courage to force survival on her. But there were Sophie and Yuri as well to think of; no calculation could balance such a reckoning. It was too late, it was done. He killed them all if he shifted now.

Chapter Thirty-two

The commission for reregistration of Party members had taken over part of Rumyantsev's headquarters, their presence permeating the building as the weeks dragged on. No one was actually arrested at a hearing but it was the frequent sequel to expulsion from the Party, and without papers few victims were able to consider escape, even had they dared leave their families behind to suffer the consequences. The humble might take to the woods as brigands but for men of high position, of dedication to the Party and the state, such a course was unthinkable.

Kolya began to wonder whether his summons would ever come, more certain with each passing week that the delay was deliberate, but in his case at least the Party's tactic of suspense had its advantages, with Anna and the children now well away.

Klintsy had been electrified to learn that the Director was sleeping in his office, and Comrade Berdeyeva was going to a surgical teaching hospital in Saratov taking the children with her. Ivan Perichev, the head teacher, even went to see the Director, tentatively trying to explain how upset Sophie and Yuri were at the upheaval, but was brutally brushed aside, as were all the other prospective peacemakers. Only Vera said nothing, watching with sympathy from shadowed eyes, her face set in deep wrinkles of sadness, far removed from the rumbustious gaiety of past years.

She came into Kolya's office one evening when he was working late on some papers; sleep only came nowadays when he was practically poleaxed by exhaustion. "May I speak to you, Comrade Director?"

"If you wish." He went on writing.

"Did you know your wife and children leave tomorrow?" She watched his hand quiver, continue to write, trail off into nothingness. She wished he would look up. "Venzher's boys helped carry their boxes to the station; the morning train tomorrow is a stopper."

He started to write again. "Thank you." It was almost a whisper.

Anna, Sophie and Yuri could not believe they were walking to the station for the last time, the track a river of mud in the autumn rains as it wound between clumps of birch and bright green bog grass. The line was dead straight at Klintsy and they could see the train coming when it was still several kilometers away, staring mesmerized, all seized with the same longing to bolt back to their tiny cottage, to burrow frantically in search of the lost warmth and happiness they had known.

"Mummy, don't you think we should have said good-by to Daddy?" Sophie clung to Anna's arm, while Yuri stood aloof on her other side.

Anna shook her head. "I don't think he could bear it and neither could we. Perhaps one day he will come to see us in Saratov and we'll be able to start again, but not yet." There was nothing left for her and Kolya, but the children at least must be able to hope. She still could not think clearly about what had happened, felt very little except the emptiness where once her love had been. And through it all she could not put the sound of his voice out of her mind, taunting her that she did not know the man she had married and trusted with everything she had. The stranger she had feared, and sometimes seen in passing, had taken over and left her adrift in the blank, black flow of life. She blamed herself as well as him, but it did not help. She knew, as they had both known, how much of their relationship had been eaten away in recent years, how the final ferocious quarrel would have been unthinkable before and would not have destroyed so much if destruction had not been already well advanced. She remembered to the shock on Kolya's face, which had told her more clearly than words, that whatever else he had used against her, the sordid memory of 1917 was hers alone.

Sophie sniffed miserably. "I don't understand why everything's gone wrong. I don't want to go away to a horrid place like Saratov. Why is Daddy so unkind all of a sudden?"

"He has done all the things he told us we must never do," said Yuri in a hard, tight voice. "He has been cruel and untruthful and he wouldn't apologize when he made you and Mummy unhappy."

"He made you unhappy too and he wouldn't apologize to you either," flashed Sophie.

Yuri's lips tightened and he scuffed at the rough timber of the platform. "I hate him."

"No," Anna whispered. Her love could have survived the long deceit of his parentage, but not the crude brutality of the way he had told her. She could have forgiven him anything, except that he would see nothing in his actions which needed forgiveness. Yet whatever he might say or do, there was too much of herself given to him over the years for her to hate, even now.

The train drew into the Klintsy stop with a howl of brakes, and there was relief in the frantic scramble up the steep steps with Yefím handing up their bags and boxes. His knowing leer slid past the window as the train pulled slowly out.

"Look!" Yuri and Anna jerked around at Sophie's excited voice and all three stared at the woods and fields of Klintsy drawing away from them, at Kolya standing silently in the shadow of the sidings to watch them go.

"Konstantin Aleksandr'itch Berdeyev, Party member since July 8, 1919?"

Kolya dragged his mind back from haunting recollections to the threatening present and the five men facing him across the table. His investigation for re-registration had come at last.

"Yes."

"Where, and in what circumstances, were you admitted?" The routine nature of the questions surprised him, as if the commission was not really interested in his answers. Although every aspect of his Party career came up for scrutiny, there was nothing searching on his earlier life, no signals of real danger.

One of the investigators unexpectedly held up a greasy Bolshevik pass. "Your earliest Party orders were signed by Rychagov of the Moscow Committee in 1918?"

"Yes." Kolya had not thought of Rychagov for years, although he knew Anna still exchanged occasional greetings with him.

"Rychagov has already been sentenced for anti-Soviet activities."

Kolya was silent. That poor old man, he must be early seventy now. A lifetime of service given to the Revolution ending in a stinking cell riven with doubt over his faults.

"Well?"

"I did not know comment from me was called for; any Soviet citizen must condemn anti-Soviet activities." Anna, he thought suddenly, could letters from Anna have been found in his rooms?

"You are married, are you not, Comrade?" The interrogator almost echoed his thoughts.

"Yes." He felt a physical chill in his stomach,

wanted to add something about Anna as a true Party member, but stuck grimly to his policy of minimum answer.

"But she and your children are no longer living with you?"

"No."

"Why not?" The voice was tight with anger at his monosyllables.

"My wife is a doctor and wished to take advantage of an opportunity to follow a surgical course. The children have naturally gone with her."

"There has been no political disagreement between you?"

"No." For the first time he wanted to hesitate, to think about his answer, but he did not dare. Would it be safer for Anna to imply that there had been disagreement, or would it merely involve her in further investigation?

"Had she any reason for choosing this time to go?" Instinctively, for they were immensely skilled at their job, they sensed he was on the defensive.

"Yes," said Kolya slowly; he had thought about this. "There were reports in the paper some months ago about Nazism and the menace of fascism in Germany, a call for Soviet preparedness. This was her contribution." It even had the merit of being partly true; they had frequently discussed the threatening situation beyond Soviet frontiers.

You did not feel inclined to follow her example and apply to come off the reserve?"

"No." Kolya turned gratefully to the latest questioner, the change of subject an enormous relief. "I have been at Klintsy nearly eleven years now. I feel my best service to the Soviet state is there."

For the next two hours they took him step by step, almost month by month, through his actions at Klintsy. They sidetracked him into discussion on Marxist dialectic, slipped in a sudden, dangerous question on his vote for Kirov in the 1934 Congress.

"You have a long list of undesirable acquaintance," remarked the Chairman dryly, Kirov apparently qualifying for this category. "You knew Army Commander Yakir in the Ukraine, didn't you?"

Kolya blinked at the change of subject; he was by now very tired and his reactions were not as fast as they had been. He had been standing, concentrating on every word and every intonation, for nearly four hours. But, as he well knew, the longer the interrogation went on the more crucial, the more lethal the questions were likely to be.

"Yes," he said finally.

"You appear reluctant to admit the acquaintance?"

"Not in the least. He was my commander in the later stages of the revolutionary struggle in the Ukraine."

"Where he has since built up a satrapy."

Kolya flushed. "He is Commander of the Kiev Military District and a full member of the Central Committee."

"He is a Jew, is he not?"

"I don't know. Under the new constitution all races of the Soviet Union are officially equal so it makes no difference anyway."

"Would it surprise you to hear that he is under investigation for counterrevolution and espionage?"

"Yes, it would." He could feel the shock loosening his muscles. Yakir, hero of the Revolution and one of the most brilliant leaders of the Red Army and the state, if anyone was to be safe surely if must be he.

"Under what circumstances did you meet him?"

"I only met him once, in the winter of 1920 at Gomel. I reported to him and was reassigned to winter duty."

"Did he express satisfaction at the victory of the Revolution?"

"Yes, of course. We were all delighted."

"You sound as if some were more delighted than others."

Kolya cursed himself, he must not relax, must not say a single unnecessary word. "We were all delighted," he repeated.

"What did you speak of apart from your mutual delight?"

"I don't remember. About building a true socialist state in Russia, I think."

"Did he express any views about the sort of state he wished to see built?" There it was, suddenly all five pairs of eyes were fastened on him, this was what they really wanted. His doubts about the questions he had faced crystallized abruptly. The whole miserable charade was directed at obtaining a few disparaging words about his former commander from an unknown cavalry officer, whose very existence Yakir would never remember, so they could form the basis for an unexpected question or trapping switch of subject in Yakir's eventual interrogation.

"He expressed only the desire to serve the Party and fulfill its ideals," said Kolya flatly, disgust a physical sensation. It would be less degrading if accusations abandoned all pretense of being connected with the truth.

"Comrade Berdeyev." The Chairman picked up a file. "I have here your application for renewal of your Party card. As a result of our investigations today we see no insuperable objection to this, but you should always remember the duty of vigilance laid on us by the Party. We wish you to search your recollection particularly in connection with Yakir."

There was a long silence. On the one hand safety, not just for himself but for Anna and the children too, since little interest was being shown in his own actions. On the other hand . . . could anything he said about a man he had not spoken to in fifteen years matter one way or the other?

"No," he said at last. "I can recollect nothing of our very brief conversation except what I told you. Army Commander Yakir showed true devotion to the Party." After he had said it he was swept by relief and remembered also the jar of fat. Yakir would have a family too.

"You have nothing else to say?"

"I am anxious to help the commission in any way I can." He flogged his mind into attentiveness again.

And so it continued until he lost count of time, of day and night. He was refused permission to visit the lavatory, the humiliation of soaking clothes and animal smell added to mental and physical stupor. The most bizarre aspect of the whole affair was the way in which it was conducted with such courtesy and formality. The procedures for the reregistration of Party members were rigidly followed, there were no threats or violence, he was addressed throughout as a colleague and senior member of the Party. The commission affected a well-bred indifference to his lack of bodily control, as one would to an unfortunate happening at dinner, as if the hours he had stood before them did not exist. After all, reregistration was a formal occasion, for which members always stood during the short time it usually took.

Before he entered the room for his hearing, Kolya had made a firm resolution to hold onto his temper, but it was becoming increasingly difficult. He had first commanded men at the age of nineteen and had long since become used to having his judgment respected, his authority questioned but not flouted. It was quite intolerable to be treated like a pig in its sty, for achievements to be regarded like a row of mud pies to be kicked aside when they had served their purpose, to see his beliefs debased for the homicidal purposes of these self-satisfied, cynical functionaries.

Anna. For her sake he must somehow preserve the façade of indifference. The longer he escaped arrest, the longer their separation was established, the safer she and the children must be. He closed his eyes an instant, summoning up a thousand images of them through the years, which rushed at him with the force of an avalanche so he swayed and nearly fell.

"Do you feel ill, Comrade?" The exaggerated concern in the man's voice infuriated him anew.

"Yes," he snapped, all his resolves finally forgotten, "and I have a day's work to do at Klintsy when you've finished wasting my time here."

"It would be unfortunate if this commission discovered that you considered Party investigations a waste of time. It might necessitate revision of the favorable conclusions we had reached in your case."

He had hold of himself again almost immediately. "Your pardon, Comrades, I spoke hastily. The Party can no doubt see further than the innocence of individuals." In spite of the barbed nature of his apology he could hardly bear his humiliation in having to make it and remembered Lev's words with bitterness. He too was now completely absorbed in trying to save those dear to him, resistance on a point of principle no longer crossed his mind. Only with individuals in a similar trap, like Yakir, was he capable of unselfish action any more.

"Very well, Comrade, I am happy to approve your application for reregistration. We are grateful to you for sparing so much of your time." He signed his name, passed some documents down the table for more signatures and then handed Kolya his new card. "The Communist Party of the Soviet Union is happy to have such a distinguished member confirmed in his loyalty and service."

Kolya had little difficulty in forcing impassivity, he was too dazed, too exhausted by reaction for astonishment. He shook hands all around; while his legs would hardly sustain him he put into the hard, bitter grip of his hand all the anger he had not voiced, his contempt for this miserable farce to which the Party had lent itself.

"May I ask my comrades' names now?" He stared at the derisive secretive eyes of the chief interrogator.

He shuffled together some of the papers littering the table. "It is not considered to be in the interests of the Party in such matters as these, but I will tell you mine if you wish. Zakhovsky—Leonid Mikhail'itch Zakhovsky."

Kolya feigned surprise. "What a remarkable thing, Comrade. I had always thought it a Jewish name by derivation until now, but plainly I was mistaken." He watched the man's face change color, the quick look he shot at those on either side of him. Interrogators were no safer than anyone else presumably, the truth of the insinuation no more important than it was with those raked up against helpless victims every day.

It was a slight consolation. Only much later did he wonder whether Zakhovsky too had reached the point where only selfishness counted.

Chapter Thirty-three

He missed them terribly, more than during the weeks of tension waiting for his investigation and anticipating disaster. Physically he recovered swiftly from his ordeal, but he retained a cold, bitter rage at the contempt and indignity with which he had been treated, although it was directed at the callous manipulators of the Party rather than the Party itself.

The empty spaces of his tiny cottage were unbearable. The straw boxes where the children had slept still showed the impress of their bodies; the chill emptiness of the bed where he and Anna had shared so much joy was scarcely worse than the lack of welcome and eager chatter over the day's events when he came home. Pride and a sense of what was safe and fitting prevented him from seeking solace among the many healthy young girls on the sovkhoz who would undoubtedly have been willing enough, but when in desperation he allowed a Smolensk whore to pick him up after a Party meeting the experience was profoundly unsatisfactory.

He was no longer a boy carried away by the intoxication of discovering his own body, but a man under immense strain and still in love with his wife; acutely conscious of the injustice of his dealings with her and filled with self-disgust even while his need betrayed him. When he could bear it no longer he left in the middle of the night, chancing police patrols, repelled by the skilled, sweaty image now between him and his memories of Anna.

He did not realize how he was scanning the post until he caught himself snatching at the incoming mailbag, felt the beat of blood in his face as he sorted the sovkhoz letters with Karakhan, the new Party representative in place of murdered Chapeta. It was the last day of 1936, a year surely few could regret, and he realized with the bitterness of deep disappointment how much he had hoped for some word from Anna. Name days were no longer kept among Party members, but with his birth date coinciding with the New Year celebrations the day had always been a special one since the first year of their marriage. There were little gifts all around, masks cut out of corn sacks by the children or any other unexpected variation which Anna, ever inventive in the most difficult years, had been able to think up.

"You were expecting something, Comrade Director?"

He became aware of Karakhan peering at him and shuffled the mail together. "No, but there should be details of the flax program for next season any day now." Karakhan was a rat, a very different proposition to slack old Chapeta, he and Bezhov often in inquisitorial huddles together over the slightest irregularity.

He could not bear the thought of returning home through the New Year festivities already spreading down the sovkhoz street, and instead stayed in his office drinking moodily. Twice he drew paper toward him and started to write, twice he thrust it in the stove. He did not know Anna's address, but the main hospital at Saratov would certainly find her; what restrained him were the futility and danger of writing anything. He could post a letter in Smolensk, but no one knew who was checking what these days and he certainly felt far from safe yet. He had survived one inquiry, but only because no one had known the right pressures to exert on him, had not perhaps particularly cared with so many more important figures to hunt down first. But the whole of his youth, any threat against his family, a still raw conscience over some of the things he had been driven to do over the past few years—these were open avenues of attack against which he would have little defense.

Had she written to him, and he could not blame her for expecting the first move to come from him, then he would have had to ignore it. He must be thankful she had not forced him into further murderous rebuff. He had driven her away and poisoned their last days together with bitter hurt, but he knew her generosity of heart well enough to be certain that the slightest appeal might bring her back again.

Vera found him the following morning, still sprawled at his desk sunk beyond rousing in vodka. She hesitated, concern on her weather-beaten face. She herself had a massive headache from the night's celebrations, but she was not deceived into thinking there had been any celebration here. He was too heavy for her to lift and after a while she went out again, locking the door and pushing the key back underneath.

As the months passed he began to drink steadily. The half-closed weeks of winter were bad enough with their bleak, long hours of loneliness, but the joyous opening of spring seemed worse still, as if everyone but he had new children or lovers, or carefree plans for the future. He wondered whether Anna had sought solace yet with some earnest young doctor; she might easily be divorcing him, the procedures the merest formality for Party members. Now he remembered, as he had not for years, her casual attitude to their wedding day.

On his next visit to Smolensk he sought a woman again but it was useless, any brief physical relief too deeply overlaid by disgust and despair. The vision of Anna probably doing the same, the thought of his children learning to look to another man for affection and guidance, made him quite literally sick, his stomach wrung with fierce nervous spasms which only alcohol could to some extent alleviate.

In late May it was still light after supper and he was sitting one evening on the step outside his cottage, idly drinking and watching a pair of starlings with the nestful of fledglings, when Vera came trudging down the road.

He stood up, not entirely steadily. "Come and sit awhile, Vera."

"I was going to," she said tartly, tugging her shawl

and sinking down with relief. Gone was the slim, laughing Vera of ten years ago; she looked already old, with the sagging muscles and myriad face lines of the hard-working peasant.

He looked down at her with a twitch of amusement. "I sense a lecture," he remarked. "Yes, dear Vera, I know I have been drinking."

"Everyone knows you have been drinking," she retorted. "Haven't you seen Golikov watching you? Have you no sense any more?"

His face tightened. "I've yet to learn that drink has affected my work."

"But then you would be the last to know, wouldn't you?" She relented suddenly. "No, Konstantin Aleksandr'itch, it hasn't affected your work. Klintsy is as well run as ever. But can't you see it isn't safe in your position, at a time like this, to show any weakness at all?"

He offered her a glass and then sat beside her, holding the bottle cupped between his hands. "Yes, I can see it. I cannot help it."

"Rubbish! I beg your pardon, Konstantin Aleksandr'itch, but I know you better than that. There is very little you can't do if you set your mind to it."

He smiled faintly. "Thank you, but at the moment I am finding some difficulty in setting my mind to anything. Why do you think I work eighteen hours a day, if not to reduce to a minimum the time I can't resist a drink? If I could sleep in the six hours left I would survive, but without vodka, I cannot." He could not quite keep fear at bay, either. The chilling apparatus of violence and privation to which arrest would expose him was never mentioned, but there were few who did not now know of its existence. Caged in with loneliness, he could not always keep his mind from dwelling on what would happen to him if his name joined the many disappearing from every rank of the

Party. He could not help being conscious of the eager anticipation with which Bezhov watched him, like a cat with a bird caught in netting. Drink a toast to your grandfather if the secret police disappear in your lifetime, he remembered sourly as he poured himself another glass. Not a toast, surely now never that toast for him, but a drink at least helped, whatever Vera said.

She looked at him thoughtfully. "When are Comrade Anna and the little Sophie and Yuri returning?"

He became very still. "Vera," he said at last, carefully. "I know you are trying to help, but I wish you would not. We are old friends, but there are some things better left alone."

"Someone has to help," said Vera simply.

He shook his head, without speaking.

She heaved to her feet sighing and stood looking at him. A twinkle came into her eyes. "If I were twenty years younger I'd take you under a hedge and give you what you need, then I'd slap your face and pack you off to Saratov to fetch Comrade Anna. You are a fool, Konstantin Aleksandr'itch, a proud selfish fool to make no effort to get her back." She put her hands on her hips belligerently.

He jumped to his feet and nearly fell.

"Vodka," she said contemptuously.

He rubbed his face with shaking hands; in truth it was as much exhaustion as vodka. "Thank you for coming," he said dully. "Believe me, I don't intend to become a sot, if that's what gossip says."

"Don't forget, though, Comrade Konstantin, gossip can be dangerous."

He kissed her cheek gently. "One kindness makes up for much else."

After she had gone he sat down again to think it out, his mind groping sluggishly through the uncertainties of alcohol and fatigue. Vera was surely right:

he could not go on like this, even if the Party spared him he would destroy himself. He must not approach Anna; he had no real desire for other women beyond the temporary satisfaction of physical need, which then left him in a worse state than before. His Party ideals were untouched, but the Party under its present masters disgusted him. There could be no question of attempting to forget himself in political service at a time when this consisted chiefly of denouncing and persecuting others. He slowly tipped up the bottle and watched as the liquid was absorbed by paper-dry boards without a single trace being left: if Anna ever came back, if he were ever able to start again with her, he would not wish her to find him a trembling, alcoholic wreck.

He decided to ask the Party to reassign him when the harvest was in. With a new challenge in a different setting, perhaps he would be able to harness his energies again, escape the stalking hatred of Bezhov before it was too late. The threatening reports of fascist Germany, of Hitler's almost open drive to war, continued in the newspapers and he wondered whether he should ask to come off the reserve. He had set his mind against the army and all it stood for, had never for an instant regretted his decision, but he remembered the misery and ruin of war too well not to know that if attack came it must be stopped, and stopped as close to Russia's borders as possible. The ruthless, desperate sacrifices of the years since the Revolution must not be ground back into rubble again, whatever his personal feelings.

With decision of a sort, he regained a degree of calm. He still could not sleep in more than snatches but found the fortitude to endure it without too frequent recourse to the anesthesia of alcohol, and even to accept with good grace the smug satisfaction with which Vera regarded the change in him.

Every quarter there was a full meeting of Klintsy Soviet, attended by representatives from district Party committees and the neighboring MTS* although Klintsy only rarely used its services. The meeting for June 1937 was held under the same contradictory circumstances as had become almost normal. Outwardly all was well, the sovkhoz flourishing and supply of goods increasing; inwardly rumors abounded, the gaps in Party ranks becoming more obvious.

Kolya opened proceedings as he always did, explaining the progress of the harvest, the supplementary plans and targets which he had received since the year's production had been projected. Golikov and the other heads of department also reported on their progress and then general discussion was invited.

On this occasion, when Kolya asked for comments, to his surprise it was Yefím who lurched to his feet. Officially Yefím should not be there at all, but as the only full-time worker on the sidings he had never been discouraged from attending, as Kolya considered that the more who came to the quarterly meetings the better.

Yefím cleared his throat nervously; he looked slightly drunk. "These targets seem too low, Comrade Director. My sidings could handle twice the amount each year."

"Yes, I expect they could and there's every hope they will in two or three years' time. They were built with the future in mind." Kolya replied himself when Golikov did not make the obvious response.

"But shouldn't we be producing more now?" persisted Yefím, rubbing his nose and glancing around to see the effect of his words.

* Machine Tractor Station. Co-operative machinery, leased out chiefly to kolkhoz. Sovkhoz the size of Klintsy would carry most of their own equipment, but MTS still watched all decisions as they co-ordinated political control of a district under a ranking NKVD officer.

"The plan scaled up all requirements this year and we have every expectation of meeting them." Kolya indicated some colored charts he had brought.

"It seems sabotage to me that we don't produce more," muttered Yefím, and then suddenly shouted, his face bright scarlet, "double as much! Double as much, eh, Comrades?"

"You can't just double the crop—" began Kolya patiently, but he was interrupted by Lobrin, the Party's choice as new head of forestry.

"The Selnyi people have been allowed to sabotage our efforts; you are too lenient with them, Comrade Director. I haven't been here long, but I've heard stories of how you've failed to insist on proper effort from them."

"What stories?" demanded Kolya. "I think it's time we had some facts in this discussion."

The MTS political officer stood up. "I agree. Sit down, Comrade Director. Let us call on your deputy and head of cropping, Comrade Golikov, to give us some facts."

Kolya stood rigid a moment and then sat down. It had come.

Golikov stared at him expressionlessly and then at the meeting. "In my opinion there's no doubt that the Comrade Director has failed in his duty." His voice was slightly rough, as if long stored away and only recently released. "The Party has constantly urged the need for high production whereas Comrade Berdeyev has always understated his figures and then taken credit for achieving his targets. We could double our flax crop next year, increase our corn by thirty per cent."

Vera stood up. "Comrade Golikov, would you obtain this increase at the cost of slaughtering livestock? I notice you say nothing of them."

"We would achieve it by better socialist labor without saboteurs to hold us back! Comrade Berdeyev has shown sympathy to peasants unwilling to work properly and holds politically unsound views."

"What politically unsound views?" asked Kolya, not because he thought it would do any good, but to forestall Vera, whom he saw ready to interrupt again. "You are criticizing the Party rather than myself since my membership has been reregistered."

The MTS man intervened sharply. "It seems to me that you are guilty of treating the people with contempt if you can't even listen to criticism without interrupting." He nodded to Golikov. "Proceed, Comrade."

But Golikov was alarmed by the possibility that he might have criticized the Party. He began stuttering and hesitating until Yefím broke in again with a malice which even in normal times scarcely knew the briefest tug of discretion. "I have more to say! I wish to denounce the traitor Berdeyev! I remember years ago, the day he went to Selnyi, he didn't want to go, he pretended not to hear Party orders on the telephone. I was there, I saw him lie and say he could not hear."

"And now you say he could plainly hear everything the traitor Rumyantsev said?"

The traitor Rumyantsev. It was like a kick in the stomach. Kolya's muscles tightened involuntarily and even the shouts in the hall died away to hear the all-powerful First Secretary's name so contemptuously tossed aside.

"Y-yes," stuttered Yefím, sitting down abruptly and drinking quite openly from his bottle, so great was his astonishment.

"The swine went to Selnyi, though. He killed my husband on the way as a means of slowing the tractors with his treachery!" The high, wavering accusation from dead Valya's widow caught Kolya unaware and for the first time he looked away from the faces peering at him, down at his clenched hands, and did not hear the next flurry of accusation. He had helped Yelena Yegorovna as best he could, and always she had gazed at him with sad, uncomprehending eyes, unable to accept her husband's death even years later; never before had she shown any sign of hatred or vindictiveness. Certain Bezhov had concerted this, but now she looked quietly happy.

The incisive voice of the MTS man rasped his oblivion apart. "Is there any Selnyi man here to speak?"

"Yes!" There were shouts from several places, evidence had anyone cared that the difference between Selnyi and Klintsy was now largely imaginary. "I speak for Selnyi!" A black-bearded giant stood up. Mikhail Mikhail'itch. Kolya remembered with difficulty, the days when he had known everyone by name and personal eccentricity long since gone.

"I speak for Selnyi," he repeated with satisfaction. "When the Party came to offer us a new way of life it was the traitor Berdeyev who insisted on bringing us here through ice and snow which killed the weak, instead of leaving us to set up our own kolkhoz as we'd been promised." His gleaming, hate-filled eyes were fixed on Kolya, daring him to say in open meeting that the Party had intended to abandon them to die. He was rapidly backed by shouts from his fellows, not unmixed with derisive laughter as a few of the quicker-witted saw the irony of it, heedless of which victim was to assuage their long-cherished craving for revenge.

Golikov thumped the table for silence. His confidence was restored by the attitude of the MTS man, who, with his casual reference to Rumyantsev, was plainly high in the counsels of the NKVD and had full license to attack the Director. "I have important evidence to add, but I wished Selnyi to speak first. My accusation is very serious, no less than encouragement of banditry."

Kolya leaped to his feet. "I protest! I never encouraged banditry in my life. I can bring a hundred witnesses to testify that I frequently led expeditions against bandits in the years when this was necessary."

"Oh?" MTS looked politely interested. "It is only this charge you dispute, the others are not contested?"

"Not only do I contest them, they are contradictory. I am accused of showing favor to people from Selnyi and also of unreasonable harshness in my dealings with Selnyi itself. Both cannot be true and I deny both. I was reluctant to risk an expedition to Selnyi under very unfavorable conditions, in which four men did in fact die, but I was obedient to the Party and reached there as quickly as possible. Since then I have extended the hand of comradeship to the people of Selnyi, but they have not been free from necessary discipline either. Two were shot in 1932 on Party verdicts; others resettled elsewhere if they refused to accept the standards here." He glanced at Bezhov, leaning back in his chair, a deeply happy smile on his face.

Venzher called out from the back, "I can witness that Comrade Director led expeditions against bandits."

Kolya was pleasantly surprised by his loyalty but could have thrashed him for his stupidity. All the arguments he had just advanced were swept aside as they gratefully returned to the charge of banditry. He supposed it did not matter, the whole affair had the feel of preconception: no doubt all those who had held office under Rumyantsev were now under attack.

"This is a serious charge indeed, Comrade Golikov," said MTS with pleasure. "Substantiate it or withdraw it, if you please."

"Withdraw it?" said Golikov, offended. "Of course I will not withdraw it. When we were loading the tractors at Selnyi for our return journey Director B . . . the traitor Berdeyev deliberately pretended to blindness so he would be able to falsify the count of young men.

The women, children and the old were brought here to be a burden on the sovkhoz, while some of the fittest young men were allowed to slip away into the woods. We had a great deal of trouble with bandits the next year."

MTS peered around at Kolya. "Have you anything to say?"

"Yes, Comrade, I have." How ridiculous never to know an accuser's name. "I have witnesses that I did . . ." He had been about to say suffer blindness, but pulled himself up in time. Anna had treated him, had been the sovkhoz doctor; this was certainly the last moment to attract attention to her. ". . . attack bandits with all my force available. Comrade Golikov supervised loading at Selnyi, as did Lieutenant Pauker of the political police." He finished smoothly enough, but even to his own ears the hesitation sounded painfully shifty.

"You don't sound too sure, Comrade," said MTS immediately "And as you apparently agree that there were bandits and they did stem from Selnyi; the complaint against you would seem to show grounds for investigation. Are you suggesting that Comrades Golikov and Pauker were in charge, or did you allow them to load up unsupervised while you warmed yourself elsewhere?"

"No," replied Kolya quietly.

"No to which proposition?"

There was a long, heavy silence, as if the collective heart of Klintsy missed a beat. Kolya stood very still, he felt supremely detached. He knew he was done for, as Lev had said he would be, as he himself had known he would be all those months ago when he had deliberately torn up his private life by the roots. The direction of attack might be unexpected but it would make little difference to him, although it yet might to Anna and the children. The longer accusation, counter-accusation and denial went on, the more likely it was that they would be dragged in and Klintsy itself seared by the faction of desperation as each member sought to save himself by accusing another. And at the finish it would all be for nothing; it was the end of the road for him anyway. He looked around at the untidy clots of faces. Familiar faces; angry faces; fearful, resentful faces; bewildered, regretful faces; Vera's tearful face looking at him; Golikov's triumphant, cunning, self-satisfied face surveying his new domain. Bezhov shaken by silent laughter.

"We have come a long way together, my friends," he said at last. "I wish you good fortune, good crops and happiness in the years to come." He turned and pushed his way out of the door before anyone thought to stop him. One man spat as he passed; the others sat silent. As soon as he had gone Bezhov wrote down formal accusations to be signed by those present: he found it quite difficult to keep up with the flow.

It was June 5, 1937.

On June 9, Konstantin Aleksandr'itch Berdeyev received notice of his expulsion from the Party.

On June 11 several of the most senior commanders of the Red Army, including Tukhachevsky, Deputy Commissioner for Defense, and Yakir, Commander of Kiev Military District, were declared guilty of treason. The next day it was announced that they had all been shot.

On June 15, the *Smolenskaya Pravda* carried a small paragraph announcing the arrest of "saboteur and bandit Berdeyev, former Director of the People's Sovkhoz at Klintsy, on the urgent representations of the sovkhozniks. They demanded death by shooting for him and all other such vermin."

On November 2 the *Smolenskaya Pravda* printed confirmation of a sentence against former Sovkhoz Director Sergei Golikov, who was to be shot for failing to reach production quotas. A Party inquiry had revealed his treasonous intentions when it discovered that Klintsy Sovkhoz had fallen into such confusion it must be considered as deliberate wrecking.

Chapter Thirty-four

The van was going far too fast.

Fortunately the prisoners inside were jammed together so tightly that actual injury was avoided but the constant flinging from side to side, chained hands snagging tight at every pothole and icy slide, produced utter prostration as the hours succeeded each other in relentless sequence of misery.

The elderly succumbed first. Although they were still held upright by the pressure of their fellows, their hearts began to fail, compressed lungs to labor, blood falter in the struggle to circulate.

Then those on the outside slid gradually into coma, the frosts of winter biting deep into scarcely existent defenses, finding the occasional easy victim clad only in a summer shirt but eventually conquering even those with ragged jackets and felt boots. It took longer, but there was plenty of time. Not one of those crushed against the thin outside body work of the van would survive.

In the middle it was warmer but the pressure became steadily more intolerable. Already debilitated by months of semistarvation, filth and darkness, the mind began to cease sending the necessary signals to nerves and heart and lungs, drifted into a longing to end it all, fragmented until it could no longer function with any vestige of coherence. Ex-Director Berdeyev was packed between the sharp ribs and bones of a professor of archeology from Kursk and the Party Secretary of Mozhaysk: neither had spoken for hours and he thought they were dead. Both were over sixty and already worn out by months of imprisonment. He had increasing doubts about how long he himself could last. His wrists and hands were already numb except when bone-jarring swerves swept them with brief flame; every nerve and muscle of his back shredded with the vibration, his whole body drowning in the foul atmosphere.

He did not very much care. Six months of being crammed into the dark filth of Smolensk jail, thrown in with criminals and suspects of every description, fed on dirty water and moldy gruel, had sapped his original rage, his determination to survive and thrust down the Party's throat what was being done in its name. Only the faint spark of desire to salvage something from the idealism of the past, the desperate need to believe something could be salvaged, still sustained him. For Anna and the children, he knew it would be better not to survive.

He was unconscious by the time they reached Moscow, staggered chokingly back to awareness in the snow of a courtyard as they were pulled bodily from the van and kicked into separate piles of living and dead. He lay awhile staring at brilliant stars swinging low overhead, completely relaxed, unaware of the bitter twenty degrees of frost. It was the first time he had seen the sky since June. He would have slept and died peacefully like a child, had he not been stabbed to his feet and thrust into line by a bayonet he never saw, jostled into a passage his feet never felt, pushed into a cell his mind did not register, to collapse on an unblanketed plank bunk his body did not feel.

It was daylight when he woke, and dark when he woke again. He was so stiff he could not stand, could not even, after an agonizing attempt, turn over. His back . . . his back surely paralyzed, he thought. He lay quietly, staring at the grain of wood under his face, at the dusty granite of the floor. He even laughed slightly at the ridiculous subconscious attempt to assert human dignity by standing, not much dignity left after six months in Smolensk jail. He slept again.

When he woke for the third time his mind was clearer and he knew he had been wrong. It was a pity he had survived, but he had. The van escort had told them they were going to the Central Detention and Interrogation Center of the Ministry of State Security, the dreaded Lubyanka, and they presumably knew. He had been brought to Moscow for a purpose; he must from somewhere find the strength to face it.

Painfully he brought his arms from under him; someone had unlocked the handcuffs but he had no recollection of it.

With immense effort he put his hands against the strut of the bunk, tried to grip his knees and roll over. At the fourth attempt he succeeded, feeling a flush of triumph out of all proportion to his achievement. His cell was about two meters long by half that distance wide and besides the bunk possessed a slop pail, a chair and a small barred window. The walls were a dispiriting chipped gray; the floor ingrained with grime but at least not thick with filth like the common cell in Smolensk. Also, he was alone. He lay a long time absorbing gratefully the immeasurable luxury of being alone.

Somehow he was going to stand. The resolution coalesced slowly, like a faint pattern in sand beneath the sea; somewhere along the way he seemed to have lost the normal impulses of thought and decision. It was not going to be easy without any power in his wrists and hands, a back as rigid as the boards he lay on, and legs in which he had not the slightest idea whether any framing of muscle remained. But at least they moved, feet, knees, thighs, slowly all answered the hazy command of his mind. Arms and shoulders; he twisted against the bunk and somehow swung his legs down. A lance of agony shot through his back and into the base of his skull, making him gasp and the room darken around him. Not paralyzed anyway, he told himself firmly. No good feeling pity for his poor emaciated body; it was all he had and no one else would feel sympathy, better not accustom it to the idea. He grinned faintly at his fancy. He dug his elbows into the hard planks, stiffened and tightened every muscle he could feel. Dimly he could hear his own tearing grunts of effort. If he fell he would never be able to get up. He gritted his teeth and lurched against the opposite wall, driving with shoulder and knee, searching desperately for purchase, scrabbling with his useless hands, even striving to lodge his jaw against a slight roughness of the stone. He was up.

From where he leaned he could see a fleck of blue sky, an edge of cloud and, once, the flash of a bird. He shouldered himself from the wall to look at this splendid reward of the outside world on his own feet, owing nothing to anyone, not even a prison wall. Before he collapsed back on the bunk he shuffled twice around his cell, catching a brief glimpse through the spy hole in his door of a silent corridor, lined with identical closed doors. No guard, no movement, nothing: only stagnant air, thick and rotting with confinement.

He was brought bread and hot water masquerading as tea twice a day. A guard stood just outside the door while he labored with clumsy, unpowered hands to life his bucket into the slop container, threw him a cloth when he failed and watched indifferently until he had mopped up the filth. No one spoke.

Once he was marched along to a barber's room, too fast so that he fell repeatedly, only to be hauled, still without speaking, back on his wavering feet. Whatever the pain it was worth all of it for the incredible well-being of towels and soap and comforting, familiar strokes off the razor, even when it shaved him as bald as a stripped maize cob, body hair and all. His ragged clothes were taken and steamed free of vermin and then, while he waited in a cold concrete cubicle outside, an overalled woman came in to scrub him.

It was of course deliberately planned as the ultimate in degradation. He was naked down to the last hair, his body scraped and bleeding from rough razoring, every bone and muscle thrusting obscenely through stretched, starvation-dry skin, and her contemptuous handling threw him relentlessly back into the pit of animalism from which he had briefly crawled. All his hardly gathered strength and renascent will of the past few days, so recently confirmed by the unexpected gift of cleanliness, was dissipated in an instant.

He should have known: there were no gifts any more.

That night they came for him.

One guard ahead, one behind, he was marched along endless corridors, his hands not tied but held, wrists crossed behind his back as the guards had shown him on his first movement out of his cell. As they walked the guards made clicking sounds with their tongues; he could not make it out at first but eventually realized it was to prevent their meeting another living soul in the huge, dead building. At all times the vast warren of the inner prison of the Lubyanka, with its thousands of prisoners, functioned in complete silence.

Stairs. He received a stunning blow on the arm when, without thinking, he put a hand on the old, gracefully carved banister. He had to go down sideways, one foot at a time, keeping his hands behind him, his back still obstinately refusing to joint his limbs adequately.

They went into what had once been a large, elegant room with a row of tall windows along one side, mirrors on the other: he averted his eyes from the look of himself. Now the room was broken up by head-high partitions and there was a general mutter of voices although he could not distinguish any words. A guard motioned him to stand by the door while his escort disappeared briefly into one of the cubicles.

They stood a long time and Kolya could feel his legs beginning to shiver under him, a tight, painful knot of fear and hunger cramping his stomach. In an effort to focus his mind he glanced up at the ceiling; it was still possible to visualize the original noble proportions of the room from rusty chandelier hooks, long swags of plaster fruit and smug, well-fleshed cherubs. He looked at their fat stomachs and rounded limbs ruefully and then suddenly knew a shock of memory.

He stood transfixed, fear and hunger forgotten, feeling the blood burn his cheeks as he was swept back twenty-six years. He had come here to a reception with his grandmother and the Kobrins, his sister Lena glowing with excitement at being introduced as Vanya Kobrin's prospective bride. He had been surly, aware of his country clothes and desperately shy among the chattering throng, until his grandmother had taken him aside and told him not to be selfish and spoil Lena's evening.

"I know it is hard for you, but it never hurt anyone to look agreeable, even if they don't feel it," she had said trenchantly. "Look at those poor cherubs on the ceiling, plastered there with smiles on their faces forever and always fifteen feet away from the food. At least you can eat." He had laughed reluctantly, Kobrin had introduced him to some sons and daughters of colleagues and the party had passed agreeably enough. He struggled with his memory, heaving with sudden urgency at a mental door he had not opened, whatever his reasons, since leaving Obeschino for the last time. The Rossiya Insurance Company, that was it. Kobrin had been a director and had brought them here for Lena to make her debut into Moscow circles. Well, my God, he thought wryly, it was lucky none of us could look ahead. Life insurance is one thing none of the new inhabitants of the Rossiya will be able to buy.

Abruptly he was pushed into one of the partitioned offices, but his brief excursion into long-forgotten pastures had steadied him. In some obscure way his mind was anchored back into known circumstance at a moment when successive debasements had threatened to sweep him away into panic and confusion.

"Konstantin Aleksandr'itch Berdeyev?"

He nodded.

"Yes or no?"

"Yes."

A lieutenant seated behind the desk reeled off a succession of facts and dates. Party membership, army service, university, Klintsy. Nothing about his origins, nothing about his childhood. Kolya looked up at the cupids again and wished he could share the joke. They were about to accuse him of every fantastic crime hysterical ingenuity could suggest, while in front of their eyes, if only they would look, was imperialist and capitalist infection enough to make the NKVD's hair stand on end.

"You find something amusing, Berdeyev?" asked the interrogator curiously.

Kolya realized with alarm that weakness more easily stripped away a man's guard than anything else. "No. I was thinking that I shall be flat on my face in a minute if you don't offer me a chair."

The man looked taken aback, although he must have been used to prisoners scarcely able to stand.

"Certainly. You have writing to do anyway." He pushed across a pen and paper. "Describe all the crimes you have committed."

Kolya stared at him, halfway through the difficult business of sitting down. "It's for you to invent my crimes, not me."

"There's no need to invent. If you were innocent you wouldn't be here."

Kolya laughed aloud, hearing the rustle of paper cease in every partitioned hutch at such an extraordinary sound. "How long have you been in the NKVD?"

The lieutenant glanced at his blue epaulets. "Two years."

"Well, then, you can't possibly be as naïve as you sound." He leaned back cautiously in his chair. "What is your name? I'm tired of being accused by anonymous faces."

"Maslov," the interrogator said stiffly, after a slight hesitation. "Now you will please write your crimes and the names of your accomplices."

"I have nothing to write." He had long since decided that nothing he said would make any difference, while flat denial might be easier to hold to under stress and safer for everyone he had ever known as well as his family. The mind could possibly sustain a simple absolute when it would no longer differentiate between truth and falsehood, the safe and the unsafe. He did in fact have a good deal to hide even if no one showed any signs of looking in the right places yet.

Maslov tilted his chair and laced his hands behind his head. He was very fair, already pasty and running to fat from long hours at his desk. "So you say now, all criminals are the same. But they all remember their crimes in the end and write, so why not do it now? We're in no hurry, take your time if you wish. Writing can't be easy for you yet." He glanced down at Kolya's swollen hands.

"I have nothing to write. I've always been loyal to the Party to the best of my ability."

Maslov shook his head, sighing deeply. "You think about it." He stood up. "I'll be back later."

Hours passed. Kolya dozed lightly and uncomfortably on his chair, his guard behind him shifted from time to time, low-voiced conversation went on around them. He dreamed of food, serried piles of it on tables watched by cherubs, and woke horribly stiff, his stomach feeling like bone-dry paper wrapping.

Maslov came into the room and the guard shot the chair from under him, spilling him helplessly on the floor. "Didn't you understand?" He looked genuinely upset by the blank paper. "You had to write down all your crimes."

Kolya grunted. For the first time he understood the lack of vocabulary which made a peasant spit in times of stress. Although the guard kicked him heavily, he could not get up.

Maslov shook his head sadly. "Take him back to his cell and let him think it over." He turned his back fastidiously while the guard attempted to beat his prisoner to his feet, but was finally driven to interfere. "Fetch another man and carry him, you won't get him up like that."

He doesn't want a mess on the floor of his office, thought Kolya hazily, when he was eventually flung back into his cell.

The process was repeated the following night and then again the night after that. Each time he refused to write Maslov stared at him with deep, sorrowful regret rather than anger. During the day he had to sit on the chair in his cell, hands on his knees, or else stand against the wall. If he dozed or tried to lie on his bunk he was roused at once; if he could not stay roused then he was taken along the corridor to wash in icy water.

Interrogation always came in the middle of the night, dragging him out of the sleep of complete exhaustion to march again along the endless, clicking corridors, wrists crossed, to face Maslov's probing questions and reproachful gaze with all his faculties at their lowest ebb.

Once Maslov really shook him. "What are your relations with your wife, Berdeyev? You are formally married, I understand, although she is a Party member too, isn't she?"

"My relations with her are good," he replied after the slightest of hesitations. "But of recent years our ways have lain apart. She is dedicated to her career of medicine and is taking a course of surgery."

"So you no longer live together, in spite of that formal marriage?"

Kolya's muscles tightened with anger, but it was anger he must not show, only love would find the question offensive. "No. We have not met for some time," he replied evenly. Anna. Anna. Clouding weariness stifled his attempts to think clearly; all he could see was the image of her face. Not the cold, remote face of their last days together, but the laughing, vivid Anna of their good years.

Maslov was speaking again and he jerked his mind back desperately. "She might perhaps be willing to help persuade you to be reasonable if she is a Party member."

Kolya shrugged. "I doubt if it would matter enough to her after so long." He looked down at his staring bones. "Doctors are used to unpleasant sights." Apparently he had managed just the right amount of casual regret in his voice, for Maslov allowed the topic to drop, explaining anxiously yet again how necessary confession was, if he had the good of the Party at heart.

After his last refusal he was not taken back to his

cell but put instead into another, the same size but with three men already there. He was showered with questions but when he could not answer, his tongue clamped with exhaustion, they understood well enough and made way for him to stretch out in merciful oblivion under the bunk.

In the days which followed Maslov left him alone and he began to revive with rest and human contact again. His new companions were like himself, they had held positions of responsibility and were accused of crimes which they openly derided as being without foundation. All had confessed, though, and he began to see why Maslov had put him there.

They were surprised when he said he had written nothing. "You might as well now at later," said Grisha, a former aircraft designer. "I didn't when they just asked me, neither did Sanka here, but it isn't worth it. They get you in the end and all I have for my pains is a broken nose and an arm I shall never use at the drawing board again."

Sanka had been Director of the Minsk Institute of Biological Sciences but he said nothing, sitting all day with his head in his hands, quivering without sound if anyone touched him and only screaming in his dreams.

The other occupant of the cell was still in fairly good shape although scarecrow thin like every prisoner. "Well, what the hell," he said cheerfully to Kolya. "The whole thing is mad anyway. I've done nothing wrong, you've done nothing wrong, the other two have done nothing wrong. I confessed everything and everybody the first time they asked me. It is their imagination not mine, and the sooner the bastards are satisfied the sooner it is all over."

"Everything and everybody?" queried Kolya. "They must have wanted names from you if you confessed so much."

"Of course. I was a divisional commander of infantry, so I gave them every man's name I could remember. It's easier to show them what fools they are if you give them too much rather than too little. If you refuse to speak they think there is something to be hidden, but they can't arrest everyone."

"Oh, can't they?" said Kolya bitterly.

The other chuckled. "Not in the army anyway. There will be war within the next five years, they must know they can't destroy the army. Ridicule is the quickest way of stopping a game gone mad like this one."

Kolya thought of Yakir, of Tukhachevsky, of the army officers among the prisoners in Smolensk jail, and shivered. Could the other be right in supposing that fantastic quantities of names would stop this insanity when no accusation was too fantastic to be believed? But he could not truly blame anyone who found what he thought to be a foolproof way out of this hell's kitchen of madness in which they found themselves. He too was finding clear thought increasingly difficult: in some ways refusing to sign a confession was the only beacon he had, without it he would be lost indeed. Without God in whom he could not believe; without ideals now that the Party which had held so many of his dreams was corrupted; without family, to whom he must figure as an irrational, cruel tyrant. The human being, truly alone, like a swimmer in an empty ocean, cannot survive very long.

Chapter Thirty-five

After three days of peace they came for him again. This time he was not taken downstairs but along the same corridor and into a windowless steel cell, brightly lit and holding a table, chair and the inevitable paper and pen.

Maslov was different too. Brisk and businesslike, rapping out his questions as if he no longer cared about an answer, while Kolya stood, wrists crossed behind him, the intense light swelling his sensitive eyes until tears poured down his face. He did not even see the first blow when it came, almost welcome because the floor took his weight and the light off his eyes. In spite of his efforts, though, he could not keep silent. As the beating went on and on, with fists and boots, knotted towels and belts, anything which came to hand, but never quite flinging him over the longed-for edge of unconsciousness, he could hear his own screams. No matter how he held his breath or bit his lips in an attempt to keep them back, the next battering assault jerked them apart again.

How long it went on he had no idea but eventually Maslov and his two guards were exhausted; he could vaguely hear them thirstily gulping some liquid, scented the whiff of tobacco. He lay without moving, terrified of attracting attention, able to see out of the edge of one swollen eye the pool of blood and filth in which he lay.

A military boot blotted out his vision and for a moment nothing happened, then a poker of white-hot pain convulsed his body, seeming to burn right through his ribs and into his lungs. He clenched his teeth desperately, tried to roll and then felt it burn again . . . and again on his stomach and thigh.

He heard a voice say cheerfully, "I miss a body for stubbing out fag ends in the canteen; an ashtray is never the same."

"Try it on the wife one day," suggested another, and there was a general laugh.

The break came to an end and the beating started again but this time he began to experience a strange sensation. He could feel himself thrown across the floor with the force of the blows, but the pain seemed to become less. He began to drift somewhere above the horror on the floor, to look at it with pity . . . when he came to there was the sharp smell of disinfectant, the sound of a woman's voice and he thought he was dreaming.

"Well, Comrades, everything seems all right now," she said, a rustle of starched nurse as she rose from her knees beside him.

Everything all right! he thought with terror; that means it isn't over. He smelled tobacco and cringed: they would put out their cigarettes on him again. Through the smashed flesh of his beating he could distinguish every agonized nerve end from the first burns, as if the butts were still smoldering against his bones.

Boots. The mumble of joking conversation, a cigarette crammed into his ribs, move over for the next . . . another . . . another . . . this time the nurse must have been smoking too.

Everything proceeded in an inexorable sequence. There was no question of confession now; until it was over no one would bother to ask him again. Beating, break, putting out cigarettes, again beating, fainting, the nurse, the horror of an extra cigarette . . .

From a great distance he heard the ting of a telephone and Maslov's voice. "Send over two removal men, will you? My boys are dead-beat." A pause and yawn of weariness. "Well, I reckon we'd better get some sleep; we've certainly earned it tonight." Kolya felt Maslov's face near his but could see only the blur. "It will be like that every third night until you write."

Chapter Thirty-six

For three weeks the beatings continued while he clung to the only scrap of certainty he had left: he would not confess.

Occasionally the guards diverted themselves with whatever refinement boredom or obscenity could suggest, twice he was strapped under continuous questioning facing such brilliant lights that the skin on his cheekbones blistered and his eyes swelled to caked clay in grit sockets. Once he was systematically drowned, held under water while his lungs filled and black terror whirled away every human reaction into an atrocity of dissolving fibers, retching pipes and crushed mind; and then again, and again, until there was scarcely an instant of tearing, vomiting consciousness left to him between onslaughts. But mostly it was just crude beating, only those who might be brought to public trial had imagination and skilled manpower wasted on them.

Finally they decided he was simply not important enough to spend more time on. The Lubyanka, the Butyrki, the Lefortovo, every prison in the country was awash with prisoners swept in on nameless denunciations: some uttered in envy, rancor or hatred; some in fear, some in agony; some by coincidence; even some by conviction.

Lieutenant Maslov was censured for his failure to obtain a confession, and what was left of Konstantin Berdeyev was sentenced to fifteen years hard labor before being thrown into a transit cell to await transport to the east.

He had no clear recollection of the weeks which followed. The cell held over two hundred people in a space forty paces by thirty and he was too weak to fight his way to the bunks or away from the slop pail and the door. Grisha, the former aircraft designer, was there too and but for his kindness he could scarcely have lived. It seemed ungrateful to die after all the trouble he had taken, hobbled as he was by his crippled arm, although Kolya himself no longer thought the effort of living worthwhile.

His burns became open ulcers; his torn flesh and cracked bones mended after a fashion but his pulped muscles continued to torment him with vicious cramps. He spat blood for weeks, with every nerve left in his body curled around the congealed agony of his pulverized back and stomach.

Spring came, and instead of the cell being cold and fetid it became hot and stinking. Kolya managed to stand upright and eventually to shuffle around the exercise yard twice a week in air so fresh it almost rolled their heads off their shoulders with its sharp purity. New arrivals to the cell brought stories of the great state trial of Bukharin and others almost equally well known. Even in the transit cell of the Lubyanka there were some who gave thanks that the Party leadership had been vigilant enough to uncover such treachery and blamed their own sufferings on these enemies of the people.

Kolya and Grisha taught each other anything they knew in order to keep a grip on sanity. Kolya flogged his mind into concentration on stress and wing-loading, while Grisha listened intently to halting explanations of soil chemistry and Civil War cavalry tactics. They finally fought their way to a plank bunk, made chessmen from hardened bread pellets and played on squares scratched on the timber surface. Kolya's eyes, which had discharged thick pus for three months, began to dry up.

A breathless July and the prisoners, stuck to each other by sweat, fought savagely at the slightest provocation. Kolya dropped one of the chess pellets and a hulking child strangler ate it and seized the rest; Grisha would not speak to him for days before offering his bread one evening in apology. One night the guards became so alarmed by the turmoil in the cells that they turned the heating full on, so the bugs dropped off the ceiling completely roasted and shook in rustling dead folds out of their clothes. Only the humans somehow lived, with every juice in their bodies so squeezed that when a man breathed he could hear the dry crease of his own lungs.

August, and the first chill breeze of autumn through the one high opening in the cell wall. Surely they could not spend another winter here?

September. At last. They were ordered out, chained in groups of four, pushed into covered vans painted with bakery or laundry signs so no one in the streets would realize what was within, and driven to a goods yard in east Moscow. As they went they heard the sound of voices, once a child's laugh, the hurrying of feet on a pavement, and looked at each other in amazement. It was difficult to grasp, although they had known it, how easily the world was spinning on in near-ignorance of what was happening to them. Kolya calculated carefully: Sophie would be fifteen. Yuri thirteen. He wondered whether Yuri still wanted to be a pilot; of Sophie's music he would not allow himself to think.

They were left in the vans all night in the freight yard, then hurried to the loading bays at a frantic pace before incoming shift workers could see them, although it was impossible for railway workers to remain in ignorance of the millions of prisoners freighted past them. Their chains tripped them up, as did weakness and the excitement of movement, while the guards as usual thought that blows solved every trivial stoppage. At last they were unshackled, pushed into freight cars and sealed in with padlocked bars. There were tiered bunks, sufficient if four prisoners shared one sagging wire base, a stove, a grilled hole for sanitation.

Day after day the train rolled slowly east, shunted into sidings as others passed, often stopped for hours without reason. Food of a sort was pushed through a hatch most days; you fought for what you could get. Grisha with his useless arm and Kolya, his back still like flame out of hell every time he moved, were frequently unsuccessful in these battles and had to barter some of their remaining clothes or their services as chess instructors for soggy morsels of bread or ladles of gruel.

Otherwise there was nothing but glimpses of countryside through cracks in the boards, brilliant oranges and golds of autumn spraying over dark green forest, trotting streams, wide, wide sky.

"I always wanted to see Siberia," said Grisha, laughing a little. "I met a man once who said it was the nearest place to the liberation of the soul he knew. I wanted to find out what he meant."

"It is very big," suggested Kolya. Surprisingly, his sense of humor had surfaced again.

Grisha grinned. "Liberation for us is going to be strictly of the soul."

"There are some compensations, though," observed Kolya. "It is absurd, but it's almost a relief to know there is nothing you can say or do which holds further risk. The worst has happened."

Grisha nodded. "Hardly a thought which reflects well on the Party we both still believe in. Or don't you believe in it any longer?"

Kolya thought it over. "Yes," he said slowly. "What

the Party wants, the true Party not the corrupt corpse we are saddled with now, is such that I cannot fail to believe in it. I gave myself long ago, and that is the kind of gift which can scarcely be recalled."

"You can't call it a corrupt corpse!" protested Grisha, genuinely horrified. "Corrupt, yes. A corpse, no. It will be reborn, better than before, you'll see."

Kolya was irresistibly reminded of Anna and for a moment was unable to reply. At last he said, "I'm not sure whether such faith is praiseworthy or not. It isn't just what has happened to us and to many millions more as well, it's the corruption of the Party in petty ways which makes me despair of it. One of the reasons I landed in prison in the first place was because I stopped an arrogant lout in uniform giving one of my sovkhozniks ten years for making love in a piggery, and he never forgave me."

Grisha burst out laughing.

Kolya looked at him. "You see? Here you can laugh as you should, outside you wouldn't dare. That is what has gone wrong."

After three weeks they passed through Novosibirsk and stopped just beyond at a transit camp while the line was taken over by military convoys of guns, stores, tanks and troops.

"There is fighting with Japan on the Manchurian border already," observed a man standing next to Kolya one day, as they both stared out through the wire, trying to see something and listening to the distant rumble of traffic. "Only a few probes as yet to see if we are still capable of fighting, but dangerous and skillfully led. Next spring will see something more no doubt."

The words were difficult to catch at first, as below a prominent nose the whole lower part of his face was a mass of swollen scabs, a trail of bloody slime trickling out of the corner of his mouth from smashed teeth and lacerated gums. In the camps, however, inmates soon became used to the grotesque appearance of some of their fellow prisoners and after a moment Kolya grasped what he was saying.

"While our armies are stripped of officers or am I wrong? Have there not been many arrests in the Red Army itself?" Whatever his appearance, the other man's whole bearing suggested the soldier, and a soldier, Kolya thought, who had once had a good deal of authority.

He gave a faint, derisive hoot of laughter. "Hardly a man left above the most sycophantic adjutant, Comrade. I walked into one of my brigade headquarters a few months ago and the whole lot were in charge of a lieutenant on his first posting. He was so terrified he was three parts drunk and didn't dare answer the telephone."

"I knew Army Commander Yakir once," said Kolya. "Many years ago in the Civil War. Nothing will persuade me that he was a traitor."

"He wasn't. Neither am I." The other stared at him. "Not a soldier, are you?"

"No. I went to the War College of the Red Star after commanding a squadron in the Civil War, but I was sickened with fighting and managed to make them retire me. I've been back for reserve training, of course."

"If the Party didn't want you out, you must at least be a good strategist to have succeeded. Would you go back in the army now?"

"Now?" echoed Kolya, startled. He looked at his rags and then at the barbed wire. "I don't think the Red Army is looking for my services at the moment, though it is certainly going to need someone's if it fights Japan and then Hitler attacks while our back is turned."

"Precisely. When the time comes our army will have

to expand at a rate to make our present police masters' heads spin." He made no effort to hide his contempt. He wiped his mouth gingerly; it looked appallingly painful but he made no concession to it, speaking with the same decision to which he had obviously long been accustomed. "With most of our able officers dead the result remains to be seen, but I am keeping note of every competent officer still on his feet in these cesspool camps and when I get out, those that still live, as God is my witness I will have them out too. I have no taste for my troops to be led by incompetent police slobs who prefer to slaughter their own men rather than use their common sense."

His eyes were hard and angry above the shattered mess of his face: worn and emaciated like all the prisoners and with his shoulder and arm bundled into bloody rags, he still looked an extremely tough customer. Unusually tall and holding himself stiffly erect, when he attempted to walk it was immediately clear that he was also suffering from some undisclosed internal injury. To Kolya's eye of bitter experience he bore all the signs of one repeatedly and savagely kicked in the guts, assaulted with the special degree of obscene vindictiveness guards reserved for those who retained in their manner any vestige of their former authority.

Kolya answered the original question with careful deliberation. "I'm still on the reserve, or I was. Much as I hate war, should we be invaded I would fight if I could . . . for Russia." Honesty compelled him to add, "Whether I shall ever be fit I don't know. I've mostly healed again, but I think that three weeks' beating has done something fairly lasting to my back."

"God knows how much beating has done more than I care to think about to me," observed his companion grimly. "Three weeks, though? Do you mean you didn't confess?"

"No. In the end they wearied before I did." Kolya gave the ghost of a smile.

"Well, well." The other surveyed him thoughtfully. "Neither did I, although some swine who did probably helped put me here. I think your back is worth a gamble. Your name will be on my list when I am out if you wish it."

"You seem very sure you will be out; everyone else thinks they are here forever."

"I will be out" he said flatly. "I am one of the few commanders left alive who knows one end of a tank from the other. Besides, I have some unfinished business to complete." He touched his injured arm and spat more blood into the partly frozen mud at their feet. There was a line of sores along his jaw open almost to the bone where already bitter winds had caught the discharge from his mouth. "The NKVD does not arrest my staff, break up my command and beat me to hell and back for a pack of lies without having it thrust down their throats at the first chance I have."

Kolya felt immensely invigorated by this encounter, the squalid swamp of Novosibirsk transit camp subtly less bereft of hope because of one man determined to challenge his fate. When the other wrote his name on a piece of dirty cloth, he laughed. "Konstantin? Allow me to introduce myself, Konstantin Konstantin'itch at your service. The world is lousy with us."

"Konstantin Konstantin'itch what?" asked Kolya. "I should like to know to whom I might owe my release one day."

"Rokossovsky. Corps Commander."

During the time he was there Rokossovsky swept through Novosibirsk camp like a demon broom. He demanded food, water, planks, winter clothes and boots for the prisoners. He browbeat the camp commandant until he was locked up and when he was released, looking so ill it was astonishing he could stay upright, he forced the apathetic prisoners to clean their huts and proof gaping cracks against the fifty or more degrees of frost they would soon encounter. Although he had the kind of injury which few guards could resist, when even a spiteful jab could shred every nerve in his face and drop him in his tracks with pain, he never avoided authority as the other prisoners did, never hid his contempt for the abysmal organization of the camp or abandoned his efforts to extract the necessities of life from the administration.

Quite soon it was the guards who avoided him if they could, and in the few weeks before the Commandant managed to ship him away he handed the prisoners back a glimmer of hope and humanity. But as Kolya watched him go, he could not help but realize that hope was almost nonexistent.

For Rokossovsky was traveling westward, against the mainstream of prisoners. He had been arrested at his command in the east and because of his high position had already faced there a series of particularly vicious variations on the usual torments awaiting those from whom a confession was required. Now he was considered important enough to be sent, his face drawn with pain of his partly healed arm clamped into handcuffs, to undergo the long physical and mental degradations which awaited those who might be brought to public trial. From this process there was seldom any outcome except death: for those who remained recalcitrant after months of suffering, a bullet in the back of the neck in some squalid cellar; for the majority who eventually disintegrated under intolerable pressure the merest possibility of a trial before execution.

In temperatures plunging below zero the strongest of the prisoners were at last entrained again. Kolya did not know whether to be pleased or sorry to find he was now counted among them. He had felt boots off a corpse and a padded jacket issued at Rokossovsky's insistence by the camp; even more usefully he had enough strength to defend these possessions against the criminal prisoners unless he was unlucky or careless enough to be jumped by a gang of them, as was all too common. Many an elderly professor or eminent engineer was simply beaten to death by the criminals roaming the camps.

Grisha should not have been included in the batch for transport. Everyday he became weaker and there was little Kolya could do but lie alongside him to lend his wasted body a little warmth, and talk endlessly to keep a spark of his mind alive. Long years at a drawing board were not the best preparation for the harshness of life in the camps.

"I wonder whether it is easier to suffer punishment for being innocent or guilty," remarked Grisha one day. He was perfectly composed, almost happy to think his sufferings nearly over. "The real criminals survive better than we, and I don't think it's just because they will stoop to anything to stay alive."

"Is anyone truly innocent?" asked Kolya bitterly. "I killed a man once. At least, I killed several in war, I even murdered a woman but it was mercy for her which made me do it. I feel no guilt for them, just hatred of war, which was why I left the army."

"Yet you do feel guilt for the other one?" Grisha felt a stirring of curiosity, for his companion had said very little about himself.

Kolya nodded slowly. Haltingly he explained about Evgeni, knowing relief as he did so, a clarification of his own thoughts. At the end he added, "I haven't been punished for his death, but in a way it helped to feel I deserved some of the beatings I got."

Grisha thought of the terrible pus-filled, pitted burns, the weeks of near-blindness and agonizingly swollen joints his companion had endured, was still to some extent enduring. "I think the man you had shot took the easier path."

Kolya shrugged. "That's scarcely the point. I don't know whether I'd do the same again, but I do know I've never really believed any justification of it I made to myself."

"You have a religious conscience, my friend, not a Communist one." Grisha was only half joking. "Otherwise, if the Party approved, why should you worry?"

"I can't believe in God," said Kolya violently. "How could anyone believe who spent the years I did in a countryside where millions died of starvation? What good or ill or conscience or anything else could decide whether a soul went to heaven or hell, or even which was man and which was beast when life is like that? I know my Bible, surprisingly enough; my grandmother used to read it to me. It didn't help at all to think of Maslov and those guards as creatures created by God, or give me respect for a Deity who could create men like that."

"Yet you didn't give in to them," said Grisha quietly. "Why not?"

Kolya shook his head; he did not want to think of it. Even his uneasy dozing in the freezing misery of the freight car was riven with nightmares, nightmares many times worse now than those of earlier years, although he would not then have thought it possible. "I think I didn't dare. I knew how I had felt over Evgeni; the undoing of everyone I mentioned in a formal confession was more than I could endure, worse than the terror of that cell. So I feel I have paid a little for Evgeni. You're right, it is easier to suffer if you are guilty."

"It is easier to stand too, if you believe yourself supported," said Grisha sadly. "We had that, you and I, when we believed everything the Party told us. We shall never have it again, even though we remain true Communists. How I wish Comrade Stalin knew a fraction of what is being done by his underlings in the name of the Party."

Kolya stared at him in astonishment. "I imagine he knows well enough."

"Of course he does not! He would stop such excesses fast enough if he knew, no leader could wish . . . can you imagine him wanting to destroy the Party, the army, every scrap of thought and culture and decency we have?"

Kolya thought of Stalin's patient, impassive scrutiny at the Congress, of the jails and torture cells which had taken to oblivion every one of those who might possibly have protested against his power. "Yes," he said evenly. I think I can imagine it very easily."

"You are a traitor, then, after all!" Grisha looked bewildered but above all angry, a hectic flush dyeing his face, otherwise like peeled birch bark. "What else could make you believe that all we've done, everything we've striven for, is nothing but a homicidal joke?"

Kolya shrugged. "It was not my joke."

Grisha turned away from him on the narrow wire bunk and stared at the rough-grained timber of the truck wall. "It isn't true anyway. How could we all die for nothing but a mockery?" He did not speak again, and just before they drew into Vladivostok in January 1939, he died.

Chapter Thirty-seven

The camp to which Kolya was sent was in the Cherskogo Hills five hundred kilometers north of Magadan, itself a week's sea voyage north from Vladivostok. In every direction there was nothing but permafrost scrub and bare hills, shrouded in mosquitoes and treacherous with swamp in the brief summer, hammered by fifty or more degrees of frost in winter. In these conditions they lived in ragged tents, the outside walls packed with snow for insulation in winter, working twelve hours a day in the nearby gold mines. The criminal trusties sorted the gold-bearing ore and panned the dust, while the politicals worked in appalling conditions below ground, drilling ore out of the permafrost and hauling loads to the surface.

Kolya could not help thinking of his Uncle Gregor, whom he had never met but who he knew had spent years mapping eastern Siberia. There seemed no end to the ironies of life: one generation explored in eagerness and hope in order apparently for the next to be worked to death opening up their discoveries. Kolya could even be faintly amused to find that his administrative instincts were as much outraged as his humanitarian scruples by the prodigal wastefulness of the way life was discarded in the camps.

Every moment of the day came to center on food and there was perpetual wolf-pack fighting for the slightest thing which might be edible: a pine cone, fishbones, a strip of leather from an old military cap, someone else's ration. There was a minute daily dole of bread and watery soup which was immediately reduced if a prisoner failed to reach his allotted production quota; once on reduced rations few had the strength to reach their work targets again and rations dwindled to nothing within days.

The criminal prisoners were encouraged to prey on the politicals by the guards, robbing and killing with impunity and nearly always receiving the extra food awarded if targets were surpassed. If a political protested then the guards never bothered to find out whether he had died from starvation or disease, or from being crudely gutted by the rusty edge of stove iron the criminals kept for the purpose. But however terrible the conditions, the worst shock of all for Kolya, and for most of the politicals, had occurred before they reached Cherskogo. Outside Vladivostok, while waiting for a ship to take them up to Magadan, they had been separated by only a few strands of wire from a women's camp. At first they had thought them female criminals, but a few minutes' talk at tap or food line soon confirmed the worst fear many still cherished. These were the wives and daughters of military and naval commanders, of scientists, writers and Party officials, condemned for no offense beyond being married to or fathered by the wrong man. Yakir's widow was there, his son only the NKVD knew where, and so were Tukhachevsky's aged mother, his daughter and all three of his sisters.

Kolya had more reason than most to hope that all was well with those who had once depended on him, but even he could not be certain. He remembered Maslov's questions about Anna, which he had believed safely evaded, and sweated with a terror worse than that of the Lubyanka floor as he saw the casual assaults on the women by brutalized guards and criminals.

He had never prayed for himself even when half crazed with pain or abject with fear in the Lubyanka, but he prayed now for Anna and Sophie and Yuri. He could not hold his mind from desperate pleas for them, ashamed to turn in his extremity to something he had rejected when judgment had been his, but powerless to avoid it. He did not know whether this made him a believer or whether fear had undermined his reason and thrown him back into superstition again, but he prayed too for strength to endure, somehow, to get out and be able to know they were safe. How terrifyingly little he could do if they had been swept into the NKVD net, even if he were released, he did not dare to contemplate.

It was remarkable he lasted as long as he did. He lost count of time but it was late spring, which in eastern Siberia was toward the end of May, nearly nine months after his arrival at Cherskogo, when he finally came to the end of his strength. The soggy layer melted out of the permafrost by the sun doubled the difficulty of pulling loads of wood and ore, and the extra work which had to be done for guards and trusties in order to obtain additional rations was quite simply beyond him. His teeth loosened in his gums, making chewing the leathery bread a misery, his legs began to swell and his back would no longer support piled loads or endure the agony of vibration from pneumatic rock drills.

As a last hope—and without the urgent drive to survive he would not have bothered—he went to see the camp doctor and had his first real luck in years. The NKVD doctor was paralytic with drink and his assistant, a prisoner condemned for attending a woman kicked downstairs when her husband was arrested, certified him as unfit for heavy labor and arranged to put him on the next outgoing convoy to Magadan. When Kolya tried to thank him, he shrugged. "When the boss is drunk he'll sign anything and I can be a doctor again; when he's sober anyone who comes for treatment is thrown out with a couple of salt pills. I'm feeding him neat alcohol out of his collection of specimens at the moment."

Magadan, which had seemed the end of the world on the journey north, felt almost like a resort after Cherskogo, the air perceptibly warmer, the prisoners housed in tumble-down huts instead of tents and allowed to improvise whatever means of fishing they could in the Sea of Okhotsk, deceptively calm and sparkling icily in the thin summer sunlight. Kolya was put to water-carrying for thc kitchens, infinitely lighter work than the gold mines and also having the occasional reward of food scraps, but after a week or two he collapsed again. A three-kilometer journey heaving a tub of water from river to kitchen several times a day on legs still swollen like logs was hardly the right treatment for a man of forty certified as unfit for heavy labor.

He went to the doctor again, but at Magadan prisoners found no help from him, whatever their state. The NKVD medical captain eyed him superciliously without even stirring from his chair. "What do you think we are running here? A Pioneer summer camp?"

"No," said Kolya gravely. "I didn't think that."

"Well, then, off with you. Wasting my time with malingering tales. Register as unable to work and draw your half rations."

"How much do you think it has cost the state to bring me here?" Kolya felt dizzy and lightheaded, a hard, bright anger the only remaining emotion in his scraped-out husk of body and mind. "A tourist would pay thousands for such a journey and now after so much expense to the Soviet Union your maggoting guards steal our food and encourage criminals to attack us so we haven't the strength to repay such generosity." He watched with a shadow of amusement while the Captain tried to find something to attack in a speech they both knew to contradict its earnest words.

Of course he did not try. Konstantin Berdeyev was placed in solitary confinement on quarter rations for failing to respond to an order to leave the room with sufficient speed and respect.

When he was taken before the Commandant eight days later, although mercifully rested, he was so weak that his guard had no choice but to allow him a chair while awaiting further sentence.

"Konstantin Aleksandr'itch Berdeyev?" The Commandant had the same worried, driven face as any Party functionary.

"Yes." His voice was almost a whisper. He cleared his throat and then repeated more strongly, "Yes." On his last lap he would not give way.

"You were once Director of Klintsy Sovkhoz and formerly graduated from a course at the War College of the Red Star?"

"Yes."

"You are summoned to Moscow for a review of your case."

Kolya blinked. For the first time since he had left Klintsy, bundled into the back of an NKVD car, someone in authority had spoken to him as *vy*, the polite form of address, and it was this which drove the sense of what the Commandant had said into his consciousness. He put his hands on the edge of the desk and, with infinite care, levered himself up. "Thank you."

"I am very happy for you, Comrade."

He really did look pleased, too. "Thank you," Kolya repeated.

The Commandant came from behind his desk and put a hand under his elbow. "People think a man in my position is some sort of fiend, but it isn't true. I am pleased to bring good news to a prisoner if I can. I can't choose what I do."

"Thank you." He could not think of anything else to say, could not engage his mind into the conventional gear of words.

"I will give orders for you to rest until a ship comes and for you to have full rations again. It should be a pleasant voyage at this time of year." He was like an anxious travel agent.

Kolya shook his head, then decided that was wrong and nodded instead; the Commandant by his side seemed infinitely distant.

"Watch what you say and do until you're in Moscow. Your case is only to be reviewed; you must be careful until it is over," the Commandant continued earnestly. He ushered his prisoner out of the door like a guest. "I am truly happy for you, Comrade."

They even shook hands on parting.

Chapter Thirty-eight

Moscow was bitterly cold. A razor-edged easterly gale blew scurries of snow off the buildings and flung it in the faces of the few unfortunates still about their business. No one glanced at the closed van which had met a train newly in at the freight yards; none of the prisoners inside noticed the weather. All were back from the east for a review of their cases, not one dismayed by meeting at various transit camps those who had already been to Moscow for review and were now heading east again. After the long excitement of the journey, the unbelievable miracle which had brought them here, everyone was full of confidence that they were only hours from freedom.

Their optimistic mood was shattered abruptly by the uncompromising reception they received at Butyrki Prison. Not the Lubyanka at least, thought Kolya thankfully. They were put into the usual filthy cell crammed to overflowing, and for the first time grasped the fact that half the people there were waiting to return to the camps after having had their cases reviewed. Many were going east for the first time as arrests continued, although apparently on a diminished scale.

Konstantin Aleksandr'itch Berdeyev was called before an interrogator on February 8, 1941. The room was almost identical with the one seared on his mind from the Lubyanka, gray drab walls, metal-lined to waist height. A table, a chair, a pile of paper.

"Sit down." No politeness, no sense that anything had changed.

He sat down and stared at the paper. He really did not think he could go through it all again. The walls seemed to be closing in on him and he wiped his face with the ice of his hands.

Name, date and place of birth, army career, Party membership and number, the whole desperate procession rolled past him again. Unexpectedly the interrogator held up his old identity card photograph. "Is this you?"

Kolya peered at it; his eyesight had never fully recovered from the Lubyanka. "Yes." Anna had always liked that photograph; she had said he looked like a true director in his smart clothes yet retained the half smile of the secret lover.

The interrogator laughed. "No one but you would know it now." He leafed through the file in front of him and began another series of questions about Klintsy, which had him groping for facts and statistics long since blurred in his mind; about his army life, which he was able to answer with more confidence.

During the next few days he had several more sessions of interrogation, his answers apparently checked against his personal file, his rusty memory and slow reactions making him steadily more alarmed.

Then he was transferred to the inner prison of the Lubyanka, his feelings beyond description when he recognized its high-windowed courtyard and silent, clicking spaces.

He was put into solitary confinement, a nightmare, crawling week which left him scraped almost bare of resolve. Then he was brought, along the same corridors, between the same clicking guards, with the same remorseless routine of crossed wrists, to interrogation again.

"You don't look well," remarked the NKVD Major facing him this time.

"No," said Kolya dryly. "I don't feel well."

"That is a pity. Our investigation is complete; the order for your release will be signed tonight. Do you have any friends in Moscow where you could go?"

He shook his head wordlessly.

"We can't let you out looking like that, even at night," said the Major severely. "You must get some clothes from somewhere."

Kolya gave a gasp of laughter, his shredded composure needing to be held with every ounce of his remaining strength. He realized he was still holding his hands behind him and laced them shakingly into the tatters of his filthy padded jacket, the same issued two and a half years earlier at Novosibirsk. "You could lend me an NKVD uniform," he suggested.

The Major's face cleared. "A Red Army uniform, you have been recalled from the reserve, I see." He pushed forward a document. "You have to report at the Commissariat of Defense for assignment in two weeks' time."

The uniform when it came was that of a full colonel, but when he remarked acidly on the extent of his sudden leap up the promotional ladder the interrogator looked quite surprised. "Full officers' ranks were restored last year and you have twenty-two years' seniority," he pointed out primly. "You couldn't be less than a colonel with your record. I have arranged a room for you at the Red Army officers' hostel, and I hope you'll be able to recover there from your difficult journey. It is unfortunate that your service to the state has left you so out of health."

I should knock him down and go back inside,

thought Kolya grimly. I should murder the sanctimonious swine and take his body to Red Square and tell everyone why, but for all the hell good it would do I might as well go back into the Red Army. He could not face any more. He said nothing; he even signed guarantees not to speak of events "while in the custody of the People's Commissariat of Internal Affairs." He did not think he would want to speak of it, ever again.

It was terrible indeed to feel almost guilty about his release, to wonder whether he was walking out into another kind of imprisonment, free yet trapped by hypocrisy and ashamed of the silence in which he was abandoning his fellow victims.

He was washed and deinfested, shaved and given a military haircut, handed new papers, identity documents, money and assignment orders. It was the interrogator himself who drove him out of the Lubyanka gates and into the cold, empty, echoing spaces of a friendless Moscow at two o'clock in the morning, who helped him undress and instructed an orderly, who obviously thought him drunk, to attend him in the morning. With every mental process thrown into reverse, the NKVD Major suddenly seemed his only contact with reality and when he went Kolya was plunged into a fresh void of confusion.

In the morning it took him two hours to summon enough resolution to leave his room; it was a week before he dared enter the communal dining room, watching surreptitiously the forgotten chatter and manners of civilization and then slipping back to the safety of his room, feeling a ridiculous impostor in the ill-fitting uniform draped over his scarecrow bones.

By the date of his appointment at the Commissariat of Defense he felt somewhat steadier. He still found it impossible to join in the joking banter of the officers downstairs but he had at least forced himself to eat in company. Every mouthful was a test of endurance, though, for however carefully he ate, his thoughts alone were sufficient to wrench his digestion apart without an instant's warning and he was terrified of disgracing himself in the mess hall. He learned, too, to sit with his fellow officers instead of hunched in his room, watching and feeling the ordinary pulses of life, trying not to turn aside from casual encounters, not to evade every contact with authority.

With a degree of recovery, as the desire just to sleep, to be still and stay hidden ceased to dominate his life quite so exclusively, other difficulties began to surface. He felt desperately adrift, scarcely comprehending normal topics of conversation. He was staggered to find that Europe had been at war for eighteen months, France defeated, fascist Germany hammering at the gates of Britain and—most astonishing of all—the ally of Soviet Russia, who now occupied a large slice of eastern Poland, the Baltic States and Finland by agreement with her new Nazi friends. He did not even recognize his own face in the mirror and could well understand the interrogator's laugh at his photograph. His hair was completely white; there were lines graven so sharply either side of his nose that the whole cast of his countenance was altered, with eyes sunk deep into pouched sockets so their original light gray color was hardly discernible. Only his eyebrows were a flag to the past, still dark and climbing as strangely upward. Like my grandmother, he thought wryly; she had white hair and dark eyebrows at eighty, it looks a little odd at forty-one.

He missed Anna; no, needed her desperately. It was martyrdom to attempt the difficult climb back to health alone. He wanted above all to know for certain that she had escaped arrest, began to wonder whether there was any reason why he should not go in search of her, attempt to patch the shattered fabric of his life. He looked at his face in the mirror again and put his head in his hands. How could he come back, a cruel ghost from the past, half crippled mentally and physically, as if nothing had changed, when surely everything had changed?

Anna would have made another life for herself, a successful surgeon and probably settled with some other man long since. It would be unreasonable to expect anything else after five years, when they had parted in such bitterness and grief. The familiar cramps twisted through his stomach again and sent him retching to the slop bucket, chill with sweat and the knowledge of his continuing dependence on the dream of Anna. Where else could he ever find a foothold in love and familiarity again, attempt to poise his life back on the still center of contentment from which it had been so violently displaced?

He still had not decided what to do when he presented himself at the Commissariat of Defense, enjoying the brisk walk through Moscow's wide streets, the bustle of people, the slightly improved array of goods in the shops. It was as if the other Soviet state of the camps were a mere sick illusion which a few more days of sanity would banish altogether into the world of mirages where it belonged.

The elderly General who interviewed him was charming, obviously sympathetic, and made several embarrassed references to the "difficult and dangerous assignment" he had just completed. "You are confirmed in the rank of colonel, with back pay to January 1," he added. "You are to be assigned to the staff here in Moscow but first you certainly need some of the leave you have accumulated."

Kolya was not sure he could support much more time on his own but he nodded; the thought of the concentrated work demanded by a staff appointment was shattering. I have no experience of staff work," he said after a pause.

The General cleared his throat. "You did once go through the War College. In all our Western staffs there cannot now be more than a few dozen officers with a staff course behind them." He added sardonically, "You need have no fear, you will be far more competent than most of your fellows once you have recovered."

Kolya stared at him, thinking of all the colonels and generals and technical experts he had met in the camps, shoveling dirt and dying of starvation. "At the Red Army hostel I hear many officers predict war with Germany soon."

"It seems very likely," agreed the General, and then checked himself. "Comrade Stalin says it will not come yet, we have plenty of time." His tone was skeptical but the topic was obviously not open to discussion and he went on briskly, "I have dated your appointment for two weeks hence; the situation is too grave to give you the full time you need for recovery. There are vouchers attached for the additional uniforms you should draw. Where would you like your leave pass made out for? I understand you have no friends in Moscow."

"Saratov." Kolya said it without thinking and then had not the strength of mind to retract.

"There is a Red Army rest center just outside Saratov, with a few individual *dachas* for those who require them." The General smiled. "I think perhaps your need is greater than most and I will add a note to that effect."

For all of the two-day cross-country journey to Saratov his mind was in turmoil; he could not sleep for more than minutes at a time and felt too sick to eat. When he arrived he still had not decided what to do and drifted around the square outside the station, his rank causing all kinds of unrealized difficulties for the numerous soldiers relaxing with their girls: regulations requiring military superiors to be saluted had been reintroduced into the Red Army while he had been in prison. Usually windswept Saratov was calm and benighnly warm, although there was still snow about and might well be more before the true spring started. Most people had left off their heaviest winter clothes and looked gay and happy in the glittering sun as they strolled, chattering and laughing with twined arms along the embankment above the Volga, their slurred speech reminding Colonel Berdeyev of long distant days of Poliarnyi and the 103rd Saratovsky Cavalry.

He began to feel hot and dizzy, bewildered by his indecision, by the difficulty of coming to any decision at all. After a while sheer weakness forced him to rest while he strove to collect his thoughts into some kind of order.

"Do you feel all right, Comrade Colonel?"

He looked up uncertainly at the girl sitting on the bench beside him. "Yes." It sounded ungracious and he added reluctantly, "Thank you."

She smiled; she had twins in the pram beside her "I'm sorry, but you looked unwell. I was worried about you, I didn't mean to interfere."

He took off his cap and ran his hands through his hair; he could feel them shaking and was suddenly convulsed with loathing for the person he had become. "You weren't interfering; it is I who should thank you for your concern. You have fine twins there," he added, in a clumsy attempt at courtesy.

She laughed. "They are little devils often. You don't think there will be war, do you?"

They both looked at the innocent, sleeping faces silently. "I don't know," he said at last, with an effort. "You should be safe here anyway."

"My husband is a pilot," she said simply.

Yuri, he thought. Yuri sixteen next month, a war

will kill him for certain. He must find out about them, know Anna was safe, see his son once at least, measure how Sophie had grown, even if they never knew he had done so. "Do you know where the hospital is?" he demanded harshly.

"Why yes, Comrade Colonel." She was convinced he was ill now. "The big building over there. Shall I come with you?"

He shook his head and put his cap on again. "Thank you, no. My wife is a surgeon there, I am on leave to see her." He had no idea whether she was still in Saratov, or even if they were still married. The wife of a political prisoner was allowed to assume her husband's death without any formalities and it was almost certain she would no longer wish to be known by his name; many Soviet wives used their own anyway. In the past Anna had been exceptional in always using his, had indeed incurred Party censure by doing so; it was not a habit likely to have survived the past five years of disillusion and danger.

"Oh." Her face cleared. "I had the twins there, may I ask her name?"

Of course, the inevitable question, throwing his mind relentlessly back into confusion again. He groped for some kind of answer, knowing there was no answer he could give, before jerking out defiantly, "Berdeyeva. Anna Berdeyeva." He watched for her reaction with painful intentness.

"Oh yes, of course!" She laughed. "She is in the gynecological Department; she told me I would have quads at least!" Then she added hastily, in case he should think this a reflection on his wife's abilities, "Not seriously of course, she is much respected."

God, he was going to be sick, he was going to be horribly sick, a colonel in full uniform and medals, all over the main promenade of Saratov. He closed his eyes and clenched his muscles desperately, not daring to move while an unknown age of time went by. A thought, a scent, the slightest reflex would turn him inside out.

He felt an arm around his shoulders, the wetness of tears on his face; surely he was not weeping? He opened his eyes.

"Anna," he said thickly. "Anna, my love."

Chapter Thirty-nine

"Had I been fit I think I would have kept away," he said. "As it was I knew I shouldn't come, but lacked the strength to stay alone without you."

She kissed him. "You fool. Didn't you know I had to fight through every day holding somehow to the belief you were still alive and would come back to me?" She laughed suddenly: "I had the wife of the hospital Registrar about to be wheeled down to the operating theater for a caesarian, when that girl came bursting into the casualty and sent the sister running for me with news my husband was taken ill on the Volga promenade."

"I hope she isn't still waiting," he said smiling.

"I was talking to the head of surgery; he said he would do it. No one discusses such matters, but he knew where you had been. It was only when I saw a Red Army colonel that I thought . . . I thought for a terrible moment she must have been mistaken and it wasn't you."

They were lying in a warmly sheltered hollow overlooking the majestic width of the still partly frozen Volga. Anna had borrowed a car and after a night in the hospital which she had insisted he take, she sitting beside him while he slept from the drugs she gave him, they had driven out to the Red Army rest center and the *dacha* to which the kindly General's chit entitled them.

"It isn't quite me, you know, *vazlublenny*," he said slowly. "I am ashamed to come to you in such need. I intended to find out whether all was well with you and the children and then go away without you knowing I'd been here, or I think that's what I intended to do. But for that girl . . ."

Anna knelt beside him and put her hand over his mouth. "Then there are no words for my gratitude to her. Please, Kolyushka, let this be our day, just with our happiness. We both have so much explaining to do later."

He reached up and drew her down on top of him, astonished to feel his body stir, which he had thought long since abused into impotence. He caressed her awkwardly, fumbling at first and beginning to apologize for the roughness of his hands, his clumsy inability to give her the rapture they had once known, but she silenced him ruthlessly, blotting out thought with her own passion.

When it was over he lay a long time without speaking. "I will be better next time," he said at last ruefully.

"Don't you dare apologize once more, Konstantin Berdeyev," she said, with all the old- remembered snap. "It is others who should be ashamed, not you. I wouldn't have tried to force you today, except I thought . . . we both remember too much of what was said that terrible night at Klintsy and I thought it wouldn't come easier between us with time."

He remembered how she had looked in their Klintsy bedroom, as pale and dead as ice in the moonlight. He gathered her into his arms again; he could sense rather than feel the sobs deep inside her. "However much I poisoned it then, I knew there was never any shadow in the love you gave me."

She buried her face in his shoulder; there were flecks of gray in the bronze of her hair now and he stroked it gently. "Five long years to live with the poison, though, Kolyushka. You thought I'd be with someone else, didn't you?"

He hesitated. "Five years is a long time after the bitterness of the sort of separation we had, the lack of hope once you knew I was arrested. I would not have blamed you."

She looked up at him, tears glittering on her lashes but with a tantalizing smile straight out of the past. "No?"

His arms tightened. "Oh God, Annochka, yes I would. I was sick just thinking about it. Has there truly been no one?"

She met his eyes. "Once, but it wasn't long before I knew it meant nothing. I only learned quite how much I loved you when you were not there."

Kolya thought of the Smolensk whores who had done little more than underline his own desperation. He kissed her fingers. "A new beginning then, love, with your help. It's no good, we can't go back, somehow together we must go forward."

They lay all night in each other's arms, sleeping and waking, Anna rousing him the moment she sensed the nightmares begin to overset him, shaken by anger and pity at the different shape and edges of his body as she had been by shock at her first sight of his eroded face and white hair; he listening to her roughened breathing which betrayed the human needs which he was unable to fulfill and must not further rouse until he could.

Next day they went walking along the frost-hard sand at the edge of the Volga. It was a beautiful day again, with glittering plates of ice diving and clashing in the wake of the earliest tugs up the river, the birds wheeling and diving in welcome to the warmth of another year.

Anna noticed almost at once when he began to flag and sat down on some driftwood. "It's hot enough for real spring, isn't it? How about fanning me while I doze in the sun. She grinned at him like a twelve-year-old.

"Husbands are made to be useful," he agreed gravely, sitting stiffly beside her. "I know that medical face of yours; there's no need to be tactful. I'll be all right in a few minutes."

"I never could deceive you, so perhaps it's as well I've never really tried," she said cheerfully.

"All right, then," he said suddenly. "Tell me about the children. There's something wrong, isn't there? Why is neither of them with you?"

She flushed at the unexpectedness of it. "What do you mean? I told you, Sophie is studying music in Leningrad and Yuri is at Kharkov Technical Institute doing an Air Force pretraining course. Although he's so young it is a wonderful chance for him; boys competed for places from all over the Soviet Union."

"You can't deceive me, remember?" he said softly. "I'm back, Anna. Not just a sick husband to be nursed but a father too with a right to know what is wrong. They are not both away at their age, leaving you alone, without good reason."

She hugged her hands tightly around her knees, staring out over the white and silver water. "They loved you, didn't you know that too?" The words were almost torn from her. "They blamed you at first, but as they came to understand a little of what had happened they felt I had let you down, had left you for my own selfish ends when your need was so great. As soon as they could walk out, they did."

"Why should they blame you? What did you tell them?"

"What could I tell them?" She shrugged helplessly. "It took years before I understood it all myself. All I knew or cared about was that I had lost you; I didn't want to talk about it. It was only when you were arrested, when the arrests swept through Saratov too, that I suddenly knew in my heart what you had done and why. It didn't help with the children, though; it would have been far too dangerous to tell them you were one of the hated medieval nobles of tsardom, even if they had cared. You were their beloved father, not Count Berdeyev—as if it mattered!"

"Does it matter to you now?" He looked down at his tightly gripped hands.

"No." Her eyes were dark and withdrawn as she thought about it. "You meant to hurt me by the way you told me. Every word you spoke was aimed at tearing us apart, whatever the cost. I hated you then, you, not some rubbish about an old title, although it shocked me, I admit it. I'd always known you couldn't quite be the peasant you claimed: in spite of your love for the land there was nothing about you of the true peasant, but I'd never dreamed of anything like that. It was the terrible way you told me I couldn't bear, how you had doubted my love enough to keep it secret all those years and then taunted me as if the fault was mine. You weren't like the man I'd married any longer. I began to wonder whether you hadn't pretended other things—about our love perhaps, or the Party, since you were so good at deceit. It wasn't as if it was the first time I'd seen a stranger in you."

"Anna—"

"No, let me finish. I've never been able to tell anyone how I felt in all this; now I want you to know. I said stupid things too, but you wouldn't help me at all. I needed time to think but of course you wouldn't give it to me. You kept throwing my beliefs in my face until I was so hurt and confused I felt that if you wanted me away then perhaps I should go. If I'd been able to think I would have known a man couldn't change as you did, even though you made me believe it was because I'd never really known you. How that hurt, more than all the rest, to be told by the man I had loved and lived with thirteen years, that I didn't know him. Until I found out I wasn't mistaken. I had known you all along. But by then it was too late. To protect the children I had to stay away as you had wanted, to hope for their sake you would somehow manage to keep silent. Never for my sake; by then I would sooner they had taken me too."

He thought of the women's camp at Vladivostok. "Thank God they did not."

She turned on him in a flash. "What do you think I have felt these last years since I understood it all? Tricked into flight by the man I loved and trusted, blamed by Yuri and Sophie for all the things they didn't understand and I couldn't explain, unable to contradict them when they accused me of throwing you over to save my skin or for the sake of my ambition to be a surgeon? How could I tell them their heredity doomed them too if it became known? How explain why we quarreled without destroying every scrap of faith they need to live by? What do you think it has cost me not to come hammering at the prison doors in Smolensk, in Moscow? Oh God, I nearly died when Vera wrote and said you had been transferred to the Lubyanka. Yet no one came for us; how could I throw all your suffering in your face and send the children after you into hell? Even now I know—" She broke off, fighting for control, but when he tried to hold her she pushed him away.

"They were my beliefs you used like a row of skittles. I had shaped my life by them and by you.

Even when I knew why you had done it I couldn't bear to think how you had used me for your own ends. How could you alone decide to throw away everything we possessed without even asking whether I thought such a sacrifice worthwhile? How stupid it sounds when you suffered so much to protect us all, but it is how I felt. You should never have forced me to accept such a gift, can't you see what you did to me?"

"Anna, don't." He felt completely defenseless under the hail of words, the storm of feeling she had contained all these years. "Somehow we have to start again. We can't tell them the truth, but when we speak to them together again as one, the children will understand." He was feeling horribly sick again, a green-edged world pressing down the corners of his sight. He held himself very still, breathing carefully, then went on slowly, "Yes, I knew what I did to you. I used your love against you deliberately, your glorious generous love for me and for the Party, because I alone could judge the strength of it. It was my feelings for you and for the children which taught me of the terrible cutting edge only great love can hold. I knew no other way to make you go. Forgive me."

There were suddenly no more words for them. They clung together while the world swung past, the half-forgotten, rusty key of passion slowly beginning to grind through his body again, unlocking sickness until at last there was an approach of easement, the sweet drive of senses searching out the source of heedless joy again, sweeping aside restraints, humiliations, pain, and launching them crystal-fresh upon the sparkling ocean of delight.

Part Six
INFERNO
1941-45

Chapter Forty

The great marble Georgievsky Hall in the Kremlin was crowded with high-ranking officers from every command in the Soviet Union. Full-dress uniforms, medals and gold braid shifted idly across the polished floor, greeting, gossiping, speculating above all on whether Stalin, when he appeared, would at last say something definite about the German threat looming across the frontier.

Staff Colonel Berdeyev was employed in evaluating the mass of reports flowing in about German troop concentrations and placing markers on a situation map which now showed a confirmed strength of two million men, and quite possibly double that. He also saw, but was not responsible for, the plot of Soviet strength. On paper this was comfortably keeping pace with the potential enemy; in practice, as he knew from his contacts among the staff, short of fuel, ammunition, tanks and guns, many formations pushed forward with very little cover into territories only acquired in the last eighteen months. When harassed forward commanders protested and suggested dispersal, camouflage, the issue of combat quantities of ammunition, even the evacuation of children from holiday camps along the frontier, they met with curt refusal and accusations of attempting to provoke a war which Party Leader

Stalin said would not come yet. A kind of helpless apathy had settled on staff and command alike, as they watched the blow come, forbidden to notice it coming, arrested or shot at the slightest sign of disagreement or protest. But tonight, at last, the *Khozyain* had gathered them here, surely for official notification of crisis.

Kolya suddenly spotted an unmistakable figure in the throng and pushed his way hastily through the chatting throng to stand at attention before a tall, handsomely medaled general. "Comrade General."

The man turned and stared at him. "Well, well, well," said Rokossovsky. "I expect I recognize you better than those at home did. Welcome, Konstantin Aleksandr'itch." He moved away slightly from the group around him.

"I have to thank you, Comrade General." Kolya glanced around to see they were not overheard. "I think I owe you my life."

Rokossovsky grinned. A set of somewhat loose false teeth helped disguise a slight distortion of mouth and lower face; otherwise he appeared remarkably untouched by the further pressures of terror he must have undergone since he had left Novosibirsk. "We both look more handsome as guests of the Kremlin than we did as guests of the NKVD. It took me more than a year after I met you to get myself out and by then few on my list were still alive. I'm glad you were one of them."

"So am I, Comrade General." He would not have been able to answer with such sincerity a couple of months before. "I should like to know the trick of getting oneself out; it is the kind of information which might come in useful at any time."

"God, I hope not. If it is any consolation to you, in your case, like mine, matters were made a little easier because you hadn't confessed to any crime."

He laughed abruptly. "The only man I happened to mention in all my interrogations they became so excited over that they obediently put him on my charge as both chief accuser and fellow conspirator for good measure."

Kolya stared at him thoughtfully. "He was Stalin's brother," he suggested, poker-faced.

Rokossovsky's expression relaxed slightly. "Konstantin Aleksandr'itch, you have the trick of it. He had been dead fifteen years, and those stupid swine never even bothered to check. Of course, you first have to get yourself a trial of some sort and make them believe it is worth risking something to make the execution legal," he added blandly. "You need to be a Corps Commander at least for that."

Kolya laughed, but there could be no doubt that Rokossovsky had achieved a truly remarkable swindle in a process from which he could not have been expected to emerge alive. "They asked me all the wrong questions too. Who needs to use even common sense, when it is easy to beat whatever you want out of a prisoner?"

"Yes," said Rokossovsky deliberately. "I rather think they did." He took Kolya's arm and propelled him across the crowded hall; only someone who had seen the sweat turning to flaked ice on his face as he labored to walk ten paces at Novosibirsk would have detected the scrape of remaining stiffness in his movements. "I have something to show you. I saw it during the last reception here when we all sat on our asses for hours, wasting time."

"I hope we don't waste time today," observed Kolya. "I think there is very little left."

"Everyone in this room, except one, knows there is no time left at all. God damn it to hell, I can hear them revving up their engines in the woods just over the frontier when I visit our apology for a frontier guard."

He shrugged. "Unfortunately, that one exception is rather important as you and I know to our cost. I have just been told to disperse my troops for summer maneuvers, those not already scattered in barracks from which I am forbidden to shift them even for training."

Kolya knew that Rokossovsky had been recently appointed to command the 9th Mechanized Brigade in the Ukraine, the best hope of immediate reinforcement for Soviet frontier defenses if the Germans should choose to drive on an area well known for its lukewarm support of the Moscow government. "What will you do? I beg your pardon, Comrade General, it is none of my business."

Rokossovsky scowled angrily. "I'm told it is none of my business either, but I take a somewhat different view. My summer maneuvers are going to have a singularly undispersed nature." He had herded Kolya over to the other side of the room. "You are usually known as Kolya, aren't you?"

"Yes, Comrade General," said Kolya, mystified.

"Unusual isn't it for a Konstantin? I should know."

"Well, yes, Comrade General. I should have been Nicolai after my grandfather but there . . . there was a family quarrel so I was Konstantin instead, but the nickname stuck."

Rokossovsky nodded. "I remember thinking it odd at Novosibirsk, but I reckoned you might have your reasons. I was sitting here the other day, as bored as hell and looking at these plaques for something to do." He indicated the marble slabs all around the hall which bore the names of those awarded the Order of St. George, Imperial Russia's highest award for gallantry. Here the Revolution had left untouched the military heroes of the past. "Look at the one above your head when you are unobserved and keep quiet about your grandfather's name in future. We both have cause to be thankful for NKVD incompetence, but you more than I perhaps: even after a trip to the camps you do not look like the Oryolsky peasant your file says you are." He disappeared back into the throng again.

Kolya was aware of several people watching him curiously, surprised by an unknown colonel in animated conversation with a brigade commander, so he affected disinterest and went in search of vodka, which his stomach, although much improved, would not in fact permit him to drink.

Suddenly the hall stirred and stiffened. Stalin appeared. Everyone clapped and Kolya was glad of the excuse of a glass for his own token performance. He had managed, with reservations, to hold on to his Communist faith but he acknowledged real personal hatred for Stalin, the image of the camps, of the corruption of the Party, held bitterly in his mind. He watched Rokossovsky sardonically. He was standing very stiff and upright, applauding with exemplary vigor.

Stalin stood for some while in mutual applause; when he stopped, there was instant silence.

"Greetings, Comrades! I welcome you here today." He moved over and spoke to one or two commanders individually and then walked out.

There was complete, astonished silence. No word on the German build-up, no acknowledgment of danger, whether imminent or distant. Covert glances were exchanged but no one dared say what was uppermost in every mind and after a few minutes they began to straggle out of the hall. The reception was over.

Hanging back politely to allow his seniors passage, Kolya glanced up at the plaque Rokossovsky had indicated. It was headed 1843 and the third name down was Major Count Nicolai Berdeyev.

He told Anna about it, without mentioning Rokossovsky, as they walked home together after he had met her from her shift at the hospital. She had accepted a more junior appointment than her experience entitled her to in order to follow him to Moscow, and they were living in a small room overlooking the Moskva River.

"Didn't you know he had the George?" asked Anna. "It seems the sort of thing any tsarist military family would know."

He shook his head. "My grandmother loved him so much she could seldom manage to speak of him. He had been killed thirty years before I came to live with her, but his memory was as close to her as if he were still living." He did not want to discuss why his father had never even mentioned his grandfather's name.

She squeezed his arm. "I can understand that, especially if he was at all like you."

He thought of the long-burned portrait, wishing suddenly he was able to look at it again. He dimly remembered harsh, deeply lined features and wondering what his grandmother could have seen in such a disagreeable-looking man to carry her through the years. With a deep sense of shock he realized that his own face must now look somewhat similar, the features different but the cast of countenance almost identical. "I remember thinking what a grim, hard face he had in the picture I saw," he said slowly. "I wonder now what the devil he had to endure which made him look as I do after the Lubyanka and the camps. I think we both were very fortunate to find the grace of women like you and my grandmother to love us." And I should like to talk politics with him too, he thought with a certain wry amusement, clouded recollections of some of the things his grandmother had told him faintly etched in the back of his mind.

"How you look!" she said contemptuously. "It is what you are which carries my heart, hers too no doubt. But I don't know how I could bear thirty years' widowhood."

"And I wasn't able to support more than a couple of weeks alone once I could return to you." They smiled at each other as if the strolling crowds around them did not exist.

"Let's go on to our bridge," suggested Anna.

"The possessive adjective is something no true Communist should need to use," he teased her as they leaned over the parapet where so long ago they had met and kissed and quarreled about a ceremony of marriage.

She flushed. "Even my thoughts were once the Party's, but now I find that you have everything first."

He kissed her, heedless of where they were. "I wasn't mocking you, my love."

"I never realized there might have to be a choice before all those terrible things happened to us. I know now that the Party can make mistakes and lose its way; we must judge it even if we still believe in what it wants." She smiled faintly. "There is no judgment I can make of you; it is over and done. All of me is yours and in the giving of it I found out something you already knew. There was a core of truth in what you said at Klintsy, wasn't there? Otherwise it wouldn't have hurt quite so much. Always before something of me was held back, which wasn't mine to give." She laughed lightly, joyously. "It's mine now, so it is yours like everything else."

He stared down at the bright Moskva water, flowing sluggishly now, for the summer so far had been dry. "The gift beyond price," he said softly. "However far we are separated it will make no difference."

"What do you mean?" She knew him too well to think he was speaking idly.

He hesitated. It seemed a wretched response to such a declaration, but they had determined never to suppress the truth between them again and he faced her squarely. "It will be war, and soon. I haven't spoken to you about my work, not because it is secret for I trust you with my life, but because we've had so little time to speak of many things which to us have been more important. But hardly anyone on the staff is in the slightest doubt; only the date is uncertain. Stalin will not speak of it or allow precautions to be taken, but even he thinks it will come, next year perhaps."

"And you?"

"A few days."

She went white with shock. "You won't go to the front?"

He smiled slightly at this instinctive personal reaction. "No. I expect I'll stay on the staff. In spite of all your efforts I'm not really fit for active duty." This was certainly true. He had recovered a remarkable degree of health and strength, contentment a medicine no drug could equal, but the weakness in his back remained, his sight was adequate only with glasses and his digestion still reacted fiercely to the slightest nervous stress.

She pressed her hands to her eyes. "Those camps . . . strange if I have to be thankful for them."

"Well, I won't," he said feelingly.

She laughed shakily. "Are you sure about this?"

"Yes, as sure as a man can be. It is dry enough for tanks now and I don't think the Germans fools enough to delay a single unnecessary day. You mustn't speak of it, though."

"No," she said dully.

He looked around him at Moscow shimmering in the sweep of summer sun. Would they truly be at war by the time the water brushing quietly through the arches under their feet flowed into the salt of the Caspian? "Yuri," he said at last. "I had hoped so much to get away to see him before it started. I don't think I will manage it now, although Sophie anyway should be here from Leningrad at the end of her term.

I've written to them both as you know, but one can say so little in a letter."

"He is only sixteen! There's no danger for him!"

"It is going to be a long war, Anna," he said gently. "A very long war."

Chapter Forty-one

The German army poured over the western frontier of the Soviet Union just before sunrise nine days later.

At Supreme Headquarters Colonel Berdeyev, unwanted by his map of German dispositions, watched as confusion struck like a hurricane across tables and maps, threw papers and files and contingency plans aside, crossed circuits on the communications network, tossed frantic appeals for help and reinforcement into a limbo of unpreparedness, and finally recoiled in a backwash of hysterical paralysis as hours passed and the Kremlin refused even to believe that war had broken out. Officers reporting themselves under fire were reprimanded, often forbidden to fire back, but otherwise the Party Leader left his armies to flounder in panic and a blank void of silence.

By the time a Committee of State Defense was formed and a coherent, if wildly optimistic, series of orders began to be issued by the leadership, a week had passed and the scale of disaster was unimaginable.

The tragedy deepened and widened every hour, the speed and weight of attack shattering all attempts at defense or delay. Within a month the Germans had occupied an area twice that of France and were only three hundred kilometers from Moscow. Within two months Leningrad was under seige; within three months half a million soldiers surrounded near Kiev brought the Red Army's list of killed and missing past the staggering total of three million. A holocaust was consuming Russia, and with every scraped-up unit thrown into battle on the instant of its arrival it seemed as if a stable front, a moment to stand and think, a single instant without bombs and confusion and inexperienced command and German tanks appearing a hundred kilometers beyond where they were supposed to be, would never again be achieved. Withdrawal was forbidden; when withdrawal nevertheless became unavoidable, the generals who carried it out and the staff who advised it faced instant execution. Troops who fought their way out of encirclement were sometimes mown down by NKVD machine guns when they reached their own lines, since any abandonment of position was likely to be treated as desertion.

The atmosphere at Supreme Headquarters, or Stavka, as it was usually called, became steadily more incoherent with strain, overwork, terror and shock. When Pavlov, Commander of the Western Army Group was summarily recalled and shot without trial together with most of his staff, Stavka's ability to make or recommend any independent decision almost ceased.

Kolya had been transferred to a detailed situation map of the northern front, but to make sense of the reports pouring in was an impossible task. Soviet units appeared, disappeared, reappeared, were renumbered, amalgamated, detached, lost sight of with their communications blown to bits. The Germans sent armored flying columns racing far ahead of their main thrust, itself sometimes moving at more than fifty kilometers a day. The dead straight, unstoppable drive for Leningrad was terrifying as it leaped across the map, and at last Kolya took a chance when he was speaking to his opposite number in Leningrad command and asked him to try to send a message to Sophie, to tell her to get out at once before the city was cut off.

Sophie. He had worried about Yuri but he apparently was safe, the whole of Kharkov Technical Institute evacuated east quite early on; but gay, loving Sophie, whom he had not seen since she had ceased to be a child, was now full in the path of the most urgent Nazi drive of all.

He saw very little of Anna, for she too was frantically busy, gynecology forgotten and her hospital turned over to military casualties, sometimes operating twenty hours at a stretch. Often days went by without their snatched rest coinciding, but even so a touch, a smile, the contentment was not gone. It was driving worry about Sophie which brought back his attacks of vomiting, not the punishing work and turmoil at Stavka.

However hard he strove to hide his difficulties his work inevitably suffered and he was not surprised when, at the beginning of October, with Leningrad tightly beseiged and still no word from Sophie, he was summoned to the main operations room. General Shaposhnikov, the Chief of Staff, was there, standing by a huge map of all the fronts covering one wall, the black Nazi arrows— Kolya stood electrified for a moment as he had not seen a southern map for several days—just about reaching Obeschino. His eyes shifted slightly, Smolensk had fallen over two months previously, Klintsy would have harvested this autumn under German compulsion.

Shaposhnikov finished what he was saying and came over, motioning four other officers, who had also been waiting, toward him. Professionally very competent, he was an almost incredible survival from the past: an ex-tsarist staff colonel and as such automatically suspect, his power of decision ludicrously limited. It was through him that Stalin's looming presence was able to pervade every discussion at Stavka, and every field commander had learned the impossibility of obtaining any answer to their most desperate needs until he had consulted the Kremlin.

He acknowledged their salutes. "None of you needs to be told of the gravity of the situation. We are short of everything, but especially command material at all levels. You five have combat experience of some kind, you are all promoted generals of division from today and will take over reinforcement units being assembled behind Moscow for the crucial battle for the city which is soon to come. You will have very little time to bring your formations up to combat readiness, Comrades, but I know I can rely on you not to fail our country in this time of great peril."

Kolya could see his own shock mirrored on the other four faces. One was still lame from a wound; two must have been close to sixty years old. They saluted, there was nothing to be said, it was exceptionally courteous of Shaposhnikov, his face pouched with exhaustion, to take the trouble to see them.

Within the afternoon he had handed over his plots and graphs, the heart-tearing ring of black closing on Leningrad, the fragmented Soviet markers sprayed in every direction, and was on his way to draw field equipment before the difficult last interview with Anna.

She was scrubbing up before an operation, but he found an elderly nurse brave enough to take a message into the operating theater. The hospital was bedlam, even the entrance stacked with newly arrived stretchers.

"What is it? I'm just going to . . ." Her voice faded when she saw him in a heavy field overcoat, padded jacket over his arm.

"I have orders to take over a reserve division, Anna," he said gently. "I'm leaving now."

"Reserve? Not the front?"

"No, much further from it than you will be here. I can't tell you exactly where, but over toward Vladimir somewhere."

She slid her hands under his bulky coat and held him tightly. "Take care, Kolyushka. Whatever those stupid generals think, you are not strong enough to go."

He flicked open his collar. "I'm one of the stupid generals now, so you watch what you say, Comrade." He kissed her, long and deep, clinging tightly together. "You take care too. If you should have to move . . ." He hesitated. "We none of us can tell what is going to happen; if you haven't left word for me at the hospital here, I will try Saratov."

"You think Moscow will fall?" Her lips were stiff.

"I shouldn't think so for a moment," he said cheerfully. "But they might not want to leave the hospitals here. It's only in case of confusion, so we don't have to search Russia for each other. I shall expect to find you at our room, waiting for me with bread and salt."*

"Yes, oh yes, my love, soon." She laughed shakily, tears glittering in her eyes, but she would not weep. "I shall have to scrub all over again now."

He kissed her fingers formally. "Your humble, loving servant, Annochka. May God go with you." The old-fashioned farewell did not sound incongruous to either of them.

He traveled uncomfortably through the night, in a train crammed to the racks as far as Vladimir, and then by staff car back to the little industrial town of Sobinka, where the 401st Reserve Rifle Division was being formed.

It was a shambles.

It was supposed to consist of three rifle regiments, an artillery regiment and an antitank battalion, together with the usual medical, signals and other services. In practice there were about five thousand men, mostly reservists arriving in small groups from the surrounding country, enough rifles but few automatic weapons,

* Traditional Russian greeting to a returning traveler.

very little ammunition and about half the complement of antitank guns. The signalers were unfamiliar with their equipment, the officers with their men, the men with their weapons.

After a week of slogging hard work, General Berdeyev came to the conclusion his artillery was really quite good while two of the regiments, the 65th and the 85th, should prove reliable with further training. The other, the 260th, for some reason he was unable to discover, was apathetic and might even prove a danger in combat, although time was too short for any solution to be found. The communications as a whole appeared useless and he was himself too ignorant of modern techniques to be much help. He applied for an experienced signals officer but, like all his other requests and demands, there was no reaction to show they had even been received. In one respect he was fortunate: his political commissar, a cheerful Ukrainian called Boitsev, was a valuable officer and far from being the menacing bane of his commander's existence that so many of them were.

"Strange to think that twenty years ago I was a political commissar just around your home village somewhere," Kolya observed to Boitsev one day as they stood in an icy wind watching one of the regimental officers wrestling with problems of fire support, dispersion and cover for the whole division. From the start General Berdeyev had been ruthless in making junior officers carry out responsible tasks. At the height of an exercise a lieutenant was likely to find himself commanding a regiment or all the divisional officers might be forced to stand writhing beside their general while their men floundered leaderless in simulated advance or pell-mell retreat.

"All under those Nazi scum now." Boitsev looked gloomy for once. "I don't know what the hell has happened to my family."

"No, it's the hardest part." Kolya thought of Sophie, the familiar, crawling gripe in his guts making him sweat. With a physical effort he turned away from his daughter's image; he must not allow himself to be overset by his own weakness now. The time for grief had not yet come. He turned away abruptly. "Colonel Shtein!"

"Yes, Comrade General?" The commander of the 65th had been positively bubbling with anxiety as he watched one of his captains reduce the whole division to confusion.

"Not very impressive, is it?"

"No, Comrade General," he said fervently.

Kolya knew very well that his officers thought him mad to attempt training like this but, quite apart from his own convictions, he was completely ignorant of modern army drills and procedures. He knew himself incapable of handling troops in conventional ways and it seemed best to hide this fact as far as possible from men who would soon have to trust him with their lives. "Listen, Shtein, every officer must be responsible for seeing his men can act alone, for training his juniors so they can take over responsible command. On a map I have seen it happen a hundred time a day since the fascist attack: a commander is killed, no one can use the wireless properly, field telephones are churned up faster than they are mended. Within hours a unit doesn't know where it is, whether it is ten or a hundred kilometers behind the enemy advance. What do you think happens then?"

Shtein pulled at the peak of his cap thoughtfully. "They die unnecessarily?"

"No. In such a situation no one who fights sensibly is dying unnecessarily. Can't you see? There is no front to be held at the moment, often you have to fight and die just to purchase a few minutes of time for your comrades. Think again, Colonel."

"They attack?" he suggested, looking confused.

Kolya shook his head. "I will tell you, Shtein. They run away. Unless every man here is used to bearing his own responsibility, the whole lot will run at the first shock. It is not a question of courage."

"Permit me to tell you, General, my men will not run." It was Starchuk, commander of the other fairly sound regiment, the 85th.

"Very well," said Kolya coldly. "We will see."

He stopped the exercise, pulled out the 85th and gave them an hour to dig in on a flat, coverless, slightly raised plateau, hard with frost and dusted with snow. Ten minutes before the hour was up he sent Boitsev forward with orders to arrest and hold Starchuk, his chief communications sergeant and both battalion commanders. While the arguments were raging he sent in the rest of the division, throwing smoke canisters and supported by a barrage of star shells fired dangerously low over Starchuk's position. Boitsev immediately seized every officer he could see while attention was distracted, and bewilderment rather than fear opened the way to the whooping excited troops.

Starchuk was spluttering with fury when Boitsev brought him over. "By what right do you arrest me, General? Or were you afraid you might be proved wrong?"

"I wasn't wrong. Over half your men ran and the position fell."

"Only because of a trick! A whole series of tricks!" The moment he had said it Starchuk realized how absurd it sounded, as if the Germans might be expected to play some macabre game by mythical rules.

General Berdeyev let the silence lengthen, his eyes tight on Starchuk's face. "I have to congratulate you, Colonel," he said at last. "Nearly half your men held their positions under very adverse conditions. I have every expectation the 85th will not let down their comrades in battle."

"Orders, Comrade General." His aide, Fedya Seregin, had a ridiculous snub nose and a sense of humor straight out of the schoolroom. He made Kolya feel very old.

He signed the pad and took the paper with foreboding; he had an idea what it might be. "Well, Comrades," he said after a moment. "It seems we are to entrain tomorrow for the front."

Bogatkin, the commander of the 260th, or suspect, regiment, exclaimed aloud, "The front! We have nowhere near our full strength yet; you can't be serious."

"It isn't my habit to joke about such matters, Colonel. If we are called to the front after only a week of training it is because our country has desperate need of us. I am sure you don't feel yourself less ready than a Leningrad factory worker who does his shift by day and fights at night."

Bogatkin muttered something and looked at his feet. Perhaps I should relieve him now, thought Kolya. He could feel Boitsev watching him; however pleasant he might be, he would certainly report the slightest dereliction of duty to the Party. He would himself be shot if his division broke under fire; Bogatkin would be shot if he was relieved of command the day before entraining for battle. The old trap of circumstance was looming before him as it had with Evgeni. He realized they were all looking at him tensely, that the silence had stretched out for a considerable time. "Thank you, Comrades. Final small arms drill, then back to camp for equipment check."

"Why didn't you get rid of him while there's still time?" asked Boitsev as they drove back to camp.

Kolya felt a spasm of irritation; it was infuriating to be bound to explain every decision. "His men are bewildered and unstable enough, without taking away the only familiarity they have on the eve of battle. He isn't a bad officer even if he'll never be an efficient one. They are a unit, even the knowledge of being despised may bind them together in a crisis, you can't tell."

"It will be too late when you find out."

"It would be too late when I found out I was wrong to relieve him. The decision is made, Boitsev, for the moment, and you will have your hands full talking to the men tonight with your political officers."

Boitsev laughed. "All right, Comrade General. I'll be on record as thinking he should have been removed and then whatever happens, I'm clear. If he stands up in combat it's no more than is expected of a Red Army officer, if he doesn't—"

"If he does not, we suffer a military reverse at a point where the line will certainly be weak, with Moscow only a few kilometers behind our backs. We are a fighting division going out to desperate battle to help save Russia; we all have to be assumed willing to do our part unless there is solid evidence otherwise. I will not have Bogatkin shot without reason, but I would shoot him myself if I had to." He hoped it was true, but his tone was coldly angry. It was as if the bloodlust of the Party could never be appeased, that even in the death grip of war they still shot each other, a youngster like Boitsev casually suggesting a man be killed for no more reason than his inability to take a firm hold on raw troops he had commanded only nine days.

Chapter Forty-two

Their train was shunted all around the freight yards of Moscow, Kolya resolutely turning his mind from the last time he had been there, and they finally detrained at Istra. It was a scant fifty kilometers northwest of the capital, but already under fire, the night sky lit by a strange phosphorescent glow shot with red, the air vibrating until eardrums shivered uncomfortably with the pressure. The journey had taken five endless days, but Kolya took the opportunity to push his way down the crowded train at leisure, to talk to his men and sort out some of the characters who always stood out of a crowd, to give them a chance to see him.

They were nervous and jumpy, as was hardly surprising, but also quite cheerful, the younger ones tightly coiled and excited, the older occasionally resentful but more often deeply determined, especially those with homes close to Moscow.

"They say the panzers have armor that thick," a young soldier said, spreading his arms, while Kolya was talking to one group. "Our shells bounce off them."

"As your girl said last time you took her out, you will have to try a little harder, then," replied Kolya, grinning. The men laughed. "Nothing the Nazis throw at us will be too thick to get at somehow."

"What about our artillery, Comrade General? Have we left it behind?" A thoughtful, long-nosed sergeant.

"No. It is following on flatcars if Moscow gets all the switch points right." They had already spent so long on a journey which usually took less than a day, that the Moscow railway control was a sore point with most of them and there were several happy suggestions as to what the officials could do with their signals and track. He left them to it and squeezed his way on down the train, through soldiers in every attitude of sleep, resignation and boredom. He felt that he at least had not wasted his time on the journey.

Istra lay in the middle of a chain of reservoirs and flooded, part-frozen rivers, and was being strengthened at frantic speed as a fall-back line of defense, but the 401st Rifles received orders to advance straight up the road westward toward the enemy.

Kolya told his officers to assemble everyone ready to move off and went in search of a command post. Once found, it was calmer than his previous experience of army staff work had led him to expect and he was quite courteously received. "I want to verify my orders to advance at once. My artillery and much of my ammunition haven't arrived yet." It seemed to him quite absurd to push untrained men piecemeal into a chaotic battlefield when, if only sufficient troops could be found, Istra was a naturally strong defensive position.

The staff captain shrugged and indicated a map. "Look for yourself."

Kolya peered at the smudged, scribbled figures but finally had to put on his glasses. The by now bitterly familiar Soviet fragments came into focus, almost overturned by thick advancing German waves. "Why don't we straighten our line along the river and reservoirs here while there's still time? The Germans couldn't use their armor effectively in such wet conditions," he said at last.

"Why don't you call the Army Commander and tell him so?" demanded the other sarcastically.

Kolya stared at the telephone; ever passing minute was time for his precious artillery and stores to come up. "All right, I will. Who is he?" He hoped to God it wasn't Zhukov, whose brutal rudeness was already notorious.

"Rokossovsky. Good luck, Comrade." He pushed the telephone over.

Kolya hesitated; he felt Rokossovsky to be a friend and did not want to trade on this. The rapid promotion which had brought him from brigade to army command in five months of fighting which had destroyed reputations as ferociously as it had lives, confirmed his own respect for Rokossovsky's capacity. If he thought his precious reserves should be committed like meat to the grinder then he probably had a reason. But after a moments' thought he asked for the connection; the personality of the Army Commander had not altered his view of what he felt to be a basically unsound military decision.

After a long wait a thin voice snapped in his ear that the Army Commander was willing to speak to him, from the interference Army Command sounded as if it were right up in the front line.

"General Berdeyev?" It was Rokossovsky all right.

"Yes, Comrade Army Commander. I have brought up the 401st Rifle Division to Istra. I wished to confirm my orders to advance at once without waiting for my artillery and stores."

"They are confirmed." He thought Rokossovsky was going to slam down the phone immediately but he added, "The situation elsewhere in the line demands it, Konstantin Aleksandr'itch. You will have to hold as long as possible to gain time for defense lines to be built behind you. I will give you what support and ammunition I can. Good fortune, Comrade."

The following weeks had the kaleidoscopic quality of a series of shellbursts. There was the incident of the long-nosed sergeant, who stood up when his position was out of ammunition and threw himself under the tracks of a tank with a grenade in either pocket.

There was Colonel Starchuk and his men, who still cherished a grudge over the affair on the plateau and would not retreat even when ordered back to provide emergency cover for the main anti-tank positions. With communications severed as usual Kolya had to dodge forward himself to reach Starchuk and nearly killed him when he grinned and said casually, "I told you the 85th wouldn't run away, Comrade General." They both ducked as a cluster of mortar bombs landed just behind the foxhole. "You didn't believe me before."

"I believe you," said Kolya bitingly. "For the petty honor of your 85th you would let the center of the division be carried away. Now get your men out and follow me back, or I will shoot you and do it myself."

Starchuk did as he was told but he was still enjoying himself, and the 85th dispersed German infantry infiltrating down the road with a wild charge which cost him half his men. General Berdeyev relieved him of command that night and two days later Starchuk was dead, leading a group of raiders in the forlorn hope of mining a conduit behind the German lines.

Fedya Seregin was both a refreshment and a worry. As aide to the Divisional General he had to be entrusted with all kinds of vital messages, since other communications rarely worked reliably, but he was obviously shocked by his own fear and in trying to hide it overcompensated with acts of reckless and unnecessary courage. Indeed he could be excused his fear. Rokossovsky's Sixteenth Army, of which the 401st was part, stood on the main axis of the German drive for Moscow. The sheer weight of the enemy onslaught was insupportable, and when the front inexitably fragmented, individual units had to fight where they stood until annihilated. Even worse, to the north they could hear the vast roar of battle drawing behind them as the whole Sixteenth Army position was outflanked. General Berdeyev had already lost three quarters of his men as his division faced tanks with machine guns and surging infantry attacks on rationed ammunition, their flanks often uncovered by the disintegration of units on either side of them, by the collapse of their own swamped regiments. Colonel Shtein was down to eighteen men in one of his battalions.

"General!" Fedya shouted at him above the distraction of sound, indicating the field telephone wordlessly.

Kolya picked it it; it was an effort to hear. "Yes? 401st Command."

"Konstantin Aleksandr'itch?" It was Rokossovsky in person.

"Yes, Comrade Army Commander." The decimation of the past few days, the impossibility of achieving anything under such circumstances, the terrible, pointless slaughter of it all, had confirmed everything he had thought about the unsoundness of sending them into such a chaotic vortex of destruction, so it was difficult not to pour out the reproaches of hysteria.

"The 28th Division on your right has broken. Turn over command to your commissar, if he is still alive, and go and see what you can do. Pull in both under your command and then, if you can, you may retreat on Istra. If your men are not steady enough to retreat in good order and with maximum advantage, then you must stay where you are until your ammunition runs out. Is that clear?"

"Yes, Comrade Commander." It was indeed very clear. The chances of retreating "with maximum advantage" through country infested with German troops, even without incorporating an already panicked unit, were almost nonexistent. Equally, very few commanders would have taken the responsibility of allowing a division discretion to retreat in such circumstances. Rokossovsky was in effect prepared to be shot as well as General Berdeyev if the retreat could be carried out and then was censured, and some of Kolya's bitterness over the futile, bloody destruction of his men ebbed slightly.

He set out with Fedya and eight soldiers shortly after, dodging back through vicious machine-gun fire and blowing snow to the crossroads where he had hidden the few vehicles he had. The wet and cold, the constant crouching and running under fire, the dangerous, crawling visits to his scattered units with their smashed, useless communications, had played hell with his back. In some respects, though, he had stood up better than his men to the harsh conditions. As supplies became scarcer and more disrupted his stomach adapted readily to a daily ration of dehydrated corn meal mixed with half-frozen slush, a near-starvation diet which left his troops almost prostrate with weakness. It was, after all, far more palatable and generous than anything found at Magadan or Cherskogo. Responsibility, the relief of positive action unfettered by guilt, the need for constant clear decision removed the stifling frustration and helplessness which had so twisted him up in recent years. He felt, although often frightened, surprisingly relaxed.

The road was lined with Soviet artillery, dangerously far forward as the struggling infantry in front of them was overwhelmed, but left until the last moment to give what support they could and firing now with open sights straight over their heads. The noise was immense and Fedya had to shake his arm to attract attention: "Look!"

A block of men was coming down the road, not running, just heads down, apathetic, only the fact that several were without weapons revealing anything unusual.

"Slew the truck across the road," Kolya ordered the driver. He put on his glasses and looked carefully: there were a lot of men there, perhaps twice the number remaining in his own battered division. He climbed out. "Spread across the road, Fedya. You by the truck, the rest either side of the ditch. Don't fire unless I say."

He stood in front of the truck, greatcoat open in the freezing wind to show his rank. When the leading fugitives were close enough he ordered a halt in the loudest parade-ground shout he could manage, but the effect was considerably spoiled by a salvo of shells at the same moment. The men did stop, though, huddling around him with a kind of dazed curiosity. Without giving them time to think he ordered them to lie down under cover, a welcome enough instruction to men obviously in the last stages of exhaustion. A few shouted inquiries as to what was going on came from the rear; there was one shot, fortunately past before he realized how fearfully close it had come, tearing the loose collar of his coat as it went.

"If that is the way you shot at the Germans, no wonder they are at the gates of Moscow," he said caustically, feeling his hands shake; it was no good threatening or shouting at men in the state these were in. There were a few scattered stirs of amusement among those who could hear, but mostly they just lay, not retreating but exhausted beyond further effort.

"Where is your commander? Your officers?" he demanded, having to repeat his questions several times before one of the muddy, tattered figures lurched to his feet.

"Back there." He indicated a slight ridge about five kilometers away. "They stayed."

Kolya stared at him, thinking hard. The man was honest and made no attempt to disguise their desertion, perhaps he was just too tired. It was damned dangerous standing up like this; although just out of German machine-gun range, the density of other fire was increasing and the enemy must soon exploit their opportunity up the road. He pulled the man aside and crouched with him in the ditch, shouting to Fedya and his men to do the same.

"Tell me what happened. How long have you been without food?" It did not need an expert eye to tell that these men were starving, physically so weak they could scarcely even desert. "What is your name?"

"Morozov, Corporal, Comrade General." He scratched his head. "A week more or less, but we've fought back almost from the frontier. We were in Minsk when war broke out."

Minsk, for God's sake. No wonder they had not a spark of effort left in them, but it was no use showing pity. "Right, Morozov," he said briskly. "My men stay here and shoot anyone who tries to go past them. I'm going up to your command post and when I come back, any man who can show me he has a weapon, I will lead out of this trap. Those without weapons stay here to be killed. Tell them."

With Morozov as guide he found the command post, terrifyingly exposed on an open slope. German tanks and black lines of infantry could be clearly seen against the snow moving up for an attack, the barrage already easing slightly. A captain, five or six junior officers and a signals sergeant were huddled together on the frozen firing step.

"What the devil is going on here?" he demanded, although it was painfully obvious and not particularly discreditable. The command had been decimated in the long retreat, communications had collapsed, ammunition and food then ceased to arrive and when the men finally broke, the officers and n.c.o.'s had deliberately stayed behind to make their final stand.

The Captain pointed out his pitiful remnants, quite cleverly disposed in overlapping bunkers, the three remaining antitank guns grouped around the command post itself. His only fault was that, battle-shocked and twenty-two years old, he had not been able to force exhausted men to stay in icy holes to be killed once they also began to starve, and he had not had the ingenuity to scrounge them food by whatever means possible.

Kolya borrowed some binoculars and studied what he could see of the German strength. Fifteen tanks at least, he thought, and a lot of infantry although exactly how much it was impossible to know, even had his sight been a great deal better than it was. "How many shells for your antitank guns, Captain?"

"Eight rounds altogether, Comrade General."

Eight rounds. "Very well," he said at last heavily. "You must stay here and hold as long as you can, while I re-form your division up the road."

"Three divisions, Comrade General. We absorbed the 261st at Smolensk and the 183rd last week, which accounts for the number of n.c.o.'s I have here. We fought out of encirclement twice."

There was nothing to be said. Three divisions reduced to less than two thousand men, bled white of will and energy in five months' murderous fighting. And now he had no choice but to leave what was left of its courage here to die while he patched what he could from the rest.

As he drove back down the road he heard the firing intensifying again behind him.

Chapter Forty-three

When Anna Berdeyeva let herself into the cold darkness of the hallway leading to their room she was too tired to take much notice of her unwelcoming, lonely surroundings. It was the smell which first alerted her, made her realize something was wrong. It was a rank, pervasive smell she could not place, although it also reminded her of something recently familiar, had she not been too tired to make the mental connection. She slid open a drawer in their shared kitchen and took out an old scalpel before cautiously opening the door.

"Kolya!" She could not believe it, hugging him without words as if he might slip into disembodiment any second.

"My God, Anna, if you welcome me home from every campaign with a knife in your hand I'm not going to survive for sure." He pulled the scalpel out of her fingers, a graze along his neck mute witness to the forgetfulness of joy. "Two months at the front without a scratch; an hour at home and my wife nearly cuts my throat." He shook his head seriously. "It's sabotage, love, that's what it is."

"Oh, Kolya, Kolyushka you fool, Kolya my love!" She could do no more than sob his name over and over until at last he soothed her quiet in his arms. "I'm sorry to make such an idiot of myself," she said at last. "I'd heard nothing for so long, the fighting has been so terrible. All those shattered bodies in the hospital, every one of them I thought was you."

"Generals don't get killed in war, perhaps unfortunately," he said shortly. It was not true. The Red Army had lost a terrible toll of its remaining commanders and in addition they faced the swift shot of retribution for failure in police headquarters, but he had never seen Anna the self-contained so upset. Love indeed made the strongest vulnerable. He pushed stiffly off the bed. "I'm sorry to have muddied everything up. I was so damned tired I didn't even wash."

"I know." She laughed, restored already by the sight and feel of him. "I thought a herd of goats had broken in." She knew now why the smell had seemed familiar. It drifted even into the antiseptic parts of the hospital from the scores of men lying in the corridors waiting for basic cleansing before they could be treated.

"Of course," he agreed, stripping off rapidly. "Any goats one finds on the third floor of an apartment block should be instantly attacked with a scalpel."

"Oh, Kolyushka," she said softly, voice breaking. "How did I live without you again these last weeks?" She noticed his awkward movements and went over to help. "Your back?"

He grimaced. "Sometimes. Considering the wreck I was, it has lasted remarkably well, but for various reasons a warm night in bed will be very welcome."

She laughed and gathered his filthy uniform off the floor. "I shall have to burn these."

"I should think you would; it is more than a month since I took them off." He began to shave with the swift strokes she remembered so well, while she stood and watched for the sheer pleasure of studying every dear familiarity of him.

"Sophie," he said, when they were eating later. "You have heard nothing?"

She shook her head. She had not intended to say anything while he was still so weary but could not stop herself, blurting out in a rush, "I heard someone say they had nothing to eat in Leningrad but one slice of bread a day, made from dust and dirt. Then another pushed in and said there was cannibalism already. I have heard it several times since."

He stared at his plate, his face gray. After a moment he pushed it away and held her hands across the table. "She is young. At Stavka they are sure the ice road across Ladoga will run more smoothly with the heavy frosts."

"One road across a frozen lake to supply a city of two million and three defending armies!" She held his hands against her wet cheeks. "I'm sorry, it is as hard for you as it is for me."

"Strange things happen in war," he said gently. "The tough and determined often survive against the odds, and from what I remember of Sophie she would not be the sort to despair, whatever happened." He had not intended to tell her much of his experiences during the past few weeks but now he began to do so, emphasizing the shifts of fortune and sometimes inexplicable escapes of the battlefield. She did not need to be told of its carnage.

He told her of the last stand of the officers and n.c.o.'s of the shattered division from Minsk, how they had died while he gathered up their shocked, exhausted men and made junction with his own division, knowing the Germans were bound to burst through the line to his right, however brave its remaining defenders. How he had led the combined remnants of the four divisions in a fierce attack on the Nazi flank exposed by their penetration, and known the savage excitement of advance for a brief half hour before they clashed with German motorized infantry following up the initial assault. How they had used captured German transport and stores for the brutal business of withdrawal when they were so closely attacked that each unit could only be disengaged at the cost of sacrificing another. He told her the story of Colonel Bogatkin and his derided regiment, always an anxiety, the first to lose contact, the last to have its ammunition replenished, its food distributed, down to a hundred men by the second day after they had started to pull back. Of Bogatkin's calamitous mistake when he failed to blow up a causeway across a reservoir and let the panzers in on top of them.

"What happened?" asked Anna, fingers tight and tense in his.

"They knew what they had done," he said grimly. "I think before Bogatkin had always believed, and his men with him, that I was unreasonable, too exacting, but this time they knew." He remembered the appalling chill of realization as the panzers had come racing down on their flank, the bitter self-blame he had felt because he had not acted to remove Bogatkin before. Then the instant of stillness which had frozen every man who had seen the figures of Bogatkin's remaining men advancing out of cover, charging tanks with rifles and automatic weapons, placing mortar bombs under their tracks, climbing up to die tossing grenades through driving slits, seizing one tank and turning the gun back down the causeway and continuing to fire even after it was enveloped in flame. Of the 260th Rifle Regiment not one man had straggled back to their lines.

Anna wiped her eyes. "We can't lose with men like that."

He levered himself up cautiously and wandered restlessly around the room. "You have heard the salutes, the bulletins, how our counteroffensive has started. We're already fifty kilometers into their lines in places."

"So it may be over before Yuri . . . ?"

He shook his head. "Those Nazis fight like mad dogs and with a lot of skill. We are just beginning and we have lost so much it will still take years. Why do you think I am here and not at the front if there is an offensive?"

"I thought you were long past needing a rest," she answered tartly.

"Rest? Our people have forgotten the meaning of the word. I am here because I brought out three hundred men and one antitank gun, all that was left of four divisions or perhaps thirty thousand men a few months ago. I have no command left, and it is the same everywhere from Rostov to Leningrad. We will win, but dear God, the cost."

"God?" she queried.

He shrugged. "I don't know, who can believe in anything but the brutality and courage of man himself in such savagery? In the camps . . . I had to pray for you all, I couldn't help myself. Afterward I thought that if I couldn't help it then perhaps it was evidence of God I shouldn't deny once I was free and you were safe. Now I'm back in confusion again, standing and holding where I can to whatever seems right at the time. The Party—" His face tightened with sudden anger. "One thing I do know is that the Party, or possibly it is just Stalin, is grinding our young men into fragments with insane orders when they have hardly the strength to crawl. I was angry with Rokossovsky for sending us forward in such confused fighting it was impossible to hold a position, when with enough troops to man it the Istra line was really strong. I learned afterward that he had gone to Stalin himself to beg to be allowed to bring his men back into the line and was refused. He took his life in his hands to go to Stalin on such an issue, but it made no difference. In the end we hadn't enough troops to hold Istra even twenty-four hours."

She sat, shadowing her face with her hands, feeling her own anxiety and sorrow intensified by the depth of anguish she sensed in him at the destruction of the men under his command. "How long are you home?" she asked at last.

"Two days."

"Two days!" It was a cry of desolation which wrung his heart.

He held her tightly, his strong, dauntless Anna seemed all at once painfully frail and worn. "Come, *vazlublenny*, we have not traveled so far, you and I, to be defeated now. I will be back; you must have the strength to keep something together for us all. Sophie and Yuri as well as I need you. You, the Anna we all know, who will have to fight alone to be true to herself just as hard as Yuri and I, perhaps Sophie, will have to fight in other ways. You have to be strong for us all."

She covered her eyes. "When you are here, I can face anything. Alone . . ."

"So long as I live you are not alone." His tone was

insistent, hands tight on her shoulders, willing her to strength. He had not yet told her he was ordered south to take over a new division near Tula, two hundred kilometers from Moscow. In an army where leave was unknown, he might well not be back before the end of the war.

She sighed and stirred under his hands. "What a pair we are. Five years apart . . . five months together . . . now perhaps five years apart again." She smiled at him waveringly: "Come and make love to me, and in the morning I will try to be strong for you."

Chapter Forty-four

The hideous weave of the first months of the war was continued without remission for a nation driven to the limits of its endurance. In Leningrad fifty thousand people a month died of starvation alone. In front of Moscow the Soviet counterattack triumphantly drove the Nazis back and then battered itself into living shreds against savage, entrenched defence. To the south, as the summer of 1942 drew on, the whole of the Ukraine was engulfed by further German advances, the Red Army splintered into more hundreds of thousands dead. And when at last the tide turned, with further sacrificial horrors at Stalingrad, at Kursk and Bryansk, the full dimension of the destruction of Russia itself was revealed.

Scarcely a town was recovered undestroyed and sometimes a hundred villages would pass without finding a single cottage left standing; only here and there a handful of tottering brick chimneys stood like gravestones over the ashes and rubble. It was impossible to imagine such a wilderness of desolation as stretched from Moscow to Smolensk, from Kursk to Kiev, from Leningrad to Minsk.

By ill fortune Oryol was the first city General Berdeyev saw which had been gutted on this shattering scale. His new division, the 196th Rifles, stormed in as one part of a pincer movement on August 5, 1943, and he recognized nothing of familiarity from his youth. No building, no road, no angle of square or garden, nothing. Fierce fires were burning and explosions still shook the ground as last-minute mines detonated. Wherever you looked there were only the silent piles of dead, the stark bones of brick and timber and twisted steel girders; the only markers for disappeared street corners the swaying obscenity of strung-up corpses.

Later, the figures began to appear. Black, bent women with tear-stained faces touching the soldiers with fearful joy; the first spate of denunciations and unexplained murders of private revenge; grinning, emaciated children clumping in German boots dragged off the dead. In the winter Kolya had even seen children sledging on frozen German corpses, and now in Oryol they sat nonchalantly on decomposing bodies to watch the Soviet tanks go by.

"What sort of little monsters are we breeding?" Fedya demanded. "Kill the fascist scum, yes, but that—" He shuddered and wiped his face. Fedya Seregin had won two Red Banner Orders before losing an arm as a company commander and had come back as his staff captain the month before.

"Can you wonder if we are all monsters?" said Kolya sharply. He was trying to work on a mass of paper as the car bumped over shell-pocked, half-obliterated roads, and with the strains and emergencies of the past two years his temper had become steadily shorter. He looked up suddenly and tapped the driver on the shoulder. "Stop at the next bend, Corporal."

"Yes, Comrade Commander." Morozov, the man he should have shot at Istra for being one of the few n.c.o.'s to join the desertion of his regiment, had firmly attached himself and been his driver ever since. I bloody well would shoot a corporal in the front rank of deserters now, he reflected. The war had become a matter of statistics and trigger fingers; mercy for a confused corporal had no place any more. Five thousand to the attack, a hundred thousand encircled, two hundred thousand attack again. Ten, fifteen, twenty million dead. What chance for a lop-eared, terrified corporal to claim anyone's attention?

He needed Fedya's help to climb out of the car, had to hold onto the roof with the force of effort necessary to straighten his back: he could not go on much longer like this. He leaned against the open door of the car and watched his men moving along the road. They looked tough and competent, some were ragged and several roughly bandaged, hospital treatment was not possible for the slightly wounded. But their weapons were well cared for, they looked intent on the matter in hand: most grinned or saluted as they passed for he had continued his practice of familiarizing himself with every level of his command. With the tide only just turning, with three quarters of the task still to do, he did not want to give them up. Whatever his own military shortcomings, he knew another commander would not take the endless trouble he did to see that every life spent was spent with the parsimony another man's life demanded.

The past eighteen months had been punishingly hard. First of all clinging beyond the hope of reason to the shattered wreck of Tula, then, when advance had at last begun, it was sheer, brutal hacking at kilometer after kilometer of fortified defense. There was no short cut, no inspired generalship, which could lessen the appalling mercilessness of advance from Tula to Oryol.

The Germans had to be cleared, firing post by firing post, tank by tank, house by house, and suffering flesh forced through a flaming mesh of reinforced concrete and tearing metal. Like every division on the front, the 196th had been decimated, reinforced, decimated again. Yet still, to its general at least, it retained a distinctive spirit and he did not think his men had ever felt him heedless of their sacrifices. For himself, apart from the steady deterioration in the condition of his back, he had been extraordinarily lucky: perhaps the fates really did perform some inscrutable calculation to balance life's hazards. His car had been twice blown up and once plunged into an ice-filled shell hole; several times he had been caught with his advanced troops by an unexpected German attack, but except for some shrapnel through the hand and a painfully dislocated shoulder, he had been untouched.

He walked slowly down the road, dust kicked up by every movement: it was stupefyingly hot. A wood, a rutted, shell-torn crossroads, a finger post with words obliterated by weather rather than war. Birds were singing languidly in the heat and down the faint left-handed turning for once there was not even a body or a splintered tree, the filthy debris of war which accompanied them everywhere. It might have been a crossroads almost anywhere in Western Russia but he would have known it without any clue of map or grid reference. Just ten versts to the south lay Obeschino and even the branches seemed to lie in a different, beckoning mosaic as he stood and stared into the patterned shade along the track. How long, dear God how long ago, he had come back along here every summer from St. Petersburg, had turned up there with Lena and his grandmother on his first journey to Moscow.

"It is good to leave the sounds of war for a few minutes, Comrade General." It was Antonov, a political representative on the Army Military Council,* always the harbinger of fresh attack, but for the moment quiet and contemplative, off-guard as he was himself.

Kolya nodded slowly. "I didn't think a single branch of birch could be untouched by the past thirty years . . . my old home is but ten versts from here. I feel like a dinosaur surviving from another age."

"But surviving from a worse to a better age, Comrade." Antonov's moment of relaxation was over.

Kolya recollected all the dangers of discussing the precise location of his home with a political officer. "I wouldn't want to go back and see it now."

Antonov shrugged. "It would probably be destroyed anyway. It is better to stay here and not know." He had lost two sons with the Red Army and his home was still deep behind enemy lines. "Now, Comrade General, we must discuss this next movement the corps has planned."

As they walked back to the car together Antonov lit a cigarette and Kolya winced involuntarily. He still found the smell of tobacco repellent, the sight of smoldering butts hard to ignore and, although they thought his aversion unreasonable, his officers had long since learned not to smoke anywhere near him. Today, with pain eating remorselessly into his back, Antonov's constant smoking was more difficult to ignore than usual. Although he knew the thought absurd, Kolya even began to wonder whether he did it deliberately. As a political officer, Antonov would certainly be familiar with every aspect of his police file. But it was useless to think about it, to allow himself to be distracted; he had to concentrate afresh, however hard concentration was becoming.

They spent the afternoon in a purgatory of discom-

* All Soviet armies and fronts (i.e., army groups) had military councils made up of military, political and NKVD representatives, with whom major decisions had to be discussed and who could make sure Stalin was kept fully informed of every detail.

fort for Kolya, crouched beside the road over maps and diagrams, Fedya and Lopukhin of the artillery working out firing patterns, two generals of neighboring divisions arriving to be co-ordinated into the next stage of the advance.

As Antonov was about to leave, Kolya detained him. "I've ordered my men to keep off the corn where the military situation makes it safe to do so. Could we have an Army order to that effect!

Antonov laughed. "Whoever heard of an army the size of this one keeping off the corn? What are you, Comrade General, a peasant farmer with his nose on the plow?"

"I have yet to hear that a peasant has cause to be ashamed of his ancestry in our Soviet Republic. But yes, if it interests you, I am a farmer, a sovkhoznik by inclination rather than a soldier. With victory I hope to have my choice again."

"I will inform the Army Commander of Divisional General Berdeyev's orders to his men to tiptoe around the corn instead of pursuing fascists, and of your suggestion that the whole front do the same."

Kolya flushed heavily with anger. The army had rid itself of commissars watching every step of the command, but the political staff officers fulfilled the same function. "And I will inform Oryol Party administration that there are some elements in the army heedless of the fact that there will be five million starving people here next winter, and suggest they take the matter up with the Central Committee."

"Your pardon, Comrade Colonel, there is an urgent NKVD signal for you," Fedya broke in. "The connection is very poor."

Antonov went off muttering, to wrestle unsuccessfully with the eternally unreliable field communications system. "The corporal promised to route him halfway around the Moscow network," said Fedya dreamily.

Kolya shot him a sharp look; he had become used to Fedya Seregin by now. "There was no call? You bloody fool boy, don't you realize Antonov is not the stamp of man for your jokes?"

Fedya looked injured. "Corporal Goiko and I fixed it up as a useful diversion last time you had a row with Colonel Antonov; we thought you might need it. He knows the NKVD call signs but the line is too bad to be able to trace any further origin. It's safe enough."

Kolya gave a gasp of laughter, the first, he realized, in weeks. "Which is more than you can say for me if I go on tangling with Antonov?" He sobered almost at once. "I'm grateful for the thought but don't ever try it again. You are in Goiko's power now if he chose to use it, and Antonov would never believe you twice. I'll invalid you from the army if I catch you attempting anything again against our political representatives."

Fedya grinned. "I hope he sweats the rest of the week wondering what top priority order has gone astray."

General Berdeyev went back to his maps and orders for the next offensive; he had already learned it was practically impossible to repress Fedya for long. That night he sent for his major of engineers and ordered him to have some kind of support made for his back. They produced a thick lacing of canvas and steel which, although at first stiflingly heavy and uncomfortable to wear, worked surprisingly well once he had become used to it, and the 196th Rifles soon became known as Ironback's Own. The only trouble was that it was impossible to bend or sit in it for more than minutes at a time. But Fedya soon became accustomed to fixing everything to walls or the sides of trucks; the divisional engineers although with lurid curses, accepted the idea that command posts in the 196th would have to be dug a meter deeper than those of neighboring units, and he managed to acquire an open-hatched armored car to supplement the more usual command car.

A week later he had an ecstatic letter from Anna to say she had heard from Sophie. At first he could not believe it: in a world so filled with destruction it seemed impossible anyone should escape. "*She was flown out over a month ago,*" wrote Anna, "*but was too ill to know where she was or think how to contact us. She says she is recovering well but I rang the sanatorium at Kazan where she is, and they do not advise a move to Moscow for some time yet. Oh Kolya darling, it is like the first drip of water off the eaves in spring, can we really be coming to the end of it so you too will soon be home?*"

He stared out of the creaking barn door of his present command post, unashamed of the wetness of his face, the curious looks of his officers. "My daughter," he said at last, gruffly. "She has been in Leningrad during the seige, but she is safe."

"I'm glad, Comrade General," said Fedya sincerely. "It's not so often we have good news like that." It was true, the yellow slips of paper from the Central Casualty Commissariat arrived in thick wads for men of the division every week. In past months they had mostly announced the death or crippling of sons, brothers or fathers in action; now with the advance often they conveyed brusque information about families who were dead, deported or wiped off the face of the earth leaving no trace behind them.

Yuri had written months ago, triumphantly announcing his acceptance for advanced flying training and he was now with a squadron at Astrakhan, working up to combat readiness.

*

Early in 1944, Kolya was promoted Lieutenant General and given two more divisions to form 60 Corps, which was then transferred to the army gathering on their right, the First Belorussian under Rokossovsky, whose name after Stalingrad and Kursk was now a household word.

Rokossovsky greeted his new corps commander characteristically. "Well, Konstantin Aleksandr'itch, I hear we shall all be standing in holes in the ground doing our staff work on the mantelpiece."

"I have taken off my corsets for the occasion," replied Kolya gravely. "I am reasonably flexible today, Comrade Army Commander."

"In several ways, I hope. I have a plan I wish to discuss with you and my other commanders." Rokossovsky again had changed very little in spite of the strains of high command over the past grinding years of savagery, the agony of a shell splinter in the spine during the fighting for Bryansk.

The plan which he revealed to his assembled corps commanders was extremely bold; a double envelopment of the whole of the German center in terrain which was well suited to defense.

"Wouldn't it be preferable to concentrate on one thrust instead of two, Comrade Commander? It seems madness to divide our strength when the fascists have six hundred thousand men facing us," asked one of the men on Kolya's right.

"They are strongly entrenched and still well supported," agreed another. "Surely we've learned that we must concentrate our strength if we're to gain success."

Rokossovsky looked at them meditatively. "Boris Ivan'itch, I think you know this country?"

"Yes, Comrade Army Commander, I was born in Bobruisk." He was a thickset man with an oiled face, like a well-handled wooden doll.

"Describe what it is like."

"Beautiful, Comrade Commander." There was a general laugh.

"Yes, well, I will visit you and admire it when the war is over. Tell us what it is like."

"Woods. Woods and swamps," he said slowly. "Little wooden huts by slow streams which spread out where-ever the ground is flat. Strips of sunlit meadow and forests where a man may be easily lost a hundred paces from the track, for one part is like another and every-thing is torn in pieces by more streams. It is beautiful," he added defiantly.

They all stirred slightly; somewhere in his description he had touched on a fragment of the Russia they all knew. "Good partisan country," said Rokossovsky thoughtfully. "But not country in which I could con-centrate three quarters of a million men for a knock-out blow against nearly the same number of cleverly entrenched Germans with every advantage of terrain. I can only make best use of my strength, use the men and superiority in artillery I have if I divide. It is dangerous perhaps, but I don't think so. The prize could be thirty German divisions encircled and the center dropped out of their line. If we achieve it, there's nowhere much short of the Vistula where they would make another stand and we would have Russia cleared of them this summer."

They went back to their maps and began discussing detailed planning. Some were still doubtful but it was plain that Rokossovsky had made up his mind. He was open to modification of detail and timing, but on the main concept he was not to be moved.

"Well, there it is, Comrades," he said at last. "Let me have your observations within the next three days. I fly to Moscow to discuss the whole offensive with the Generalissimo* on Saturday. General Berdeyev, a word with you if you please." Rokossovsky's courtesy to his officers was a byword in an army used to chiefs

* Stalin awarded himself this rank during the war.

of staff being slapped and kicked, the threat of shooting used for every failure.

"You made no contribution to our discussions, Konstantin Aleksandr'itch. Does that imply disapproval?" Rokossovsky said when the others had filed out, his tone slightly edged.

"No, Comrade Commander, it seems to me to have an excellent chance of success." Kolya had indeed been struck both by the skill of Rokossovsky's dispositions and the imaginative daring of his plan. After the brutal slogging of past years the chance of victory on such a scale was exciting, and if it were successful then losses would be a fraction of those incurred in a frontal assault for much greater gain. "I have very little theoretical knowledge, however, only some experience of handling fairly small formations in battle."

"If I didn't value your opinion I shouldn't have appointed you one of my corps commanders."

"I am sorry, Comrade Army Commander." Kolya hesitated. Rokossovsky was obviously too shrewd not to know there was something wrong and he was entitled to an explanation. "I found it hard to concentrate. I received news yesterday that my son had been killed in action." It had not been a shock so much as bitter, bitter grief; deep in his heart he had known that Yuri had scarcely a chance of survival.

Rokossovsky's face tightened; he stood up and walked over to a map. "There are never any words, I have learned that in three years of war. How many of our young men will be left when this is over?" He turned abruptly. "Does your wife know?"

Kolya shook his head. "I'm trying to write to her. When Yuri was posted to a combat squadron he put only my name on the next of kin form."

"I'm going to Moscow at the end of the week as you know, to discuss my plan for this offensive with Stalin and the War Committee. I will take you instead of my Chief of Staff to help in the presentation if you will familiarize yourself with all the details of it."

"Thank you, Comrade Commander." Then he added, he could not help it, "I hadn't seen the boy since 1936." A blurred face at a train window, turning toward him as it pulled out of Klintsy sidings.

"There is no cure for it, Konstantin Aleksandr'itch," Rokossovsky put his hand on his shoulder a moment. "Go and start work on those plans."

There was no cure for it indeed. Bright-headed Yuri, whom he had scarcely known for the first few years of his life and then come to know so well, with his serious, considering expression and sudden delight in absurdity; the way he had stood in his short nightshirt on the cold floor of their Klintsy home in stiff accusation and hidden plea for understanding. He had hoped so much for the chance to straighten out the whole miserable mess with him face to face, to say all the things which letters left unsaid, to see the fine promise of his son unfolding.

Not yet nineteen, Yuri was dead.

Chapter Forty-five

Anna was so delighted to see him, joy releasing such a torrent of relief, of respite from loneliness, that he had to exert all the harsh will forged over the past eight years of inhuman stress to keep command of himself, to wait, to seek the right moment to tell her what he had to tell.

Of course there was no right moment to deliver such a blow and even before the news of Yuri's death he had lost his ability to relax or switch his mind easily from the agony of suffering he had witnessed, from the weight of his own responsibilities. After more than two years' abstinence he had a driving bodily need, a fierce urge to lose himself in the quickening desires of life in defiance of the death by which he had been surrounded for so long, but, torn and physically sick again from the knowledge of what he was keeping from Anna, he could not.

Anna told him about Sophie, how they had spoken for a few seconds on the telephone, how she would come to Moscow very soon now. She told him of her work at the hospital, desperately hard, often tragic, sometimes inspiring. Of the great salutes and fireworks in Red Square greeting every Russian victory, of the misery of cold and food queues and shortages which she at the hospital mostly escaped. She told him about a letter she had had from Yuri a few days before describing his new squadron.

"Anna," in spite of himself his voice was rough and harsh. "Anna . . ."

She slid out of his arms and stood looking at him. "It's Yuri, isn't it?"

He nodded, staring at the floor. "He's dead, Anna. I heard a week ago."

"No hope?" she whispered.

"No." He had spoken to the Air Fleet Commander.

"I knew there was something wrong," she said dully. "I chattered and chattered, hoping and begging in my heart it was just the strain and separation of the last two years between us." She dropped her head in her hands, her body racked with sobs. "Yuri . . . he never forgave me . . . if you could only have seen him . . . explained . . ."

He sat there, graven, unable to speak or offer comfort. Along the way he had also lost the ability to comfort his wife on the death of their son.

There is no cure for it . . .

Later in the day they walked out along the Moskva embankment and onto their Kamenny Bridge, scarcely speaking, for had they spoken it would have been of Yuri and that was a weakness neither could afford. At the corner of the bridge an old woman was selling bunches of early spring violets and Kolya stopped and bought one, pinning it on Anna's shabby, scuffed jacket, and for the first time since he had told her of Yuri, she kissed him.

The Moskva ice was showing thin shreds of dark water and under the bridge could be heard the brisk gurgle of life and spring calling the land from its winter death.

"Kolya," said Anna at last, "do you think there could be anything in what the churches say? Perhaps there is another life for them to live?"

"I don't know." He spoke slowly; even to help Anna in her grief, to help himself, he could not lie about such a thing. "No one knows, not even the Party which says it is not so. This slaughter . . . would it make more sense if there were another life?"

She began to shred the violets down into the icy oblivion below. "You told me once you prayed for us in those camps. Well, I have prayed for all of you. I prayed in anger, not because I believed, but just in case there is a God, to leave no stone unturned to appease His malice. Write it down, full Party member for twenty-seven years, Anna Berdeyeva went down on her knees and prayed."

"And did it help?"

"Obviously not," she said shortly, "since Yuri is dead."

"But did it help you?" he persisted. "To bear your burdens of sorrow and fear and loneliness?"

She shrugged and then said reluctantly, "Yes, I suppose it did then. It makes me angry now, though, as if I had been cheated."

"Why?" He smiled faintly. "We both still consider ourselves Communists, in spite of the Party as it is now, not because of it. If you obtained some comfort then you were not cheated. A Christian is a Christian in spite of what his God inflicts on him; it is the ideals, the hopes, the aspirations of a faith we must try to live by, not what some of its servants do. No matter what we call it we have to hold to the truth of the vision within us; we must not be trapped by events into abandoning it. That is what caused me such anguish over Evgeni: I betrayed what I thought was right for what other people thought was right. It wasn't really a question of how I could have avoided the choice. My father was trapped the same way, through him a man was killed because others convinced him it was right, and he was never able to pull his life together again."

"Tell me," said Anna quietly. "If you can. I should like to know. Evgeni was my sacrifice to principle as much as yours."

So, dropping his voice, and watching glinting, ice-edged water rather than her face, he told her how an Imperial general of the old regime had died, only then suddenly thinking how strange it was that he too should be a general, the very last direction he would have expected his life to take. "Now I know something of how he felt, I think my father greatly to be pitied," he added when he had finished. "At least I can feel I have paid for what I did, however indirectly, if it is possible to pay for such actions. But he had to live all his life under a burden of debt which would crush any man. Sent away to safety believing all was well and then shielded by the victim, forgiven by my grandmother but never by himself. No wonder he was glad to go off to war."

"But where did we all go wrong?" demanded Anna. "I have never asked you this before, the weeks we had together were so precious and I didn't feel able to face such questions then. Now, even if you say you don't know what to believe, you seem more certain in your mind that I am. What your father wanted was more noble than your grandfather's aims of quiet administration, our vision finer than the selfishness and greed of the peasants. Yet in the end, who was right and who was wrong?"

"I don't know," he said again. "I wish I did. You say I seem more certain in my mind, but if I am it is only because I have at least gained a greater understanding of what is wrong, rather than a knowledge of what is right. There's a saying my grandmother told me once: *Turn thine eyes from his face and thine ears from his lips and watch his hands.* She hoped I'd never find out what it meant."

She looked at him curiously. "But you think you know now?"

"Perhaps. A man betrays himself by what he does, not what he says. Our ideals are noble but killing Evgeni was not a noble deed; our revolution was no longer true to itself when it did that. A revolution brought about by men who tried to force a son to kill his father would not have been a revolution worth having, whatever they mouthed of their ideals. I may be a good Communist, I hope I am, but I'll never be a good Party man again." It had been suggested to him that, with his distinguished war service, he should apply to rejoin the Party, but he had not done so.

"Kolya," she faced him squarely, "will you promise me something?"

"If I can."

"After the war, will you promise to stay in the army?"

"Stay in the army?" he echoed, completely astonished. "Of course I will not. I detest soldiering. I can't wait to get back to the task of making things grow again."

"And if you did, how long would it be before you couldn't do something you were told to do? I can't bear any more, Kolya. I have a right to your promise."

"But how would it help if I stayed in the army?"

"The army has so much prestige after its victories, even the Party would not dare attack it. Surely after all the disasters which followed the purge of so many of our officers, the army at least they must leave alone? Surely the army itself couldn't be so stupid, now in all its strength, to let them do it again. If you are to be safe anywhere you must be safe there."

He looked down at his hands, tightly laced on the parapet of the bridge. How often in all the endless desolation of Western Russia had he looked at pitted fields, spoiled crops and blackened villages and longed to get his hands on a tractor or surveyor's level again? His hands, once musician's hands, but all those hopes and dreams abandoned for the Party. Then the hands of a farmer, tough, work-hardened yet answering again the call of his spirit; convict's hands, torn, swollen and bleeding. Now soldier's hands, he looked thoughtfully at the star-shaped, ridged scar left by red-hot mortar fragments at Tula, an overlooked sliver grated on the bone still if he clenched his fist too tightly.

Lover's hands, the long, long bond of flesh and mind and spirit which he and Anna owed each other.

"I promise," he said curtly. "If they will keep me. The army will be much smaller after the war. I shouldn't hold such a rank in peacetime."

She slid her hand between his. "It isn't your rank but your life I cannot do without. You are trying not to resent the way I made you promise, today when you could scarcely refuse me. You hurt me bitterly once for my own good, because you knew no other way to make me go. I know no other way to keep you with me. Forgive me."

Forgive me. The very words he had used to her on

the banks of the Volga so long ago at Saratov. He drew her arm through his. "Let's go home, love, it is a little public here. I shall be swept up by the military patrols for undignified conduct; not a very favorable circumstance for a general meeting Comrade Stalin tomorrow."

"Stalin? Not really, Kolya?"

"Rokossovsky brought me here to help present the plans for his summer offensive," he explained. "The Chief of Staff would normally come but he was considerate enough to offer to bring me."

"I'm very grateful," she said briefly, and then sheered away from the subject. Their grief was only bearable together, yet would be immediately unbearable if either mentioned it again. "It's an honor all the same."

"The Chief of Staff was delighted for me to take his place. From what I hear these trips to the Kremlin are an ordeal for everyone."

He learned just how much of an ordeal the next day.

Warned by Rokossovsky, Kolya had borrowed a parade jacket since he possessed only field service uniform and Anna checked every detail of his appearance. Privately she thought he looked very fine; the tight, guarded lines of his face and white hair which caused her such personal regret did not seem out of place with so much grandeur of smooth cloth, red piping and gold braid.

Their car entered the Kremlin by the Borovitsky Gate and crossed the ancient cobbles of Ivanovsky Square, where Stalin's apartments and personal office were to be found. Rokossovsky sat silent and obviously tense. Although nothing in his attitude revealed it, Kolya thought that he probably found the inevitable close contact with the Kremlin the most trying aspect of his present high position. It was, after all, impossible for Stalin even to look at him, old scars still faintly visible around the mouth and with teeth which never quite fitted the uneven line of his jaw, without recalling that this was a man only a few years before almost beaten to death on his orders.

The corner doorway to Stalin's private quarters was unpretentious and Kolya, carrying maps and briefcases, scarcely had a chance to look around him as they were hurried through various offices and anterooms, up some stairs and finally into a guardroom.

"Any arms?" demanded one of the guards rudely.

"No." Rokossovsky's tone indicated clearly enough the fury he felt at such offhand treatment.

"How about him?" The man flipped a finger at Kolya, who realized with sudden horror that it had never occurred to him not to wear an ordinary service belt incorporating a revolver. It was only now he noticed that Rokossovsky was wearing an old-fashioned General Staff sash in place of the usual belt.

"I have my service revolver," he said hastily, putting down the briefcase and reaching for his holster. He was instantly grabbed from behind, the weapon pulled out and thrown on the floor.

"What's this?" the man behind him demanded. He ran his hands swiftly over his clothing and of course felt his metal brace. He had wondered whether to wear it, but had finally decided that he almost certainly would not be asked to sit down, and whatever the discomfort of tightly laced canvas and steel in a heated atmosphere, he was no longer capable of standing for hours without support.

"General Berdeyev has a serious spinal injury and requires to wear a brace," said Rokossovsky coldly. "His wars have not been spent in a comfortable guardroom."

It made no difference. He had partly to strip before the guards would let them through, endure rough investigation of everything he wore until they were satisfied. Rokossovsky stood waiting, his face stiff with anger but quite powerless against Stalin's personal bodyguard. Later he apologized. "I didn't think to warn you about carrying any kind of arms here. I wear this damn silly sash because I don't choose to be searched by some pimply little swine crawled out of a back gutter. It was an insult to the Red Army but I could do nothing about it."

Although angry, Kolya did not feel particularly insulted. He was no murderer, but sometimes wondered whether this was cause for shame rather than congratulation. He would have felt nothing but pleasure at the death of his Party and national leader. To him, trust from such a man would have been more offensive than suspicion.

Stalin's office was not well lit but it was large and quite comfortable, with a desk in one corner, maps on the walls and a long table down one side covered with files and papers.

Kolya stood rigidly at attention by the door while Rokossovsky made his report, glancing around surreptitiously to identify the various people in the room. He recognized Marshal Voronov, head of Soviet artillery, looking careworn and exhausted. A repulsive-looking squat general he could not place until Rokossovsky referred to him as Poskrebyshev, then realized he must be the loathed and feared head of Stalin's private Cabinet office, widely thought in the army to have personally supervised many private murders in the upper hierarchy. There was Molotov, Deputy Premier and Foreign Commisar, looking precisely like his inscrutable, pernickety photographs in every Soviet newspaper. The other civilian present was seated while everyone else except Stalin and Poskrebyshev stood, a sure sign of superiority and influence. He was flabby and darkly greasy, and Kolya at first placed him as a secret policeman. He later realized that he was not far wrong, Georgi Malenkov was well known for his close links with Beria, the head of the NKVD, mercifully not present.

Stalin listened quietly to Rokossovsky's report, grunting from time to time. These reports were a severe strain on commanders, since everything had to be done orally, down to the most precise details, some of which had been independently checked beforehand, an occasional interjection designed to probe the slightest hesitation or weakness.

When Stalin finally stood up after half an hour of this cross-examination, Kolya was struck afresh by his small stature and by the effortless way he dominated the room. "Your plans for the summer, Rokossovsky?" Stalin alone defied the custom of using name and patronymic to anyone he knew at all closely.

"I have them here, Comrade Generalissimo."

"In words, Rokossovsky, in words first."

Rokossovsky embarked on an endlessly complicated description of the German positions, the terrain, his proposals for a double-pronged assault and envelopment. "We have a small bridgehead beyond the Dnieper," he concluded. "We can pivot an increasing strength there as we gain ground; the other half of my front will drive to meet it from the region of Vitebsk. I would like to demonstrate my detailed proposals on the map."

"The German defenses must be breached in one place." Stalin spoke flatly, with no offer of argument. "One place only, with our main strength."

"If we breach it in two places, Comrade Stalin, we shall gain many advantages."

"What advantages?" demanded Stalin contemptuously. "Divide our strength and we are beaten. Six hundred thousand Germans by your own intelligence reports. Seven hundred and fifty thousand Soviet troops. In your piece of insanity"—he flicked his fingers at the briefcase Kolya was carrying—"we are three hundred thousand in each blow and both are beaten separately. What sort of cow dung is this for a general to bring me?"

"If we breach their defense in two sectors we can bring more forces in total to the attack. The ground is so wet and cut up it would be impossible to concentrate the whole army for one overwhelming blow." Rokossovsky's tone was completely neutral. "If you would consider my detailed proposals I think you will agree that we have an excellent chance of deploying our troops to full advantage and so exploiting the possibility of a massive encirclement of the enemy's center."

"And that is what you call advantages?" demanded Stalin roughly. He took his pipe from his mouth and stabbed it at Rokossovsky's face. "What cowardly parade-ground maneuvering is that? What punishment do you think waits for cowards in our Soviet state?"

"I am no coward Comrade Generalissimo," said Rokossovsky after a pause.

"Well, then, think it over again if you wish to prove otherwise. Think it over now." Stalin stared at him unwinkingly out of eyes like slime at the bottom of a pond, and repeated deliberately, "If you wish to prove otherwise you prove it now."

Some unspoken message passed between him and Poskrebyshev as he turned away and it was Poskrebyshev who ushered them out of the room. "This way, Comrade General." He opened the door of a dark, airless office, tightly curtained against the sunlight, just down the passage. "Comfortable enough for second thoughts, I trust? Comfort is such a relative thing, is it not? Here today and gone tomorrow as they say." The corner of his lip lifted slightly and he shook his head in mock regret. "I've always found the twists and turns of life fascinating, how someone high one moment can be brought so low the next." He stared at Rokossovsky with open malice and then turned on Kolya. "Who are you?"

"My staff officer," said Rokossovsky. "Wait outside, Konstantin Aleksandr'itch." He turned and went into the room, leaving Kolya standing in the passage outside.

"You bloody generals," snarled Poskrebyshev. "You think because of all your fancy soldiers you own the earth. It will need a few more of you shot before you learn your lessons again." He beckoned a sentry to stand outside the door where Rokossovsky was confined, then blundered back into Stalin's office, slamming the door behind him. Nothing could have demonstrated more clearly the uniquely privileged nature of his position.

Kolya stood in the quiet passage with only the sentry for company, his thoughts on his commander in his lonely isolation. Within the day both of them might easily be dead, Rokossovsky's name added to the list of those revered one day and execrated the next, he himself shot for no better reason than the misfortune of having been present at a conference where differences were settled with a bullet.

Kremlin meetings were notorious for their tensions but he knew Rokossovsky well enough to be sure he would not have brought him if he had expected such a reception. He could only guess at the nature of Stalin's prejudices, military conservatism, and possibly the inner Kremlin politics, which would surely kill them unless Rokossovsky were prepared to compromise.

As well as alarm and fear for Anna (what indeed would she do if he never reappeared, husband and son lost within twenty-four hours?) he felt cold anger that far-reaching military issues and the lives of thousands of soldiers should be decided by such crude pressures as these. Rokossovsky's plan was daring, he might be wrong, but no effort had been made to discuss its merits or understand its conception.

The minutes lengthened into half an hour, an hour, two hours. It was a miniature variation of the old Lubyanka technique to which, of course, both he and Rokossovsky were particularly vulnerable. There was a continuing murmur of voices in Stalin's office, the occasional hurrying clerk; otherwise the building was deathly quiet. It was hard to grasp that most of the major decisions of the war had been taken here.

At last a red-faced major came out of Stalin's room, shoved the sentry unceremoniously aside and curtly called Rokossovsky's name. As they were ushered back into Stalin's presence Kolya saw that Rokossovsky, for the first time in his experience, looked tired and resigned.

"Well?" Stalin glanced up irritably from his desk. "I don't know why the hell I waste time on you, eh, Poskrebyshev?"

"No indeed, Comrade Stalin. I have a department to take care of such worries for you." Poskrebyshev laughed slightly. "To encourage those who stand too long in idleness with crossed wrists, do you think, Comrade General?"

Rokossovsky's head jerked involuntarily; it was an allusion which only those familiar with certain Soviet jails would catch.

"Have you thought it through, General?" Stalin looked completely impassive, no stirring of doubt, no opening for argument.

"Yes, sir, Comrade Stalin." Rokossovsky's voice was low and very formal.

"Good." Stalin looked at him in grim satisfaction. "Let us have a look at those plans then and decide where the blow is to fall."

Kolya fumbled open the briefcase and spread out maps and diagrams on the long table, not sure whether he felt relief, anger or shame. Stalin stooped over them, considering. "There?" he suggested. "A single blow through Rogachev?"

Rokossovsky had not moved, following Stalin's finger with his eyes. "Two blows rather than one would be advisable, Comrade Stalin."

A shocked silence stretched into every corner of the room. A chair creaked as Malenkov screwed himself around to stare at Rokossovsky, while Poskrebyshev looked quietly pleased, a finger wiping across his mouth.

For perhaps as long as two or three minutes Stalin did not look up. When he did, the menace of his whole bearing was unmistakable, his voice thick with anger. "I do not have generals in my army whose military practices are unsound. You have one more chance. Go and think it over again."

Again Kolya stood in the passage. With the strain and fear of the disaster facing them added to the pain of standing such long hours, he was feeling not far from collapse. Try as he would, he could not keep his mind from the steel-lined cells of the Lubyanka or from the certainty that this time Anna would follow him into the grasp of the NKVD when she inevitably tried to find out what had happened, protested at the wall of silence she would meet. He watched with bitter fury as Rokossovsky, commander of three quarters of a million men, was pushed back into the room opposite, roughly and insultingly this time, as if the forces of violence could scarcely wait to get their hands on him, the sentry summoned as if he were a common criminal, the endless tale of time resumed.

This time they were not left quite so long. Molotov and Malenkov came out of Stalin's office and went in to Rokossovsky together. Kolya had a quick glimpse of him seated with his head in his hands before he stood up, guard slipped back into place.

"You have taken leave of your senses, General," said Malenkov harshly. "You forget who you are speaking to; there can be no will against the Supreme Commander-in-Chief." There was almost a tone of disbelief in his voice as he added, "You are disagreeing with Comrade Stalin."

"Yes," said Rokossovsky dryly. "I know I am." The past hours had completely stripped his face of color, a faint sheen of sweat outlining sharp lines of cheekbone and nose. A blood-stained cell floor was something no man who had endured it ever forgot.

Molotov spoke severely, like the elderly schoolmaster his appearance suggested. "You will have to agree, that's all there is to it. Poskrebyshev . . . you will not like the consequences if you do not."

Rokossovsky's eyes met Kolya's and he shrugged slightly. "I don't suppose I will. I am sorry, Konstantin Aleksandr'itch." He looked bone-weary as they all trooped back into Stalin's office again. Everyone fell back, leaving him alone facing Stalin, his height dwarfing those around him. Kolya had the sudden irrelevant recollection of hearing somewhere that it was his physique which thirty years before had resulted in Trooper Rokossovsky being drafted into the Imperial Dragoons.

"Well?" Stalin spoke quickly, impatiently, as if he could scarcely wait to finish with such inconvenience. "Which is better, one strong blow or two weak ones?"

"Two strong blows are better than one," replied Rokossovsky quietly.

"But which of them should be primary in your opinion?" It was a last, rather unexpected chance to escape with some degree of honor.

"They should both be primary."

A terrible silence fell. No one moved or spoke, waiting for the explosion of anger which such silences always presaged, as if they expected execution to take place in that very room.

Stalin stroked his eyebrows meditatively with the stem of his pipe. "I wonder," he said musingly, "I wonder whether two blows could really be better than one?" He laughed and buffeted Rokossovsky playfully on the back. "I think I like generals who stick to their ideas; we shall see." He snapped his fingers at Kolya. "Show me those plans again."

It was another hour before they left, walking speechless across the guardroom, through the anterooms and offices, down the stairs, past the sentries, and still without speaking were driven through the drab Moscow streets to the Commissariat for Defense.

Only when they were standing in the courtyard there, safe from listening ears, did Rokossovsky finally remark acidly, "We shouldn't have much trouble beating the Germans with all the practice we put in at home. It is a sorrow to me, Konstantin my friend, that you can only drink mineral water, for I certainly need a large vodka."

"I shall have to suck the cork," said Kolya cheerfully, emotions caught on the knife edge of reaction. "I don't think mineral water would quite meet the occasion."

Rokossovsky laughed; for all his outward calm he was probably feeling very similar. "You'd better come in and take that secret weapon of yours off; we've work to do. If this plan of mine goes wrong now, we shall both be back in a cellar with our wrists crossed." He hesitated a moment and then added brusquely, "I couldn't do anything else with so many lives in my charge, but you mustn't think I was unmindful of the position I had placed you in, of your wife particularly."

Kolya nodded. "I feared for Anna. For myself, much as I should have disliked it, I would have preferred to be shot with you today rather than see you stand aside from your convictions for such a reason."

"Thank you." Rokossovsky's voice was without expression. "But I don't recommend a firing squad as an experience. When they were softening me up for my trial I was tied up to face two of them in the space of a month; they even used live ammunition. I damned nearly passed out without more than a graze from some chippings of wall on me, and it is certainly not something which comes easier with practice. I must be one of the very few men left alive who is an authority on the subject."

God, thought Kolya, glancing at his face, rigid with memory, I think I might have found that as hard as beatings to recover from, alone in a cell. It was the only reference Rokossovsky had ever made to his long imprisonment and the lonely battle he had fought there, itself an indication of just how great a strain he had undergone that day. "Stalin knew." Kolya spoke almost to himself.

"What?" Rokossovsky came out of his abstraction.

"He would know every detail of your interrogations, how difficult you would find it to resist this particular threat yet again." One failing of which Stalin could never be accused was lack of mastery over every detail which would enable him to maintain absolute ascendancy over each individual citizen of the Soviet Union. He was a punishingly hard worker at his profession as a tyrant.

Rokossovsky shrugged. "Of course, and a good few other things I shouldn't choose to face again; you too no doubt. The trouble is the swine are so fiendishly skillful at persuading you it's the real thing each time. I expect on this occasion it was just Comrade Stalin's way of warning either the army or Poskrebyshev he is still the *Khozyain*, and he left his choice of which open until the last moment. But you never bloody know these things until you're going down the cellar steps.

I didn't find myself relishing my third attempt at execution any more than my first."

They remained standing in silence, looking at the clear sun and thawed slop of spring, lingering as if reluctant to re-enter the entrapment of buildings. Kolya felt every nerve respond to the sheer pleasure of being alive before the memory of Yuri returned to him again. At least some thousands of other men's sons might have been saved this day from the holocaust and without bidding some words slid into his mind, in English even after thirty years of disuse.

I have been a true man a long season and therefore it could not be expected I should now throw in my lot with thieves. She said it suited a Konstantin, he thought wryly. He grinned at Rokossovsky. "It seems a pity we can't tell your army they have a commander worth fighting for."

Chapter Forty-six

Later, the Bobruisk encirclement of twenty-eight German divisions was taught in Soviet military academies as a masterpiece of its kind: at the time Kolya retained nothing but a series of layered impressions. The staff work for such a massive operation was far more complicated than anything he had encountered before, and, having been present at the Kremlin meeting and subsequent discussions at Stavka, he was naturally more involved than he otherwise would have been as commander of a single corps. The immense volume of work which had to be pushed through at great speed if the attack schedule was to be met blurred events with fatigue, yet gave him an unusually three-dimensional view of the normal confusions of bombardment, advance, counterattack and reinforcement.

When it was all over and the triumphant First Belorussian Army was punched clean through a hundred-kilometer gap, leaving most of the enemy strength encircled behind them, he stood and watched his men streaming past, perched on guns and tanks, crammed into trucks, tramping caked in dust with tunics tied around their waists. The atmosphere, in spite of casualties and the grim paraphernalia of war, was almost carnival-gay. Then he turned aside into the shade of his car, pulled his cap over his eyes and went to sleep with a completeness he had scarcely known since childhood.

It was dark when he awoke. "What the hell?" He struggled to his feet, creakingly stiff.

Fedya laughed somewhere in the shadows. "Ten hours. It is three o'clock in the morning." Then he added apologetically. "I'm very sorry, Comrade General, there was nothing we could do, there were too many of them. I thought we might as well let you sleep but it's a sad ending to such a battle. Fortunately it shouldn't be for long."

Startled, Kolya looked around him disbelievingly. They were entirely surrounded by a mass of steel-helmeted Germans. He took an instinctive step back, mind fluttering with shock; the fate of a Soviet general captured at this stage of the war was likely to be singularly unenviable. His first reaction was to dive for cover in the woods; the area must be alive with Soviet troops. He opened his mouth to communicate this to his remarkably passive companions and then shut it again, some instinct warned by Fedya's stance, a familiarity in his tone. Now he was fully awake the oddity of the Germans' behavior in considerately allowing him to sleep on became obvious.

That blasted boy, he thought, torn between exasperation and reluctant amusement, feeling the pulse of his heart subside. God help him dealing with the Party in peacetime Russia. He pulled out his revolver and threw it at Fedya. "One Russian with a revolver ought to be enough to cope with a Nazi division nowadays, don't you agree, Captain? You'd better find your friends and round them up again, hadn't you?" He tipped his watch to the moonlight. "I just have time to shave and wash while you're busy with all the extra chores you make for yourself."

Fedya laughed and shook his head. "All the way from Oryol and I've never caught you clean yet!" He strolled off whistling, pushing his way through tightly packed wedges of Germans, producing guards from behind trees with the effortless ease of a magician.

"That Captain Seregin, he's worse than my kids back home," grumbled Morozov, boiling tea. "The trouble he took to borrow all those fascist scum while you slept and drive them here like sheep! A penal battalion is what he needs, worrying you like that when you were scarcely awake; there's many generals would have had him shot." He stared at his commander accusingly, although he was Fedya's protesting accomplice in most of his schemes.

Kolya said nothing but smiled to himself as he went in search of a stream. He had not felt so lighthearted in ten years, and Fedya had merely taken advantage of the mood gripping them all.

"There was a message from General Rokossovsky earlier in the night," remarked Fedya on his return.

"Why the devil wasn't I told?" demanded Kolya, returning abruptly to reality.

"The Front Commander spoke personally and told me I needn't log the signal. He said to tell you the bag was two hundred and fifty thousand to the nearest ten thousand either way."

"What the hell will happen to you if you are appointed to a general less long-suffering than I is hard to imagine," said Kolya feelingly. "Two hundred and fifty thousand? That must just about let us through for good, I should think."

"The General added another message I didn't quite understand." Fedya sounded regretful. " 'No crossed wrists.' Is that right? Is it code?"

Kolya laughed abruptly. "In a way." He scarcely knew whether it was cowardice which kept him and others like him silent, the fear of instant return to starvation camp and the brutalities of a steel-lined cell, or the aching guilt of knowing they sentenced everyone they told to the same fate.

However outnumbered and decimated the Germans might be, they continued to fight savagely and the nearer they drew to their home soil the more ferocious resistance became. It was impossible not to feel respect for such courage, but courage alone could not expunge the fearful memories of their destroyed homeland carried by every Soviet soldier. They also felt a growing rage at the thought of being maimed or killed when the war must surely be nearing its end at last, when everyone had survived such hazards it seemed unbearable to find the last stretch home so desperately hard.

There was another of the frequent shuffles of high command. To his fury, Rokossovsky, although newly promoted Marshal of the Soviet Union, was shunted off to the smaller 2nd Belorussian Front for its assault on East Prussia. Perhaps this showed that Stalin after all did not like a subordinate to be proved quite so resoundingly right; perhaps he merely wanted to give his most famous marshal, Zhukov, whom he appointed in his place, the honor of capturing Berlin. It was even rumored that it was a kind of disgrace for Zhukov, removed from central command of the armed forces at the final stage of the war. Stalin's mind, as always, was unknowable. One thing was certain, though: ever since Rokossovsky had outfaced Stalin in the Kremlin he had been saddled with a personal watchdog on his Army Council. Nicolai Bulganin, a member of the Supreme Committee of State Defense, had been sent to him as Stalin's special representative and caused endless trouble by demanding his own kitchen and all kinds of delicacies flown out from Moscow, using the authority of the Central Committee to commandeer aircraft when Rokossovsky flatly refused to allow any of his to be used.

South of Zhukov and his new command were Marshal Konev and his First Ukrainian Front, their long-standing detestation of each other well known. They could well be expected to race their armies to Berlin, to push the Soviet advance ahead at almost any cost, for the pleasure of humiliating each other as much as defeating the enemy. 60 Corps was on the left flank of Zhukov's advance, immediately next to Konev's army, and so suffered from this rivalry almost daily, with its supplies poached and Zhukov's fury sweeping over General Berdeyev at the slightest sign of laggardliness in advance. The Marshal's notoriously violent temper had become almost murderous with the long strains war had imposed upon him

In April 1945 the last great assault went in over the Oder, a strong position defended by every man the Germans could scrape up. It was made more formidable than it need have been, in General Berdeyev's opinion, by Zhukov's insistence on direct mass attack with very little attempt at maneuver, since this would have given Konev's and Rokossovsky's flanking armies the advantage. Nevertheless, in the untidy, savage battle which followed, Konev, facing lighter defenses in the south, began to pull ahead and then, still worse, to swing northward, crossing into the area reserved for Zhukov and striking direct for Berlin.

"What the hell does it matter anyway?" demanded Meretsev, Corps Chief of Staff, as he watched Fedya plotting Konev's advance as far as they knew it—the Germans were probably better informed than neighboring Soviet commands. "They're Russians too, aren't they?"

No one answered him. Zhukov's emotions were too well known and 60 Corps, facing the German Ninth Army, well dug in along a series of swampy rivers and lakes with every narrow tank approach mined to a density they had never before encountered, was lagging particularly badly.

In the late afternoon Kolya went up to a forward observation post with Fedya to see what was going on, but for the moment there was little more which could be done. Mine clearance was slow, bloody work so long as the German artillery continued to fire with the rapidity of gunners who know they will have to blow up everything they cannot throw at the enemy in the shortest possible time.

"Front Command for you, General," said Fedya.

Kolya nodded and went down to the communications bunker; Front Command seldom left him alone for long these days.

"Berdeyev, 60 Corps." The line was atrociously bad.

"Report your position and situation."

He did so, concluding: "Advance rate is increasing but tanks can't get through until the mines are cleared and my engineers cannot work effectively until German saturation fire of the approaches is smothered. There are few routes suitable for armor and every one has been presighted for long and short range fire."

There was a pause while the staff officer reported elsewhere and Kolya stood moodily fiddling with the binoculars around his neck. This was wicked fighting, but whereas before there had been no choice but to attack the Germans if they were ever to be defeated, he bitterly resented throwing his men at positions which, in his view, relatively simple flanking moves would make it unnecessary to take. Konev was already behind this German army and motoring for Berlin; surely Russia had lost enough, the suffering men and women of Russia had lost enough to cherish those who were left? 60 Corps could scarcely help making slow progress in their present circumstances, but their commander was making very little effort to hurry them up. Yuri . . . how would he feel if Yuri's life had been thrown away for a futile piece of megalomania?

"Berdeyev? Repeat the co-ordinates of your position."

He did so. Another pause. The dugout was cramped and he had to crouch, bending uncomfortably from the hips; as a forward divisional position it had not the extra depth he required at his corps command.

"Your orders are to advance to co-ordinate position Red Victory by dawn tomorrow."

He fumbled for his glasses and list of coded check lines, pulling a map toward him. Position Red Victory was nearly fifteen kilometers off, the far side of those murderously narrow tank approaches. "Dawn will give me quite insufficient time to clear routes through the mine fields for armor," he said patiently. "There are few suitable assault points for tanks in this sector and the density of mines is at least one per square meter."

"Those are your orders." The distant voice was quite impersonal.

"Well, I haven't accepted them," he snapped back, exasperated. "Go and tell the Marshal what I've said. It is impossible to make the required depth of breakthrough in the time. As we infiltrate the German positions we are increasing our rate of gain but I can't possibly reach Red Victory in less than . . ." he calculated swiftly, "sixty hours. The enemy will probably pull back before then as the threat of encirclement grows."

"You have no choice but to accept them; they are orders, Comrade General." The man on the other end of the line was obviously too terrified of Zhukov to take such a message.

"Ask the Marshal whether I may speak to him direct." The whole communications dugout was shaking with the force of the German shelling; whatever might be the case elsewhere, resistance was not slackening here. He set his teeth as his eardrums snapped viciously to a burst directly in line with the entrance. Perhaps because of faint memories of a Galician wood in 1917, he always found this kind of close bombardment particularly hard to endure, but at least the noise was too great for the signalers around him to hear much of what was being said.

"Zhukov." The voice was thick and angry.

"Comrade Marshal. Berdeyev, 60 Corps."

"I know. What the devil do you want?"

"Your orders, Comrade Marshal." Kolya spoke carefully. "You have my situation report, the density of mining and co-ordinated artillery fire on the only tank approach routes—"

"What do your clearance squads think they are doing? Going to a tea party instead of a brothel?"

"They are dying, Comrade Marshal, even with all the covering support I can give them."

"You reach Red Victory by dawn tomorrow, is that clear? If you are then too weak to advance further, I will order another corps through your ranks to take up pursuit."

Kolya took a deep breath. "There is no possible means by which I could reach Red Victory by dawn, Comrade Marshal, with or without my corps. I need between fifty and sixty hours to clear enough mines to let the tanks through."

"Do I have to instruct you in basic military techniques? Send your infantry through first tonight, they will explode the mines and the tanks can follow over them. Your report at dawn from Red Victory, General. There are no excuses I will accept." He slammed down the phone.

Kolya replaced the instrument carefully, his whole body suddenly clammy, the muscles of his stomach contracting with the old horrible familiarity. He pushed his way out of the trench hastily, away from the staring signalers, before vomiting helplessly into a shell hole. What Zhukov had ordered was inconceivable, yet it was true. To form up his regiments and divisions one by one and drive them like beasts down those tank approaches until they died on exploding mines, and then send in the next wave, and the next, until nothing but bloody rags marked the death of 60 Corps on the altar, not of war, but of pride. Twenty thousand families all over Russia who would never see son or husband home again, the precious life-blood of a nation already almost destroyed, heedlessly thrown away when the war had only days to run. For nothing. Nothing. No possible, conceivable object. He retched again, hands spread in slime and mud; he had not had such a fearful, driving, gut-splitting attack in years.

"General?" Dimly, he saw Fedya's boots.

"Go away. Get out, leave me alone." It was a gasping effort to speak.

"You can't stay there." He felt Fedya's hand under his elbow, became distantly aware of the German shelling again, his men passing in the trench behind him, and blindly allowed himself to be pulled aside.

"I'm sorry." He fumbled open his tunic collar and tipped his face back, eyes closed. A thin rain was falling and after a while the chill wet running down his neck dragged him back to awareness again and he opened his eyes to see Fedya leaning against a mud wall opposite, his one arm hooked into his belt, regarding him gravely. They were in an abandoned foxhole off the main communication trench.

"You should go to hospital for a while; the war is nearly over. There is no reason to drive yourself so now, especially when we can't do anything here except sit and wait."

Kolya shrugged but said nothing, there was nothing to say. He straightened his tunic slowly; he had been sick over his binoculars. He threw them away violently. "Give me yours."

Fedya handed them over. "There's nothing to see. It's raining enough to give us a little cover, but it doesn't make much difference." With their guns already sighted, visibility was not essential to the Germans.

They walked back to the observation post in silence, Kolya only belatedly realizing from some of the startled stares he encountered how ghastly he must look.

He stood a long while studying the enemy positions, already well known to him and now partly obscured by drifting rain. The German bombardment was not quite as fierce as it had been, he suspected they were already pulling out some of their guns, but the murderous cross fire on the only possible tank routes was still intense, his corps artillery working frantically to plot position after position in an attempt to help the engineers in their fearsomely exposed task of clearing the enemy mine fields. Eventually he turned to a forward company commander out of his dugout and ordered detailed maps to be brought: massive German staff maps captured in Poland, showing every feature down to a rock the size of a man, but horribly inconvenient for use in the open.

"You'd better come too," he said to Fedya briefly. "Everyone else out, I want room to move." The bunker was small enough as it was and Fedya had to help him scramble out of his brace before he could attempt any work, while all the time minutes were slipping away, sliding past him like a thawing stream while he fumbled and sweated, unable to see any way out of the fearful ultimatum Zhukov had issued.

One by one he went over the maps minutely, considering and rejecting the various possibilities which occurred to him. The ground was too wet for maneuver or for handling tanks in unconventional ways, the German positions too strong for anything short of major assault to be successful. He frowned over tiny German figures on the maps, it was ridiculous to attempt planning such an operation in a cramped, dark, front-line bunker, but he did not want to return to his headquarters, where Zhukov's staff would be harrying him for his detailed plans every few minutes.

He took off his glasses and rubbed his eyes wearily. There was no answer he could see except the obvious one of leaving the whole treacherous business alone. Sit down and wait, form up the tanks ready for breakthrough and take the day off. The Germans must be alarmed already as Konev sliced into their rear and the threat of encirclement grew. In twenty-four hours, thirty-six at most, they would be pulling back as fast as they could and he would reach Red Victory almost without losing a man. From Zhukov's point of view the snag was that by then Konov might well be into the suburbs of Berlin.

A signaler came in. "A message from Front Headquarters, Comrade General. Also Colonel Meretsev is anxious for you to return to Corps Headquarters as Front wants to maintain direct contact."

He waited until the man had gone and then tossed the message over to Fedya. *Report your preparations for attack*. The code groups were very familiar.

"Attack?" exclaimed Fedya. "You've been ordered to attack down there?"

He nodded, eyes still on the map.

"My God, it'll be a bloodbath! How can you get the tanks through? They must know the mines can't be cleared until some of the cross fire is smothered."

"Front Command suggests I send infantry through first to explode the mines for the tanks." He met Fedya's shocked gaze evenly. "Which is for your ears only. You tell no one else, ever, do you understand? There is one exception I will tell you of presently."

Fedya's eyes narrowed. "You're not going to do it?"

There was a long silence and then Kolya shook his head slowly, conscious as he did so that this time there would be no escape for him: how ironic that Anna had thought he must be safe in the army. "I need a clear twenty-four hours, though, or someone else will come and do it instead. I will draft a message for Front Command in as ambiguous terms as I can and you code it up; anyone else would know I was reporting nonsense. My advance line is Red Victory by dawn tomorrow—when is sunrise?"

"Zero-five-fifty-eight," said Fedya after a moment. "Thirteen hours' time."

Kolya clenched his hands suddenly. "By tomorrow evening the Germans will be pulling out, I'm sure of it. If then someone else pushes the corps through, at least the engineers will be able to work. I have to gain the whole of tomorrow somehow." He stood up. "Help me back into that thing, then when you've done your coding get Meretsev and a couple of his staff up here. Everyone is about to think me mad, but I'm going to so confuse this corps it will take half the staff officers of the Front to get it untangled again when they eventually realize what has happened, or rather not happened, about six o'clock tomorrow morning."

Chapter Forty-seven

In fact it was nearly eight o'clock before a curt message came through from Front Command ordering General Berdeyev to report himself forthwith, having handed over 60 Corps to General Cermek, who was already on his way to assume command.

When the news that Old Ironback was sacked spread through the corps it was met with disbelief. To be sure everyone had been thoroughly bewildered by the futile blunderings of the night, which had thrown every unit into blasphemous outrage as assault troops tangled with mobile kitchens, tanks were pulled back behind heavy artillery, regiments broken up and spread around the sector in confusion. But the corps as a whole, not only the original 196th Rifles, regarded themselves as Ironback's Own, proud of their record and of their commander, who had brought them through eighteen months of continuous fighting to the point of victory.

"They can't take you away from the corps now!" Meretsev had large, sad eyes like an owl at a funeral. "What are they thinking of when the war will be over in a week or two?"

Kolya leaned back against the sodden mud side of the forward command post dug during the night, hands in pockets, staring out over the saturated Spree countryside. "There will be many changes with the end of the war, I daresay." He felt quite relaxed, although very tired. He grinned suddenly. "I'm afraid I've left General Cermek quite a mess to sort out." He could not imagine what Cermek would say when he saw the disposition charts of the corps.

"Don't you think we should start to do something now, before he comes, Comrade General?" Meretsev had prowled around the bunker all night, querying orders and mopping sweat off his face with a dirty towel as the full enormity of his commander's orders dawned on him.

"No," said Kolya shortly. "The artillery is doing very nicely where it is."

"Yes, Comrade General, but . . . but the whole sector is clogged with it, nothing else can get forward. Whatever will a new commander make of such dispositions? What am I to tell him you had in mind? I must confess I am not clear myself." He could not understand the almost flippant attitude of his normally exacting commander.

Kolya laughed. "Not quite up to War College standard are they? You carried out orders, that's all you need to tell him. I'm going to wash and shave; the signalers will warn us when the new man arrives." Fedya had strict orders to gain every minute he could on the long trek forward with Cermek, and of all the officers in the army there could be no one quite as well suited for such a task as Fedya.

Ten o'clock.

Eleven-thirty.

Twelve-fifteen and a furious message from Zhukov's H.Q. demanding to know what was going on.

"Tell them I am still awaiting General Cermek in order to hand over the corps." General Berdeyev had been spending the time wishing his men well and it took the perspiring runner nearly an hour to find him.

Thirteen-fifty and even Kolya was beginning to wonder what the hell Fedya could have done with Cermek, while his officers had subsided from ill-concealed hilarity to a heavy foreboding as they realized Old Ironback could only be so exposing himself for some deadly serious purpose.

"Comrade General?" It was forward artillery observation.

"Yes? Berdeyev here."

"The Germans, Comrade General, there are very heavy movements to the rear. It looks like support formations pulling out."

"Any signs from the forward positions?"

"Not exactly, Comrade General, but you know how it is, you get a feeling after a long time at this game. I think they are thinning out although there are no positive signs yet."

"Who is reporting?"

"Major Suvalki, Comrade General."

A very sound man; if he had an instinct about what the Germans were doing, he was almost certainly right. "Very well, Suvalki, keep me informed." He turned to Meretsev with a faint smile. "All right, Aleksei Pavl'itch, you'll soon be able to start sorting it all out again. Engineers and tanks can start moving now; infantry still stay where they are." By the time the corps was handed over and Cermek had digested the situation it would cause even worse confusion to try to reverse this fresh movement. Orthodox methods surely should be inescapable.

Fourteen-fifteen. Fourteen thirty-eight. At least five hours to sort things out; it should be just about right.

To say Cermek was angry when he finally appeared would have been short of the truth; even Fedya looked chastened and his nose had been bleeding. General Berdeyev did not inquire too closely into their journey forward but he gathered that Cermek had finally lost his temper and knocked Fedya down when they had been delayed half an hour by tanks, traveling nose to tail and churning the ground to bottomless sour cream borsch directly across their route. The handing-over ceremony was brief to the point of rudeness, Cermek merely remarking with unconcealed satisfaction, "There is an escort with my car, General. They have orders to take you to Front H.Q."

"Under arrest?" Meretsev looked at his former commander very hard.

"Naturally," said Cermek coldly. "What else for those who disobey orders? I shall want to see all your logs and reports, Colonel, to judge your own blame."

"Blame for what?" Poor Meretsev looked quite bewildered, while the rest of the staff and assembled divisional commanders exchanged startled glances.

"We shall see," said Cermek grimly. "This corps should have been fifteen kilometers into the enemy positions by now."

"Fifteen kilometers? Why, that's impossible; it would have meant . . ." The words died on Meretsev's lips and he swung back to stare at Kolya again.

"Precisely," said Cermek. "Your general saw fit to disobey his orders and now he is going to pay the penalty. The last commander Marshal Zhukov caught out in dereliction of his duty went to a penal assault battalion as a major and was killed three days later." He stared at them without expression.

"I remember it," said one of the divisional commanders unexpectedly. "The Marshal recommended him for a gallantry award after he was killed." He spat on the floor deliberately, an inconceivable insult from a man of his rank.

Cermek flushed a deep, violent red. "What sort of a corps is this I have taken over! You are relieved of your duties! You"—he turned to Meretsev—"make out the papers at once."

"It was one of the best corps in the army." It was impossible to tell who had spoken and Cermek hesitated, made uncertain suddenly by the ring of hostile faces.

"Come, Comrades," said Kolya quietly. "We have come a long way together, don't let us bicker at the end. I'm grateful for your support these past eighteen months and wish you well in the peace you have won. Now, General Cermek, perhaps I might just have a last word with you over the disposition of forces." He did not really wish to linger, but if Cermek were distracted now he would not know who he had relieved of his duties, could hardly search the corps for an unknown officer, face partly hidden by a soft-peaked cap, who had spat on the floor. Meretsev could certainly be relied on not to prepare papers if the matter were dropped.

The headquarters car had an escort of two armed soldiers and a motorcyclist. "They must think I'm much more dangerous than I feel," remarked Kolya, observing this.

"Comrade General," Fedya swallowed. "It has been an honor to serve you."

"And it's certainly been a privilege to watch you in action." Kolya laughed suddenly. "I'm sorry you had your nose punched in the end, but over the years I reckon you earned it."

Fedya did not smile, he looked on the edge of tears. "Comrade General, is there nothing we can do?"

"For God's sake, no! Anything you attempted would only make matters worse. There is one thing you can do for me, though." Fedya nodded eagerly and he went on slowly, the escort very near now. "I don't know how things will go for me, the war is nearly over so the time for suicide battalions is probably over too, I may get off quite lightly." He was sure he would not; Zhukov did not forgive those who disobeyed his orders. "If things go really wrong, will you see my wife for me? Tell her exactly what happened so she will know I had no choice. It will be very hard for her, but if she might perhaps understand why . . . it will help a little I think."

Anna. He could not stop thinking about her all

through the long uncomfortable journey. Hard for her. It was difficult to sustain the knowledge of her anguish, of what his death for such a reason would do to her. Anna, who had said she could not bear any more, who had thought to keep him safe in the army. Watch their hands and not their lips. I hope, Kolya, you will never know what I mean. But I do, Grandmother, I do indeed . . . What a lesson to spend your life learning. Your century, I really think things are easier . . . perhaps you will be the first Berdeyev to be able to do for Russia what he really wanted to do . . . the cost too dear lightly to give it away. I can't bear any more, Kolya, I have a right to your promise . . . Where did we go wrong, Kolyushka?

Exhausted, he slept uneasily.

No one knew what to do with him when his escort turned him over to the Provost Major at Front Headquarters. Zhukov had left for the forward area, where Konev's tanks were reported into the suburbs of Berlin, and there was no time for a single discredited general who was, nevertheless, still ranked as a corps commander and could not yet be thrown into the common cell.

In the event, General Berdeyev passed the next days in complete peace and comfort, resting in some absent colonel's room with a guard discreetly huddled into a corner of the passage. He slept and woke and slept again. He distantly heard, with a certain cynical amusement, the wave of near hysteria which swept over the building when news broke that Konev had beaten Zhukov into Berlin by a full day. He began cautiously to eat again and wrote a long, loving letter to Anna without any mention of his present danger, only the certainty of peace within days. There was no way he could prepare her for the shock to come, no censor who would pass any explanation he chose to make.

It was his first rest free from responsibility since the

two days he had spent with Anna at the height of the battle for Moscow three and a half years before, and long-accumulated exhaustion mercifully prevented him from brooding too much on the seriousness of his position. Had it not been for anxiety about Anna he would not have cared too deeply. He knew he could have done nothing else and the moment of victory, when he also knew himself still deeply loved however long their separation, did not seem an inappropriate time for his forty-five-year struggle with his century to end. He was not afraid of death; only, now, very much afraid of life on certain terms.

But he knew this resignation to be bitterly unfair and selfish. For Anna's sake he must still fight every step of the way, even if it was hard to see how he could again survive. It was this which roused him from his lethargy before he was fully rested, set him pacing and scheming, and brought him full realization of just how little chance of escape he had left himself. There was no possible excuse or explanation he could offer Zhukov which would be accepted for a moment.

He knew at once when Zhukov returned. The whole vast complex of Front Headquarters was cast into a pool of silence, broken only by racing feet. Nothing was dropped, no casual clatter of equipment, such speech as was necessary confined to signals and operations rooms. Zhukov, with his will of steel and one of the best military minds in the Soviet Union, was a swine to serve.

"General Berdeyev?"

"Yes." It was two o'clock in the morning but he was fully dressed, expecting a summons at any time of day or night.

"This way, please." He had to wait in an anteroom and then again in the main operations room. Both Konev's and Zhukov's men were well into the suburbs of Berlin, he noted, studying the situation map with interest. He looked down at the Spree Valley and the markers for 60 Corps; as far as he could make out they had advanced about eight kilometers in four days. At that rate Cermek would soon be following him into the punishment cells. It seemed weird and unearthly to be standing, waiting for God knew what, while the map calmly recorded the greatest triumph Russian arms had ever known, the culmination of all the suffering, all the blood and heroism of four unspeakable years. See you in Berlin, the careless farewell of millions of Soviet soldiers had come true, although more than twenty million Soviet citizens had not lived to see the day. See you in Berlin, and now they were there. It was over.

"This way if you please, Comrade General." The aide was almost painfully polite, and Kolya wondered wryly whether it was an instinctive reaction to serving a man like Marshal Zhukov.

Zhukov's office was large and comfortably furnished—a distinct improvement on the Kremlin as a place of execution was his first, rather cynical reaction. The second was complete astonishment. Rokossovsky was sitting alone on the edge of the desk.

"Comrade Marshal," he said after a moment. "General Berdeyev reporting to Marshal Zhukov."

Rokossovsky gave a flickering smile. "Perhaps you would prefer to report to me?"

"Yes, very much prefer it, Comrade Marshal, but my orders are for Marshal Zhukov."

"The Marshal has agreed that I should listen to your case, and in the circumstance does not wish to see you."

"I think you must have come all the way from Second Army to do this for me," said Kolya slowly. "How did you know?"

"That fiendish little captain of yours, Fedya Seregin, came to my H.Q. yesterday with what he said was a message from you. It turned out to be nothing of the sort, and to make matters worse your former chief of staff had provided him with fraudulent movement papers. He told me a story I found it hard to credit, but a conversation I had on the telephone with Georgi Konstantin'itch* suggested there might be some truth in it. I should like to have your version."

Kolya told him, not omitting his deliberate confusion of 60 Corps before he handed it over. Rokossovsky's mouth twisted slightly at that but he heard him through in silence. "What a mess," he said finally. "You have committed just about every military crime in the book. If it goes to court-martial you will be shot. How many know the full story?"

"The Corps staff realized part of it when I was relieved of my command, but nothing more than they could see. Only Captain Seregin knew it all, and now you. I told him not to speak of it to anyone except my wife," he added pointedly.

"Just as well he did," said Rokossovsky shortly. "I had another corps commander once who fell foul of Zhukov and I practically had to go down on my knees to save him. You should be a little easier if no one else knows."

"Marshal Zhukov knows," said Kolya grimly. "I don't see what difference it will make in the circumstances."

"Court-martial proceedings don't have to be instituted unless he insists. If they were, the verdict would be inescapable. Flat disobedience on the field of battle, deliberate mishandling of your troops in the presence of the enemy, you wouldn't have a chance whatever your reasons. I'd shoot you myself if I were on the panel. As it is, all I have to do is bring the necessary pressures to bear on Georgi Konstantin'itch."

"But—" Kolya stopped and thought about it care-

* I.e., Marshal G. K. Zhukov.

fully. "He is your superior," he said finally, "and must be in favor with Comrade Stalin since he gave him your army to have the honor of capturing Berlin."

"That was six months ago," pointed out Rokossovsky. "I don't think there will be much place in the Soviet Union after the war for a marshal who is popularly regarded as the savior of Russia. It will not be long before complaints against the great Marshal Zhukov are welcome in high places; he won't be too anxious then for the orders he gave you to be publicized. How else do you suppose I made him let me see you? If I do make a bargain with him, though, you'll have to keep your mouth shut forever on this, whatever your feelings may be." He laughed suddenly. "Just as well we can be sure that Georgi is too good a soldier not to have secured his office against possible listeners. We shall all have to redouble our care now the war is over."

"You are no favorite of Stalin and the Central Committee, Comrade Marshal. You are already closely watched, I would not like you to expose yourself for me."

Rokossovsky rubbed his nose reflectively. "I was once a stonemason's laborer, the son of a Polish railway worker. This may have helped put me in prison as a suspect foreigner, possibly even one tainted with Catholicism, but the position is somewhat different today. The Red Army does not have so many solidly proletarian marshals with Polish blood. I am going to be very useful to the state after the war, with all the troops and interests we now have in Poland. I shall be safe enough. Meanwhile I have to decide what to do with you."

"I knew what I was doing," said Kolya stiffly. "As you say yourself, I have no military defense. I'm afraid I'm not a very military person."

Rokossovsky looked at him thoughtfully. "No, although the Red army has scarcely been the loser from your service during the war. I also understand that you have applied to stay in the army. The papers came for my recommendation."

"My wife made me promise to stay in; she thought I would be safer with the Red Army to protect me," explained Kolya, straight-faced.

Rokossovsky gave a sharp crack of laughter. "I wonder which would give her the most confidence, an insight into the methods of the Kremlin or into those of Georgi Konstantin'itch? Let us see then where we stand. My private verdict is that you acted correctly; the kind of order you received should never have been given. I would probably have done the same. However, whether you like it or not, you are a soldier, and as a soldier you have no defense. However reticent you were, in the way of the army enough has certainly been guessed or rumored to make your reinstatement impossible, neither would it be proper under the circumstances. To leave you with Zhukov would be dangerous; to take you into my own command would publicize the whole affair and be a deliberate insult to a marshal who has, whatever his faults, deserved well of his country."

He hesitated and then went on slowly, "I have served with Georgi many years. I was once his commanding officer before I lost my seniority in jail. It was he who had the courage to draw Stalin's attention to the fact that I had made a nonsense of the charges against me when, as you know, innocence alone made little difference to whether a man was shot or not. He is a naturally ruthless man: it was not Stalin but he who refused me permission to pull my men back at Istra during the Moscow battle and at the time I found it hard to forgive. But he did win the battle when someone less ruthless might have lost it. He is an exceptional soldier who is probably about to be shamefully treated by his country. This he senses, and if it does not excuse his orders to you it perhaps helps explain them. I do not wish to be a party to discrediting him and any open action of mine which helped you in this situation might be brought up in the months to come so I would have to testify against him. Do I make myself clear?"

"Yes, Comrade Marshal. Entirely clear."

"Very well, then. I will inform Marshal Zhukov that in my opinion there should be a suitable position for you, in a reduced rank of divisional general, in one of our rear areas. Everyone is so used to him demoting and dismissing people it will not cause more than momentary comment in all our police reports. In return I expect your word to keep silent about the whole occurrence. I have already extracted a similar undertaking from Captain Seregin."

Kolya stood to attention. "You have it, Comrade Marshal, I am very grateful. To come all this way . . . that is twice I owe my life to you."

"It was my debt this time for nearly throwing it back down the Kremlin drains for you. In any case, my judgment of your value to the army when I helped you get out of the camps was not at fault. You will not escape too lightly, though; from my experience of Georgi Konstantin'itch I'm sure he will go to great trouble to find you the most unattractive base appointment he can. I'll tell him you have put in enough time in the east to excuse you from that at least." He went out swiftly, with over a hundred kilometers to drive over war-torn roads before dawn. Kolya hoped he had left his Defense Committee watchdog, Bulganin, in a sufficient stupor of food and drink for his absence to pass unremarked, although Stalin would certainly hear of it within hours from someone.

Chapter Forty-eight

General Berdeyev was sent to Leningrad to take charge of heavy construction troops helping repair the city and of the German prisoners who had been set to work clearing some of the devastation they had caused. Zhukov no doubt considered such an assignment sufficiently discreditable to fulfill Rokossovsky's prediction, command of pioneers and prisoners of war being regarded as virtually a convict posting, but Kolya was delighted. To help rebuild the city of his birth, which he had loved so well thirty years before and never since seen, to be away from fighting and the disagreeable duties of administering sullen, frightened German and Polish populations, to turn his mind at last to the problems of peace and a chance to see Anna and Sophie again: he could not think of anything he would like better.

He flew by way of Minsk and Smolensk. Sunshine poured over the unfolding land, reflecting brilliantly from thawed pools, rivers and swamps. Grass and trees were bending in the rough, sweet wind of a Russian spring, flaunting yellow rather than green so fresh were they with new life.

He sat hour after hour looking out over the vast plain of Russia through a small, scratched perspex window, feeling the pulse of the land hesitantly beating again in village, farm and town. He was thinking too of the concourse of dead in mound and common grave; charred and blown apart, lives expunged in an instant, tormented boys begging to die, old men and women hanged, deported and murdered. Colonel Bogatkin at the reservoir before Moscow in 1941. The long-nosed sergeant, whose name he had never known, who had thrown himself under a German tank with grenades in his pockets. The swaying bodies on the gibbets of Oryol. A complete battalion he had lost to an unexpected German attack near . . . near . . . he was shamed he could not even remember where. The thousands of soldiers he had never come to know who had died or been maimed under his command.

As the aircraft came lower for landing the false tranquillity of height disappeared. The brilliant yellows and greens were more often weeds than spring corn; the countryside lay silent and devastated with scarcely an animal in the fields or movement in the smashed villages. Minsk was recognizable as a city, with cleared streets and about a third of its houses intact; Smolensk, familiar, ancient, shabby Smolensk, was scarcely recognizable as anything. Gutted walls like skeletons gave a false impression of continuing life from the ground, but from the air it could be seen that nothing but rubble lay behind those façades which still stood. The beautiful, upright block of the cathedral was shattered, its golden clusters of domes dropped into rubbish, two or three snapped-off semicircular curves against the sky all that were left of their grace.

Kolya picked his way through the littered streets oppressed with sadness. Smolensk had been liberated for nearly two years yet very little had been done: the people looked tired and old, they were so few and equipment almost nonexistent. It annoyed him to see soldiers lounging about, the masses of tanks and guns parked everywhere; surely the army could have converted some of its vehicles and set these men to work, there were no battles for them to fight.

He found Party headquarters huddled into a warehouse and introduced himself. "I used to be Director of Klintsy Sovkhoz before the war. Could you tell me what happened to it?"

"Klintsy? Where is that?" A harassed-looking girl, surrounded by the ocher and purple files of Soviet bureaucracy, flipped over some papers helplessly.

"On the Roslavl-Bryansk railway, about seventy kilometers down the line."

"In that case . . . Comrade General, there's nothing left down there. In 1941 the front line was held in that area for two months and then again in 1943 the fighting . . ." She shrugged. "I was a partisan but we couldn't operate there. Everything, even the forest, is smashed."

"Has Klintsy Sovkhoz been re-established now?"

"Comrade General," she said patiently. "There is nothing left. No people, no animals, no cottages, nothing. If you went to look you wouldn't know when you reached it, what were fields are twice your height in weeds and trees." She softened slightly at the expression on his face. "We'll get it back, but we can't start in such a place. We are concentrating now on areas not quite so completely destroyed."

Her earnest faith was touching. A partisan, now a district official and not yet twenty, he guessed. "Thank you, Comrade. I'm sure you will." He hesitated. "Do you have any record of the fate of Party members in the Smolenskaya?"

"We are building up our files again, as you can see." She waved her hand despairingly at the mass of paper littering her cramped office. "But naturally they are incomplete. What did you want to know?

He gave her the names of Vera, Perichev the schoolmaster, Venzher and Pyotr the stockman, whose pride at being accepted as a candidate Party member he just remembered before his arrest.

After about a quarter of an hour she came back with a slip of paper, folded, and gave it to him. "I have written it down for you, Comrade General. We will build it up again, never fear. Come and see us again in two or three years' time." The sympathy in her face, the way she gave him the folded note, warned him that there was nothing good to hear and she had the intuition to know he would not wish to hear it baldly stated by a stranger.

He was back on the aircraft and flying directly north for Leningrad before he had the courage to open the paper and read:

Vera Lesichina . . .	Hanged in Smolensk Dec. 1942 as hostage against partisan activity.
Illyrion Venzher . . .	Military service from July 1941. Killed Kursk 1943.
Ivan Perichev . . .	Reported with partisans 1942. No subsequent record.
Pyotr Keremenko . . .	Military service from June 1941. Invalided 1942, severely burned. Retrained as telephone operator, Tiflis.

The sun was setting now and below the land looked blank and desolate, a thick haze enveloping the horizon as if the earth itself could not bear to show its grief. He shivered suddenly. God, it was going to be hard to build it all up again, to feel at a worn-out forty-five the faith of that girl in Smolensk.

*

Leningrad airbase was running fairly smoothly, with an obviously massive traffic flow, but transport into the city was a different matter and in the end he spent what was left of the night in an uncomfortable officers' bunkhouse, a thin cardboard partition the only concession to rank. In the morning he shared a car with some talkative Aia Force officers who had been stationed in Leningrad during the seige and took an almost proprietorial pride in the ruins they had helped to cause, and had survived.

The suburbs were one long shock after another: Tsarskoye Selo (Pushkin now, he remembered hastily,) the Moscow section, the great observatory, the ring of outer railway stations, all were utterly smashed, huge piles of rubble hastily thrown back to clear the road, no more.

He began to feel sick again, the airmen's lighthearted banter unbearable.

"Where are you going, Comrade General?" asked one of them.

"The General Staff building," he replied briefly, wondering whether that too was shattered, its yellow plasterwork and elegant arches dropped into powder, the marvelous flow of buildings along the Neva lost forever.

"We'll drop off here, then: nice to have known you, Comrade General." They scrambled out, still chattering, too used to devastation to find it remarkable.

Obrodny Canal. The Yusupov Gardens. The turning leading to the Sadovskaya, where his grandmother had lived. He stared out of the window, his heart lightening with immeasurable relief. It was battered, peeling, shabby, with odd painted false-board fronts concealing some of the damage, but it was recognizable. The clang and roar of a tram brought back a wave of nostalgia, jostling crowds trading in heaven knew what in the jumble of the Haymarket were gesticulating and shouting with all the old Petersburg verve. The steel-gray Neva looked calm and detached, cradling its city with the same translucent serenity he remembered; spires, domes and quays flickering reflections in light which was not sun, yet was not quite the absence of sun.

He stopped the car in Palace Square and walked across to Palace Bridge, leaning against the pitted balustrade, staring as if he could never see enough. The sword point of Admiralty spire was clumsily daubed with gray instead of gleaming gold: how the hell had anyone climbed up there with a can of paint? The long façade of the Winter Palace, canvas tarpaulins flapping dismally across holes in the roof, one end crumbled, but with half-shut eyes it was possible to imagine how it had been, how it surely would be again. The fortress and church of St. Peter and St. Paul across the Neva, scarred with bombs and its silhouette differently shaped, but indisputably there. When he walked out along the bridge he could see the great bronze horse of Peter the Great back on its plinth, the stretches of shimmering quayside graciously hiding their scars in the mist of distance, great ladies from the past exerting the poise of age to make a wandering son feel home again.

*

He was to take up his command the following morning, and so in the evening he went to a concert. He had not listened to music, would not on any account let himself listen to music, since *Russlan and Ludmila* in Kiev in 1918, but that night he felt completely content. In the absence of Anna, music seemed the only suitable benediction for his mood. When he saw the posters outside the Mariinsky he succumbed to overwhelming temptation.

Inside the theater the atmosphere was so extraordinary he could only stand and stare, like the schoolboy he had once been in the top gallery. The chandeliers were remounted and lovingly polished, many of the people looked ill and shabby but they were carefully if not smartly dressed, the girls gay in cotton dresses even when they were discreetly patched. The old sharp arguments in quick Petersburg tones tossed backward and forward, quarreling about artists and exhibitions, striking like fantasy on his ears, the polish of manners automatic to most of the crowding audience.

He had underestimated the appalling impact of music on his unguarded mind: within minutes he knew he had been a fool to come. The program was not particularly ambitious. The players were either very young and playing with more excitement than discipline, or else old and lovingly dedicated to every nuance of the score and visibly annoyed at what they plainly regarded as a rather slapdash performance, but on Kolya the effect was shattering.

Whether the music was well or badly played made scarcely any difference. It was music, and a whole side of his nature and temperament, which in other circumstances would have dominated his life, was let out of the cage in which it had been clamped ever since he left Petersburg, so many years before. To listen, to criticize, to allow himself laboriously to attempt untwining the strands of melody, to marvel at the intricate pattern of composer and instrument and be flicked in an instant into speculation as to how else it might have been done: this was release, this was the feeling of God on the seventh day. The long, long guard on feeling dissolved almost unnoticed, his emotions so deeply involved withdrawal became impossible.

Surprisingly enough, it was Chopin's First Piano Concerto which finally overwhelmed him. Not perhaps a work it was easy to associate with emotional upheaval, but to him it was a symbol he could not avoid. It had been in the final concert of the 1913 Conservatoire Summer School and he had been in the orchestra, his grandmother in the audience. Even after so long every note came fresh out of his mind, where he had not known it was still stored. The poignancy of the early theme blended with the immense sadness he had known flying over the ravaged plains of Russia the day before and pitched him into a fearful unraveling of the years between. It was not so much the music speaking to him as he speaking to the music, pouring out of his heart all the feelings he had never been able truly to express in thirty years, because to him the ultimate expression remained the rejected fabric of sound.

He found himself crying. Warm, comfortable and without pain, he was crying as he had never done in the Lubyanka, the starving Ukraine, the steel hell of the battles for Oryol or Moscow. As the music remorselessly unlocked door after door he had thought safely slammed shut forever, he was powerless to hold on any longer to emotions so long guarded that tonight he had forgotten the need for watchfulness. He wept for lost faith, for the great Party of his youth and manhood, to which so many had given everything and been betrayed. He wept for what he could have been and now was not, for Yuri and countless millions of others like him, dead in camp or cell or war; for the new, terrible efforts a suffering people must now make yet again to rebuild their shattered lives and country.

He struggled desperately for control, to still his twitching face and close an aching throat on tears. A few faces stared at him curiously and then looked away: had he known it Leningrad was not unused to the emotional frailties left by war.

Afterward he tried to ring Anna from the call phone in the foyer although earlier the lines to Moscow had been too congested to get through. His desire to hear her voice had become an urgent need and the endless delays of the exchanges infuriated him, still upset and off balance from what he now regarded as an utterly inexplicable disintegration into weakness. He scowled moodily at the floor, still the old delicate rosewood inlay, anger an instinctive reaction from humiliation. Then, reluctantly, he began to feel a certain wry resignation. What the hell, he thought, surely enough has happened for tears in the last thirty years? What of it if I wept? Today is for weakness, for the weakness of memory, of loss and remorse; tomorrow I have to start again, we all have to start again. Of what then should I be ashamed?

The telephone seemed completely dead and he put on his glasses to read the instructions glued to the wall; he was long unfamiliar with civilian instruments. While he waited he studied the concert program, flipping through trite summaries of the works played —how useless words were to express the impact he had felt.

He froze, eyes on the names of the performers.

One of the violinists was Sophie Konstantinovna Berdeyeva.

Chapter Forty-nine

By the time the exchange had told him there was a four-hour delay on calls to Moscow, he had of course missed Sophie at the theater. The first doorkeeper he asked for the lodgings of the young ladies of the orchestra plainly cherished the darkest suspicions about his morals and denied all knowledge of their whereabouts; by the time he had tracked them down to a dingy hotel near the Summer Gardens it was past midnight. There, however, the desk porter was a figure straight out of the past. It was easy to imagine him in the cossack outfit affected by some of the grander hotels in old Petersburg for their doormen, twirling fierce mustaches and unshocked by the most outrageous demands from the hotel's guests—he certainly palmed a tip in the manner born.

Waiting in the hall while the porter went in search of Sophie, Kolya felt ridiculously nervous. The lecherous disbelief with which he had instinctively known the porter would greet an explanation that it was her father wishing to speak to Sophie Berdeyeva had deterred him from offering any information at all, and he wondered whether she would even recognize him. Would he recognize her? He put on his cap, thinking suddenly that his white hair would certainly be a shock.

She came down the stairs slowly, obviously made wary by the late hour and comments of her companions.

He took off his cap again without thinking.

"Sophie." He would have known her.

She stopped dead, lips framing a query but no sound came.

He stood quietly and let her take her time; it was no good thinking a relationship could be rebuilt with a hug and a kiss after nine years of separation, during which each had been exposed to extremes of stress. Like everything else it would have to be laboriously constructed anew. There was pleasure anyway in just looking at his daughter, seeing how much had changed, how much was still the same.

"Father?" She found her voice at last; light, shaken, uncertain.

He nodded and then smiled. "How ridiculous after all these years not to be able to find anything to say."

She came forward slowly. Apart from the eyebrows, she did not really look like either himself or Anna, he decided. She was nearly as tall as he, and, still painfully thin a year after the end of the siege, but her face nevertheless subtly retained the gaiety and rapid change of expression he remembered. It was set and somber now, looking him over carefully.

"You look very different from what I remember," she said flatly.

"Yes," he replied quietly. "I expect I do."

She gave a gulp, part tears, part laughter. "I'm sorry! I didn't mean . . . I would have known you anywhere all the same."

"Well, that's clever," he said cheerfully, in an effort to keep the emotional temperature at a bearable level. "For I certainly don't recognize myself sometimes."

Impulsively, she put her arms around his neck and laid her cheek against his. "Don't. Please don't feel you have to set me at my ease as if . . . as if we didn't belong together however long we've been apart." She stood back again quickly. "I'm Sophie, not some girl you've got to keep quiet in case she has hysterics all over the hall."

He discovered that a hug after all could rebuild more than he had thought. "You're Sophie all right," he said gruffly. "You haven't changed a bit." They both laughed and after a moment he added, "Would you like to come out for a while or are you too tired after the concert? I think perhaps we both need a little time to get used to each other again."

She headed straight for the door and slipped her arm into his. "A white night* in Piter, it seems just the right way to meet again somehow." She chuckled, "That porter would have thought me very choosy if I hadn't gone out with you; it isn't every violinist who gets picked up by a general."

"I should think myself that elderly generals are to

* The white nights of the north are those when it is never completely dark.

be avoided at all costs by a girl of twenty-one," he observed, more sharply than he had intended.

She looked at him in amusement. "I know I've got a father back now."

He was silent. The last right he had after nine years of absence was any shadow of a right to criticize her conduct.

She squeezed his arm. "No generals, I promise. Although I know your age as well as you know mine. I wouldn't call you elderly exactly."

He laughed. "Sophie Konstantinovna, I rather think you have grown up into a minx." Although it was so late the luminescence of the summer night had brought many out into the streets, drifting in groups and couples just as he remembered from so long ago. "You called it Piter," he said suddenly, "do people still call it that?"

"Of course," She looked surprised. "Leningrad is a name of honor now, but to those who love it, it will always be Piter."

"And you love it?"

"Yes," she said simply. "It was terrible here in the seige, but even then I wouldn't have been anywhere else. As soon as a friend told me there was a place in this orchestra for a violinist I jumped at the chance to come back." She laughed, "I can't think any other city would have poetry readings in the middle of such shelling, or mount a special expedition to rescue astronomical instruments from the very edge of the German lines! When we were starving in the winter of forty-one, when there was no wallpaper anywhere because the glue had all been licked off, the university wouldn't allow their collection of seeds to be used for food."

"I loved it too, many years ago." They went across and leaned on a balustrade overlooking the Neva. Earth, sky and water were one opal glow together, the air scented by lime from the Summer Gardens behind them.

"I didn't know you'd ever been here before." She looked puzzled and he cursed himself for such carelessness.

"Yes, but long before I met your mother. I left when I was fifteen," he replied carefully, after a minute.

"Father," she hesitated, and then plunged abruptly, "could you tell me about it?"

"About what?"

"All of it," she said impatiently. "All the things I don't understand about you. Yurka and I—" She broke off.

"Ah, Yuri," he said, staring out over the water. "How I wish I had seen him before he was killed." He regretted bitterly that he had not gone to Kharkov somehow, instead of taking those idle few days by the Volga at Saratov. At the time it had not been clear it was the only chance he would ever have of seeing his son again; he had felt so ill that the thought of a further cross-country journey to Kharkov had seemed impossible, the rediscovery of their love between Anna and himself has been overwhelmingly important. Now, he could not quite forgive himself for not going.

"We talked a lot, Yurka and I." She kept her voice even with an effort. "Such barriers grew up between us and Mother after we left Klintsy, there never seemed anything we could say to her without the most terrible rows. I want to ask the questions we both intended to ask when we saw you again. For months we thought it would be tomorrow, next week perhaps, but it never was."

He drew away from her and took off his cap again, the strengthening light falling on his white hair and lined face. "Curiosity is a dangerous fault in the Soviet Union," he replied at last. "What is it you want to know?" Having set out hours before to attend a concert, he was not wearing his brace; for some time only the intense emotions of the evening had overlaid the fact that his back was hurting savagely.

She was angry suddenly. "I have a right to know; it was my life as well as yours which was smashed up. Mother always told us we shouldn't be ashamed of you, that you had done nothing wrong, but if so, why did she run out on you? Why did you go to prison? People don't go to prison without good reason. I think we never really believed you had been arrested, it seemed so fantastic. We thought it must be a stupid story Mother had thought up because she wanted to do surgery more than stay with you and she never quite contradicted us. Those quarrels you had at the end . . . were they because you were angry she wanted to go away or did you really do something and she was frightened of the consequences?"

"But now you do believe I have been in prison?" He had no idea how to answer such a ruthless battery of questions. This new Sophie, at once perceptive and naïve, could certainly not be burdened with knowledge of the camps or the dangerous treachery of his birth, of the methods of the NKVD or his reservations about the Party she had been brought up to revere, the disclosure or discussion of any of which would inevitably lead to her own destruction.

She looked at him and nodded. Her first shock at his altered appearance had subsided; as they talked it was familiarity which gripped her and brought back flooding memory, but the physical difference was inescapable nevertheless. "Yes, tonight when I saw you, how you had changed, I knew it was true."

"Sophie . . . yes, it is true. I served three and a half years and ten days ago I nearly went back again." It was more likely he would have been shot, but he was scarcely worried about strict accuracy. "I found it then, and find it now, far from easy to do just what I am told. The more responsibility you have, to me, the more carefully you should think about what you are doing and why."

"Well, of course," she said, surprised. "What about it?"

He felt completely at a loss; she seemed to have no grasp at all of the ruthlessness of the state she lived in. "If that is your attitude," he said dryly at last, "you don't need me to explain what happened. You will find out for yourself."

She thought it over carefully and this time he did recognize a likeness to himself. Anna had always teased him about the obvious way he withdrew from a conversation to consider some piece of information. "You said you nearly went back ten days ago, yet you are a well-known commander. I've even heard your name in some of the communiqués. I still don't understand."

"I'm one rank of general down now from what I was a week ago," he retorted lightly. "I must be the only man in the army to end the war with the same rank he held four months after it started."

She laughed. "So what did you do this time?"

"Oh, for heaven's sake, Sophie," he said impatiently. "I've told you once, you'll just have to accept it. I cannot blindly do what I am told, I don't even think it right to do so. I'll always be in trouble, I daresay although for your mother's sake I try to survive somehow."

"And mine."

"Thank you, my dear, but I don't think I've quite earned that from you."

"It was because Yurka and I believed Mother when she said we mustn't be ashamed of you that we thought she must be at fault."

"She was not." He eased his position carefully against the balustrade and then held himself very still. "When you are very much in love one day, you will learn that there is nothing quite so bad as the hurt given by the person you love. I used the greatest hurt I knew to make your mother go and take you both with her because by then I was certain I could not last. Everyone in authority was at risk and I had made enemies by querying some of the things which were done. Sooner or later I was bound to be arrested but she didn't realize it. Had I asked or begged her to go, or tried to explain the position I was in, she would not have gone."

"But if you were arrested, why should we be in any danger?"

He stirred restlessly, thinking of the women's camp at Vladivostok. "Because that was the way it was, and could be again."

"You aren't going to tell me, are you? Not what really happened. Perhaps you might have told Yuri, though." Her tone was bitter.

His lips tightened. "Sophie, you are behaving like a spoiled child. I have told you as clearly as I can, you're not a fool. You may not so far have chosen to look around you with more than your eyes, but you know well enough some of the penalties the Party can impose, if it wishes to and for no other reason. If I sent you all away, placed an intolerable burden on your mother and bore what I did bear, it was because it was the best I could do at the time to protect you all. I am not going to put it all at risk simply to satisfy your curiosity, when the details do not matter anyway."

"If they didn't matter you would tell me," she interrupted shrewdly.

He shrugged and then held his breath at the thrust of pain. "For the essentials of what is between us, they do not matter. I could not do the sort of things which might have allowed me to avoid arrest; even if I had the whole thing became so hysterical and meaningless in the end, it wouldn't have made much difference. I

know it spoiled your life, it spoiled your mother's and mine too, but I owe you no apology. If I could go back, all I could hope for is the strength to go through with it again. I have done wrong in my life, there is much I am ashamed of, but not that. I can't make you believe me, you'll just have to take my word that there are some things it is better for you not to know."
It was a miserable end to what should have been an encounter to delight them both, but nine years was too great a chasm to bridge with an unknown daughter when littered with so many bones of the past.

There was a long silence and then he realized she was laughing softly. "I remember how angry you used to be with us sometimes at Klintsy. Over the years you'd become a cardboard figure, still loved, but not quite a person any longer. I'm in no doubt now I'm back under parental authority."

"I didn't mean it to be like that," he said awkwardly.

She kissed his cheek. "I like it. Don't you see? There's no one else on earth who could have dealt with me as you've just done. I told you earlier, we still belong together."

"Yes." He was smiling too. "I really think we do."

"You're in pain, aren't you? I watched you trying not to let me see, to argue it out without appealing to pity."

"You're too damned acute for your own good," he said ruefully. "Deceiving the secret police is one thing, deceiving you is going to be something else again. Sophie, I'll be in touch with you in a day or so. I have a command to take over in"—he glanced at his watch—"four hours' time."

"And I've kept you out most of the night when you aren't really well yet," she said remorsefully.

"I'm as fit as I'll ever be; you'll have to get used to it as I have had to." He knew his words were ungracious and added grudgingly. "I have some steel strapping I usually wear but it is almost impossible to sit down in. As I went along last night expecting a quiet couple of hours at a concert, I wasn't wearing it. I shall be all right when I have it on again."

She did not reply, aware of his instinctive recoil from sympathy, alarmed by his obvious difficulty in even standing upright. Nothing her mother had mentioned of the changes she would see had prepared her for such physical weakness, its extent disguised until now by the way he completely ignored it.

She had cherished an image of him over the years in which he was both perhaps an overidealized, beloved father and the tireless, vigorous director of Klintsy, the framework for the earlier, happy years of her life. Only following his accident with the tractor did she ever remember him unwell and then she had been so disconcerted that for weeks she had refused to see him without shaming tantrums. Dimly she began to realize that a mere prison sentence could not possibly explain such a fearful change, to feel on the edge of her mind the unimaginable implications of what must have been done to him.

"Were you injured in the war?" she asked. It was a faint hope, surely she would have been told that at least.

"No," he said shortly. "I've had trouble with my back for years, don't worry about it. My divisional engineers made me enough armor to brace up a tank; when we meet next I shall be so damned upright you won't recognize me.

They parted outside the hotel taken over by the Red Army where he was billeted. "I'm sorry not to see you home," he said apologetically. "How long are you in Leningrad?"

"I'm looking for a permanent job at the moment. I know quite a few people in Radio Leningrad. I was here nearly four years, studying and in the siege."

"Are you hoping to work as a musician?"

"I don't think it is quite the driving force with me that it once was with you," she replied gently. "I love it, I should never wish to be without it, but I know I'll never be one of the very best. In a way, I think I wanted to do it for you more than for what was inside me."

He stared at her, completely taken aback; his daughter seemed to have the power of continually astonishing him. "For me?"

She frowned and then said simply, "We missed you so much. Even at Klintsy I know how much my music meant to you, though I didn't quite understand why. Mother told me later that you could perhaps have been a great composer."

"Perhaps not," he interjected. After last evening, he now thought the attempt to put his feelings into music over the past twenty years would have destroyed him.

She shrugged. "Who knows? It was what you wanted to do above everything and you never had the chance. I was a fool perhaps, but I needed to hold onto something I knew you wanted me to do. I'm afraid I'm just not quite good enough."

He put his arm around her shoulders, the first gesture of affection he had allowed himself. "Perhaps it's not inappropriate for a concern to bring us together again."

She laughed. "Perhaps, but I'm not keeping you standing here any longer. If you're ever free in the middle of the day, I usually have a cup of whatever passes for soup at the Shkid on the Nevsky, although a general might feel a little out of place there."

"I hope I'm not as pompous as that yet," he observed. "You called it the Nevsky—I thought it had become 25th October Street, or is it like Piter and goes on all the same?"

"It did," she said, smiling. "But the day the siege

ended the City Soviet proclaimed all the new names abolished and all the old ones, which everyone still used anyway, to be put up again. It isn't just the Nevsky Prospekt, it is Sadovaya again not 3rd July; Suvorosky, Ismailovsky and all the rest are back too. It seemed just the right gesture somehow, although I was so ill I had been flown out of the city by the time I heard."

He looked across at the still splendid buildings on every side. At Kazan Cathedral colonnade opposite, where as a boy he had read of the stirring of armies which led within days to the First World War, absorbing again an atmosphere which he now believed even ruin would not have destroyed. "Piter the eternal, who could have doubted it would survive somehow?" He spoke almost to himself.

"Like you?" she suggested.

He laughed. "Hardly, but I shall be proud to think so. I'm very happy I will be helping rebuild it, in however small a way."

As she walked back through the lightening streets, pallid with reflected haze, chill with a dawn breeze off the Gulf of Finland, Sophie's thoughts were in confusion; simple, long-accepted absolutes for the first time eroded by uncertainty. She had had a life already full of chances and heartbreak, had touched the edge of death, lain in terror under bombardment and in weakness without hope of food. But she had trodden a path clearly signposted, accepting the struggles in which she was engaged as the price which must be paid if the Party's dream of a new future for all mankind was to be realized.

She had never doubted that one day her father's disappearance would be explained in ordinary terms, but now it was his frail figure which was throwing its shadow across all this, suddenly making all the old landmarks throw their shadows too. They were unfamiliar shadows she had never dreamed existed, but which she would never now be able to avoid again.

Chapter Fifty

The Georgievsky Hall in the Kremlin again, candelabra reflecting a million sparks of light from gilded decorations, polished marble and glittering full-dress uniforms as the senior commanders and high Party officials of the Soviet Union celebrated their victory.

The contrast with the last time General Berdeyev had stood in this great hall was extraordinary. Then, everyone had been tense, overborne by a sense of impending catastrophe, and he had been an uncertain staff colonel, ignorant of military affairs and one of the most junior officers present. Now, after four years of the most brutal war known to man, there was everywhere the happy, proud exhilaration of victory won. Dignified, decorated officials and high-ranking officers shouted greetings, shaking hands and embracing each other. Many had scarcely known what fate had overtaken friends and colleagues in the cataclysm they had all lived through. Kolya found himself greeting men who had secured his flank at Tula, spearheaded the tank advance after Oryol while his riflemen sweated to keep up, commanded the many other corps in Rokossovsky's Bobruisk encirclement. He was swept away as they all were by the elation of the moment, by the dimensions of their achievement, the achievement of their people. His reinstatement in rank had come through the previous week without explanation, together with an invitation to this official Soviet Government reception for its victorious commanders and a notification of his place in the following Victory Parade—as one of Rokossovsky's corps commanders, he noticed with amusement, not Zhukov's

There were tables piled high with every kind of food, beautifully decorated with flowers, and as the time for the appearance of Stalin and the Politburo drew near they straggled over to their places, shouts and ovations greeting the appearance one after another of the famous. Stalin looked so genial, laughing and drinking toasts with the Politburo on the raised platform, that Kolya found it almost impossible to realize it was only just over a year since he and Rokossovsky had narrowly escaped being murdered in this same palace of the Kremlin. I don't wonder Sophie finds it hard to grasp the contradictions of our state, he reflected, looking around at the immense enthusiasm on every side. How indeed can we reconcile ourselves to the way we live if we do not close our eyes to part of it? The courage of these men around me with the secret fears everyone in authority has to live with, Stalin above all perhaps? The pride and achievement of our revolution, the way we all, myself included, want to build it up again, with the fact that many of us know this was not what we really wished to build when we started out along the revolutionary road? The implacable, terrible endurance of our people with the way they recklessly give themselves so much to endure?

Molotov began to give the toasts, benignly schoolmasterish now. To the Party . . . to the soldiers of the Soviet state . . . to the sailors . . . the people . . . the Politburo . . . the marshals. One by one as he called their names the marshals rose from their places and, to thunderous cheers, were invited to the table occupied by the Politburo. Kolya could not help wondering how many besides Rokossovsky had feared for their lives in the various crises of the war, how many were not there because they had paid the penalty for mistakes which were often not their own.

Nevertheless, it was a truly splendid occasion, an occasion to remember all one's life, an evening which fittingly reflected the feelings of everyone present. For once gaiety without shadow, enthusiasm without reservation, for Kolya even music with pure enjoyment unmixed with strain, as great artists like the ballet star Ulanova were casually alternated with charming, unsophisticated folk acts and songs. In some subtle way the very essence of Russia and of the Soviet Union was blended together and caught long enough to leave an indelible impression of itself, for once without the harsh trammels of the state intruding. Kolya glanced up at his grandfather's name carved on its marble tablet and sipped his private toast, watching Beria and Malenkov on the platform and wishing it could also have been the promised toast on the disappearance of the secret police.

It was two o'clock in the morning by the time the Politburo finally withdrew and by then General Berdeyev, with the regard he had to pay to his stomach, was one of the few sober officers in the hall. Another was Rokossovsky, who would certainly never allow himself to relax while a guest of the Politburo, and sent a message as Kolya was about to leave, asking him to wait.

There was a brilliant moon floating low over the crowding domes, turrets and rooftops of the Kremlin, throwing cold whiteness over dark stone. After the heat and conviviality inside, the chill austerity of wall and battlement was strangely welcome as he stood waiting in the courtyard.

"Ah, Konstantin Aleksandr'itch, I knew I should find you on your feet, whatever may be the case with most of our fellow commanders." Rokossovsky appeared from a side entrance, having presumably accompanied the Politburo to their anteroom. "Prison stomachs have some advantages. Would you feel like walking part of the way home with me?"

"Of course, Comrade Marshal. I should be honored."

"I may have spent the evening with the Politburo, but you don't have to talk to me as if I were a police spy," said Rokossovsky irritably. "Are you able to walk or shall I call my car?"

"Thank you, Comrade Marshal, I am well able to walk. My daughter produced some Leningrad University professor who specializes in structural steelwork for bridges and he has at last designed me something I can sit down in. You should have seen it, pages and pages of calculations, all carried to six places of decimals. It made my engineers' efforts look a little crude."

Rokossovsky laughed. "A gift through the agency of Marshal Zhukov; he would be very disgusted. He certainly found you a swine of a command though; what have you now, ten thousand Germans?"

"Rather more, fifteen thousand, I should think."

"What are you doing with them?"

"Feeding them, Comrade Marshal," Kolya replied grimly. "As usual the idea seems to be that prisoners work better when they're so starved they can scarcely stand. I've had brawls with everyone from the Party and the NKVD up to the City Soviet, but I finally produced God knows how many charts proving that we obtained five times as much work from prisoners who were not actually on the edge of death and it seemed to satisfy them. The ration scales are just about adequate now.

They were walking slowly down the slope from the Borovitsky Gate toward the Moskva River, the pale green of very early dawn just touching the sky to the east. "I am appointed to Poland," said Rokossovsky abruptly. "I will command our troops there and start work on re-establishing the Polish army. Would you like to come as my deputy? Your application to stay in the army is approved."

"I speak no Polish," objected Kolya, taken aback by the unexpectedness of it.

Rokossovsky shrugged. "What do you think? They are going to have to learn Russian."

Kolya shot him a glance, the contrast with the banquet was complete: the normally buoyant Rokossovsky looked tired and depressed. Poland after all was the land of his father, even if he himself had been born at a time when Poland was part of the Russian Empire.

"You are very generous, Comrade Marshal," he said after a pause. "Considering we are both agreed that I'm not a very military person. I owe you so much and I should always like to serve with you, but—"

"But?"

"I am forty-five, Comrade Marshal," said Kolya carefully. "With luck and the six places of decimals holding me upright, I have something over twenty years of useful life ahead of me. I don't want to spend them building up armies and turning millions of Germans out over the new Polish frontier. I would prefer to stay with my heavy construction troops. There is certainly more than enough for them to do.

"My God, you are not a military person," said Rokossovsky feelingly. "Who ever heard of a general who preferred squads of pioneers to a field command? And one thing you can't do with that back of yours is shovel rubble for a living."

Kolya grinned. "I've got fifteen thousand Germans to do it for me," he pointed out. "Very conscientious they are, too, shoveling it all away with as much enthusiasm and discipline as they knocked it all down. The best architects and engineers of the Soviet Union are in Leningrad; I'm learning as much as I can from them and later I might take some kind of military engineering course. We're trying to piece together the old plans of Tsarskoye Selo at the moment and they are all amazed at my intuitive grasp of what it must have looked like. Naturally I haven't told anyone I once went there to an Imperial reception."

Rokossovsky glanced around the empty streets. "Just as well we're not in my car," he said dryly. "Your answer is no, then?"

"If you will accept that answer, Comrade Marshal." Kolya felt ashamed to have a choice when Rokossovsky plainly had none, and gratitude alone should have made him accept an offer clearly made because his company would have been welcome in a distasteful assignment. But he knew he must refuse; he was no longer capable of acting as the vanguard of the Party. In a situation of repression such as Poland he would be a useless danger, the ineffectual betrayer of all he touched. Of Rokossovsky, who might try to save him, of Anna, who would stand by him, of all the unknowns who might be encouraged by attitudes which they would find out too late he was powerless to translate into deeds: all would be dragged to destruction because of what he was no longer able to do. Friendship and sympathy were as much a trap as ever idealism had been.

Rokossovsky appeared unsurprised; there were few unknowns in personalities who had shared a prison barrack and the fear of death together. "Why not? You are probably right after all. May I give you one piece of advice?"

"Of course, Comrade Marshal. I should be grateful."

"Don't stay in Leningrad too long."

"Why?" asked Kolya bluntly. "You think someone might remember my grandparents? It is too long ago surely."

"Oh, God no," said Rokossovsky impatiently. "I must be the only person who could thoroughly betray you now. If the NKVD is too stupid to see what has been under its nose ever since you joined the Party, it isn't likely to find out now. They'll never lack grounds for arresting you without searching through your parentage, especially if you are prepared to fight them even over rations for Germans. How the hell you got away with all those half truths on your papers I don't know, I damned near laughed when I read them, but you have. I'm warning you of something which should be obvious to you too: Leningrad is bound to have a purge within the next two or three years."

Kolya felt the blood drain from his face; now Rokossovsky had said it, of course it was obvious. Proud Leningrad, which had emerged from its supreme trial more self-confident than ever before, with its own ideas and dreams, the sometimes expressed opinion that the capital should be transferred back there from dour, half-Asiatic Moscow; the audacity with which it had abolished revolutionary street names. The Party would never let such a challenge of mind and spirit stand unscathed.

"You see?" Rokossovsky was watching his face, and then added with apparent irrelevance, "What did you think of Comrade Stalin's speech tonight?"

Kolya stared across the Moskva at the Kamenny Bridge, their bridge, where he and Anna had stood in so many of the crises of their lives. "Whenever we want to talk freely we will have to seek the open air. The camps of Magadan are still waiting for us." It had in truth been an extraordinary speech, praising the Russian people without once mentioning the other nationalities of the Union. However many millions of Ukrainians or Siberians had died in the Soviet victory, it was clear that the welcome given by some outlying parts of the Soviet Union to the invaders had been neither forgotten nor forgiven and vengeance was not now far off. Stalin had scarcely referred to the Red

Army, to the galaxy of famous commanders around him; Zhukov's name had not been mentioned again after Molotov's individual toast. Such things did not happen by accident in official speeches.

Rokossovsky nodded. "I don't think even the open air will be either safe or pleasant in Poland." He held out his hand. "Be careful, Konstantin Aleksandr'itch. Try to survive for your twenty years of useful service to Russia, I think they will be needed. I don't expect our ways will cross very often in the future, but you know that if I have the power to help you then you need not fear to ask." His mood changed suddenly, setting aside depression. "I command the Victory Parade next month and Georgi inspects it on the most handsome gray horse you ever saw, while I've no doubt he'll make sure I have the most unmanageable animal in the army. We rode a race together once out of Leningrad Cavalry Barracks over all the cafe tables in the outer boulevards, and he beat me then, damn his eyes. You'll have to be ready to scrape me up off the cobbles; it is all of eight years since I sat in a saddle."

"I'll be much too busy holding on myself. If Marshal Zhukov has time for looking at horses for the parade, words won't express what he'll find for me," responded Kolya in the same light tone. He stood back and saluted stiffly, "*Vsevo khoroshevo*, Comrade Marshal, every good fortune."

*

Anna woke up as he came in and smiled mischievously. "Home with the dawn, Kolyushka?"

He sat on the edge of the bed and kissed her. "Stone cold sober and home with the dawn," he agreed. "How do you like embracing a chestful of medals and a pebble beach of bold braid and buttons in a night-dress?"

"And a bristly chin." She ran her hand over his face. "So long as it had you inside it I would embrace a suit of armor."

His hand closed tight on hers, holding it against his cheek. "Peace, Annochka. Peace to return to living, peace to live with you, to have and hold the gift you long since gave me. To see Sophie wed perhaps, a new generation born without the burdens we all carry with us. A future to build again, but for us a future together again at last. Now and for always, my beloved."

They lay together in love as the city stirred to life around them, as sunlight splintered over streets and parks, over the gold and green of domes and swift-rushing Moskva water, over ruins already softened by rioting weeds and signs of human life struggling back into patched celler and blocked-up, tottering walls. It spilled over fields showing the first green spears of growing crops; over a shabby, battered, indomitable people who must turn their thoughts yet again from the fearful cost of what they had won to the unimaginable task of restoring what they had lost, to forging a worthy heritage for their children amid the beckoning treacheries of high ideals and harsh reality.

Epilogue
1968

What a strange day this has been. I came to Moscow in sadness for the funeral of my old friend Konstantin Konstantin'itch Rokossovsky, who had written to me shortly before he died of the cancer which was destroying him. I think perhaps he was not sorry to know his time was nearly finished, although of course his achievements, even since the Great Patriotic War in which he made his name, are too well known for me to describe. It is not every soldier who ends up as Deputy Prime Minister of a country not his own, but I do not truly think it gave him much satisfaction, and for the past few years he has been living in some obscurity. So I came feeling depressed already, the more so because it is not yet a year since my beloved Anna died leaving me desolate, and although my loneliness is always with me, this day and occasion seemed to make it more so.

Yet now I am writing in the quietness of my hotel room and I do not feel depressed. Partly it was Moscow, so changed with the people looking happier and not haunted by fear, although I have no doubt there are some among them who are fearful. Things have not changed so very much after all. I have been away so long, and Anna and I have been so happy in the twenty-two years we had together after the war, that I still associated Moscow with the bleak grayness of the last years of Stalin's rule, the fierce vendetta which shattered yet again the leadership of Piter, then and always the city of my heart, just as Konstantin Konstantin'itch said it would. But Moscow today was not like that at all. After the brief funeral I walked along the Moskva and out onto Kamenny Bridge, which Anna and I always regarded as peculiarly our own. It was a beautiful day, and there were more people than I ever remember strolling and talking, holding hands and making me feel very envious. I even resented them, wishing to be alone with my memories.

....After a while I heard a group of young people discussing Czechoslovakia, and for the first time I realized a little of what we are doing there. On the pipeline in Uzbekhistan, where I am at the moment, we just hear the official bulletins and receive the local Party newspaper, which very few bother to read.

What struck me first was the way they were discussing it quite openly, anybody could have heard them, certainly I did and Red Army generals do not usually receive the confidences of complete strangers. As I listened, though, I could not help interrupting; what they were saying was so extraordinary. I had heard on the radio bulletins how our Czech friends had asked for our help to put down some violence which had arisen in the course of unmasking a foreign plot in their country. I had not believed it, as a habit I believe very little of what I am told, long experience has taught me the need for skepticism when dealing with officials. Nevertheless, I had vaguely thought it to be some approximation of the facts and had not given the affair much attention for it seemed fairly slight. My friend Vanya Gulianov, the commander of the Uzbekh Military District, told me that he had been ordered to send a locally raised division west; it seemed odd but that was all.

Now, one of those boys told me he had been with the Soviet troops sent into Czechoslovakia, of the terrible shock they all felt when the people, not just a few rowdies but the people themselves, had greeted them as betrayers, had tried to lie down in front of their tanks and poured buckets of slops into the ventilating slits. His division was so shaken, their belief in the ultimate rightness of ideals they sincerely held so undermined, that they were pulled out a week later and replaced by the Uzbekhs, who mostly speak only military Russian and are scarcely politically literate, although I like them.

"It was just rape," the boy kept saying. "Rape of your best friend who trusted you. We went in there believing we were going to help and instead were betrayed into being criminals. They were not capitalists or reactionaries; it was the people who did not want us." Only those who have been born and brought up in the Soviet Union, only the very best of our citizens as that boy was, who believe with every fiber of their being in the place and purpose of the Soviet State in man's pilgrimage toward the ideal, can understand the misery of disillusionment he felt. Long, long ago I felt the same when I had to accept that the Party and our ideals were not the same, in fact were often directly opposed, and with every effort to establish our ideal all we seemed to do was strengthen the ogre in our midst. Yet that is not the truth either: our people and the Party together have achieved so much of which they can be proud. Twice in my lifetime we have pulled ourselves out of a cesspool of destruction and built anew, turned our backs on twenty million dead and striven afresh to create a better life for our children. I do not know if any other nation on earth could have done it, and it was the Party which led us, its vision as well as its brutality which would not let us rest.

I have been lucky in many ways. I was very deeply

in love so I did not lose everything when I lost the Party, and with all the vicissitudes of our lives Anna and I only became closer; together we never lost an idea at least of what we wanted to accomplish. Also, when I would have been at a loss as to what to do for the best, the path before me has always suddenly become so clear that there has been no doubt about which was the way forward. Christians would call this Divine Providence, but I am still quite unsure about many things they claim as being beyond doubt; all I do know is that the older I became, the more certain I was about what I must hold to, and what name you call it does not seem to me important. When I came out of the camps, there was no doubt I must help Russia in her extremity and fight to the best of my ability, although I loathe war. After the war, when I was in despair to see the Party more vindictive and ruthless than ever, still there was little question in my mind that I must contribute as best I could to bringing the people of Russia out of the abyss of destruction in which they lay. In the years to follow there has been no time for despair, in our love, no room for it.

Sophie my dear, I am writing this because I promised those young men that I would join them in a protest they were planning against what the Soviet Union has done in Czechoslovakia. I know this will sound like an old man's senility to you, for it can do no good and the consequences are inevitable. But a general of the Red Army can give them the standing and perhaps even a little of the publicity they need, will turn a brave, naïve, futile martyrdom into something which cannot be completely hushed up. I feel that probably the only useful thing I can now do is lend my name, such as it is, to the first attempt I have seen in the Soviet Union by ordinary citizens to set their voices against official policy. Out of small beginnings . . . if when the precious seed of conscience appears we all fear ridicule and retribution too much to dare water it, how can it ever grow? This effort will do no good, but there will be others. They will do no good either, but strength comes only from the use of those faculties we have.

Sophie, I am not putting this very well. I am old and tired now, often in a great deal of pain. I do not see very well nowadays and I am lonely. So long as Anna was alive the constant struggle to keep on my feet was a battle we won together and infinitely worthwhile; alone I do not think I can face it very much longer. You must not mourn me; above all I do not want you to attempt to help. There will be nothing you can do, nothing I want you to do. I have been very happy to see your joy in your marriage to Fedya and I hope that what I am going to do will, however slightly, help toward a better future for your children. Kiss them for me; I am glad to hear that little Nicolai has the Berdeyev eyebrows!

Give my best wishes to Fedya; he is the only architect I know in the Soviet Union with the ingenuity to trick officials into letting him try adventurous designs and then convince them it was socialist realism all along. On no account must he think he can do anything for me. He saved me once long ago (he had to promise to say nothing about it so it is no good asking him) but he cannot do so again. His duty now is to you and your children. I would not do this if I did not believe the regime to have changed enough for you all to be safe if you keep quiet, but of course you will be watched, so be careful. Destroy this letter.

Perhaps one day you and he will have to make your own stand, but now it is my turn so feel no regrets. When your time and place come, which I trust they never will, you will know. We all have to try to live up to the best within us, otherwise life is meaningless we all fail but somehow have to try again. It would, after all, be very dull if we did not.

Thank you, my dear, for all the love and happiness you have given me through the years; from the day of your birth you had your very own place in my heart.

Your loving father,

Konstantin Aleksandr'itch Berdeyev.

I am giving this to my old driver Morozov to bring to you; do you think you could look after him for me?

This Book Is Dedicated to
Pyotr Grigorenko
General of the Red Army
Confined to an asylum
for the criminally insane 1970
for public criticism of Soviet policy.

Historical Note

Apart from Kolya, Anna and their family, almost all the characters in this book are either historical personalities or based on actual individuals. Although Rokossovsky's private dealings with Kolya are fiction, the main framework of his career follows the actual sequence of events very closely. He was arrested in 1937 and severely tortured, losing most of his teeth and, according to a subsequent KGB defector,* having a chair leg driven up his rectum as well as the more normal brutalities of interrogation. Solzhenitsyn remarks on common camp gossip that Rokossovsky was twice led out to execution in an effort to force a confession out of him.

It was apparently his own ingenuity which exposed the fraud of the charges against him, although this did not prevent him being sent to the notorious forced labor camp at Vorkuta inside the Arctic Circle. Mrs. Kuusinen, who was a fellow prisoner although wife of the virtual head of the Comintern, encountered him there as late as the spring of 1940. Almost every Soviet memoirist who came into contact with him during the war comments on his humanity as well as his military

* *The Nights Are Longest There*, A. I. Romanov (pseudonym). Hutchinson, 1971.

ability and courage, or else recalls quite trivial encounters with him in respect and affection. His meeting with Stalin in 1944 is well documented, notably in an interview with Rokossovsky himself published after Stalin's death in the *Soviet Journal of Military History*, 1964. This kind of scene was not uncommon although few commanders attempted to maintain their own opinions against those of Stalin for long: it is probably true that the degree of risk which Rokossovsky attached to this particular encounter was more usually experienced by commanders rather earlier in the war. The Bobruisk encirclement was naturally only part of a complex campaign extending over several weeks and involving other Soviet fronts, but the broad essentials were as depicted.

Marshal Zhukov is, of course, well known. He told General Eisenhower after the war how he had used his infantry to explode mine fields, rather than allow his assault on Berlin to slow down. Even minor characters like the Commandant at Magadan, the doctor at Cherskogo, the NKVD interrogators or the peasant boy accused of sabotage for lovemaking in a piggery—no one intervened in reality and he got ten years in a labor camp—are reflections of actual events and people. The Smolensk region between the wars is quite well documented as the Germans captured some of the Party files and these are now in the U. S. National Archives.

Although I have necessarily simplified a vast mass of material, I have made ever effort to ensure that the simplification process has not led to falsification of fact. Obviously, come of Kolya's interpretations are arguable, but I have been careful not to give him the benefit of hindsight, or to include information and views which could not have been available to someone in his position at the time.

The question must remain: what made men like

him, like Marshal Rokossovsky, serve the Soviet state so loyally in spite of such savage treatment and all the disillusion which went with it? The obvious answer is that they had no choice, no possible alternative: even Foreign Commissar Molotov's wife was in exile for years while he continued to serve as Stalin's right-hand man. But there is more to it than mere fear, for fear alone would not explain the quality of service so many gave. Part of the answer, of course, lies in the nature of the German invasion immediately following the purges, when the fearsome sufferings of the Russian people made victory, even with Stalin as the beneficiary, preferable to total servitude under Hitler. For the army, professional pride undoubtedly played a part too—it is difficult indeed for a conscientious and able soldier to refuse his duty of defending his native land out of hatred for its leader, as the German army also discovered.

Another remarkable fact is that many of those who had been most shamefully treated retained their belief in communism intact. The question they asked themselves was: "How can the Party have gone so astray?" not whether the system itself was such that it was likely to give rise to such enormities. Had the invader been different, the reaction might have been different too, although this remains uncertain. The Germans were not initially received as enemies in some outlying parts of the Soviet Union; it was their own atrocities which rapidly changed this attitude—in Odessa, where the Rumanians were the occupying power, Soviet reconquest was greeted with apathy or outright hostility.

A further element in the problem is probably that the Russian shock factor is simply higher than our own. They expect their rulers to behave with callous brutality. A British ambassador to the Soviet Union once remarked that Russian governments through the ages may have been able or stupid, ambitious or passive, corrupt or idealistic but one thing they never are is humane.

It is difficult too for a Westerner to realize just how little standard for comparison even Russians in responsible positions had in those days—or indeed nowadays. Very few survived from families which had enjoyed a reasonably comfortable or cultured background before 1914; after the purges there were almost none. There was no unbiased factual information on events, little possibility of knowing that the final death toll for forced collectivization and the subsequent purges was in the region of fifteen million. Party members felt themselves part of a great endeavor, an inevitable historical process which was not just right but unquestionable and unavoidable. To attempt to set puny individual judgment against the collective wisdom of the whole of human experience as they believed it was quite simply impossible, and Stalin *was* the Party, just as the Party *was* present, future and the whole destiny of man. When he was shot Yakir is alleged to have called out, "Long live the Party! Long live Stalin!" and there is no particular reason to doubt the story.